LAVENDER MOON

NATALIE PARKER

Natalie Parker

Copyright©
Copyright 2023 by Natalie Parker
Cover Design by: Lori Jackson
Photo by: Wander Aguiar
Formatting By: Paula Dombrowiak

Editor: Katy Nielsen

This is a work of fiction. Names, characters, places, incidents, and organizations, are a product of the author's imagination or used fictitiously. Any resemblance to actual events, locales, or persons, living or dead is entirely coincidental.

All Rights Reserved. In accordance with U.S. Copyright Act of 1976, the scanning, uploading, and electronic sharing or distribution of any part of this book without the permission of the publisher is unlawful piracy and theft of the author's intellectual property and hard work.
Thank you for your support of the author's rights.

PLAYLIST

Not Easy - *X Ambassadors, Elle King, Wiz Khalifa*
Queen of the Night - *Hey Violet*
Jack and Diane - *John Mellencamp*
Fast Car - *Luke Combs*
Good Girl, Bad Boy - *Florida Georgia Line*
What if I Love You - *Gatlin*
Fever Dream - *Jillian Rossi*
If I Don't Laugh, I'll Cry - *Frawley*
Different For Girls - *Dierks Bentley, Elle King*
Hard To Love - *Lee Brice*
Take My Name - *Parmalee*
Breathe Again - *Harrison Storm*
Hate Me - *Blue October*
Out of Tears - *The Rolling Stones*
The Black and White - *The Band Camino*
Kiss the Rain - *Billie Myers*
Heart Medicine - *Judah & the Lion*

FOREWORD

This story was originally going to be a collaboration between myself and another author and I want to take a moment to give appreciation to Celia Pereira. We came up with the idea of this story together and while I was excited to write it with her, another world of characters was calling to her at the same time. With Celias explicit support, and encouragement, I struck out to write Luna and Kaleb's story on my own, and if she hadn't, she wouldn't have been able to bring the beautiful story "When Souls Collide" into this romance world.

While the words are mine, the idea for the synopsis was ours.

Celia, we hatched the idea for this book together and I want to thank you for trusting me to give it wings.

CONTENT WARNING

This book contains themes that some may find triggering including domestic violence, addiction, and PTSD episodes.

Please read cautiously.

PROLOGUE
KALEB

My heart turns to ice and drops into the pit of my stomach when I roar into the driveway, finding her car gone. Cutting the engine, I dismount the bike and hightail it as fast as my sore thigh will let me up the front porch steps.

"Luna?" I call out, not recognizing the desperation in my own voice, surging from the back of my throat. You just saw her car wasn't here, you fucking idiot, my brain tries to tell me, but I bash the thought away because my heart doesn't care and wants to call out to her. I make myself stop in the open floor space, looking around the main living area. None of her shoes by the door... her gym bag isn't here either.

I whip around, trying to jog down the hall to the bedrooms, despite the screaming muscles in my leg. I charge into my room first, looking around for any obvious evidence that she's not gone. Her purple panties aren't on the floor where they were this morning. None of her clothes are on the chair, there's nothing.

I quickly dart to the spare room - her room - as my heart starts to crack, one fissure threatening to spread and branch out into more. And when I push through the door, it splits wide open. Everything is gone. All of her clothes, art supplies, easels, canvases, brushes... they're all gone. The room is completely sterile. The bed is made, and there's just one art piece left behind. The one I hate. The one that represents what I did to her. I walk towards it, my eyes fixated, even though I want to pretend this painting doesn't exist, let alone look at it. All the darkness that takes up the canvas, all the blacks and greys twisted together... I feel sick to my stomach as I run my finger over one of the brush strokes, trying to feel what she must have been feeling when this came out of her and onto the textured surface... because I deserve to feel that way, not her.

I chipped away at her for all of this past year by being a pathetic, self-loathing bastard, and just when I thought we were both healing, today I gave her the final blow, smashing us to smithereens.

The dark monstrosity turns fuzzy as my vision blurs with moisture, and I angrily try to blink it away. No... this can't be over. It can't be too late.

Whipping around, I storm back down the hallway on a mission. Reaching the kitchen, I scan the surface of the round dining table, as well as that of the kitchen counter. It's not here. It has to be around here somewhere, please tell me I'm not too late, that I can fix this. Please tell me she left it behind...

Beginning to panic, I head for the desk in the foyer, rifling around for the large 8 x 12 envelope that holds my future inside it, but all my efforts come up empty. I stand here, my entire body heaving with the deep breaths necessary to fill my lungs. I feel the back of my neck go hot and my fists clench as I look down at the dark oak of the desk, my mind itching to reach out and overturn it, sending it and its contents crashing to the floor. Mere weeks ago, I would have done just that, and though I have the urge, I'm able to tamp it down. Luna did that. She brought me back home and helped me to no longer be a slave to my anger. While part of me tries to say it shouldn't matter now that she's not here, I can't bring myself to let go and go for it because the other part is telling me if I act on it, I'll only take myself further away from her. I can't go back to that if I have any prayer of being with her again… which means that part of me still has hope.

1

KALEB, AGE 10

I remember feeling completely amped as the counselors strapped a harness around me, adjusting carabiners while I fiddled with the strap of my helmet. I loved climbing and did so on anything I could. Bookshelves, the roof of the garage, and no tree in town was safe from testing my weight. I loved being up high. It was my escape. Any surroundings, no matter how boring, seemed beautiful from a certain height – and I enjoyed the quiet. It was for sure like being in my own little world.

As I gave the helmet strap a final jerk to secure it in place, I thanked my lucky stars one more time that Pops was able to send me there to Mystic Hills, and I was looking forward to two whole weeks doing things like this ropes course. There was no better way to let out my adventurous side without getting into trouble, not to mention it kept me safe while Pops dealt with my shitshow of a father.

"Kaleb, we've found you a partner," Sheila, one of the senior counselors, announced as she walked a brown-haired girl over my way. She looked to be my age, with wide brown eyes that looked like they were swimming in contained terror as she pressed her lips together so hard they mottled white. She walked tentatively, leaning back slightly on the hand Sheila had on her back as she ushered her toward me. "This is Luna," she introduced the girl when they stopped in front of me. "Luna, this is Kaleb."

Luna attempted a half smile and a nervous wave as Sheila walked away.

"Hi," I said, taking in the way she wrapped her arms around herself nervously. I could tell she was trying not to shake. "Are you scared?"

She nodded. "I don't like heights."

"I love heights," I shared with her, but it didn't change the frightened look in her eyes, despite her efforts to hide it. "It won't be so bad," I continued. "We'll be harnessed together and I climb all the time so we won't fall, and even if we do, the ropes will catch us," I tried to reassure her, and to my satisfaction, her face did relax slightly as she drew in a breath.

"What do you climb?" Luna asked as we approached our first obstacle, a rock wall, that leads us to the rest of the rest of the course.

"Whatever they tell me not to." I gave her a cheesy grin that actually made her smile and her slim shoulders shake slightly with a giggle. "For real," I surged on as I grabbed onto one of the foot holds and she did the same. "Last week I figured out how to get on the roof by grabbing onto the gutter from our back deck railing. My pops was super pissed." I smiled at the recent memory of Pops yelling up at me from the ground to get off the damn roof.

"No way," she laughed at the same moment her foot slipped, turning it into a terrified yelp. She grappled tight to the holds, scrambling to find her footing, and I could practically hear her heart galloping as she hungrily panted for air.

"Don't look down," I gently instructed, holding a hand out for her to grab. She looked at it and then at me before taking it and letting me pull her up a little higher so she could get her feet secure before letting go to grab back onto one of the hand grabs.

"Just watch my hands and my feet and do what I do. It will be okay," I reassure and give her another smile.

I didn't know why I cared so much when I hardly knew this girl. For some odd reason, I wanted her to be okay. I'd never had much need for friends, being so used to being on my own and entertaining myself, but something about helping her made me feel something good. And it got better and better the more I saw her laugh at my jokes as we climbed, forgetting about how high up we were. She got shaky again on the Burma loops, but I offered to go behind her so that I could watch out for her and stay close as she got across. With each element she conquered, I felt a sense of pride in her, as well as feeling good about myself. Both feelings were foreign, but surprisingly welcome. The endorphins they produced surpassed the ones I got from climbing tree tops and roofs – and maybe even the ones I got from careening down the midtown death hill on my skateboard.

After an hour of yakking and laughing while maneuvering ourselves to around thirty feet in the air, we completed the course with all of our limbs still intact.

"Thank you," Luna said sweetly with a grateful smile, and held her hand up which confused me for a moment, until I realized what she was waiting for. Feeling another rush of that unfamiliar sensation, I brought my hand up to slap it against hers. High-fives were yet another thing I didn't come by often;. not by my peers, anyway. They mostly steered clear of me at school, and I didn't miss the looks their parents gave me when they picked them up afterward. I expected as much there at camp, but Luna was treating me like a friend she'd known all her life within the duration of one ropes' course.

"What swimming group are you in?" I dared to ask her after we'd discarded our climbing gear and given it back to the counselors.

"Green," she beamed brightly back at me, looking proud. " What about you?"

"Green too," I was happy to tell her, excited I might see her again in the green swim zone.

"So where are you from?" She asked, clasping her hands behind her back while we walked. Her question caught me off guard. I wasn't used to having an interest taken in me. At home with Pops, I was to help out or stay the hell out of the way, either around the house or in his shop where he repaired Harleys.

"You probably haven't heard of it," I mumbled down at the path. "It's a small town in Indiana about an hour from here."

"What's it called?"

"Coyote Creek."

"Sounds cool. I sometimes wish I lived in a small town," she mused with a twinkle in her eye.

"So where are you from?" I asked, happy to turn the focus back to her.

"Detroit," she sighed, and I found myself feeling a little bummed that we didn't live closer. The camp was in Ohio, close to the Indiana border, and I'd heard of some other kids that came from farther away than Luna. It was pretty well-known in the region.

"Alright, campers! To your cabins! Be ready for the lake in fifteen minutes!" Zach, the senior counselor that was in charge of the boys cabin I was in, shouted.

"You heard him, girls!" Hollered the bubbly blonde counselor from Luna's cabin as she clapped her hands.

All the other campers started scampering around us, pushing and shoving gleefully to their respective cabins while Luna turned to me, a shy smile on her face as she looked up the full inch and a half I was taller than her. "See you at the lake?" She asked, a hopefulness to her tone that about knocked me over.

"Yeah," I nodded, catching myself when I thought I maybe looked too eager. I wasn't sure how to react to someone excited to spend more time with me.

"Great! I'm going to go get ready!" Luna announced, flashing me that sweet smile before skipping off in the direction of her cabin, brown ponytail bouncing against her back.

I didn't realize it then, but I was already smitten.

Two girls, whose names aren't worth remembering, gave matching dirty sneers to Luna as they walked past where she and I sat on the dock, dangling our legs in the water after equally clobbering each other racing laps. We seemed to be equally matched in swimming, which Luna said made her feel a little better about being a scaredy cat on the ropes course with me. Her words, not mine.

"What's their problem?" I muttered, looking from their retreating forms back to Luna.

She shrugged, looking uncomfortable. "I'm sitting with you," she responded absently, and started drawing hearts on her knee with her finger, likely trying to distract herself from her discomfort.

"That's nothing new," I grumbled, before taking a bite of my apple.

"What do you mean?" She looked up from her knee, a confused expression marring her forehead.

Rather than go into how people didn't like to associate with me, I did what I had taught myself best: shoving it down in my inner basement and pretending it wasn't real. "Never mind.," I shook my head, trying to give off the best don't care vibe I could. "They're not anybody," I shrug off.

"I'm used to it anyway," she sighed, shaking her head but not meeting my eyes. "Most girls don't like me."

That got my attention, and I looked up in astonishment while I chewed thoughtfully. "How come?" I finally asked after swallowing.

"I don't know," she clasped her hands together between her knees, her voice rising just a little in frustration. "I play basketball, but other than that, I always thought I was just like them," she confided. "Do you play any sports?" She rolled her shoulders like she was trying to shake off the subject.

I shook my head, looking out at the lake that rippled a pretty orange from the afternoon sun. "We could never really afford it," I explained, but before she could even have a chance to feel bad for me, I added, "they never really interested me, anyway. I prefer just running and climbing and stuff."

"The next Ninja Warrior?" she asked, smiling with interest and beaming even more when she sees me light up.

"I love that show," I professed, grinning. "I watch it with my Pops some nights when it's on."

"Is that your dad or your grandpa?" She asked, looking innocently curious.

I was quiet a moment before finally looking away and answering. "Grampa."

"Oh, do you live with him?" She leaned forward, seeming genuinely interested, and not like she wanted to give me hell for basically being an orphan who lived with my grouchy grandfather who struggled to make ends meet working on Harleys.

"Yeah," I answered, turning my apple over in my hands a few times before taking another bite.

"That's so neat," she said wistfully. "I never really had grandparents that I saw a lot until last year. My dad's parents moved over here from Seattle, and I really like them. Especially Granna."

While listening to her, the part I found myself zeroing in on most was how she beamed when she said the word dad, something I would never do in my life.

Before I could comment further, the two snotty girls plopped down on the wooden dock just behind us, this time with another boy with them.

"Do you guys want to play Truth or Dare?" The one with the French braid asked with a very knowing smirk and a very entitled tone.

Luna looked to me before addressing them, pulling her legs out of the water and turning to face our new companions. "How do you play?" She asked, bending a knee to tuck a foot beneath her. I opted to keep facing the lake but leaned back and turned towards everyone a little bit.

"You have to pick one, and if it's truth, you have to answer whatever question we ask you," the boy explained nicely, folding his arms on his knees.

"And if you choose dare, you have to do whatever the other players dare you to. Whoever doesn't answer their question or take their dare, loses," concluded the dark-haired girl with the low ponytail.

Again, Luna looked to me first before shrugging. "Okay."

This made French braid smile wickedly. "Luna, truth or dare?"

Luna looked around at our surroundings while she gave it some thought, humming with her bottom lip between her teeth. I saw her eyes land on the ropes course in the distance before quickly turning back to the group. "Truth."

I smiled to myself that she chose truth at the possibility of having to do something up high, but the smile on French braid turned downright malicious, as she eyed her dark-haired friend before looking back to Luna.

"Truth. Do you like him?" She asked nodding in my direction.

I could feel my own face going all shades of pale as the blood drained from it and straight down to my stomach, but the sinking feeling was quickly replaced by a shot of surprise, when Luna straightened up, squaring her shoulders and answered. "He has a name. And yes, I like Kaleb."

She didn't even bat an eye as she continued to stare down the girl. I felt myself gulp as I looked to the boy who gave me an amused look, complete with raised eyebrows. By the way he tucked his lower lip in, my guess was he was afraid to comment, but as was stoked as I was to see the looks on the other two girls faces when their plan to embarrass Luna was foiled - or as stoked as I would've been if I hadn't been so dumbfounded by

Luna's admission. More like the way she said it. She liked me, and wasn't afraid who knew it.

I didn't have much time to revel in the notion however, when the girls turned to me, trying not to look put off. "Kaleb,. Truth or dare?," the head biotch tightly bit out.

Knowing how different I was from the rest of the kids there, I didn't feel like I wanted to share any truths, but thought a dare could be fun. Maybe they'd dare me to climb to the top of one of the towering pine trees and jump in the water.

"Dare," I declare, before biting into my apple again.

"Okay," the girl responded, looking oh so superior. "I dare you to carve Luna's name into the side of the senior counselor's cabin," she finished, looking triumphant; like she had me. Like I'd be too afraid to take the dare and lose.

"Fine," I shrugged like it was no big thing, and got to my feet. Chucking my apple in the nearest trash can, I began the march up to the counselor's cabin.

2

KALEB, AGE 18

"I still don't get why the hell you have to do this," Cheyenne complains as she crosses her arms and pops her hip out. I still don't get why she thinks she can intimidate me with that pose. It's never worked before, and it's not going to now.

"I don't have to do this, I want to do this," I correct her, as I roll a flash light up in a thin green rain jacket.

"So you're going to go to some camp and play around with a bunch of kids instead of spending your last two months here with me," she states in disbelief, and I can't help the gust of air that huffs from my throat. I've been nothing but straight with her. She's known all along since we started fooling around a few months ago that my end game was the Army, and that this wouldn't turn into anything more. She gives good head, but she's been nothing more to me than a distraction.

"Yeah," I look up with a raised eyebrow. "Like I've told you at least a handful of times, that's what I'm doing." Crouching down, I push the rolled-up bundle into one of my bike's saddle bags. "And last I checked, I'm the one who decides how I spend my time."

"But why?" she whines, and it makes me wince. "I don't get

why that's so important after the last few months we've spent together."

"It's what I do every year." I straighten up and hold my arms out, exacerbated at this point. I've gone back to Mystic Hills ever single year without fail since I was ten years old. Pops got lucky with a good commission that first year, and it was good for both of us. But every year since, I'd done paper routes, mowed lawns, and whatever else I could to be able to afford to go each summer. Most recently, that included helping out at the tattoo parlor on the edge of town, helping the artists with drawings and designs that were overtly complex.

Every year when it got close to that time, Luna would ask in her letters if I was going, and she's the one person that I never, ever wanted to let down. At least, that's what I tell myself. The truth, no matter how much I try to ignore it, is that I could never bear the thought of missing a chance to see her.

A moment or two of silence falls over the atmosphere as I continue prepping the bike and Cheyenne stands there watching, absently playing with a strand of her blonde hair.

"I saw the letters," she finally pipes up, and when my head whips up to regard her, I'm stunned at how she doesn't look the least bit ashamed. If anything, she looks self-righteous and entitled.

"What the fuck, Cheyenne?!" I exclaim in a grumble, and it earns me squinty-eyes and a head tilt.

"Funny how you know exactly what I'm talking about," she sneers, and it makes me feel red-hot rage begin to ignite at the base of my spine. "So this is about some little ho named Luna." She spits the name out as if Luna is some kind of battery acid.

I take a furious step towards her, ready to explode all over her when I stop myself, thinking better of it. This is just what she wants; I can tell by the smug, expectant look on her face as she continues to play with her hair.

For the better part of this last semester, Cheyenne has enjoyed pushing my buttons in between fucks, picking fights with me if that's what kept me around longer. She'd push me to a certain point and then turn sweet and apologetic, totally fucking with my head. Sometimes, I'll even admit, it had me totally confused as to what exactly our relationship was. But never once did I let her think we were something we weren't.

And then I'd get a letter, and with a few words from Luna, my head would be clear. I'd be reminded of what an honest, level-headed person was like; a genuinely good person that saw good in me and made me like myself. Then I would ride that high until the next time Cheyenne came along with her mind games.

This is the first time, however, that she's brought up seeing the letters. Now she stands here, waiting for me to unload on her so that we can draw this out.

I don't know if it's the knowledge I'm going to see Luna in less than two hours that is taking effect on me or what, but it doesn't matter. I immediately tamp down my fury at this girl in front of me invading my privacy with no remorse, and school my features to represent indifference.

"It was good getting to know you, Cheyenne," I convey calmly, giving her a friendly smile. "Take care of yourself." I only catch a flicker of her hardened eyes and tightened mouth before I turn away just in time to see Pops walking out of the garage, wiping his hands on a shammy cloth.

"You good to go there, boy?" he asks gruffly, the years of cigarettes making his voice come out raspy.

"Yes, sir," I smile, squaring my shoulders as he comes in for a manly, back-slapping hug. As I grew older, I became less of a responsibility to him and more of an actual grandson. He always cared, hence the reason I was never in the foster system – or worse, with my abusive drunk of a father. It was just incredibly stressful for him having to start over raising a small kid while trying to keep his shop afloat and dealing with his trainwreck of a son all on his own. Trying to keep me safe and provided for in that exceptional situation made him put his game face on for those first few years, but as I got older and more self-sufficient, he relaxed some. And when I got old enough to help him with some of the responsibilities in the shop and the house is when we bonded and became something resembling family.

"I'll have your ruck sack at the airport for ya," he husks, referencing my leave for basic training after the counselor stint at the camp is over.

"Thanks," I say, turning to swing my backpack on. I swing my leg over my Harley and ignore Cheyenne still standing there, having pretty much dismissed her at this point.

"Say hi to Luna for me!" Pops yells, just before I stomp my foot down on the kickstart, and I don't even try to hide the sheepish smile that pulls at one side of my lips at the mention of her name, nor do I bother to check Cheyenne's reaction as I roar out of the driveway.

Luna

"CHARLOTTE, YOU HAVE ROBIN'S NEST," Rob, one of Mystic Hill's managers reads off as he hands Charlotte her list of campers, before continuing down the line of counselors. "Nolan, you have the Frog Pad. Luna, you're taking Squirrel Hollow, and... Kaleb?" He looks up from his clipboard and scans the rest of the clearing we've congregated in to receive assignments, coming up empty, and I feel the nerves that already had a grip on my chest and shoulders dig in a little deeper. "Has anyone seen Kaleb Shane yet?" Rob asks, looking around to each of us for some kind of answer.

"He should be coming," I offer up, before discreetly pulling in a deep breath to calm myself.

Rob looks to me with a questioning eyebrow raised. "You've spoken to him?"

"Sort of," I hesitantly nod. "I got an email from him a couple of days ago, and he said he'd be here. Maybe he's just running..." I trail off as I hear a faint rumbling, and for a moment I'm confused. It's a perfectly sunny afternoon, that can't be thunder. But as the sound gets gradually louder, it starts to click. I feel my body relax and my lips tugging at the sides.

In our letters and emails, Kaleb had mentioned resurrecting an old Harley that had come through Pop's shop that everyone thought was a lost cause. And as we'd seen each other over the years, he'd grown a little rougher around the edges each summer, but it still doesn't prepare me for what I see when the motorcycle rolls up over the small hill from the access road.

A cloud of dust blows forward as the bike comes to a stop and Kaleb brings his feet down to steady the machine, showcasing his badass motorcycle boots and long, jean-clad legs. Cutting the engine, he swiftly dismounts, swinging one leg back, and before I even realize it, my legs are moving, I'm closing the distance, meeting him halfway between the bike and the group.

I only have a few short strides to take in the countless changes in him, despite our last time together being only a year ago. A collection of tattoos take up the space of his left arm that weren't there before, he's even taller yet, and a piercing glints from his right eyebrow. There's a light dusting of scruff along his jawline, and the way his body carries itself is more confident. He's never been the most social creature, but his stature conveys that he has no problem with anyone or anything.

We stop, leaving less than a foot of space between us, and everyone else seems to cease to exist. It's just him and me standing in the middle of these beautiful trees as I stare up into those absolutely beautiful green eyes I have yet to find a pair like. The smile on his face is faint as his hooded gaze searches mine, but it speaks a million words. I know because it's a smile I know by heart by now. It doesn't matter how far apart our visits are stretched; each one is packed with that smile.

"Hey, silly girl," he finally greets quietly, his smile turning up on one side just a little further.

"Hey, soldier," I greet back just as a throat clears, ripping both our attention away from each other.

"You Kaleb Shane?" Rob asks, holding his camper list out to him without waiting for an answer. "You have the Hawks Perch," he informs him and turns away, again not waiting for any kind of acknowledgement. "Campers will be arriving in the next thirty minutes, counselors! Head to your respective cabins and get squared away!" he barks out, and the rest of our fellow counselors quickly disperse, leaving Kaleb and I standing by his motorcycle.

Kaleb slowly drops his backpack once everyone's far enough away with their attentions diverted, and his arms are around me before my heart even has a chance to take its next beat. His long arms wrap as far as they can around, holding me tight and flush against his lean frame. A small giggle bubbles out on the breath being squeezed out of me which just makes me laugh harder against his shoulder, and holy shit, did he always smell this good? The closeness wakes something up inside of me, making a thrill swish through my body.

Our reunions have always been joyous, but I'm finding a special little zing dancing up my spine with this one. Maybe it's because I know it's the last time, at least here at camp. If we see each other after this it likely won't be every year, due to entering adulthood and all the bullshit that comes with it.

Kaleb straightens up, pulling me with him and lifting me off my feet a moment and giving me one more squeeze before setting me back down and taking a step back.

"You look great," he tells me, giving me a quick once over, making my heart burst out a few rapid beats.

"Thanks, so do you. And you're going to have to tell me about this," I wave a hand at his very decorated left arm.

"Promise," he utters softly, amusement dancing in his eyes.

Not giving myself a chance to get caught up in this moment, I turn in the direction of the cabins, glancing at him to join me, and we find a casual pace, walking easily in step.

Kaleb and I have always known that what we have is more than a friendship, but neither of us has dared venture to find out exactly what it is. I think we've always had an unspoken agreement not to mess with what isn't broken. It's just special.

"Remember, you promised to do all the dangerous stuff with the kids," I remind him of what we've discussed in our emails.

"Of course," he answers. "I've got the ropes course and the derby race, and you take all the pussy shit – ow!" He hollers when I cut him off with a smack to the arm. He retaliates by giving me a shove that has me stumbling a few feet.

"Just go get ready," I order exasperatedly as I shove him in the direction of his cabin, and he obliges, chuckling at me over his shoulder.

AFTER ALL TWELVE of my ten-year-old girls are settled in their cabin, I head to the main staff cabin that has the internet signal and phone line to do my first nightly check in with the parents. Some campers stay for only a week or two, and some stay all summer, so I know I'm going to have quite the variety of little people filtering in and out of my cabin for the next couple of months.

I click send on a group email to all the parents and guardians that we had a good first afternoon, all their kiddos are accounted for, what I have planned for the week, and rise from the chair.

When I exit the cabin, I don't immediately head in the direction of Squirrel Hollow, but instead, venture around the side. When I get to the far East corner of the building, I pull out my small flashlight. The sun hasn't completely set, but enough so that it's hard to see what I'm looking for, even though I know without a doubt it's right where it's always been, year after year since I was ten.

Skimming my fingers along the wooden siding, I click the light on just to see it with my eyes as I touch it. And without fail, there's my name etched into the wood. Luna is carved in extremely tiny letters with the beautiful imperfection of a ten-year-old boy using the edge of a flathead screwdriver he'd concocted for the job.

Taking a moment to glide my fingertip over it, I smile at the memory that cemented an eight-year friendship.

3

LUNA, AGE 10

"*A*re you kidding me?" Kelliann griped as Kaleb stepped away from the staff cabin. "That is too little to even see!"

Kaleb quirked a small half-smile as he raised a shoulder. "You didn't say how big I had to make it." His smile is small but proud as Logan snickers.

As for me, I stood off to the side, smiling, feeling a little relieved as I clasped my hands together in front of me. The whole walk over here I tried to talk him out of it, that it was just a stupid game and I didn't want him to get in trouble.

"That should not count as a dare," she continued to protest, sticking her hands on her little hips.

"I like this game," Kaleb softly chuckled over at me, making me laugh.

Our shared amusement pissed the girl off even more. "Whatever," she huffed as she turned away. "We're not playing with you, if you can't do it right. Brynne, come on!" she snapped, and the dark-haired girl scampered to catch up.

"Technically he did the dare!" the other boy that had originally accompanied them called after their retreating backs, holding his hands up in a shrug as he followed a few paces behind.

No love lost there, but still, it kind of burned every time my friendship felt rejected. Too young to realize it then, it was because of my athleticism that boys wanted to be friends with me, pissing off all the girls that had crushes on them. As far as I knew I wasn't a tomboy; not at all. I was just as girly as my female peers; I just happened to like sports and chose basketball over girl scouts.

"Do you have any friends here?" I asked him as we both started walking back to the main trail that ran and sprawled in all different directions throughout the whole camp.

Only a headshake was his answer as we walked down the hill back in the direction of the camp, and I didn't push it further. I did, however, stick to him like glue for the rest of my two weeks. What he did on the side of the staff cabin meant things to me that I was too young to even understand. His smart thinking kept him out of trouble, save both of us embarrassment, and weeded out a few personalities we did not want to hang with.

We fell into some kind of natural companionship, like we'd known each other all our lives, if you'll forgive the cliché. With each hour we got more comfortable, even picking on each other, and ignoring all the other kid's sneers about us being inseparable.

We played on the black top where I showed him out to shoot a layup, and he showed me how to ride a skateboard without killing myself. We sat next to each other in the mess hall at meal times, and by the camp fire each night. However, our friendship turned a corner when we were having an arts and crafts hour at one of the outdoor picnic tables.

Art had always been my passion, my jam if you will, and I was excited to have free time to create whatever we wanted. I loved using colors, whether it was markers, pastels, or paints, but even if I had access to nothing but crayons, I'd happily make do. One thing I avoided like the plague was drawing and sketching. I struggled with utensils that were fine-tipped and could not seem to construct an image the way I saw it in my head.

I would occasionally come back to it and make an attempt, but it always ended in frustration. I tried to chalk it up to just simply not being my strong suit and stuck to making abstract art, even though, to me, it felt like it wasn't up to par with being an actual artist.

So when I saw Kaleb drawing an amazingly intricate wolf that day, I was in awe – and a little bit of envy.

"Wow, that is so good," I mused, leaning forward with my arms tucked under me against the table. "How did you do that?"

Kaleb shrugged while continuing to move the pencil in mesmerizing strokes. "I don't know, I've just always liked drawing. I'm not sure how I got good at it."

"I love art, but I can't draw," I admitted glumly, and twisted my mouth at the corner as I continued to watch his work.

"Want to color it in when I'm done?" he asked as he looked up, his eyebrows slightly lifted.

"Sure!" I felt myself light up, even though with Kaleb's incredible knack for filling in and shading, it seriously didn't need it. I think my little ego just needed a boost.

I waited patiently for the next little while for Kaleb to be done, but the lunch bell rang, signaling our craft hour was up.

"Here," he'd said, folding it up and handing it over to me. You can do it in your cabin or something."

"Thanks," I said, looking at our hands touching as I took it from him. "Do you care how I do it? What colors I use?"

"You can do whatever you want," he said and looked down, giving me that serene smile with his lashes coming partway down over his green eyes for the first time.

Little bubbles of excitement creeped through me, and I could think of nothing else but making it something he'd love. "What's your favorite color?" I asked, as we started strolling side by side to the mess hall.

"Black."

"Oh," I looked down at the path, not expecting that answer. I loved colors and I wanted to do something special with his favorite. My aunt had taught me to use every shade of a single color all on one picture, and I was immediately hooked. The end product was always so cool. But there were only so many shades of black.

As if sensing my trepidation, Kaleb's face took on a quizzical expression. "What's your favorite color?"

"Purple," I rattled right off while I still stewed over what to do with the wolf drawing, but very quickly, it came to me. I had the best idea.

Kaleb

THE HIGH OF being in virtually another world was starting to get jaded by the impending reality I'd have to go back to as I rolled up my sleeping bag. It's crazy how my own day-to-day life had never bothered me before, but here I was, almost dreading going back to it. For the last two weeks I'd gotten to see what it was like to have someone by my side. Pops meant well, but looking back, I know that Luna already knew me worlds better than he did in much less time.

I barely registered a rap at the cabin's screen door as I finished stuffing random items in my backpack, but perked up when Logan called out, "Kaleb, Luuuuuna's here!" in a mocking voice. He clearly did not make the distinction between girlfriend and girl friend.

Ignoring him, I approached the door to find Luna's face reflecting my exact sentiment with a bored roll of her eyes. Offering up a smile in solidarity, I opened the door and came out to meet her on the front porch.

"I brought you something," she chirped, holding out a familiar-looking folded up piece of paper. Pulling it open, I half expected I'd find the wolf I drew that she colored in, but it took my breath away anyway.

It was the coolest wolf I'd ever seen with streaks of purple against black in all different shades. Grape, lavender, pitch black, violet, charcoal, even a color you couldn't quite tell was black or purple… they all gave a certain essence to the wolf. It looked mystical yet dangerous. Dark, but beautiful.

"I love it," I breathed out, not even thinking about my words as my eyes stayed fixated on the paper.

"I'm glad you like it," Luna's voice echoed softly as I continued to catalog each line and curve. Still not satisfied, but not wanting to spend our goodbye staring at something I'd have the rest of my life to look at, I looked back up at her.

"Thank you."

"I was thinking, we could keep in touch?" She lifts a shoulder and squints her eyes shyly. "I could write my number at the bottom. I only get limited privileges with my cell phone, but we could text each other and call and stuff," she offers, sounding hopeful.

"Um…" I stammered, trying not to acknowledge the sinking feeling in my gut while I found a way to explain. But when I looked in those expectant brown eyes that I just now noticed had a few gold flecks, I realized this was the person who'd embraced everything about me from the start. "I don't have a phone," I confess.

Luna didn't bat an eye at my admission, and brightly suggested, "We could write letters then."

"Yeah, sure," I agreed and piped up at the idea, dashing back to my bunk to get a paper and pen. After scratching down my address, using the flat rail of the porch, I handed the pen to her and watched as she started to write down her own.

Luna Conlin, she wrote down before quickly scribbling out the last name and starting over.

"Did you forget your last name, goof?" I teased her, watching her cheeks turn a little pink.

"Yeah," she chuckled at herself, but not looking up. Instead, she busied herself with the task of writing her information down. "I'm still not used to writing my new last name."

Luna Isaak her name now read, when she finally handed the paper back to me.

"Why did you change your last name?"

"Well… my dad… my dad just adopted me last year."

"Oh…" started off my brilliant response. I was totally stunned. "Cool."

Her smile beamed as she nodded in agreement. "Well, I should probably go," she said, starting to step away, when I thought of something.

"Wait." She stopped as I held my hand out, making her slow backward steps come to a halt and her eyes regard my hand curiously. "Give me your hand."

"Okaaay…" she obliged, cocking a sassy eyebrow at me. Taking her hand in mine, I grabbed the pen and started drawing on her palm. I took my time with each line and detail, drawing out our last moments as long as I could. When I finished, I curled her fingers in, closing her hand.

"Don't look until you're in the car, okay?"

"Okay," she agreed again, this time on a lighthearted giggle. "Write me?" she asked, backing away again.

"Of course."

She gave me one last wave, which I returned, before she took part of my heart and skipped away; out of my sight, but not my life.

4

KALEB

Dear Luna,
I'm back home, about to start 5th grade. I really had fun at camp with you and I hope you liked what I put on your hand. Our black and purple wolf is taped to my wall, and while I was gone, Pops hung a tire swing for me in the backyard. It's awesome!

Dear Kaleb,
I begged my mom and dad to let me go back to camp again next year and they said yes! Will you be there too? I'll ask my dad if he can hang me a tire swing too, it sounds fun. I have a pet cat named Buster. Do you have any pets? I really don't want to start school this fall. Yuck...

Hi Luna,
How is school? It's going okay for me. I've made a couple of new friends this year. I don't know if I can go back to camp, but I'm going to try. I hope you like this

picture of a skunk I drew for you. Maybe you could make something and send it to me. I like your paintings...

Dear Kaleb,
It was so cool seeing you at camp again. I think I'm getting better at the ropes course. Guess what? My mom is pregnant, I'm getting a baby brother! But don't worry, I'll still be at camp again next year...

Dear Luna,
Your uncle is NOT in Turn it Up! There's no way you're related to a rockstar! Nice prank, though. I love their music. Pops usually has a rock station playing in the shop and they come on a lot. Oh, and one of the guys that works with him on the cars has a lot of tattoos and said he likes my drawings. It makes me want to get even better at it, so I'm signing up for art as an elective in middle school...

Dear Kaleb,
Oh yeah?? Check out this picture I sent you! That is ME on my uncle MATT's shoulders! And did you forget that my last name used to be Conlin?? He also signed this t-shirt for you, so you're welcome!

Kaleb, Age 18

Over the last eight years, one thing I could always depend on was letters from Luna. We'd make it a top priority to see each other each summer at camp for two weeks, three if we could manage it, and in all those letters in between, I got to know her better than anyone else.

And the funny thing is, after that first summer meeting her, making friends at school came a little easier to me. I was still perfectly happy to spend time on my own, but getting to know other kids came a little more naturally after her.

I've still never felt the need to get a cell phone, even after I started to make some money. I could see all the drama that came with having one from my friends that all had them, and I felt no need. My town was small enough that people knew where to find me, and I sure as hell didn't need any of that social media garbage. I guess I'm just a simple guy when it comes to that kind of thing, and I'm seriously glad to not have one right now with all of Cheyenne's antics. Besides, there's something to be said about snail mail. Getting a letter from Luna was always something to look forward to, yet a welcome surprise whenever one came.

Now here we are in the flesh, a week into counseling together, and some new, irritating feeling is coming over me that I don't like one bit. It's hard to describe except that I feel partially sick to my stomach and grumpy as fuck. I've been feeling it since I noticed that one of my fellow counselors, Michael, started sniffing around Luna earlier this week.

It started when I noticed him staring a little too long at us when she and I were on lifeguard duty together. I couldn't quite blame him as she was a sight for sore eyes in her royal blue one piece swim suit, with the sun glinting off her silky, tanned skin. I had to hide my hard-on by holding my buoy in front of me. But seriously, dude, move the fuck along. Then he just had to demonstrate good lasso throwing technique to the kids by tossing his rope around her, followed by a joke about keeping her. While she humored him with a laugh, the accompanying smile didn't reach her eyes, and any moron could read that she was just being polite and not swooning over his flirting attempts.

He was all over her during a cornhole tournament, pretending to be scared and hide behind her during the water balloon wars, and I damn near blew a gasket when he wiped a smudge of marshmallow off the corner of her mouth from her S'more the other night. He kept touching her a little more than he had to, and I was ready to knock his lights out. And with each interaction he's talking, talking, talking.

The idiot clearly knows nothing about her like I do. For example, if she wants to know something about you, she'll ask you.

I'll admit, I'm kind of enjoying the sour expression he's shooting our way as she and I sit at the end of the picnic table while her campers and mine write out letters to their families. He needs to get the hint that when Luna and I are here in this place, she and I belong to each other.

Seeing her when I first rolled up last week took my breath away. I tried to tell myself it's just because another year had gone by, and because this was our last time at this place I was getting nostalgic about the first time, and comparing how much she'd changed.

She's still slim and lithe, I'd wager about 5'7" to my 6'2" now. Her face is all high cheek bones and a delicate jaw, while her eyes hold a certain maturity that I must have missed gradually building over the years.

And her body has not gone unnoticed. Toned, smooth legs, breasts that are just the right size for both her frame and my hand, and a dynamite ass. And don't get me started on her skin. The smooth canvas is both begging for ink but also looks so damn good as it is; perfect and untouched.

"Do you think you can help me out in art later?" she asks, jarring me out of my lusty haze, but instead of looking at me, her brow is pulled into a scowl as she looks down at something she's trying to draw in her notebook. I'm not sure what it is, but it looks like a partially deflated soccer ball with flippers.

"Yeah, with what?"

"I have this great step-by-step painting of a beach for the kids to do, but I want it to have a baby sea turtle crawling towards the waves and - uggghhh! I just can't get it right," she grits out, flipping her pencil over to furiously rub at her drawing with the eraser.

"What do you want me to do? Draw a turtle on their pictures for them and they can paint it in?" I ask, coming around to her side so I can get a look at the poor turtle she's deforming.

"Yeah, would you?" She huffs out a breath, blowing a wisp of brown hair from hanging down in her face.

"Sure thing," I assure her as I sit down close to her, straddling the bench, my crotch flush against her hip. "Here," I hold out my hand across her. Looking up at me over her shoulder she tries to hand over her pencil, questions glowing in her honey-brown eyes, but rather than take it from her, I guide her hand back down to the paper. "Hold it like you're going to draw," I instruct and she obliged with no hesitation. I chance a quick look up to Michael, who's still giving me a death stare while he's supposed to be working with his campers on knots.

This is what years of bonding and trust looks like, fucker. Get the fuck back to your ropes.

Looking back down at Luna's notebook, I grip the pencil just above where her hand is. Without verbal instruction, I just start drawing a sea turtle the way I see it in my head, and it just appears naturally on the paper. Luna, however, is taking in every single movement and it's resulting mark on the page. For sure, she's going to try it on her own later. She's forever striving to further perfect her craft.

I continue with the general outline, pretending I'm focusing on the picture, when really, I'm letting her scent cast it's spell over my senses. Sunscreen mixed with florals and the musk of her shampoo make up my favorite scent on earth, and I never knew it. Our closeness gives me a dreamlike feeling that's having an effect on more than one part of me, and I just hope to God she doesn't feel it against her hip.

When I glance up from the paper to the side of Luna's face, I see that she's smiling down fondly, and I wish I knew if it was our turtle making her happy, or the act of doing something like this; our hands touching while they create something together. Despite myself, I hope to hell it's the latter.

Luna has no idea how close I hold her inside. She's special to me, and it's because of that I've never let her all the way in. Don't get me wrong, she knows a lot of things about me that no one else does, but when it comes to emotions, I've been very reserved. It's one thing to know facts about someone, but something down in my self-conscious must think that because I've worn my armor so long, I'm afraid to be something other than what she's always known.

To her, I'm Kaleb who will take any dare before he tells any truths, and she seems to be fine enough with that to still be here.

"Voilá," I announce in a low voice when the turtle is complete.

Luna is still looking down at it smiling when her lips part and her eyes dart off in the distance for moment. "Wait a minute..." she says, turning in her seat so that she's facing me and grabs hold of my left arm. The warmth of her hand sends a pang through my chest I'm sure she's oblivious to as her eyes scan up and down the artwork on my arm.

"You did these tats, didn't you?"

"Guilty," I quirk a smile at her and feel that thrill again when she looks up and down between me and my arm with a radiant smile. "I've been helping out at the tattoo parlor back home, and they've let me practice on myself."

"Oh my God, K, you should do this! Like, for a living..." she shakes her head in awe and my heart swells at the sight. This is why she's my Luna. Cheyenne sneered at the idea, not that I gave any fucks what she thought.

"Well, after boot camp, I may go back there and do an apprenticeship unless I get stationed somewhere else," I shrug, not missing her blink at the words boot camp.

"I want a tattoo," she mumbles softly, rotating my arm a little so she can see more of the designs.

"Why don't you have any? Will your dad kill you?" I tease, raising an eyebrow.

"No, blockhead, I just don't know what to get. I have too many ideas." She's watching her language in front of the kids. Normally she'd call me something else. It's the mark of a true friendship when you can give each other shit.

"Ah, the life of an artist," I lament. "The struggle is real."

"Looks like you have the same problem, only you just decided to go with them all," she quips taking one last look, but before she lets go, her mouth goes slack as her eyes widen. "Oh my God… Kaleb?" She looks up at me with a look of wonder I'd been waiting to see on her face since I etched the crescent moon into my skin. "That's the moon. I mean, obviously, but the moon you drew on my hand! This is the same one! Exactly!"

I look down at the design of the white moon peeking out from some dark clouds with a few twinkling stars keeping it company.

"What made you put that on your body for all eternity?" she marvels with a shake of her head and lets go of my arm, much to my inner chagrin.

"Excuse me, is that not a sick-ass drawing for a ten-year-old?" I ask rhetorically. "That had to go in my little record book. Besides, it reminds me of when I met you," I add as casually as I can, already feeling a pang of anxiety at giving her even a partial truth of how I feel about her… the whole truth being that I had heard what the name Luna meant, and decided that she was my moon. My Luna.

"Yeah, it's time I handed the gun over to someone else though, so I can get this other arm done." I change the subject and nod at my right arm. "It looks like I dipped one arm in ink."

"Well whoever does it, make sure they're the best. Don't trust just anyone with your designs."

"Don't worry. Remember Logan?" I ask, and she rolls her eyes skyward for a moment.

"From our first year here? He was hanging out with the two twits that taught us truth or dare?"

"Yes," I chuckle, bending a knee and folding my arms over it. "Anyway, his town isn't too far from mine, and his old man has a shop of his own. I'll probably go there."

She tucks her lip in and nods thoughtfully, her tell that her mind is racing a mile a minute. "Would you come up with a design for me?"

"For a tat?" I ask, dipping my chin forward a little and she nods her affirmation. "You're going to saddle me with that impossible task, huh?"

"Please?" she begs, giving me the cheesiest grin she can muster.

"Fine." I roll my eyes acting like it's a hardship, when in reality, there's nothing I wouldn't do for her.

"Yes!" She celebrates by doing her double fist-pump thing she's done for as long as I've known her.

"You owe me though," I say and give her an admonishing look, to which she tilts her head.

"Yeah, right," she tilts her head and squints her eyes up at me.

"I'll collect," I tell her, just to piss her off. It's fun. "Might be tomorrow or five years from now, but I'll collect."

"Oh, you..." she looks around at the campers as they fold up their letters into envelopes, "butthead," she finishes.

"So what about you, goof?" I ask as we stand just in time for the dinner bell to ring, and she starts collecting all the envelopes from the kids.

"What do you mean?"

"What are you going to be doing while I'm learning how to kick your ass at boot camp?" I ask as I follow her around, and a couple of wide-eyed campers swivel their heads my way. I look between their slack mouthed expressions and up to Luna to see her widening her eyes at me with a hard set of her jaw.

"A year of college, and then hopefully a bomb art school," she answers my question without meeting my eyes as she arranges all the letters in the bin tucked under her arm.

"Okay, I get the art school, but why lose a year going to college first?" I ask, feeling my eyes squint, trying to process this. I just don't see Luna in a library, studying her ass off. She is and has always been a hands-on kind of girl.

"I just…" she starts to twitch, still not looking at me, "promised my parents I'd try college for a year. They're worried I won't be able to make a living as an artist and think I should go to school for some kind of degree that's more in demand. I've told them I don't want to and that I'd rather make peanuts doing what I love, but… they've done so much for me and I don't want to let them down, so we compromised." She lets out a hard breath before finally looking at me. "I promised I would try it for a year, and if I don't like it – which I know I won't – they'll help me transfer to an art institute."

I stare down at her as she shifts her weight between both feet awkwardly. I want so badly to point out that she just minutes ago told me I should go for it with my drawing, but I don't.

"It'll be good," she nods, and I can tell she's trying to convince herself. "Maybe that year at a university will help me get into a really good one."

I let a moment pass, telling her with my solemn stare what I really think, before finally letting out a resigned sigh. "Cool."

She knows that response is full of shit, but she takes it as her free pass, smiling at me before turning away to take the letters to the office.

5

LUNA

*A*fter the last of the campers leaves in the back seat of their respective sedan, minivan, or SUV, the rest of the counselors and I hurry to close up the camp for the fall. We get to stay one more night, sans children, and so as you can imagine, we're eager to get the work part over with.

When the lane ropes and life vests are put away in the boat house, and all the Tough Mudder-type obstacles are cleaned and put away in the barn, I march over to the boys' cabin and obnoxiously bang on the screen door.

Kaleb comes sauntering from somewhere in the back, slapping hands with a couple of the other guys.

"M'lady?" he grunts as he opens the door to join me on the front porch.

"You've been torturing me for the last seven weeks, and it ends now," I gripe at him between my teeth which only makes him stand straighter and give me a smug look as he jams his hands in his pockets.

"I don't know what you're talking about," he bullshits, and I roll my eyes.

"You've been telling me you've got something up your sleeve for tonight and it's been driving me up the fucking wall all this time! It was worse than when you leave one of your letters on a cliffhanger!"

"We better get going then," he says off-handedly as he strolls past me.

"Where?"

"To the beach," he tosses back, referring to the lakefront property where there's a sandy area, a camp fire pit, and the dock with swimming area where we conduct all the water activities.

"Kaleb Dominic, I don't like this one bit," I scold from behind him.

"You will," he promises, and I hate to admit it, but I'm thrilled to see a large air mattress set up by the grassy area behind the sand in the clearing of trees. It's loaded down with pillows and blankets with a cooler nearby.

"Okay, I'm not sure if you're aware what decade we're in, but that day I said I owed you one, I didn't mean you'd get laid," I pop a hip out and wave a hand at the setup he has going on.

"Relax, you don't owe me shit," he waves me off. "I was fucking with you."

"I hate you so much sometimes."

"I know, but I figured I could make it up to you by…" he pauses, clearly for effect by the way he's eyeing me, as he bends over to pull one of the blankets back to reveal a laptop computer laying beneath it.

"Are you sending prank emails to the Pentagon?"

"No, wiseass, we're watching a movie."

"Ooh! Which movie?" I ask and gleefully skip closer.

"Dead Scared Four."

"Yes!" I double fist pump, looking forward to watching a scary-ass movie in the dark woods. "And what's in the cooler?"

"Beer, what else?" He gives me a shit-eating grin I haven't seen since we were little.

"Kaleb," I huff out disapprovingly, even though I don't care that he has beer, nor am I worried about how he got it. Upper management is actually pretty chill once we're off our contract, which we are as of this afternoon. "What the hell am I supposed to drink?"

"You still don't drink?" he asks, flipping the cooler's lid.

"That's right, I don't," I say adamantly, refusing to let him be the nine hundredth person that's given me shit or tried to make me feel like a loser about it.

"Well then, good thing I also have the kind you drink in here," he snickers, holding up a brown bottle that I immediately recognize as an old-fashioned root beer.

I smile warmly at him. "You remembered." I waste no more time and hustle over to him, quickly relieving him of the bottle. I'm an absolute sucker for root beer, and I have no clue which letter or conversation I revealed that to him, and I don't care. It gives me a warm glow when I realize how much he's paid attention over the years.

What I've never told him is why I don't drink. It has nothing to do with being underage. It's actually kind of petty, because if he ever asked, I would tell him. I trust him like no other, and I have nothing to hide from him for worry of him pulling away from me. What bothers me is how much he knows about me, and how much I don't know about him. I've never pushed him to tell me anything, but an immature part of me doesn't like how unbalanced the scales are. So while I've revealed things during our ongoing truth or dare game, I've kept little pieces to myself. I also can't help but wonder if maintaining a little mystery will keep this bond burning bright.

I do wish Kaleb would let me all the way in, that he'd realize there's nothing he can tell me about himself that would change anything. I've always assumed his life hasn't been puppies and rainbows. It's not hard to figure out when he's let things slip about money being tight and no mention of either parent growing up. But then, I suppose part of being a true friend is just being there and caring for them whether they tell you things or not. Besides, he tells me through actions how much he cares about me. While part of me aches to know him deeper, I know I have a special part of him.

"Come on," he beckons as he lowers himself to the makeshift bed and reclines back against the pillows with one arm tucked behind his head. "Let's get this rolling."

"Okay, just one more," I say, sitting down and holding the phone out to take a selfie with Kaleb in the background. I make a goofy face, winking with my tongue out – it's kind of my thing with selfies – while Kaleb's brow scrunches with narrowed eyes, as if to say, really?

Satisfied with the perfectly imperfect image saved on my phone, I tuck it away and accept the root beer he holds out to me.

The sun is just beginning its descent as we get comfortable, drinks in hands and movie cued up. We spend the next hour and a half scaring the shit out of ourselves and each other, and when the credits roll, I go over to the pit to fire up the logs and newspaper Kaleb had already prepped. He meets me back on the mattress, holding out another root beer for me and a real beer of his own before reclining back with an arm tucked behind his head. The inside of his bicep is on display, lines of muscles and tattoos being picked up by licks of firelight. It's flicking on all sorts of switches on my insides, and I pretend not to gawk as I curl up on a pillow a couple feet away. I've seen him grow up in such gradual phases, and last year, I saw a change in him for sure, but this year it's impossible to see him as a boy. He may only be eighteen, but he's definitely a man when I look at him. Pair that with the close connection over the years, and God, is it doing things to me.

"How long are we staying out here?" I ask conversationally as I look out at the reflection of the moon, crinkling on the surface of the water.

"All night if we want."

All night together… on a bed.

My mind nervously flits to a vision of Kaleb and I curled in close together under a blanket, trying to keep warm as I breathe in that scent that makes me want to grow up right along with him. To be a woman to his man. He snaps me out of it by hauling himself off the mattress. After placing his empty bottle in the trash bin, he reaches behind him to pull off his shirt.

"Uh... what are you doing?" I ask, cocking my head to the side.

"Let's jump in the lake," he suggests, tilting his head in the direction of the water.

"Um, no thanks, I'm good." I turn my head away, busying myself with a drink from my bottle. I don't know why his disrobing is giving me flutters all of a sudden when I saw him without a shirt for half the summer when we had to do swim activities with the campers. Maybe it's because it's just him and me in a semi-romantic atmosphere.

"Come on," he beckons, dragging the second word out as he looks down to unbutton his shorts.

"Oh my God," I look away again, holding a hand up by my face as a blinder.

"Pffft... please. You've seen me in my swim trunks, don't tell me my boxer briefs are too revealing for you."

"Just... trying to protect your modesty." I give my tone a joking lilt as I hesitantly drop my hand. Since he's cool with me seeing him in his underwear, I let myself look while trying not to make it obvious, or openly gawk. "Nice skivvies," I tell him, arching a brow as I mentally catalog the form-fitting cotton material hugging his hips and thighs.

"Yeah, whatever." He brushes off my teasing as he kicks his shorts to the side. "Come in with me," he implores again in a steady voice.

"Nope."

"Chickenshit," he sniggers, lifting a challenging eyebrow at me.

"Fuck you," I huff back, still nervously chuckling. And your biceps.

"What are you so afraid of? Getting your hair wet?" he jeers as he starts backing slowly in the direction of the dock.

"No..." I shoot back, annoyed.

"Getting caught?"

"No."

"Having a dare blemish your dare-free record?" he teases, his tongue poking out at me from between his teeth.

"You're not daring me, so I'm all set," I inform him smugly as I stand and slowly start following his leisurely backwards pace.

This makes him stop and level me with a hard look. "Lu, seriously... When are we going to see each other again after this? Don't you want to remember this as the night you did something unexpected?"

Ooh. Playing Jedi-mind tricks, are we?

For a quick second I humor him, and try to mentally fast forward to myself years in the future looking back at this night, and telling myself I just hung out on the bank; that I couldn't even be talked into a simple night swim.

"You coming?" he prods further, and I barely have a second to register the look on his face as he shifts from the firelight and is promptly backlit by the moonlight that kicks off the water. His eyes have gone half-lidded with a lazy smile that does something to my insides, lighting up my senses with endorphins.

I close my eyes and let out a nervous sigh that quakes my body. "Fine," I concede, dropping my head back.

"Yes!" Kaleb celebrates, clapping his hands a couple times in triumph. I feel a tug at the corner of my mouth and a flutter in my abdomen at his excitement. In fact, I feel a quite a few new sensations at the idea of him wanting me to come in the water with him. Even so, I avert my eyes as I kick off my sneakers and undo the clasp on my jeans.

I can feel his gaze on me without looking as I work the denim down my hips, trying not to feel self-conscious or nervous for him to see me half-dressed. I try reassuring myself that it's dark out here anyway, and he probably can't see much. We're too far from the fire for him to take note of my purple bikini underwear, yet I still find myself tugging at the hem of my t-shirt that refuses to come down to even my pelvis.

Kaleb spares me any reservations when he tackles me out of nowhere, wrapping his arms around my legs and briskly hoisting me up on his shoulder. I let out a startled shriek as he whips us around in the direction of the water. My heart is flopping around somewhere between my chest and my throat as he howls with excitement and charges down the dock with me over his shoulder.

I try to steady the bouncing by bracing my arms against his bare back. I squeeze my eyes shut but squeal in exhilaration as I anticipate us nearing the dock's edge. And then sure enough, in the next second, we're sailing through the night air, Kaleb losing his hold on me as I pitch over his shoulder, and we fall the rest of the way into the water.

The shock of the cold water surging up around me is invigorating as I kick my way to the surface, emerging with a deep gasp of air. I turn, looking for Kaleb, and immediately find him treading water on my left with a shit-eating grin on his face.

"Asshole," I exhale with a grin as I catch my breath.

"Whatever, I know you love me," he chides, dipping his head back to slick his long hair off his forehead, and before I have time to register the zing that statement sends up my spine, he's immediately back to our game. "Okay, where were we – oh yes, it's your turn. Truth or dare?"

"What? No! I just jumped in the damn lake!"

"But it wasn't a dare. It doesn't count, remember?"

"Oh my God," I huff out, rolling my eyes. He's such a pain in my ass. "Fine, truth."

"Are you still a virgin?"

My head snaps up as a wave of adrenaline blows through my body. "What the fuck, Kaleb?" I exclaim as he chuckles up at me. He's never asked me a question like that.

"Hey, we don't know when we're seeing each other next, I intend to win this game."

"Oh… taking it to the cutthroat level are we? Asking me a question you don't think I'll answer. By the way, I didn't miss how you already had that one locked and loaded. How long have you been pondering the state of my hymen?"

"Is this you refusing to answer?" he lifts an eyebrow.

"No, you're not winning that easily," I blow out as I drop my head back, soaking my hair in the water. "Yes. Truth or dare?" I quickly fire back before he can give me shit for not drinking and not having sex.

When I'm met with silence however, I peer up and find him treading in the same place, with a small smile gracing his lips. It's definitely a knowing smile, but it's absent of any of the cockiness I was expecting. His half-lidded eyes give it a certain fondness, like this information makes him appreciative and he's proud of me or something.

"What?" I ask, feeling self-conscious.

The moon reflects off the bare shoulder he lifts out of the water in a half-shrug. "Just glad to hear you're still a good girl," he winks, confusing me on how I should be taking it.

"Shut up," I mutter, smiling sheepishly as I look away again.

"Relax, Lu," I hear him sigh out behind me. "It's a good thing."

I know what he's trying to say, and have no idea why I'm taking such offense. The first thing I can think of is I don't want to be seen as some proper, boring, uptight girl.

"Right," I mumble cynically.

"Seriously."

I feel a hint of irritation flicker inside me and I try to hide it, leveling him with a dubious look. "Well, maybe you don't know me as well as you think. I'm forgetful and I don't plan for shit, I fly by the seat of my pants, I'm a B student, I drive too fast, and hell, I made out heavily with my prom date! Hands were everywhere …" I trail off when I notice the way his eyes widen and drift downwards a moment before he seems to blink out of it.

"Hey, I said you were a good girl," he interjects, raising the eyebrow that's adorned with the small silver hoop. "I never said you were perfect. Hell, you can't draw for shit –"

He's cut off by me dousing him with a whoosh of lake water that I whisk into his face with a sweep of my arm. I feel a breath release from my chest and a grin spread on my face as he sputters and wipes water out of his eyes before looking back at me.

There's a short pause before he adds, "You kind of suck at basketball too."

His dumb taunt is cut off by splooshing bubbles this time as I propel myself up and bring my hands down on his head, dunking him under water. And just like that, I've forgotten my self-conscious discomfort. How Kaleb has the talent to pull me out of my comfort zone and toss me right back in it is a phenomenon, especially considering how little we see each other.

We splash and shove at each other for a moment or two, slowly drifting back closer to the dock before we both relent and a comfortable silence falls over us. Giving myself a break, I reach one hand up to grab onto the planked wood to steady myself as Kaleb's face takes on a sort of pensive expression while his green eyes seem to search mine.

"What?" I ask.

His eyes shift downwards in a hesitant moment before glancing back up at me. "What's so bad about being a good girl?"

Ugh. Okay, this is worse than the virgin question. This is a truth that I seriously don't want him to know, that I find myself giving a huge fuck about what he thinks of me. I see him and have a very good idea of who he surrounds himself with – girls, in particular – and it's not the goody-goody type. I don't want to be seen as someone who never takes risks and plays it safe. Not by him.

Instead of answering, I hit him back with, "It's not my turn," and cover up any residual uneasiness with a smirk.

He lets out an airy chuckle, his grin giving my insides a squeeze, and I feel my heart beat faster in my chest the longer he stares back at me.

Something is happening in this moment. I can't tell if it's a good something or bad, but… we're changing. This is the longest we've ever just stared at each other, and my heart is starting to ache with every pound. Whatever plane Kaleb and I have always been on is moving, but it's so hard to tell in which direction.

I'm almost relieved to see his face change to one of mischief.

"Fine," he concedes. "Go ahead."

"Truth or dare?" I fire off as my shoulders relax, feeling like I'm off the hook.

"Dare."

"Duh. Okay, I dare you –"

"Dare me to kiss you," he cuts off without even blinking. In fact, he's never looked more confident.

A sharp gasp expands my lungs and my abdominal muscles tighten. I feel my features pull together in confusion.

"What?"

6

LUNA

*I*n disbelief of what I just heard, I vigorously shake my head, as if I fell asleep for a moment and dreamed that he said that. "That's not how it works. You're not supposed to choose the dare yourself," I puff out, flustered by the curve ball.

"So I'm breaking a rule." He shrugs a shoulder before grabbing onto the dock with the same arm, mirroring my position. "Break it with me," he challenges with a playful jut of his chin, as his upper body drifts towards me just slightly. I grip the dock a little firmer, but don't let my own buoyancy move me away from his, chancing to see if he'll keep moving closer. And he does. It's slow and casual, giving me plenty of time to move away, protest, or smack him away.

"Wha…" I shake my head, still trying to wrap my brain around this, not to mention the different sensations pinging and zigzagging through my body. "Why?" I finally ask.

"Look how long we've known each other." He levels me with this look like this should be simple math. Who knows, maybe it should be. "Haven't you wondered what it would be like if we kissed?"

I have, I immediately respond to only myself with no question. I have a million times, but I want to keep that to myself for just a few seconds while I search his face, trying to see if he's for real; genuine. He's so hard to read with the many masks he switches between to keep me guessing.

A resigned shadow falls over his eyes as he blinks slowly, shaking his head. "Never mind. I get it, that's a bad idea, we can just –"

"Yes," I breathe out before he can finish. Because for a blink of time I saw it, his real face. He may hide it a lot, even from me, but I know what it looks like. And I just saw it, in that split-second as he backtracked. He brought up the kissing because he wanted to.

After my acquiescence, his gaze now darts between my eyes and my lips, queuing me to do the same. Droplets of lake water cling to parts of his gorgeous lips, and the front strands of his wet hair graze my temple as his forehead comes to rest against mine.

"Why?" I ask in a hushed tone, hoping to the stars above that I'm not killing this moment – a moment I never even knew I wanted until we got here. "Tell me why."

"I chose dare, not truth," he rasps back, not realizing he told me so much by telling me nothing at all.

We hang suspended in the moment, both of us clinging to the dock, bobbing close to each other with the crickets and water lapping at the dock as our soundtrack. My heart is quaking in my chest, threatening to give out and making my breath ragged as I breathe him in, the breath coming just in time for him to softly place his lips on mine, brushing them together with a softness that suggests he's feeling me out; gauging my response before taking it deeper.

It feels surreal and dizzying and I press into him, moving my lips with his to signal that this is good; to keep going. I'm breathless, yet I don't want to take my mouth away from his to take a breath, and I'm reassured that the feeling is mutual when his free hand comes down to grasp onto my waist beneath the water.

His mouth opens and slants over mine, pushing deeper and consuming me in bliss.

Caught up in our movements, I feel my knee brush against his hip, and that one touch ignites my core and makes every cell of my skin awaken. I feel so alive in the darkness of the night, and a small whimper escapes when Kaleb's hand grips my side tighter and pulls me into him. He groans approvingly into my mouth in response as the few inches between us is erased when he wraps his lean and muscular arm securely around my middle.

I startle slightly when I feel the hard ridge of his cock pressed against my lower abdomen, and my gasp forces us to break the kiss, both of us breathing heavily, and I realize we're moving. Our bodies are moving together so subtly that I can't tell if it's from the motion of the water or if we're doing it intentionally.

We look at each other a moment, our breaths coming in deep rasps. With each second that ticks by, my body aches more and more in a way I didn't know it could. It's rapt with need and I'm not naive enough not to realize what it's chasing after, no matter my level of inexperience. My body wants Kaleb, and it's demanding the rest of me to stop living in denial and admit the same.

Kaleb squeezes my body close to his, and then releases before doing it again, his eyes never leaving mine. I can see him trying to gauge my reaction as he repeats the motion again. I hold his stare with my own, willing him to see what I'm feeling.

It's okay... keep going.

As if to demonstrate my consent, my legs wind around his legs and I close my eyes in ecstasy as he keeps rubbing and pulling me against him and I feel like I'm in a dream that's the sweetest blend of fluid and vivid. Beautiful shades of blues and creams flash and plume behind my eyelids as we rock together before I feel his lips closing over mine again as his motions pick up.

A muted moan escapes my throat and hums between our lips

when I feel his hardness rubbing against my sex beneath the water; the friction of our undergarments heightening the pleasure. As our lips remain locked we breathe harder through our noses, desperate for breath, but even more so for what we're giving each other in this moment as our tongues massage against each other.

The water sloshes around us as I feel myself get closer. Unable to breathe, our mouths break apart, giving each other just enough space to draw in breath as Kaleb pulls me tighter against him, our cores still grinding against each other. Seemingly letting go of some of his control, he groans into my neck with each thrust, making my breath come out in a staccato sequence of gasps.

Letting go of the dock, my arms come around his neck, holding on for fear of tumbling out into another orbit as my orgasm crashes through me. I cry out, trying to muffle it against his shoulder as my whole-body hums with the reverberations.

Kaleb propels his body harder and faster, moaning into my neck. His cock is so hard and rigid against my sex it almost hurts, but in such a primal way it elicits cries of pleasure from my throat. He drives his groin against me several more times, drawing each one out slower than the last. The moments it takes for our breathing to slow are endless, as we cling to each other, drifting and bobbing with the gentle waves we created. I don't know if it's the cold lake water or my blood slowing, but I'm hit with a sudden shiver and it seems to jolt us both out of our post-orgasmic fog.

"You're cold," he pants, resting his head against mine. "Let's get you back by the fire."

Kaleb

I don't like to admit truths out loud, and even try to conceal them from myself, but I can't deny that there's a rogue voice in the back of my head shouting that I could hold Luna in my arms forever.

The tender taste of her lips and the sweet moans that escaped them when she came apart melted my soul if such a thing were possible.

Luna unwinds her arms from my neck and paddles the few feet to the dock's ladder.

I reach under the water and shake out the front of my briefs, trying to rinse most of the cum out of them before swiftly swimming after her. By the time I reach the ladder, she's just pulled herself out of the water, giving me a stunning view of her wet purple panties clinging to her perfect ass, droplets of water making individual paths down her long slender legs.

After hauling myself out of the water, I pull her close before she can walk away.

"Are you okay?" I whisper against her lips, and though she gives a subtle nod, she looks up at me with clouds of confusion in her brown eyes.

"What did we just do?" she whispers and attempts a nervous smile.

You just made me come inside my damn boxer briefs.

"Something amazing," is all I can think to answer, and I add a playful snicker to my delivery. She shakes her head like she doesn't know what to do with me. Hell, I don't know what to do with me, but being or even looking vulnerable is not what I do, especially not in tense moments, so acting cavalier is both a habit and a defense mechanism.

Rivulets of water skim and drip down her body and onto the dock as she continues striding away, pulling her long, wet hair to the side. She's walking carefully, as she always does on the dock since she almost drowned once as a kid. The summer before she and I had met, she'd slipped on a dock and hit her head before falling in the water. She told me about it during one of our countless conversations over the last eight summers. It's made her forever cautious not to slip, but also easy for me to catch up to her.

"Lu, don't you dare freak out or get weird on me," I huff out as I fall into step next to her. I don't want what she and I have to change, one way or another. It's the one thing that's been constant in my life. She's the one person besides Pops I've been able to depend on.

"I'm not," she promises, but she doesn't meet my eyes while she tries to feign being casual, wringing out her hair before tossing the wet strands back over her shoulder.

"Luna, that was no big deal." I wave an arm at the lake to indicate what we just did, because I'm a stupid eighteen-year-old. She whips her head in my direction, her amber eyes wide and questioning. "I didn't mean that," I hold up a placating hand. "I just mean it doesn't have to change anything. We're still us, right?"

She goes quiet a moment as we reach the blanket and she looks around distractedly while holding her wet t-shirt away from her stomach. "Yeah."

I don't believe her but I don't prod, as a certain instinct makes me move, one that always seems to kick in around Luna and I bend down to our blanket to grab my t-shirt. "Here," I hold it out to her and her eyes light up again with a small smile that shows her appreciation.

She turns her back, and though I try to put the cocky pervert in me aside, I can't help but stare as she struggles with her wet shirt, the clingy material inching up the damp skin of her back. I try to busy myself with getting the fire blazing again, adding a couple of shards of dry wood and more paper. But as I'm stoking at the building flames with a stick, I can't help but notice how alluring the sight of the firelight is, reflecting off her now completely bare back as she unclips her bra, a simple black number.

The damp ends of her hair tickle at that silky-looking skin as she turns my grey t-shirt around in her hands, getting it straight before lifting it over her head. As the soft cotton falls down around her body, she starts to turn and I quickly look down at the business of stoking the flames.

Luna comes to stand beside me, holding the shirt up slightly, facing her ass towards the fire, but away from me. Her eyes close as the emanating heat caresses up her skin, presumably taking the chill out of her body. Seeing her in my shirt does something to me, hitting me somewhere inside that's never been touched before. It's like she's been claimed as mine without me having to do anything, and it transports me to a different plane where she's my girl and I'm her man.

Deciding to get out of my own wet boxers, I straighten and walk over to where I discarded my shorts a few yards away. In the darkness away from the fire, I trade them for the wet briefs and stalk back over to the blanket where Luna is curling back up on the mattress and wrapping one of the blankets around her shoulders.

Normally the quiet between us is comfortable. There have been times we've swam or hiked and gone short whiles without feeling the need to fill it. But this particular silence is deafening, and it's making my heart pound in a way I don't like. My nerves are going haywire at the idea of us not having what's always been there. Desperate to take the edge off, I cross to the cooler and pull out a beer, as well as the other bottle I hadn't felt the need to touch yet.

As I unscrew the cap and bring the bottle up to my lips I hear Luna's voice, so soft, but cutting through the thick silence. "You brought… that too?" she asks as I take a hearty pull, shrugging as I tip the bottle back. Where I'm from, there's seriously nothing to do but hang out in my buddy, Alex's, garage, catching a good buzz while shooting the shit. Having no one around to stop us made it even less of a big deal.

I swallow down the strong liquid, letting it burn like fire down my throat to my gut, and take utter relief in the way it torches the cold nerves. "It's just Jack Daniels, Lu," I dismissively sigh out, enjoying the after taste on my tongue as I return the whiskey and crack open the beer I pulled out, taking a hearty swig. Grabbing a drink for Luna, I hand it to her as I join her on the mattress.

I lie down close to her and feel a twinge of warm relief when she curls her body towards mine, and I rest a hand on her bare thigh. She looks down at my thumb as it skims back and forth on her smooth skin.

When I feel a substantial amount of nerves lift away from my orbit, and a thin veil of fuzziness settles over my mind, I'm finally ready to test the waters.

"What's going on Lu?" I grumble softly, deciding I could already do with another long pull of my beer. I want to know what she's thinking. Obviously we just crossed a line we never have before, and I want to know how she feels about it. No one, including us, ever said we couldn't cross it, but all the same, we hadn't before tonight.

"Mmm?" She barely reacts, tilting her head an inch in my direction, her eyes still fixated on my hand on her thigh.

"Come on," I give her leg a gentle shake, trying to bring her out of wherever she's hiding, and her shoulders draw up, stiffening.

"I'm just," she pauses, closing her eyes as if searching for something behind them. "I'm just feeling so many different things at once, and I can't keep up."

"Like what?"

Her lips press together as her eyes get glassy; the flames of the fire dancing in their reflection. "I'm scared to talk about it. There, that's one thing," she huffs apathetically and drops her head back, looking up at the dark blue of the sky while she tries to blink away the moisture.

"Just tell me, baby," I prod, turning more towards her. "I mean, come on, it's me."

Lowering her head, she blows out a long breath between pursed lips. "I can't," she whispers, closing her eyes.

"Why the hell can't you?" I tilt my head, and try to check my tone. I'm feeling frustration starting to simmer up in my blood, but that won't get me anywhere here, and the sooner we get past this awkwardness, the better.

"Because I don't want us to change, and I feel stuck, right here in this moment, afraid to move!" Her voice rises along with mine as she sits up straighter.

"We're fine, Luna," I huff out, starting to get exasperated as I feel the comfortable haze I was in start to thin. I roll my legs off the mattress and stand to go for the whiskey again. Things with Luna have always been so easy; natural. Now here I am, needing shots to get through this conversation. I don't like what's happening.

"Something happened between us tonight, K. And I want to know how you feel about it."

I tip the whiskey bottle back and take a big glug before recapping it. "Why?" I respond on the exhale. She and I have never addressed anything deep, involving me, anyway. I always just kind of assumed she understood that wasn't really something I did easily and was leaving it be. Then again, this is something that involves her too. Still, it doesn't keep me from squirming at the idea of exposing what I like to keep on the inside.

"Because I never know where you're at." The frustration in her voice is prominent, even after that second shot.

"The fuck you talking about? I'm right here, Lu." I crawl back onto the bed towards her, but the face she gives me when she looks up at me tells me she's not fucking around.

"I mean in your head, Kaleb; your feelings."

"Lu," I huff out a heavy sigh, weighted by all the discomfort I'm trying to clear out of the air between us, but it's like bailing water out of a leaking boat with a thimble at this point. "You should know how I feel, we've known each other since we were ten."

"And that whole time, you've been hiding from me," she murmurs, the notes of discord in her voice growing louder.

I pause a second, narrowing my eyes as if I'm seeing someone different all of a sudden. "Where the hell did that come from?"

"A lot's changed since we first walked out here, Kaleb," her eyes cautiously lift to mine. "And I can only read body language and vibes to a certain point before I need you to talk to me. I don't know how to act with you right now, or where we're going after tonight –"

"Well then talk to me. Tell me how you feel," I urge her.

"See? You're doing it right now!" She lifts a finger to me and I don't like it one bit. It's like having the spotlight on me. "You won't answer or address what I'm saying. Instead, you turn it back over to me!"

I grab onto her finger, my own wrapping securely around it as I open my mouth to spew out a witty comeback when the alcohol clears a space for a hit of reality. That's exactly what I'm doing. Fuck.

We sit there, staring each other down, neither one of us wanting to be the next one to speak… until she finally does, albeit in a whisper. "Why do you never choose truth?"

"How come you never pick dare?" I challenge, setting my jaw.

Her beautiful pink lips part, and she looks out at the inky lake as if it will give her an answer.

"Because you're chickenshit," I snicker, trying to keep the upper hand.

"You're chickenshit," she fires back, this time the fire in her eyes is her own. "You're a fucking pussy," she leans away and stands, putting space between us. The sudden distance makes me feel oddly disarmed.

"How's that when you're the one that will never take a dare?" I scoff back.

"Fine," she throws her arms out, her voice deep with an

emotion I'm hating the sound of. "I'll admit I'm scared to do something scary or humiliating," she lifts her shoulders in a shrug, "but you're afraid of yourself," she bites out, folding her arms over her chest and looking out at the water.

"How do you figure?" I feel my jaw go slack and my brows knit together.

"Well," she blows out, somewhat haughtily, and turns back to me. "Clearly you don't want to share any truths, enough so that you will choose to commit to an unknown challenge rather than share something about yourself that is anything other than surface level, every. Single. Time. You're afraid to be seen."

I have to say, the conviction in her voice is more of a knife to the gut than her actual words. They hit me like a tiniest pinprick, straight to my heart, stunning me.

She's still for a moment, and I barely hear her breath hitch below the light symphony of frogs and crickets. The heaviness that has suddenly fallen over us makes me feel a little remorseful, enough to throw out the tiniest of bones.

"I didn't want you to feel sorry for me," I spit out quietly, and immediately grab my beer back up and draw from it. Anything to distract myself.

"What do you mean?" Her eyes soften, not with pity, but with an attentiveness that I'm not sure I can take either, and it makes me look away.

"If you knew everything," I clarify in a mumble, taking another drink.

"Why would I feel sorry for you?" she pushes, stepping closer again as I drain my bottle and chuck it in the empties. I don't answer as I open the cooler, retrieving another cold one from what is now melted ice water. I feel every muscle in my back and shoulders tense as I tip it back, chugging as much as I can. Hell, the one in my chest too.

"Kaleb!" she prods again, a certain pang in her voice that makes me inwardly flinch.

"What? What do you want?!" I explode, turning towards her

in time to see her body emit a small quake. "You want me to spill my guts? Bare my soul about what a shitty childhood I had? You want to hear about how my mom died when I was one, and my dad turned into an abusive drunk that took to smacking me around as his new pastime?" I rant, all the while secretly scanning her face for that damn look I don't want to see. The one that would make this entire relationship feel like a sham.

One thing that's always made me keep Luna close is that she's never seen me as the poor, disadvantaged kid that came from a broken home. To her, I was always just the kid that helped her when she was scared of heights and drew her pictures. The friend she clung to every summer, and wrote sweet letters to every year in between.

And while now, her eyes definitely mist over as I continue unloading on her, I see no sign of that dreaded pity. Instead, her glassy eyes stare hard at me as if she's not entirely surprised, but feels for me nonetheless. She's a loving and caring person, and her empathy is to be expected. But that absence of pity is what makes her the Luna I love.

"You want to know that ever since he broke my arm when I was seven, my grandfather became my guardian and has had to hide me from him while he cruised in and out of jails and rehab centers?!" I persist, still looking for that look. At this point, one might think I'm actually hoping for it so I have an excuse to detach. I've loved Luna so much all these years, and right now the possibility of her seeing me as anything other than the Kaleb she knows is screaming in my face.

"I want to know you, Kaleb!" She leans forward as if to physically help get her point across.

"You do know me," I gesture at my chest, willing her to see. She knows me, she does. She doesn't have to know the ugly parts too, does she?

"I know camp you," she argues, "while you know almost everything about me! Don't you understand how vulnerable that makes me feel – especially after that switch got flipped tonight?"

I don't have an answer, but I choose to smolder back at her instead of admit it.

"Yes, it sounds like you had a shitty start to life and mine can't compare to that, but it wasn't perfect!"

"Is that so?" I snidely throw back.

"It is! But none of what's happened to either of us matters! At least, it shouldn't!"

"Easy for you to say, your dad chose you, while mine saw me as a punching bag," I cynically mutter, trying not to wince at the acid in my own voice. "Then you got raised in a loving, well-off home, so excuse me if I don't want to sing and dance about my tragic past," I impart in a mocking tone while I feel the alcohol start to make my temper hot.

"You're leaving out one important detail, you fucking dick," she shoots back menacingly. Guess I'm seeing something other than camp Luna as well. "The fact that my dad didn't come into my life until I was nine! What the hell do you think was happening before that? I was raised by a single mother who juggled a job that barely paid the bills, raising me all by herself, and fighting addiction!"

Okay, damn. That was one hell of a bomb she dropped on me, and yet here I stand, with what should be a comfortable buzz (far from it), looking unfazed because that's what I do best... just like Luna said.

"Yeah," she nods, pinning me with more of her fiery gaze, and I can almost see her inward struggle to keep the tear that pools in her eye from falling. "I know a thing about addiction myself, seeing as how both of my biological parents live with it. The jackass that got my mother pregnant left her as soon as he heard about me."

The things I'm hearing from her knock me sideways as I think about what life might have been like for her before she met me. But my ego still won't give in. "Wow," is my impressive retort when I finally find my tongue. "Look who's also been holding back her not so pretty past." I lift a scrutinizing eyebrow at her. "And here you're trying to make me feel like shit because I didn't let you in on mine."

"I'm giving you shit for not letting me in on anything," she clarifies. "I never said you had to tell me all your sorrows, but I at least let you see me! You've never had to question anything in regards to how I feel. You get to ask anything you want in our stupid little game because I choose to let you, and I answer you with a truth every time. Anything you've ever wanted to know, you've asked and I've told you." Her voice is weakening, the fight going out of her. The only problem is I'm too buzzed to do what her Kaleb would do, which is take her in my arms and tell her she's still a tough cookie.

But because I'm a fucking teenaged jackass with whiskey running through his veins and fucking with his brain cells, I throw out a surly, "Well, guess we don't really know each other at all, do we? This is probably too intense to go any further," I grumble, keeping my regret out of my voice.

"Is that what you want?" she asks quietly, and my stubborn ass won't let myself rush to her when that tear finally falls.

"I'm just saying, camp is over," I drone on, talking out my ass at this point, "and look at us…" I wave my hand that clutches my beer between us. "It's already getting ugly. Maybe we weren't meant to be more than… whatever the hell this has been," I wave my arm around. I need to check out of this conversation soon before I make a bigger ass of myself, if that's even possible.

Luna doesn't even respond, instead moving to grab up her jeans, slipping a leg in each as she refuses to look my way.

"Where you going?" I demand, as she stuffs her feet into her sneakers.

"To my cabin," she answers, barely audible as she starts taking strides to the trailhead.

"Why?" I call after her, holding my hands out.

"Because you called it." She doesn't look back, but I can hear the tears making her voice thick. "And I can't believe I ever loved such a fucking asshole."

Even though I've got Jack Daniels whispering in my ear to keep right on up with the dickhead act, those last words she said broke through every wall I've put up tonight. And it fucking hurts like a bitch.

"Come on, you can't walk back alone," I grunt as I stumble around in a circle, wondering where in the fuck I left my shoes.

"I'll take my chances with a bear rather than spend another second with your pitiful ass!"

"There are no bears out here, you moron!" I bellow back.

"You're the fucking moron," she yells, storming back all of a sudden, and I actually feel a traitorous hopeful flutter. "And by the way, I would actually love to have a beer with you. The reason I don't is because there's more than a fifty percent chance addiction has been passed down to me, so I don't take the risk!"

"Good for you, you're such a good girl," the venomous words slither out of me like the snake I am right now. And the look on Luna's face looks as if she's just seen a person she thought she knew morph into just that.

But she squares her shoulders and toughens her veneer before speaking one last time. "Just so you know... the only person feeling sorry for you is you!" She turns back around, her beautiful brown hair swinging behind her as she goes. But unlike that first summer at camp, this time she's taking my whole heart with her.

I turn back towards the fire, trying to fight off the pain that is effectively breaking through the forcefield of intoxication that had been protecting me from vulnerability. The pain is so potent, I lash out against it, drawing my arm back and pitching my beer bottle into the fire, watching the exploding sparks rise into the night.

7

LUNA

I watch as Kaleb preps his bike, checking gears and oil and all sorts of things I don't have the first clue about. After making sure his saddle bags have everything, he straightens up and turns to me while pulling his jacket on.

I blow out a breath as I relax back against my black Mazda, both wanting to get this moment over with and draw it out at the same time.

"Good luck at training," I murmur somberly as he comes to stand only a few inches in front of me. "Don't let them cut your hair too short." I quirk an eyebrow, trying to lighten the moment.

"You like this?" He tips his head forward and tugs at one of the longer strands of hair he has up front. Now waiting for an answer, he stares down at me, much like the way he did when he arrived at the beginning of the summer. Finally, he brings a hand up to cup the side of my face, his thumb brushing over my cheek bone. "Truth or dare?"

"Hmmph," I can't help a small snort at the idea I would possibly choose dare at this moment. He'd probably dare me to go up on the ropes course naked. "Truth."

"One day you're going to pick dare," he says gruffly down at me.

"That will be the day you pick truth."

"Fair enough. Alright, truth. Do you swear nothing's changed between us?"

I take a moment to think about my answer, because I want to it be one hundred percent whole-hearted. A few things did change between us. There was a definite shift in our dynamic bond, but that's to be expected as you grow and get older. The important thing is I'm unequivocally certain Kaleb is going to stay in my heart, the way he always has been.

"Nothing's changed, K. And it never will."

His barely-there smile and the slight shift of his shoulders as he lets out a breath are a balm to my heart; a sign that he feels the same.

"Your turn," I tell him.

"Dare."

"I dare youuu..." I draw the last word out to buy me some time while I decide whether to dare him to kiss me again. But after our pact for nothing to change, I think better of it. "I dare you to keep writing me. At least every month until you get a damn phone," I finally spew out with a smart look.

"We'll see," he mutters reluctantly. All those years of not having a phone, Kaleb decided he preferred it. He'd told me one summer he just didn't feel the need, and was happy in his own company. I'm hoping now that he's off to boot camp in South Carolina, however, he'll get one so that he can stay in better touch with his granddad.

When he drops his hands, I reach in my back pocket and produce a ballpoint pen before handing it to him.

"This again?" He looks at me dubiously, but he's full of shit. He lives for this as much as I do.

"Don't fuck with tradition," I say holding my hand out.

"Wouldn't dream of it." He clicks the end of the pen and takes my hand in his rough one, clueless to the fact that I'm filing the feeling of his touch away in my mind as he begins to draw. The pen sweeping and dragging along my palm tickles, and like always, he folds my fingers in when he's done. "You know the rules."

"Yup."

He reaches towards me again, placing his hand on the back of my neck and pulling me into him, placing his lips on my forehead and letting them linger there. My hands find purchase on his hips as I feel his warm breath against my skin.

"Bye, silly girl."

"Bye," I say back before turning to climb into my car. I start the engine and watch out the window as he fires up his Harley, giving me a last wink before he pulls out of the lot. When he's out of sight is when I look down at my hand and find the iconic crescent moon doodled into my palm next to the words, Still My Luna.

    The cold ache in my chest registers before my eyes even flutter open. The woodsy and somewhat dank smell of the cabin is one of the first things to greet my senses, contributing to the realization that things are not okay. Resenting waking back up to this bitter reality, I pull the covers closer to my chest and turn my face into my pillow. The movement wafts another scent into the mix, and I realize I'm still in Kaleb's t-shirt. Last night I'd gone to the bathroom where I cried, splashed water on my face, and repeated that a couple of times before coming to bed and crawling under the covers without another thought – except for finding unconsciousness.

    I slipped in and out of restless sleep the few hours I had in the twin bed I'd slept in all summer. It was a vicious cycle of nodding off, only to jerk awake and realize the actuality that Kaleb might not be in my life anymore.

    I went from replaying our fight over and over to drifting off and having faint dreams that all was okay between us, to waking up to the realization that they were far from it.

    While part of me would love to just lay in bed and stare at the wall all day, the part of me that wants to be done with this revolving misery wins out.

    Throwing the covers back, I sit up, my body feeling like rusted metal. I'm drained and only half conscious as I brush my teeth in the communal bathroom before packing up the rest of my toiletries and carrying them back to my bunk.

    "You came in late last night." I look up to see one of my co-

counselors smiling at me from across the room where she stuffs folded clothing into her duffel.

I clung to Kaleb so much this summer that I didn't spend a lot of time with Cassidy, and I'm all of a sudden regretful I didn't get to know her better. She's extremely nice, and I just know my mom would dig her hair that's blonde with black tips.

"Oh," I stall, looking down at my packing. "I just… hung out with Kaleb for a bit before I came to bed." I awkwardly raise a shoulder as I stuff his t-shirt into the bag. I had thought about leaving it somewhere for him to find it, but a selfish, masochistic part of me wanted to take it along and wouldn't let any other part of me argue.

"Oh that's cool," she comments, grabbing her toiletry bag and adding it to her duffel. I take the generic but well-intentioned response as a window to get my head away from the whole thing.

"So what do you have going after this?" I ask, trying to put on an interested face, and she lights up right away.

"I'm going to this fine arts institute in Indianapolis," she reports gleefully, and I feel a few butterflies that somehow survived last night's nuclear blast wake up in my belly.

"Really?" She nods. "That's amazing. I wish I was doing something like that. What are you going to do there?" This is the best subject for distraction, and I want to hear more as I stack my comforter, duffel, and pillow on top of each other.

"Creative writing," she sighs contentedly, and I nod while I gather everything up as she follows suit. "What about you?" she asks as she follows me out the door, and we make our way down the wooden steps.

"I'm going to Eastern for a year, and then I hope to do something like you," I sigh as we fall in step with each other, our arms loaded with our camp gear.

"You do art, right? Painting?" she questions as she looks over at me.

"That, and a couple of other things." I nod and tell her about my work with pastels, and how I also want to learn charcoal, and maybe even pottery.

"Well the school I'm going to looked like they had a really great creative program for all that," she notes. "You should join me there."

I force myself not to look in the direction of Kaleb's cabin as we pass it, and pull my eyebrows together harder than needed. "Really? Is it hard to get in to?"

She shakes her head. "Not too bad. I mean, you need to know how to do more than work with crayons," she giggles, and I force one with her. This sick and dreadful feeling in the center of my sternum is still making itself very well known, but talking about future possibilities is slightly soothing, even if only minimally.

"Yeah, you know you could probably take a couple of art credits while you're over at Eastern and transfer over when you're done – unless you have other art schools in mind." She holds a placating hand up. I do have some in mind, but I like the idea of moving a small distance from home yet having a friendly face where I end up. I should look into this place. I ignore the fact that it's in Indiana where Kaleb is from and shake the thought away. That doesn't have to matter.

I gratefully accept the information Cassidy writes down for me, including her email and phone number.

After giving me a little hug, she gets in her car, and pulls away.

As I stand in the dirt lot, I'm suddenly hit with the finality of this moment. I'm about to leave without knowing how to write to Kaleb. All I know is his basic training is in South Carolina, and he doesn't know where my dorm is because I haven't even gotten that information yet.

I glance around the lot, probably looking like a lost child as I hold my pillow and bed linens to my chest with my duffel hanging off me.

We could have that sweet goodbye I dreamed about. We

could laugh off last night and put it behind us, and one day it will be just some stupid fight we had once because we were stupid teenagers. Our friendship is too sacred to throw away over that.

My heartbeat elevates as I continue turning and walking aimlessly through the lot, looking for Kaleb or his bike. Neither is to be found anywhere as I walk around, hoping for any little sign, because once I leave… that's it.

I wait. I watch several people come, get in their vehicles, and leave. I even see a couple of Kaleb's co-counselors from his cabin, and they say they haven't seen him at all this morning.

So this really is ending, like Kaleb said last night, only I'd hoped he'd just been drunk and angry. This was always meant to end.

Feeling as if my whole chest has been hollowed out, I finally make tracks to my car, holding my chin up, even though it's for no one but myself. After getting all my things settled in the back, I open the front door and slide into the driver's seat. I sit for a moment, shaking my head at myself. Every moment I wait, the stupider I feel. Holding my left hand up, I look at my bare palm and rub my thumb against the empty space where there should be a sweet little drawing.

Dropping my hands, I blow out a breath and turn the engine over. Cranking the radio up so that the music can blast away the sad and dismal thoughts trying to take over my mind right now, as I pull away and onto the road.

Kaleb

My fingers lace together, grip tight, and then release as I sit on the picnic table, feet on the bench and forearms on my knees. Closing my eyes against the morning sun, I draw in breath of the crisp air, willing it to cleanse my body of the toxins that have infected my spirit.

Little by little, I feel my head start to clear and my heart get heavier when I pick through my argument with Luna. We had some serious firsts last night, and sadly, that was one of them.

I never knew the dark side of her life because she never told me, but just because she didn't offer it up, didn't mean I couldn't ask. I just always assumed she had a charmed life. She's been open to anything I wanted to know, and maybe some screwed up part of my subconscious didn't want to know anything other than the bright light she has been in my life. How naive was I to assume she didn't know what a hard time looked like? No, her biological dad never hit her, but he abandoned her. Her real dad loved her so much that he wanted to make it legal, and that's the part I always focused on. I never let myself stop and think that she'd been rejected by the one that shares her DNA. And in this moment, I'm facing the fact it's because I didn't want to believe that I wasn't alone in my hardships.

After she stormed off last night, I felt the worst sinking feeling in my gut that I was desperate to escape. I wasn't too drunk, but did have enough to make my head a little hazy, and all I knew was that I needed to sort this out.

I needed to get on my bike, something that always seems to clear my head. But while I don't have the good sense to lay off alcohol altogether like Luna does – seeing as how it turns out both our piece of shit sperm donors are addicts – I was smart enough to throw myself back in the lake to sober up, and the walk to my Harley helped finish the job.

When I got on the road, with nothing but me and the single headlight on the asphalt, I went through every possible thing I could or should have done differently… like tell her I've never been with a girl that was anything more than a placeholder between those times I'd get to be with her; grabbed her and held her in the water after we made each other feel amazing, fighting away any awkwardness that tried to destroy us.

I reach beside me and grab the paper cup and drain the rest of the black coffee I bought from some little stand about fifteen or so miles down the road from Mystic Hills. The bitter liquid is stone cold, and I grimace as I swallow it down before crushing the cup between my hands and look out over the grassy meadow before me.

Luna said she loved me last night. I always felt that she did, but that was the first time I heard it. And I love her too, so much it hurts.

Over the last eight hours, my very being seems to have split off into several different segments, each one arguing a different point.

She's too good for me, and she'll never understand me.

She's never given a shit about where I'm from, or what I've been through, but she loved me anyway. I'd be a fucking imbecile to give that up.

We could call this what it was, be the story each of us tells about the special friend we had at camp that became pen pals until that part of our lives was over and we went our separate ways, to our own next chapters.

Going back there this morning and asking her to be my girl, despite the time and distance we're facing, would mean letting her see more than camp me, as she described it.

She'd have to know how much Pops and I struggle, and the only options I have laid out before me are taking over his bike shop or joining the military in the hopes of getting some schooling out of it. She'd have to know that my dad came back into my life a changed man. Loving, attentive and responsible. Pops would let him move back in so he could get back on his feet and fix things with me. I'd had my dad back… twice. And twice he broke my heart when someone would offer him a little coke and a lot of alcohol, and he'd leave me; the scary monster from my nightmares appearing in his place. Each of those times hurt worse than any slap or broken arm. All hope I had in the one person that was supposed to care about me was obliterated twice when he tried to change. I wasn't worth not picking up the glass.

As far as Pops was concerned, that was his third strike. He wouldn't let him near me after that, hiding me in closets or cupboards whenever the asshole came around. Then coming home with ice cream after he'd dropped him off at a bus station or rehab center.

And here I am, treating Luna in the opposite way she's come to depend on from me.

Pops provided for me, Luna showed me friendship and love. The girl who never let me down… partly because I never gave her the opportunity.

Keeping her means letting her see all the ugly parts of me; telling her how I live my life this way because I grew up thinking I wasn't worth anything better. I would have to let her see all of it. She wouldn't care about it one iota, but she'd still see it.

And she'd still be my Luna.

Fuck.

I need to get to her. She came into my life when we were ten, and she does not get to leave. I can't let her.

I jump to my feet and make quick strides towards my bike, chucking my coffee in a nearby waste can along the way. Hopping on, I fire up the engine and tear off back onto the road, the engine puttering furiously as I go. The cold breeze on my face only drives the sentiment home. I can't be without her. She's worth all of it, even admitting I was the dickhead of the century last night and begging forgiveness.

We'll keep going, her and me. We'll take this thing as far as it will go, even if we have to do it miles apart for a while… shit…

I never gave her my address in South Carolina, and I didn't get her dorm info. I don't have her phone number – Jesus!

I rev the engine, picking up speed, barreling my way back as fast as I can.

Dust kicks up as I finally turn down the dirt road that eventually opens up to the main building of the camp, and I feel panic rise in my chest; my heart pumping overtime when I see very few vehicles remaining.

Yanking my Colts hat out of my back pocket, I slip it over my windblown hair and hightail it to Luna's cabin. Tromping up the steps, I yank the screen door open to find it barren.

I feel my heart plummet into my stomach, along with the disheartened breath I blow out. It sits there and turns to ice as I descend the front steps and feebly look around my immediate surroundings, knowing damn well I'm too late. There's no glimpse of her anywhere.

"Dammit!" I roar, as I rip off my hat and kick at the dirt.

She's gone. I fucked everything up, I'm too late.

Feeling uncontrolled self-anger and infuriating despair, I dash back over to the parking lot, checking one more time that her black little Mazda is really gone.

My body feels the defeat and I start to feel it give out as I walk back towards the counselors' main cabin, needing one small dose of her, one last time.

I find the spot on the back corner that no one knows about except those that were there that day. I find Luna's name, still there, undisturbed, in tiny letters. I run my finger tip over them, closing my eyes and letting myself go back to that moment when it was just she and I standing here, and how now I'm here again – alone.

Reaching for my belt, I unclip my pocket knife and extend the blade.

Then, with all the feelings that terrorize my mind, body, and soul, I start carving and slicing at the old weathered wood.

8

KALEB

"Call the house or the shop when you're able," Pops orders in his endearing rumble as I hand my rucksack over to the airline attendant for checking.

"I got it, Pops," says not me, but Alex, my best high school friend, or I guess I should now say my only best friend. We went with the whole Buddy Program route when we enlisted so we get to go to Basic and Advanced Institute training together. "I'm making sure this asshole actually gets a phone when we land." He shoulder bumps me and I return it with a headshake and a well patented eye roll.

Pops grabs the bill of his hat and rubs the back of his gnarled hand against his forehead before replacing it.

"How's Moon Girl?" he asks, referring to my summer with Luna.

I shake my head, trying not to meet his eyes. "We're growing in separate directions," I say and try to give a shrug. "She just wasn't the one."

I jam my hands in my pockets and finally look up to find an expression I can't decipher as exceptionally sour or just his usual resting grouch face. "What?" I raise my shoulders defensively.

"You're a fucking idiot," he deadpans.

"I know."

"I mean it, I'm going to kick your ass when you get home."

"Yes, sir," I acknowledge firmly as he extends an arm, pulling me in for a hug.

"I'm proud of you," he mutters as we pull away.

"For what, serving my country?" I raise a sardonic eyebrow.

"For doing something with your life, no matter what it is."

I give a thoughtful nod as I pull my small carry-on duffel up onto my shoulder, and Alex and I turn, heading for the security check point.

Once aboard the plane, I take the window seat, yearning for that childhood escape I always sought. Watching the ground grow farther away, I'm up higher than I've ever been and I concentrate on tuning out my awkward surroundings and just take it in.

When we've penetrated the cloud cover and there's not much else to see, I pull my pencil and notepad out of my duffel, intent on drawing to pass the time. I let myself zone out, just letting my hand draw what it will in strokes and scribbles; light lines and dark ones.

"It just wasn't the right time, man." I hear Alex's voice break through the din of the engines, and it jars me just a little.

"What?" I respond without even looking up.

"You've known each other since you were kids, and that's all you know."

What in the hell? It sounds like he's referring to Luna, but I never talked about her much. I kind of liked keeping her to myself.

"Are you on something, man?" I finally look up and furrow my brow at him because he's not making sense.

He rests his head back against the seat with a smug grin. "Cheyenne's been throwing some little prissy girl tantrum the whole summer while you've been gone," he explains, "about how you ditched her to go be with your pen pal, Luna, for the summer."

"Yeah, well, Cheyenne's a nosey, insecure bitch with a really big mouth," I spew out, bitterly.

"Yeah, and she's hung up on you. Couldn't stand that the big, shit-eating grin you get every summer just before you leave for that camp in Ohio wasn't for her."

Again, what the hell?

I cock my head towards him again, willing him to elaborate.

"I've known you for six years... you think I didn't notice?" He pauses, taking in my pensive expression. "Anyway, you'll see her again. You'll both be older, and there will be something different between you." He gives me a smart look before popping his earbuds in, signaling the end of this little heart-to-heart, and I gaze away, turning this over in my head. I always thought Luna was the only friend that cared about me. In my mind she's still irreplaceable, yet I didn't realize that Alex was more than just someone to hang with, and that he's actually been paying attention the last few years. That says a lot. That says that Luna may be the most important person I've had in my life, but she's not my only friend. That said... I have her to thank.

Before her I didn't care to make friends. I felt better in my own company; safer. But then she pranced into my life so freely like she'd always belonged there, and it gave me a certain confidence – a quiet confidence, but it's there nonetheless, thanks to her.

Looking down at my notepad, I take in the two dark eyes that dazzle back up at me from the page. Deep set, with up turned brows and thick, dark lashes, they smile up at me without the need for a set of full pink lips.

A sudden twinge has me leaning forward and rifling through the side pocket of my carry-on before I feel my fingers wrap around the ballpoint pen I stashed in there.

After sitting back up, pen in my hand, I click it open. A sharp pain digs through my chest at the recent memory of this morning resurfacing. Luna and I didn't say goodbye. I didn't draw a picture on the palm of her hand to look at on her way back home.

If I believed in things like bad juju or curses, I would think this break in tradition has left us both doomed. I don't, but it still gives me a restless, unsettling feeling. Who knew I was a guy who needed closure?

Not caring how inane this idea sounds to myself, I hold up my left hand and start gliding the pen across my palm. Like I always did with Luna, I take my time, curving the stroke of the pen, drawing what I always knew I would on this last visit while also drawing out the moment. I sweep the pen side-to-side in a repetitive motion, getting the shapes and the shading just right.

My mind barely registers the sound of Alex quietly snoring beside me as I put the finishing touch just below the crescent moon that peeks out from between dark clouds. Just a single word:

Mine.

The next two months are therapeutic in a way I never even dreamed of. The strict routine, no bullshit, hardcore environment leaves no room for daydreaming or dissecting any emotional aspects of my life.

It's not that I never think about things or people. I think about them plenty. I just don't have time or space for them to consume me.

When I needed motivation, I thought about Pops and how I wanted to make something of myself for him. When I needed aggressive strength and force, I thought of my sperm donor. Every pull-up, punch, press, jab, kick… I think of that fuckrag. How I would beat him into the ground if I ever saw him again. If given the choice, I'd never have the chance; I'm fine with him being essentially dead to me. Beating the shit out of him would just be my consolation prize if I had to come face-to-face with him.

And of course, I think of Luna. Though she tries to break into my thoughts when I'm training, I save her for my private moments. At night, when I'm drifting off to sleep, she's my escape. The one thing that keeps me from going into complete tunnel vision. Thoughts of our joint climax in the lake have brought me back there time and again in the rare moments I can lock myself in a bathroom stall to find release. When I'm marching in military step, I imagine the chance encounter I fantasize of us having later on down the road. I drive and push myself to become the man I want to be for if that ever happens.

Luna, Age 20

THE SOUND of the front door opening invokes a shiver of adrenaline zinging up my body, and I can't help but give a small start. I look up from the task of shoving random supplies into my art bag and meet my grandmother's eyes. She holds my gaze steady, reminding me we've got this under control, and she briefly pauses, placing my folded sweaters into my duffel to reach out and lay a comforting hand on my arm.

I'm still for a moment, letting each quiet breath that enters my lungs infuse my nerves with incremental steel as I wait. Finally, I hear it. The door slams and I try to stifle the reactive jolt of my shoulders. No question, he saw the box on the kitchen table. It's go time.

Exhaling the last of my nervous energy through pursed lips, I grab up the bundle of paint brushes from the dresser and shove them in their rightful compartment. I'm so ready for this, but I'm even more ready for it to be over.

"Right behind you, kiddo." Granna sends behind me as I turn with squared shoulders toward the bedroom door.

"Luna?!" Carter's bellow echoes down the hallway as I venture down its length, putting one foot in front of the other, adjusting the strap of my art bag on my shoulder. When I emerge into the kitchen, I find pretty much the exact sight I was imagining I would. Carter stands before the kitchen table, steely eyes set on the box half-full with some of my odds and ends. His jaw is set, and his eyebrows are pulled into each other. As he stands with a hand on his hip and the other clutching what looks like today's mail, hanging at his side.

I know he detects me in his peripheral, but he doesn't do me the decency of acknowledging me. Ever the narcissist, he needs to control the interaction and make me squirm while he drags it out for dramatic effect.

Not this time, dipshit. I've seen the light.

Instead of giving the toddler his cookie, I head towards the lucky bamboo plant on the far end of the counter without a look or a word. Grabbing the plant in its slim glass vase, I walk it over to the table and carefully place it in the corner of the box with my other belongings as he continues to watch in silence.

That's right, fucker. It's exactly what it looks like.

"And just what the fuck are you doing?" Carter finally grumbles out, blinking first, so to speak.

As much as I don't want to, I lift my chin and look him square in the eye as Granna told me to.

"I'm leaving." The response comes on a shuddery exhale but I don't care, and divert by turning to lift one of my framed art pieces from off the wall; a speckled owl with black, downy feathers that I drew with charcoal; its wide, yellow eyes standing out from its dark, fluffy face almost looks like it's thanking me for taking him with me as I place him in the box.

"You're not fucking leaving," Carter spits and shakes his head as I start folding down the cardboard flaps, and my head actually snaps up, not at what he said, but the confidence with which he said it.

"You don't get to decide that – I do," I grit out, giving him what I hope is a good death stare, and I'm mildly satisfied that it makes his eyes widen slightly in surprise.

This is what Granna pointed out to me one of the last times she was around, and I can't believe I didn't see it. Carter has been engaging control over me so gradually that I didn't even notice it happening. I didn't want to believe her at first, but two nights ago... I found the smoking fucking gun.

"Obviously," he says snidely. "I mean tell me why you're leaving so that I can fix whatever the fuck you think it is I did wrong." He tosses the mail on the table right when my head shoots up to regard him.

All of a sudden, the nerves I had about facing him are gone. I'm no longer worried about him saying something charming to try and suck me back in like he has with so many other apologies that I was stupid enough to believe were sincere. I'm not dreading him putting me down, yelling at me, or slamming his fist against something to try to scare me.

Nope. His cavalier attitude about whatever the fuck he did wrong, as he put it, has flipped a switch and rage has taken over.

"Oh?" I ask cynically. It feels like acid is flowing through my veins, but I welcome it, envisioning it fueling me and transforming me into a monster like him as I thrust my hand into my purse and snatch out the thick paper that's been folded three ways into a rectangle. Shaking it open, I hold it up in front of him. "Can you fix this?"

He sets his jaw, and props to him for keeping his stoney expression intact, but he can't hide the way his complexion just paled as he looks at the letter I'm holding. The real letter I received from the Novel Institute of Creative Art in Indianapolis – the one that says I was accepted.

"Can you fix the year you took away from me, from my career?"

"Luna, it's not a career –"

"Shut up!" I cut off his careless words and dismissive headshake and actually make his shoulders jerk a little in surprise. Good. I won't stand here and listen to him tell me I can't make something of myself with my art even one more time. "Every word out of your mouth is bullshit, Carter! You actually stood there and told me that my art was brilliant and that they were idiots not to accept me, while I cried over the letter that you typed up and put in their envelope, you son of a bitch!"

"Luna..." he sighs, looking down pensively, and I can see it. I can see the shift. "Honey, we had just got something going and you had made it clear that NICA was your future, and nothing was going to stop you. I needed more time to prove myself to you, that you could be happy here with me." His voice is somber, but I know now it's deliberate. He's been playing me for the better part of a year, changing his demeanor to make me react in whichever way worked in his favor. Right now, he's trying to appeal to my compassionate side so that he can get the upper hand again. But I'm impervious now. This is unforgivable.

"Again, Carter, every word I hear is bullshit. Do yourself a favor and shut the fuck up," I tell him through clenched teeth as I fold the paper back up.

"Luna, see, right now I'm trying to explain why I did what I did... the lengths I'd go to be with you because I love you, and you won't even listen –"

"I don't need to listen to you!" I cut him off again. He doesn't get to control this conversation. "I know everything! You found my acceptance letter and switched it out with a rejection that you typed up so that I would feel exactly that – rejected! Then you came in like the comforting hero that was going to pick me up and dust me off," I mutter, shaking my head as I close up the box. The anger infused spike in my adrenaline is starting to gradually taper down, and that's fine. I've shown this asshole what I'm capable of, and now it's time to really drive it home with a cool veneer. Nothing says I'm dead fucking serious more than being as calm as fuck when you deliver your message of finality.

"Alright, Luna," Carter says as he grips the bridge of his nose and rubs at his eyes with one hand before regrouping and squaring his shoulders. "I know what I did was fucked up on so many levels..."

"You act like you just forgot to pay the water bill," I insert in the middle of his crap proclamation, "You betrayed and deceived me all the while continuing to knock me down! I could actually sue you for what you did, and not even your lawyer cousin would be able to get you out of that one," I spit out, not even looking at him as I turn towards the fridge to retrieve my pint of Ben & Jerrys. I absolutely love the bitter bitch I'm being right now. Speaking of...

"As I was saying," Carter picks back up, annoyance in his voice. "I know what I did was all kinds of wrong, but can we try to have an adult conversation about all this? I mean, I've never seen you act like this. This isn't you," he declares, waving a hand in my direction.

"Actually, it is," Granna corrects him calmly as she strolls into the room with my duffel hanging off one shoulder, a suitcase trailing behind her, and a shoe box tucked under her arm. "Luna is being herself for the first time since she met you," she informs Carter.

A brief flash of surprise passes over his face before he juts his chin in her direction. "Who asked you?"

"I did," I snap, getting immediately protective, even though it takes a lot to freak out my Granna.

"And she can sue you for not only meddling with her mail, but forgery on behalf of an accredited institute," Granna continues on. "But lucky for you, we were able to contact the admissions office at NICA and her acceptance still stands. There's a place for her starting in the fall semester, so my good-hearted granddaughter is content to simply remove herself from this toxic situation so that you can both move on."

"Please, she's not even your real granddaughter," Carter splutters, hitting below the belt in reference to my adoption on my dad's side. He's grasping at straws.

"I've been helping to raise her for most of her formative years, and we share a last name," Granna calmly defends. "That's as real as it gets."

God, I love her.

The thing is, Granna is a psychologist, and the first couple of times she heard me talk about Carter and how he'd do things like come to my dorm with scones from my favorite bakery and walk me to my first class, or how often he would text to see what I was up to and tell me he was thinking about me... I can tell now that at the time she was trying to be happy for me and not jump to conclusions. But after meeting him a couple of times and hearing more about how he'd show up to my pottery class to see what I made that day, and all the things he'd say and do, she voiced her concerns that he was love bombing. I didn't want to believe that of someone who was being so sweet to me, but here we are.

Finally satisfied that he had me where he wanted me, Carter started to show me his ugly side, just a little bit at a time. Before I knew it, I was walking on eggshells trying not to upset him, and if I dared go anywhere without him, he would text me incessantly, making sure my attention still stayed on him in some way, and getting irritated when I wouldn't respond fast enough.

For the next couple of weeks, I didn't act on anything but I kept my eyes open. And then I found the letter. And now, I'm taking my life back.

I draw in one more long breath, and look the guy straight in the eye. "Goodbye, Carter," I say calmly and move to walk around him, hauling my huge art bag and my box, but he steps in front of me.

"Luna, stop. You've got to–"

"Step out of my way and let me leave Carter, or I'll call the cops to have them come do a civil standby." That's right, I did my research and came prepared. "And I'll follow through with telling them about your federal offense while they're here," I lay out for him, firm and simple.

My ultimatum is met with a look of malicious fury blazing in Carter's eyes, and though I keep my chin tilted high, I'm shaking in my shoes. Just when I thought I'd seen every face he had...

"Well done, my girl," Granna congratulates me as I flop back against the passenger seat, blowing out a breath that I must have been holding way down at the bottom of my lungs. "I mean it, you did good," she adds, and I absently raise my hand up to her and she claps it with her own before pulling down her seatbelt.

"Thanks, Granna," I murmur, still trying to decompress. Carter was angrier than I'd ever seen him, and clearly, he was trying to intimidate me. But it turned out he truly was more afraid of what I had to offer than I was afraid of him. And as we left, my petty ass might have thrown in how dim he was to hide the letter in one of his Ammo magazines and forget about it so that I could find it one day.

"Now," she begins and puts her game face on as she turns the engine over. "Let's get you back to your life."

9

KALEB, AGE 21

"Congratulations, Corporal," Alex murmurs, as he pins my new rank insignia to my uniform. "I'm sorry it's me and not Pops," he adds somberly for only my ears before saluting me. Ramrod straight, I return the sharp movement before he falls in beside me.

I don't react, taking my role seriously in front of our superiors as I'm handed my certificate and snap off another salute to my unit commander. Stone-cold, staring straight ahead.

Over the last three years, I've erected a steel fortress around my heart and soul. I haven't become an emotionless machine or anything, but I can compartmentalize like a motherfucker.

I miss Pops to the point of aching, but I don't let it weaken me. Instead, I envision that ache as a fire that only reinforces my protective armor. The fire had been steadily burning low all my life, occasionally stoked and fueled with surfacing memories of my father. Then the first pound of the hammer came when I blew my relationship with Luna. Then another when I found out Pops was gone from hundreds of miles away while stationed in Oklahoma. Several harder hits when I found out it was from a heart attack in his shop and he wasn't found until the next morning by Jackson, his assistant manager.

Pops had no one in this world to try to save him but me, and while my brain knows perfectly well that it wasn't my fault, my heart blazed hotter, pounding away at more steel to make me stronger. Both knew that the tragedies in my life could easily be my downfall, and worked together to make me stand stronger against them.

So I buried Pops in the town cemetery with a handful of people from around Coyote Creek in attendance, including the firefighters from one of the two stations in town who dressed in their official uniforms to send him off. They were grateful for the few years Pops volunteered before his asshole son showed up on his step with his grandson. Speaking of the dick, I thank my lucky stars that he didn't show up. The loser probably had no way of finding out, or better yet, is dead himself.

In fact, the biggest worry I have is that he is still alive, as that poses something of a problem with Pops gone now. It makes Rick Shane officially my next of kin.

"Ready for the flight out tomorrow?" Alex asks as the ceremony concludes and we start heading in the direction of our barracks.

"Hell yeah," I exhale heavily as we go. We've spent the last couple of years stationed here, training for our impending roles as gunners on the infamous Blackhawks. And now the time has come. In three weeks' time, we ship out to fulfill the duty we've been training for. In the meantime, we get to head back home to be with our families, not that I have any to speak of anymore. But I do have the house, left to me by Pops in his will, as well as the repair shop that I need to check in on. I'm actually looking forward to checking in on things with Shane Automotive to see how Jackson is doing running the place until we can find someone with more time and energy, and fixing up things around the house like Pops taught me before I leave for my year-long tour. It will be peaceful and satisfying and just the right reset. Add in blowing off some steam with a few beers and maybe a good lay, and I'll be good to go.

"Remember Ryan and Parker?" Alex asks, referring to a couple of guys we used to run with, and I look over and give him a nod. "They asked us to go to Indianapolis for the weekend. They want to party it up at that place, JJs," he elaborates.

I've heard of that place. It's a four-story establishment hub for all sorts of entertainment. The first floor hosts a bowling alley and arcade, the second has some kind of nice restaurant and bar. And the other floors have an expansive sports bar, and the top floor is a lively night club.

After the last three years of strict routine, back-breaking work, discipline, and a dead grandfather, it sounds like just the ticket. Perhaps the drinking and debauchery will come first on that list in Mission Reset...

Luna

My content smile is totally complicit with my mood as my body lightly bounces and sways to the angsty but sweet country song playing on the radio. Wisps of my hair hang in my face – some brown, some purple – that have fallen loose from my top knot, and I puff them out of the way as I reach up to smudge a little of the light yellow of the sky on my canvas.

I'm in my happy place; my element. Never have I felt more secure and confident in every aspect of my life, and dancing in my studio apartment while I create something beautiful on my beloved easel while the evening sun shines through the dirty windows is the cherry on top.

I love my classes with their challenging projects. I love the group of friends I've made here, including of course, Cassidy from camp. I love my little hole-in-the-wall apartment with its open floor plan, tiny kitchen, and exposed brick that my dad and little brother, Matthew, helped me move into a year ago.

I hear what is meant to be a light knock, but comes out as a couple of bangs, due to my metal door, before Cassidy pops her head in.

"Helloooo!" she sings before letting herself all the way in, and I smile in greeting as she closes the door. "How'd I know I'd find you here with your hair a mess and your overalls on?" she teases.

"Do not knock my process," I snipe back teasingly as I point a soft pink oil pastel crayon at her before turning back to scribble and smudge a small cloud in my sunset sky. "Respect the overalls," I add, squinting my eyes in concentration as I smear and smudge the lines a bit. My ratty, paint-splattered, blue denim overalls are my personal uniform for when I'm working, and they've proven lucky for when I'm creating. How dare she...

"Fine, I respect the sacred overalls." She holds her hands up as she hops up on my tiny countertop and crosses her legs at the ankle. "But you're going to have to get out of them for what we have planned tonight, darling."

I twist one side of my face up in a remorseful scowl. "I don't think I'm going to make it," I inform her regretfully as I turn to take in her gussied-up appearance. "You look nice though," I note before I turn back to my work. She looks dynamite in her black tank dress, and her hair – still blonde, but now with black, pink, and purple streaks – styled in soft curls.

"Bullshit," she curses behind my back, and I cringe. "Why?" she demands.

"I'm in the zone," I argue, lifting a shoulder. "I can't stop until the inspiration runs dry, and I'm on a roll right now."

"Dude! You have until next Friday to get that done. A week! You have plenty of time to get back in the zone!"

I sigh, continuing to add a ribbon of dark purple to my sunset.

"Come on!" she prods with a huff. "I'm thirsty and horny and I need my wing woman!"

"Joanie and Beth will be there," I reminder her.

"We need an even number."

"Why?" I laugh gently at her ludicrous reasoning.

"In case we get separated, it's easier to keep up a buddy system."

"You so just pulled that out of your ass," I sigh in mock disapproval.

"I did, but you gotta admit that's pretty good." I hear her chuckle behind me. Ugh. She's blowing my concentration, and my music – which varies from country to alternative to reggaeton, depending on my mood – that usually drives my art, is now failing to do its job over her protesting.

"Alright," I sigh. "Go find me something to wear and plug in my curling iron."

"Yes!" she shrieks, and I hear her drop to the floor and skitter in the direction of the corner where my bed and closet reside.

I may act annoyed, but who am I kidding? Without Cassidy, I'd become one of those reclusive artists that never leaves their hole.

10

KALEB

"Down 'em, soldiers!" Ryan commands, holding his shot up in the center of the round, high-top for us all to clink against. I fucking hate tequila but he bought the round so I go for it, downing the small glass, grimacing as it goes down. The burn doesn't faze me, but I pick up my beer to chase away the nasty taste.

"Another one!" Ryan shouts, raising his hand to signal the waitress, but I interject.

"Not me, I'm good."

"What?" His jaw drops. "Shane, you ship out in a few weeks, this is no time to be a fucking pussy."

"Hey now," Parker speaks up. "Maybe he's not being a pussy but rather wants to pace himself so that he's not too soft to actually get some of it later!"

"I was going to say I don't want to be too plowed to make the hour drive back, but sure, let's go with that." I cross my arms over the table with a lazy half-smile.

"No way, man," Ryan chides. "We're getting a hotel. Live it up! You've got a lot of oats to sow before you deploy. Build that stock pile, bro."

"Like I'm going to sleep in a bed with any of you fucks," I joke, sweeping the neck of my beer bottle at all of them.

"No worries, I plan on going home with a random lady tonight. That frees up some space," Parker assures us.

"Is Miranda still coming out?" I ask Alex about the girl he's been casually seeing in our hometown that he's considering getting serious with.

"Yeah, she's going to call when she's close."

"Doesn't she always?" Ryan spews and laughs hysterically at his own stupid joke while I knock back the rest of my beer in dismay.

With my bottle empty, I turn in my seat to see if I can spot our waitress. Instead, my gaze is drawn to a brunette beauty across the way, sitting at a high-top table. Her little dress with the black and grey zigzag design allows me to see she's got legs for days, and though I can only see a side profile at this moment, I'm feeling a serious twinge at the sight of her; something intuitive. She's so animated as she lays her palms on the table top and leans forward to hear what one of her girlfriends is saying before her eyes crinkled closed in laughter.

When her long, closed lashes accentuate her delicate cheekbones, I get another twinge, this time with a flash.

I know you.

When a waitress stops by their table, the girl turns in my direction to regard her... and then boom. The stunning realization of who I'm looking at hits me like a nuclear blast I've had no way to train for. When she smiles up at the waitress while tucking a strand of her soft brown hair behind her ear, all the blood goes rushing to my heart when I see that it's unmistakably Luna.

There she is. That's her. My mind races right along with the blood in my veins.

Having no clue what my buddies are chattering about around the table, because all I can see is Luna and the changes she's clearly embraced over the last three years, and the way they swirl beautifully with the ways she's stayed the same. Like that bubbly smile and the way she talks with her hands. The coy smile that goes along with her laugh. It's all so surreal, and I'm still not completely sure I'm not dreaming or imagining her. My chest is tight, not wanting to move air in and out, and I can feel the rest of my body buzzing with a nervous excitement.

This is the moment I always fantasized about to get me through the drills when they were at their hardest, but I never thought it would actually come true.

I have to see her.

No matter how we left things between us, not taking this once-in-a-lifetime chance to go to talk to her is not an option. Even if she smacks me or tells me to get fucked, I would never regret going over to say hello. I would only regret not doing it.

I polish off my beer and after I set it back down, I tap my knuckles on the table top a couple of times to get Alex's attention.

"I think I see someone I know," I talk loudly over the din of the music and crowd.

"Yeah right, you just see your next conquest of the night," he guffaws, and it heats my blood slightly.

"Shut the fuck up," I growl loudly over the noise and point at him as I start backing away. On a normal night, he wouldn't necessarily be wrong, but when it comes to Luna, apparently I never lost my protective instinct.

I side step through the crowd of faceless strangers, all of them clueless that I'm inching towards the girl I never stopped thinking about.

When there's finally a short and clear line between me and her, I realize I have no idea what I should even say. All of a sudden, the usual acceptable salutations seem so incredibly awkward and stupid.

With the clock ticking, I finally decide to go with a nonverbal tactic. I'm not sure how she's going to react to this particular greeting, especially from me after three years, but here goes.

Before any of her friends can warn her that someone is behind her, I reach forward with both hands and tickle either side of her rib cage. The action makes her jump a foot off her stool and let out a shriek. Before even looking behind her to find the culprit, she puts her hands over mine. Probably to anchor them so they don't continue their assault, but I like the feeling all the same.

"Oh my God," she pants out, "what the…" she turns her body just enough to look over her shoulder, and her lips part when she sees her attacker.

I hear a sharp breath hitch in her throat as her eyes search my face.

"Hey, silly girl," I stare back at her with a small smile as I await my fate.

"Kaleb…" she finally exclaims and instead of getting a drink thrown on me, I get her instead. She's in my arms in half a second, her body crashing against mine. The impact and her arms roping around my neck is so beautifully rapturous and I feel like I just found my home after wandering around lost for three years. I don't let the surprise take away from soaking this moment in though. I have my arms wrapped completely around Luna Isaaks. My face is burrowed in her hair, and I can smell that she still uses her mom's salon shampoo. That smell is now mixed with some kind of flowery orange scent that I could absolutely get drunk on.

"Oh my God, it's been so long!" Her voice is as warm as her hug as she utters them right next to my ear, and it almost feels like a lullaby. "How are you, soldier?" she asks, breaking away and bringing her hands up over her mouth, her eyes radiant with a smile. Even under the neon lights, I can see that her cheeks have gone a little pink, and I realize I still haven't done any talking.

"You look amazing," I tell her and I'm about to inwardly

curse myself out for not even answering her question, but fuck it. I'm at a loss for words, and she does look amazing. I grew up seeing her in all the casual outdoor clothes, and her swimsuit was always a treat, but I never imagined what it would be like to see her in a sexy dress like tonight, and it makes her look feminine on a different level. Yes, I have to remind myself to keep my eyes on hers, and not let them venture to where they yearn, but it's the essence she's giving off that's doing me in.

"Thank you," she blinks coyly with a soft laugh. "That's really sweet."

"Sorry," I clear my throat, "I've been alright. How about you?"

"Really good, thanks," she nods with a smile so genuine I know she's telling the truth, and not just saying it because she's supposed to. She looks radiant. My attention is deterred however, when one of her friends at the table clears their throat.

We both turn to the raven-haired girl on the right, giving us a sly look while she stirs her drink with her straw.

"Okay, Luna, you've got some explaining to do."

Lu gives a shy chuckle and blinks and my heart thumps out a few hard beats when I realize we both still have a hand on each other. "Everybody, this is Kaleb," she holds her other hand up at me, and I hook the thumb of my free hand in my jeans pocket as I give each one a nod. "We've known each other since we were kids."

"Kaleb from camp!" the girl on the end pipes up, and it's hard with the flashing lights in the club to tell what color her hair is, but it looks blonde with some other colors mixed in. I think I remember her though. She was a counselor in Luna's cabin. Cassie? "I totally remember you! You and Luna were inseparable!"

"Lucky Luna," a redhead, hipster-looking girl sings out jokingly as she eyes me up and down, and Luna cracks half a smile, shaking her head at her before turning to me.

"So… do you live here now? I mean, you're not stationed anywhere?"

I blow out a long breath, raising my eyebrows which earns me and endearing, closed-mouth smile from her up at me. I want to tell her everything, but a noisy bar with her friends present is hardly the time and place. "It's a long story," I finally settle on before leaning in closer and giving her hip a squeeze. "We should catch up."

Before she can respond, her friends call her name and wave for her attention at the same time Alex appears at my side.

"Kaleb,"

"Yeah?"

"Miranda's waiting for me at the hotel, I gotta go," he reports, though I barely hear him as I'm staring at the way Luna's dark-haired friend is whispering in her ear. Her eyes dart to mine and her pink lips press together.

"Alright, man, you good to drive?" I finally tear my eyes away from her to listen. We slap hands when he assures me he is, and I turn back in time to see Luna's friends all standing from their stools and grabbing their belongings. "What's going on?"

"I'm being abandoned because my friends think I need to catch up with the hot soldier as they put it." Luna rolls her eyes endearingly, and my heart inflates just slightly at the word hot.

"You haven't seen him in how long?" Cassidy, that's her name, points out with a wave of her hand. "And you run into each other by chance? You guys have to hang."

I knew I liked her.

Luna looks to me, her brown hair swishing around her bare shoulders, and looks up at me with those soft brown eyes. "We can do this anytime you want, K, you don't have to stick around." She shakes her head offering me an out. "And they're my ride, so… " she tips her head in their direction.

"I can take you home," I cut her off before she can bow out. I know she's trying to save us both some awkwardness, but she's not going anywhere. Not after how long I've waited. "Stay with me, Lu." I give her the stare down, a small but playful smile in place, just like I always did before. "I've got nowhere to be and all night to get there. I'd love to spend time with you and hear what your silly ass has been up to," I add firmly.

Her smile is tight but warm as it slowly stretches across her face, and finally she nods. "Okay."

"The bar on the second floor is a bit quieter," I recall, giving her a knowing smile. "Can I buy you a root beer?"

Luna

I CAN'T BELIEVE I'm sitting here with the boy from my summers as our knees brush against each other under the bar. As we made our way down here, my blood warmed as I noticed he now walks a bit taller and straighter, but still looks like the Kaleb I last saw in those well-fitting jeans and tattoos all over, only his eyebrow piercing is gone now and he's filling out that Henley a bit more. Before he was lean and fit, but now he's grown to be so muscular and strong. I felt in his embrace when I threw myself into his arms when I realized I was looking at the special someone I never thought I'd lay eyes on again.

Even now, I still can't believe I'm looking at him as he tells me about his budding career in the military. My heart both beams and hurts for him and the things he's accomplished, but also what he's had to endure to do so.

"I'm sorry about your granddad," I tell him in a low voice that reflects the heaviness in my heart.

He nods dismissively as he deflects, taking a sip of his pint as I twirl the straw in my own drink.

I'd only met Pops a handful of times at camp drop-off and pick-up over the years, but I'd always liked that he seemed like a badass grandfather. Even with his perpetually stoney face, the way he'd look over his shoulder a last time at Kaleb before he'd leave showed me how much he cared. I'm only sorry I didn't get to know him better.

We're about thirty minutes in and we've told each other so much, yet there's so much left to learn, and I yearn to get back to that place he and I once were.

Sensing he'd rather not dwell on losing Pops, I inwardly grapple for a way to change the subject, and probably for the tenth time, I find myself taking in his shirt stretched deliciously across his chest. "You look really good, Kaleb," I tell him, forcing my eyes away from his solid frame and up to his green eyes instead.

"So do you, Lu." He nods sincerely at me, and our closeness gives me a subtle whiff of his scent. The clean musk and sandalwood smell makes me want to raise his shirt and lay across his chest all night in a confusing way that's both comforting and sexual. "Listen," he looks down at our legs for a second while resting an elbow on the bar and gripping both sets of fingers together. "About that last time we saw each other…"

Oh God.

I feel a nervous sing radiate up the center of my chest. I knew this would come up at some point as it always needed closure, but I was still dreading it.

"We were stupid teenagers, K." I blink slowly, shaking my head as if to dissipate the heavy tone of the conversation. "We had a dumb fight."

"A dumb fight we had because I was a dumbass that didn't know how to vocalize his emotions," he amends with regret casting a shadow in those green eyes. "You just wanted to know me deeper, and I pushed back in the shittiest way."

I nod thoughtfully. "But like I said, we were young, and I was so inexperienced and just didn't know what it meant to live in the moment, so when we…" I scrunch my face and peek up at him for the right words.

"Did what we did in the lake," he fills in, trying to keep his smile warm, but I can see that twinkle of cockiness in his eyes and I have to contain my grin from splitting my face.

"I had it in my head that we needed to know what came next, or I needed to know, and I pushed," I shrug with a headshake. "I felt insecure that you had so much of me, and I felt like I had so little of you. But looking back, I understand the reasoning you had, and I feel stupid for that younger version of me." I laugh gently, looking down at the tiny bubbles fizzing to the surface of my root beer.

"Maybe, but Luna," he pins me with a solemn stare, leaning towards me slightly. "I was the asshole that night, not you, not in least. You taught my stubborn ass a lot that night." He looks at me fondly, and I feel good about this moment. I feel like a vice that I forgot was in the pit of my stomach just made itself known to me by releasing the hold it's had on me for a long time.

I suck in a long breath and let it out before regarding him. As healthy as it has been to address this, I just want to be past it and have my Kaleb back, at least in some capacity.

"Can we just... be okay now?" I ask, letting go of my straw and clasping my hands together in my lap. I've felt overjoyed since laying eyes on him tonight, but it's been just a little shaded by how we left things, making me unsure how to act around him.

"Hell yes," he sighs out, a relieved look relaxing his face and making him look as grateful as I feel. "I've got less than three weeks, and I'm going to need my pen pal back," he jokes with a wink as he reaches for his pint glass before polishing off what's left.

He'd told me shortly after we sat down that he deploys really soon and that he came home to take care of his house and Pop's motorcycle shop. While I felt a cold pang at the idea of him leaving just after we found each other again, it made me so thankful that we did at the same time. Our paths might have never crossed again if not now. It's also got me wishing I could help him out with all that before he goes and soak him up a little longer. I don't bring up any such idea, though. We've only been catching up a little while, and while I'd love to pick up where we left off, I don't know if his head and heart are in the same place as mine. He could even have a girl that hasn't come up yet, and I inwardly cringe at the sinking in my stomach that gives me.

"Of course," I assure him, shaking off my trepidations. "You know if you have by chance wised up and gotten a phone, I can do even better than that." I widen my eyes teasingly, and with an eyeroll, he shifts on his stool while reaching in his back pocket. His smile is one of faux annoyance as he holds up a cell phone in presentation. "Aww, I'm so proud of you," I tease some more, and he shakes his head while laying it on the bar.

When he turns back to me, something seems to catch his eye and he reaches forward. My eyes follow his hand, and the rest of my senses all buzz to life as he reaches beside my neck. The brush of his fingers against my skin makes goosebumps break out down my back.

"What's this?" His narrowed eyes examine the strand of my hair his fingers are now sliding down, and I try to hide the way it makes me shiver.

"Ah, you found my purple hair," I beam at him.

"Yeah," he lets out an amused chuckle and I turn in my seat, my back to him as I raise the sides of my hair up to show him the layer underneath I have dyed in a multitude of purple shades.

"That's beautiful." His voice is low and velvety behind me as I feel him leaf through more strands. "I see your favorite color hasn't changed."

"Never," I give a playful growl over my shoulder.

"And still no ink," he says as I drop the rest of my hair and turn to face him again. "Not that I can see anyway," he adds and we exchange a flirty look.

Oh my God. I don't know what's with me right now, but I'm going with it. I may not have understood living in the moment before, but in the year since Carter, I sure as hell do now. And I intend to spend each moment tonight with Kaleb as natural as can be.

We stare at each other as a few moments beat by, and it's not a bit uncomfortable. It's like we're still having an entire conversation with our eyes before that look of mischief narrows Kaleb's eyes in the same old way.

"Truth or dare?" he asks.

Fuck.

11

KALEB

The wry, half smile Luna is giving me, her brown eyes alight with the golden ambers that have always lived within, is making a dormant lust thrive to life inside me. The kind of lust I've never felt for anyone else I've been with. The kind that makes me want to pull her close and breathe her in while we take each other to ecstasy.

"Truth," she finally decides, shaking her head.

I'm not surprised, but I'm also not disappointed.

"Is there someone waiting for you that would be upset that you're here with me tonight?" I ask her. I want to know right now if tonight comes with any restrictions or boundaries – not because I'm planning anything, but because I don't want to do anything to overstep and ruin this thrilling reunion. I don't know how she feels about the term these days, so I don't bring it up, but if Luna is still the good girl I always knew, then she'll appreciate that. And now I find myself holding my breath, hoping to hear the word no.

My whole body seems to lighten when she shakes her head.

"No," she affirms and I nod in appreciation.

"Surprising." I feel my eyebrows lift and a flirty smile try to tug at the corners of my mouth. I'm trying to behave, but I am surprised and can't seem to refrain from letting her know how alluring she is. She's fucking radiant, like she's found her place in this. And now that we seem to have fallen back into our old dynamic, she's relaxing into it more by the minute, and it's a thing of beauty.

"I mean," she lifts a shoulder, like she's playing off what she's about to say as casually as possible. "I had a not-great experience with that, and I guess you could say I've been fiercely independent ever since. Love yourself first and all that." She wobbles her head facetiously before taking hold of her root beer and bringing the straw to her lips.

Alright, where is this guy so I can pound him? I don't need to know what he did to give her a not-great experience, as she puts it.

"What about you?" she asks on an exhale, setting her drink back down and looking at me. "Should someone know you're here with me?"

I shake my head. "No, there's no one. I promise."

"Good," she concludes with a sneaky grin. "Truth or dare?"

Oh shit, we're still playing that. Never mind that I started it too.

"Dare," I blurt out without giving it much thought. Hopefully she doesn't dare me to do a full-Monty striptease on top of the bar.

She sits up high in her stool, glancing at something over my shoulder. A smile pulls at her parted lips and I chance a look behind me to see what she's got in store. All I see is a rooftop patio behind the glass door where I can hear muted music coming through, and there seems to be people idly dancing - wait…

"I dare you…" she gives me a knowing look.

"No."

"To dance," she finishes, a triumphant smile on her face as she reaches for her stupid root beer again.

"Come on," I plead.

"Dance," she volleys over her straw.

"No, you're supposed to dare me to go base jumping with my ass on fire or something," I lecture.

"Then it looks like I win." She smugly switches her crossed legs – which doesn't give me a semi at all – rolls her shoulders back and bites teasingly down on her straw.

"What?" I retort after mentally shaking myself out of the arousing stupor she put me in for a minute there.

"I win our eleven-year-long game of Truth or Dare," she announces on a satisfied exhale.

"No, you don't."

"Then do the dare."

"No."

"Then I win. This is why I pick truth," she whispers smugly as she leans in.

"You pick truth because you're too chickenshit to do anything," I retort and tilt my chin at her.

"Says the man afraid to dance," she taunts.

"Ugh," I grunt, getting to my feet. "I'm going to make you pay for this one," I grind out.

"Yes!" She gives that double fist pump she's always done as she slides off her stool and joins me in the walk of doom toward the outside dance floor.

The music blares louder as I open the door and usher Luna through. The DJ is playing some kind of oldie that I'm sure I've heard on the radio in Pops's shop. Luna turns to face me, and taking my hands in hers, shimmies her ass backwards until we're on the hardwood space.

Swinging our hands between us, she dances horribly just to annoy me bouncing back and forth while I barely move, giving her my best resting bitch face. My eyes continue to shoot lasers at her as she swishes her hips back and forth before twirling herself under my arm.

One thing I've never liked is moving to music. In fact, I despise it. Anytime someone even suggests it, I feel so fucking stupid. Seriously, why couldn't she dare me to run down the street naked?

The song mercifully comes to an end, fading out and transitioning to something slow, and I see a few guys pull their women close. When I look to Luna, that idea doesn't seem so bad.

"That does not count," Luna insists, dropping my hands. "You didn't even move, I did it all!"

She's cut off when I swiftly step into her and throw and arm around her back, pulling her securely against me. That same thrill I got when we hugged earlier is back, only this time, I have an excuse to bask in her closeness and her scent a little longer.

"This counts," I declare and eyeball her, defying her to argue.

"Fine," she mumbles, and rests her hand on my bicep as I take hold of her other hand.

This is surprisingly nice, and I realize I'm slowly turning us with almost no effort at all.

"So…" I look down at her as we sway in the summer night breeze. "Truth or dare?"

"Truth," she murmurs, her hand sliding up a little higher on my arm.

It's no surprise to me that I'm feeling this way with Luna right now. I always knew I would if I saw her again. No matter our past, I've always romanticized her and without a single picture of her in my possession, I relied on my memory to keep her face vivid in my mind over the last three years. Now she's in my arms, moving slowly with me while soft music plays under the night sky. I'm more nervous to ask her this truth than I was to take her dare. But all the feelings I ever had for her have come flooding back – with reinforcements – and who knows when I'll get another chance?

"Have you thought about me?" I finally ask in a gentle rasp. She stares back up at me, searching my eyes for where this question came from. Showing vulnerability is even harder now after the training I've been put through, but I silently will her to understand it came from the love I've been carrying for her.

Her eyes dilate, and I see conviction in their depths as she licks her lips before answering, "All the time."

I let out a breath, and with our bodies pressed together, I can feel her do the same. "Truth or dare?" she asks me, her voice raspy.

I keep looking at her another moment, wondering what would happen if I chose truth just once. "Dare," I barely whisper instead, praying to God she'll dare me to do what I want to do more than anything in this world.

"Dare you to kiss me," she whispers back, and without any hesitation, I lower my head, touching my lips to hers.

Her kiss is exactly how I remember. Sweet. Full. Gentle... and it turns my world upside down. Endorphins swirl in my chest and disperse throughout the rest of my body, and I want more of the high. I part my lips open and she follows suit, as if by instinct. My heart is racing, and just like when we kissed in the lake, it's the strangest mix of comforting and exhilarating. I'm safe at home, yet I'm on an exciting adventure.

Nothing has ever felt more right, and when I push my tongue into her mouth to stroke against hers, the rest of the world could crumble around us and I wouldn't be bothered to care. Like a drug addict taking a hit for the first time, I'm immersed. I want Luna. I want her tonight.

Luna

"Fuck, Luna," Kaleb groans in my ear as his mouth ravishes my neck. The windows of Pops' old Chevy pick-up are steamed to opaque as I straddle Kaleb's lap in the driver's seat. "I can't believe it's taken me seven years to get you like this."

"You've wanted this since you were fourteen?" I laugh gently between breaths, leaning back to give him access to my chest. God his mouth feels so good on my skin. It's soft and hot and every touch of it sends one flash of arousal after another through my body.

"Fuck yeah, I have," he murmurs against my cleavage.

God, this is the pleasure I've been waiting for. After my experience with Kaleb in the lake followed by the immediate heartbreak, I didn't want my first time to have any emotional ties. So when a make-out session with a guy from my bio class at a party was going well, I let it go all the way. During my reflection time after Carter, I was all the happier I made that choice. The first time was fun, but still, it was a first time. Carter was selfish most of the time, and way too fast.

Right now, with Kaleb... I didn't know a guy could make both my body and soul feel so good at the same time. When you feel about somebody the way I do about him, it's like a fantasy come to life, and it's happening all over you.

"Early bloomer..." I sigh, my breathing getting shallow with my increasing heart rate. "I'm not surprised," I tease, and he chuckles lightly in my ear with its lobe between his teeth.

"When it came to you, yes," he rasps, moving down my neck and fisting his hand into my hair. The soft sting on my scalp makes a moan escape my throat, and Kaleb pushes his jean-clad hard-on against me.

I don't know who wants this more, but it's happening. Regardless what happens in the morning, Kaleb and I were always meant to have this moment, and I'm not giving it up.

"How far to your bed?" Kaleb pants against my throat as my fingers grip at the back of his neck.

"It's a sixteen-stair hike," I inform him.

Our kiss on the dance floor had continued through to the end of the song before I pushed up on my toes and told him I was ready to go. More kissing ensued when we got into the cab of his truck before he put it in drive, and now that we're parked on the street outside my apartment, it's getting more questionable by the minute if we'll make it upstairs.

"That's too far," Kaleb groans as his hands slip under my skirt, his fingers kneading my hips.

Case in point.

"Well, should I just say goodnight then?" I challenge playfully, though I sure as hell hope that's not the case. I lean in and nibble at his jaw, just in case.

"Not a chance in hell, baby," he growls, leaning in to maul my chest again, drawing out a shameless moan from deep down in my chest.

"Fuck, I want you, K," I sigh out.

"Not as bad as I want you," he responds, palming my breast and splaying a kiss against it, and it makes my sex clench from the rush of pleasure.

"Ah," I gasp out.

"How do you want me, Lu?" Kaleb asks as he tilts his head back to regard me with his green gaze that's shadowed in lust as his other hand comes up to squeeze my other breast. "I'll give it to you however you want it. I want you to love every minute," he finishes, leaning in to place another kiss on my lips.

"I want you to do what's natural," I tell him honestly. I want whatever he has to give; to do with me whatever makes him feel good, whether it's slow and tender or fast and furious. "Whatever will leave you thinking about this every night of your tour," I boldly whisper, cupping his face in my hands.

"Fuck, baby, are you sure?" he rumbles against my lips.

"I want us to be completely free with each other," I affirm as I feel his hand go under my dress again.

"That's my perfect girl," he moans his approval as his fingers find the front of my panties, teasing at the edge.

"I'm not perfect," I moan at his touch.

"You're perfect for me," he admonishes, hooking his finger in the front of my dress and nudging it down. "You've always been." His mouth comes down over my exposed nipple and I whimper out it pleasure as his fingers nudge my panties aside to rub against my slit. "Mmm, but those stairs," he muses.

"What?" I pant out, feeling light-headed from what both his mouth and his fingers are doing to me.

"They're going to have to wait a few minutes," he elaborates as two of his fingers are now gliding up and down my wetness.

"Oh God, K," I'm writhing now, my body slowing rolling against him.

"Fuck Luna, I want you to come first."

Dammit, I never thought I'd be in Kaleb's lap while he spoke to me in this way but the shock at how much I love it is an aphrodisiac. It's like he's peeled back several layers and is showing me the being that's been hiding down in his depths craving me. Maybe he doesn't show me much of himself with his words but his actions right now… I could get drunk on the things I'm seeing with them.

"More," I exhale, my throat growing dry and he shifts me in his lap, pushing up against me again. He's harder than steel and it makes me feel empowered.

"You need to come baby," he says again and God, his words are both tender and dirty and so fucking perfect. "I want you nice and wet when I get inside you upstairs."

"Oh fuck K, please," I beg as he glides two fingers up and down my clit before nudging them through my opening. "Oh my God," my words are a strained whisper.

"Lu you're so fucking beautiful and perfect like this, fuck," he growls as he pushes his fingers deeper and I begin to ride them without a conscious thought. He dips his head back down to nibble at my breast again as my back arches with the mind-bending pleasure.

"Kaleb," I cry out hoarsely as he continues to pump his fingers in and out of me and I roll my hips in counter movements.

"Mmmm, are you close?" He moans against me and I nod. "Are you about to come?" Another nod because my heavy breathing leaves no room for words and his free hand comes up to cup the side of my face. "Look at me, look at me," he beckons urgently just as my climax is about to crest and I obey. "Show me those pretty eyes, baby," he gently orders right when I erupt, crying out and riding each wave of my orgasm on his hand.

Kalebs mouth closes over mine and he moans into it as the pleasure wanes, little by little with each pass. When he feels like he can withdraw his hand, he rights my skirt back down over my thighs and his arms come around me, wrapping me close against him as if he's treasuring this moment.

12

KALEB

The trek up to Luna's apartment bought me some time where my hard on is concerned. Watching a flush creep up her neck as she came in my lap damn near made me go off in my boxer briefs - again.

There's still a pink tint to her skin now as she turns the key in her lock and pushes the metal door open to reveal a small but open space with exposed brick and big windows that show off the city lights. I can see the far corner is where she does her creations, with the drop cloth and easel set up with a mess of brushes and papers, as well as a large metal cabinet that must hold more supplies. A small kitchen is off to my right, but I'll have time to take all this in in the morning. Right now I'm only interested in her bed where I can make love to her all the ways that I want.

I don't know what tomorrow has in store for us, but I intend to worship her and wrap each other in bliss all night long. Luna turns the lock on the door just as I spot the bed against the wall to my left and turn to take hold of her once again. Pulling her into me, I waste no time invading her mouth with mine once again as my pulse pounds in my ears.

"Am I going too fast?" I check in with her between kisses and she shakes her head and starts stepping backwards, leading us in the direction of her bed that adorns a white down comforter and pillows encased in a light purple linen.

My thumbs stroke along her delicate jawbone as we move along, not wanting to break our connection.

I should take this slow. I should make it last but then I'm not going anywhere tonight. I plan on ravishing Luna as many times and ways she'll let me take her.

Our time downstairs only made me look forward to this more when I got to see how damn responsive she is, and unafraid to let me know what she wanted. Not to mention she practically demanded I simply give into my instincts without holding back.

"Are you on the pill," my words come out on a ragged breath as I start inching the material of her skirt up, my hands craving the feel of her ass in their grip.

"Yes," she breaths back, and though the revelation destroys the very unreasonable fantasy of her saving her virginity for me, I console myself with the realization I get to be bare inside her. She starts pulling the front of my shirt up, her hands skimming along the ridges of my abs. I release her a moment to reach behind me and help her off with the rest of my shirt. Once I'm rid of the garment, Luna explores my bare torso with her sweet lips and while her fingers curl around the waist band of my jeans. Meanwhile, I reach back down and take hold of her dress and lifting it up over her body.

When I drop it to the floor, my dick jumps when I see she's braless with lace panties the same color as her pillows.

"God damn," I huff out as I take her hands in mine, looking her up and down. This is my first time seeing her naked with the exception of her panties and it's better than any vision I've daydreamed of. "So fucking beautiful," I say, taking in her alluring form in the dark of the room as her eyes blink up at me. "And you're all mine," I add and she can take it however the hell she wants. Tonight, forever, however long she'll allow.

"Kaleb please," she whispers up at me, releasing the snap on my jeans and when she goes up on her toes, I take her pleading lips with my own, jumping back into our fervent exploration of each other's senses. My tongue plunges into her mouth with no abandon, enjoying the way she moans around it in response. I grip onto her ass, her hips, her back as she works my zipper down, opening my fly. I grunt into her mouth when she finds my painfully stiff cock and palms through my boxer briefs.

"Fuck," my voice is gravel as she runs her nails along the cotton before gripping onto it again. "Baby, what are you doing to me?"

Every inch of my body aches to collide with hers as I tilt her chin back and suck on her neck and take hold of her left breast. It's a perfect handful and I get a rush, squeezing and massaging it.

"I want you," she pants, her breathing staggered. "I want you inside me Kaleb." Fucking hell, just when I didn't think my dick could get more painfully hard she goes and says that.

"Lie down," I order in a raspy growl and I work my jeans down as she sits on the mattress before scooching herself back. My dick springs free, jutting out towards her as I lean over and take hold of her panties pulling them down her hips as she lifts her ass off the mattress for me. Her fingers tunnel through my hair as I come to hover over her. "You ready for me?" I ask, notching my tip at her entrance. I could feel how tight she was when I got her off earlier and I'm glad to feel she's still wet.

"Yes, K, come on," she commands, nodding impatiently, her voice breathy. Fuck, her eagerness is going to make me go off too soon if I'm not careful.

With a swift snap of my hips, I thrust inside her, gliding through her wetness easily despite her tight channel and fucking hell, I've just entered paradise.

"Ah!" She cries out, tossing her head back and her mouth falling open. "Oh my God," she moans.

"Feel good?" I ask, kissing up her neck as I inch in further and further, easing us the rest of the way to the hilt.

"Yes," she manages out between breaths. "Yes… fuck…"

I've never felt so euphoric in all my life. All the waiting and fantasizing about this moment and it exceeds my wildest dreams. From the feel of her tight warmth around me to her nails digging into my back, to my hips rocking against hers, is exquisite perfection.

"Fucking amazing," I moan out, rolling my hips again and propping myself on an elbow to look down at her. "I want you to come again," I tell her. We're only a few minutes in but fuck I love seeing her come apart. I'm greedy for her orgasms.

"What about you?" she asks grunts out between thrusts. "Are you close?"

"Don't worry about me baby," I shake my head down at her. "I want you to have another one." I roll to the side and onto my back, pulling her with me. "Take what you want my girl. I'll be right behind you," I tenderly instruct her and she immediately finds a rhythm that blows my mind. Her hips grind and roll against mine as the sound of our breathing and skin sliding together fills the room. I take hold of her gorgeous tits as she arches back, basking in the pleasure and then hold her hair up out of her face when she comes back down to kiss me.

We're so unbelievably in sync for two people that are so different on paper, reading each other so well and perfectly in tune. Her moaning gets more urgent against my lips at the same time I feel the walls of her sweet pussy begin to spasm around me. Hauling myself up to sitting, I wrap my arms around her, keeping the connection hard and tight as I pump up into her, meeting her for each thrust.

"Ohh…" she cries out, her voice dry as I dip my head down to lick at her nipple. "Oh Kaleb, I'm fucking coming," her voice strains and it's music to my fucking ears.

"That's it, give it to me," I growl affectionately, coaxing her to the edge.

"Fuck!" She cries out helplessly as I pound her through it, grunting along with her cries of pleasure.

"Feels so fucking good," I exclaim, chasing my breath. Her climax goes on forever, her sex pulsing around my dick, slowing with each passing beat. I bring her down, our hips undulating against each other until a sated look falls over her eyes and I briefly pull out and guide her to turn over on her stomach.

As I drape my body over hers, my forehead comes to rest in the smooth space between her shoulder blades. Her skin is dewy with a sheen of sweat and I breath in the beautiful scent as I guide my cock into her entrance once again.

"Oh Lu," I pant as I start to move inside her again.

"Kaleb," she whispers as I sweep her luscious locks to the side and skim my lips up the back of her neck and thrust forward. Her body slides beneath mine against the comforter. I push one hand beneath her body and find her clit, hoping to strum one more out of her. My other hand comes up and cups her throat. "Fuck baby," I moan against her ear between sharp, measured thrusts. "Fuck…"

"Harder," she beckons. "I want more Kaleb, I want you," the words rush out of her desperately and I oblige, my libido shooting through the roof. My thrusts are borderline savage as I pound harder, my mouth teasing and licking at her neck as she cries out, giving me that coveted third orgasm and it's the one that brings me home.

"Ahhh, fuck!" I roar as I come inside her as she keeps riding her own climax, crying out as it racks her body. I drive into her hard thrusting out each jet of cum, groaning with each one until I collapse on top of her.

My heart is threatening to explode and my lungs want to give out as I shift off of her slightly. Planting kisses along her shoulder as she lays her head down and closes her eyes, trying to catch her breath. Burying my face in her neck, I wonder how the hell I was existing before tonight.

"What are you thinking, soldier?" Luna whispers from her prone position across from me as I skate my fingertips across the silky skin of her back.

Resting my head on my fist, I sigh out through my nose, my world never feeling so right. It's still hard putting myself out there, but I'm not going to ruin this moment by being evasive.

"I was thinking… I should've been your first," I admit quietly and she squints her eyes and gives me a smartass half-smile.

"Was I yours?" She pulls an eyebrow up.

"Touche," I breathe out.

"You were my first orgasm if that helps," she exhales, closing her eyes as I continue gliding my fingers along her back. "Well, that wasn't self-delivered that is."

"Oh? Tell me more about that," I suggest slyly as dirty thoughts start sailing through my head.

"Shut up," she mumbles behind her relaxed smile. "And, you have so many of my firsts anyway, Kaleb. The ones that matter."

"Like what?" I lay my head completely down.

"You were the first boy to draw me a picture," she indulges me with a smile and a dreamy look in those almond eyes. "To write me a letter… to give me a movie night by the lake…my first… love…" she raises her brows and a shoulder. She smiles nervously as if to say 'there it is'.

The feeling those words evoke is a confusing conundrum of shock and elation. They both scare and excite me as I look inside myself, looking at each feeling I've ever harbored for her.

"You were in love with me?" I ask, as my fingers start swirling a new path along her skin.

She pulls in a long breath through her nose as her eyes search the space above her. "It was confusing," she starts off, thoughtfully. "Knowing you for so many years but only in one context. Seeing each other grow and change but only getting to see it in intervals without continuity. But that bond was always there; always strong and palpable. I don't know," she shakes her head with a faint smile, looking as if she's giving up on how to describe the phenomenon that is us. "Some kind of love," she finally settles on with a sigh.

"Some kind of love," I echo, as I keep slowly drawing my message on her back, willing it to seep into her skin so that she knows without me having to say it out loud.

I don't get it. I've trained to hang out of a helicopter while being shot at, but Luna's braver than I am in this aspect. She's not afraid to show her raw feelings beneath her armor, while I for some reason still feel the pain from the fallout of trusting my dad to love and care for me. I've never been able to let any part of me depend on someone else to fill any emotional spaces in my life.

She closes her eyes as I keep tracing the words I would say across her back, that faint smile still in place and I see her eyebrows lift just slightly, and as much as I love making her feel nice, I find myself not ready for her to fall asleep and leaving me with my thoughts. "What about you?" I ask, and her eyes blink open to look at me. "What are you thinking about, goof?"

"Just glad this happened before you deployed," she looks at me, honesty reflecting in her eyes. "And that you better get all my info so that it's not another three years before we talk again," she sticks her tongue out and part of me admires how she enjoyed what happened between us but isn't laying any expectations on this; only to stay in touch. And yet another part of me wants her to want more... because I do. I don't know exactly what more looks like in this moment, I just know that I want it.

"Speaking of which," she pipes up again and leans up to mirror my position, resting her head on her hand. "I was thinking about when you're gone, do you have someone to take care of the house?" She lifts her brows expectantly and the righteousness that swirls in my chest with the surprise at how casually she's asking. It's like we talk every day and didn't just have a three-year gap of absence. And the answer is that I don't. Normally that would be Alex, my only real friend in Coyote Creek, but fat lot of good that does me when he'll be overseas with me.

"No," I grumble, shaking my head. "That's why I'm back for the next couple weeks, so that I can straighten up anything that needs it. "I need to square away anything I can with the shop while I'm at it, make sure there's nothing that could fall apart while I'm gone."

"Well, if you want, I could stop by every so often," she offers, her voice light. "It's not that bad of a drive from here…?"

"It's an hour and change," I supply, the wheels starting to turn in my head as a spark of relief comes to life in my chest.

"Right, so that's not bad. I can drive down in my free time and make sure everything is as it should be," she lifts her shoulder.

"You would do that?" I ask, not about to turn down this offer. It's a huge solid she'd be doing for me, not to mention I find myself not hating the idea of her in my house.

"Of course," she murmurs, starting to trace little hearts on the space of sheet beside her. "I won't let anyone mess with Pop's house," she gives me a fierce smile and I'm overwhelmed in this moment. I don't think I ever even paused to think what it would be like to have someone else to care about my well-being besides Pops. And though she only met him a handful of times in passing, here's Luna, lying beautifully naked across from me, telling me she'll make sure I have a home to come back to.

"Come here," I whisper, all of a sudden feeling like she's too far away. Lifting the sheet, I help her shift over to drape her warm, naked body over mine and wrapping us up together, skin to skin. Never in my life have I felt so safe as I run my both my hands through her hair and trail down her back.

"This feels so nice, K," she sighs heavily, her sweet breath breezing across the skin of my chest.

"Thank you," I whisper into the top of her hair, deciding to do one small thing that scares me. I want to show her the inside of me, just a little… just to see what happens.

"For what?"

"For coming back into my life," I let the words roll out, biting the bullet.

She hums a thought in response as she starts to draw her little hearts just below my collar bone. "I was just in a bar at the right time. "You came to me, K. You came back to into my life."

I consider this a moment, my lips finding her temple as I breathe her in. Letting her know how I felt came with a small side of nerves, but it didn't hurt. On the contrary it's rewarding.

"It's a good place to be," I tell her, but I'm lying. It's the best place to be. It's home.

13

LUNA

"That's beautiful." Kaleb's raspy morning voice is close behind me as I peer in close at the small silhouette of a bird against my dusky sky, trying to smudge its wings a little.

"Thank you." I smile warmly at him before turning back to my work, trying not to get distracted by his bare, tatted torso that he's apparently been ripping to shreds for the last three years. I hear him set his coffee mug down behind me before my hair is gathered in his hands, stroking the strands before sweeping them to the side and laying his sinfully soft and warm lips to my neck before wrapping his arms around my shoulders.

"What's it for?" he asks in my ear.

"It's my final for my abstract landscapes class," I tell him, setting my crayon down and waving a hand at the unfinished project. "I'm thinking the main street of a small town will be the focal, but you know me and drawing," I chuckle. "I'm saving that for last."

"Speaking of small towns," he mumbles into my ear before giving it a playful nibble that makes shivers break out down my neck.

"Oh yeah," I recall, "when do you need to get moving?" I ask, remembering that he's got work to get done back home.

"Actually, I was wondering if you wanted to come with me…" his lips come down to my shoulder and linger as he waits for a response. Another warm shiver.

"What?" I heard him fine, I just can't believe it. I was going to take this encounter for what it was and not worry about where we went from here. I wasn't expecting him to extend it, being a guy and all.

"Come back with me," he repeats, straightening up. "We'll make a little road trip out of it."

"Well, I'd love to see where you're from, but what brought this on?" Okay, I'm a little anxious, I'll admit. I guess I just want to have a good idea where his head's at before I go driving back to his hometown with him.

"I leave in a couple weeks. You should see the house if you're going to be looking in on it," he reasons. "Plus, it will give you inspiration for your assignment," he nods at my canvas.

"Well," I begin and turn to face him, "I guess I can't argue with any of that." I raise a hand to push my hair away from my face as he gives me a victorious grin.

"Good," he pulls me close by my hips, "and if you don't have a summer job or classes, maybe you could spend some time between here and there, you know, make it look like someone's living there?"

"Totally," I nod. I work for myself for the most part, booking painting parties for people that want to do group paintings. Paint and sips are big right now, so I do alright. And of course, a little surplus of money sometimes magically appears in my bank account whether I want it to or not. Thanks, Dad. I told him when he and my little brother, Matthew, moved me in here last year that I wanted to go it alone, see what it was like to struggle a little bit and provide for myself. Clearly, he didn't give a shit about what I said.

"Perfect." He leans in to kiss my lips and whispers, "Why don't you get an overnight bag together?" causing my sex to wake up, warmth flowing towards it from the tatted god whose pheromones are suddenly wafting off his bare skin as his lips linger on mine. "I'll bring you back tomorrow night if you have a class to be back at," he mutters before pressing his lips a little harder against mine. I'm excited for this, but the way he's got me going, I'm wondering if he wouldn't mind showing me that magnificent thing he can do with his cock again.

"I need to shower," I practically moan as he nibbles at my bottom lip.

"I'll help you with that."

"My shower is tiny," I warn him.

"Perfect," he clips out before ducking and tackling me around my waist and hoisting me up on his shoulder as I yelp out a surprised laugh. Another shriek escapes me when his hand comes down hard on my left ass cheek, his palm lingering for a moment as he hurries us toward my bathroom.

WITH A SMALL WEEKEND BAG, as well as my huge art bag that Kaleb insisted I bring along secured in the flat bed of the old truck, we cruise down the freeway in the vibrant, cheerful light the sun is providing.

When I told Kaleb that I didn't have a class until Tuesday at one, he insisted I bring my supplies, just in case I was able to draw inspiration from his little town. Kaleb smiles between me and the road as we catch up on more of the last three years. I toe off my gold t-strap sandals and tuck a leg under me as he regales me with anecdotes of him and Alex in boot camp, the warmth of his hand seeping through my jeans where it rests on my leg.

My blissful basking is cut off at about thirty minutes in, however, when my phone buzzes in my back pocket, alerting me of a new email. I pull it out, intense on dismissing it so that it doesn't continue to buzz intermittently, when I see a preview of the message.

From: Carter Lange
Subject: Long time...

My heart stutters to a stop and a lump lodges in my throat.

"Lu? Babe?" I glance up to see Kaleb's face turning between me and the road, his smile gone and concern etching the features not hidden by his sunglasses. "Everything alright?"

"Uh…" my voice is shaky and my brain refuses to form words while it's trying to digest the message my eyes are sending it. "Um, yeah," the words come out serrated by my erratic heartbeat.

"No, it's not," Kaleb protests as he sits up straighter, leaning around to check our surroundings before pulling over. Putting the truck in park he turns towards me. "What, is it bad news? Talk to me," he says in just the right combination of firm and gentle to get me to comply.

"I got an email," I finally manage to say. It's Kaleb, I remind myself. I've got nothing to hide. "It's my ex, and he shouldn't know how to get a hold of me."

"This the one that made you steer clear of relationships the last year?" Kaleb puts an arm over the back of my seat.

Dammit. I was really hoping for Carter to never have to come up between Kaleb and me, but here we are, so I regretfully nod.

"Luna, what did he do?" Kaleb pulls his shades off his face and I follow suit, pushing mine up on my head. He levels me with that no-nonsense glare of his.

It's not that I'm afraid to tell him, I just didn't want this to be a thing. I didn't want Carter to have any particle in my life, let alone have him break into mine and Kaleb's private bubble. Plus, I'm embarrassed about what I have to admit.

"He was just really controlling and borderline abusive when I was with him," I impart, and when I look up to see green eyes blazing with a shocked fury, I'm quick to correct myself. "Verbally abusive," I quickly amend, and I hate the thick silence that emanates off Kaleb and fills the cab of the truck. "Anyway, when I left him, I blocked him on every avenue, I changed my phone number, and even blocked him for good measure. I even changed my email to a handle I didn't think he'd figure out so easily."

"The fact he found you then, says he was trying to," Kaleb utters ominously, his voice sounding like it's being dragged across jagged gravel.

"He probably didn't have to try very hard, he's a computer whiz," I explain, huffing out a mangled breath before I look to Kaleb again to find a confused look on his face. "I know," I hold a hand up and roll my eyes, knowing he's questioning how in the hell I ended up dating someone so far from my type. "He was just really sweet and charming at first, and…" I steel myself with a mild breath before looking up, directly into his eyes, "he didn't make me think of you."

Obviously. Carter asked me out after fixing my laptop when I had an English paper due and was so far from Kaleb in both looks and personality I thought I was safe; that he was stable and secure. Now, I laugh at the whole thought.

Kaleb's eyes go downcast a moment, his lips pressing together with an emotion I can't pinpoint before he looks back up. "So he found ways to control you after he hooked you, and now, a year later, he's not only looking for you, he found you," Kaleb grits out, I can tell, trying to keep his voice steady, but there's no hiding how dark his eyes have gone.

"I know how stupid I sound," I mumble down at my lap. "That I fell for someone's shit and didn't even realize what he was doing for the better part of a year." Another reason I don't like looking back on that time. It's the one thing in my life I feel foolish about.

"No, Luna…" I feel Kaleb's hand playing with my hair. "You're the smartest person I know, and the strongest." I scoff out a breath which agitates him. "No, I'm serious. Look at me." I look up from my lap and am relieved to see his eyes have softened. "You're remarkable, and he's a piece of shit for hurting you. That's on him, understand?" He dips his head to look at me closer, and I nod.

"I know," I assure him quietly. "I'm just glad you don't think otherwise." I grab my shades off my head and run a hand through my hair. I hate the idea of Kaleb seeing me as weak or naive.

"I could never possibly," he affirms, giving me a light kiss on my cheek. "Let's see what it says," he nods down at my phone.

"No, I was just going to delete it and block him," I shake my head, lifting my phone to do just that before he stops me.

"No, hang on,"

"Kaleb, I really don't want to even look. He's taken up enough time and energy just in the last three minutes. He doesn't get any more."

"Agreed, but we can't just turn a blind eye, either. This could get worse, and we need to cover our asses," he explains, and his use of the word we makes a small butterfly flutter to life in my chest. "Can I see it?" he asks, holding out his hand, and I hand over my phone with no hesitation.

Kaleb taps at the screen, trying his best not to react, but the set of his jaw gives away just enough. I try not to pay attention, not wanting to catch any of Carter's scumbag words, but do ask what Kaleb's plan is.

He makes a few more deliberate swipes and taps before handing my phone back.

"It's going to be okay now," he informs me solemnly, and I immediately feel the tension leave my body and my next breath cleanse my lungs.

"Okay," I acknowledge and try to give him a smile. "Thank you."

He nods. "But if he contacts you again, you tell me. Got it?"

"Got it." I smile bigger now, trying to get us away from this territory and back to our happy reunion bubble. "Now, where were we?"

"I was taking you home," he answers with a playfully wicked grin as he puts the truck back in gear.

Kaleb

THIS MORNING, I wasn't ready to separate from Luna, going completely against what I've resisted all this time: tying myself to somebody. But I just got her back and I'm not ready to say goodbye, no matter how much we'd probably keep in touch this time. I'm making the most of my time before I ship out, and that includes spending time with her. The fact that she should see the house and people around town should know her face is just convenient.

Then the way we were laughing and talking easily in the truck... that's the way it was always supposed to be between her and I, I'm sure of it. Even now, as I stare straight ahead at the road with my left-hand white knuckling the steering wheel and my other hand on her thigh, making soothing circles with my thumb, everything feels right in place. Even though one side of me is fuming at the idea of some fucker hurting my girl, no matter in what capacity, while the other side keeps her calm, I feel completely balanced.

I know all I need to know about this Carter asshole by the way the mere knowledge of his efforts to communicate shook her up. I swear to God she spaced out and looked like she was going to be sick, and it made my instincts kick in; the ones that drive me to do anything to protect every part of her being. It was clear by her following behavior that she's eager to put it behind her and do so by acting like it didn't happen, but this piece of shit is now on my radar for life. I indeed deleted his message and blocked him on her phone, but not before taking a screenshot and sending it to myself.

> *Hey girl, how are things?*
> *It's been a while, so I thought I'd reach out. I miss talking to you and was wondering if you were over what happened between us yet. If so, maybe we can get back in touch? If not, I hope you can get past it and realize just how much I cared about our relationship, and what I was willing to do for it.*
> *Hope you're taking care of yourself.*
> *Love, Carter.*

Whatever he did, there's no apology or remorse on his end. He barely even took ownership. And he sought her out by hacking, and just because I blocked him, doesn't mean he won't do it again if he was so gung-ho to do it even once. It's evident that he and I are going to have a problem, but I need to know everything. I'm letting it go for now, so that Luna can have a chance to process it all through her thoughts, but then I'm hoping she'll let me in on everything later.

Turning off the ramp, I turn left, following the green sign with the white arrow pointing us towards Coyote Creek and West Bridge, the town only eight miles past it that's bigger and has more access to certain things – like restaurants and department stores.

I navigate the truck down the long, two-lane highway as Luna takes in the rolly hills and tall trees before they open up to some farm lands and wheat fields. The wind flutters her hair, brown and purple strands breezing across her face, and she pulls them away from her eyes and leans forward as the town's first buildings come into view. The main street is lined with old, red brick buildings that consist of a bank, two bars, a salon, and restaurant that added a dining patio in the last couple of years.

"Oh my God, I love this," Luna gushes appreciatively as she looks back and forth between the two sides of the street. She points at little things from hanging flower baskets, to an old mailbox, to how even the cracked and faded pavement gives the place character. "Oh my God, you guys even have one of those cute old water towers!" she exclaims, looking out her side of the truck.

"It's like you've never seen a Podunk town before," I chuckle at her.

"I've seen plenty," she sasses back and lightly bats my arm with the back of her hand. "Okay only a few," she admits, "But I love them. They're so cozy and charming; quiet…" she trails off, looking content as she takes in more of the sights – or lack thereof. She insists on stopping in front of my high school of all places to snap a photo of the sign out front, and as we get closer to the edge of town, I turn down a side street. I go past the small park with the baseball diamond before turning down Conway – my street. A couple of empty lots pass by before I turn into the driveway of the modest white bungalow with the chipped paint on its front porch. It's old and weathered, and has seen better days for sure, but it's home. It's saving grace is that it's on two acres instead of one, or even less. There's a separate garage to the side and back a little way for when Pops would bring his work home with him, and where my Harley now sits under a sheet.

"Oh my God, there's a porch swing!" Luna gasps, a smile of adoration curving her lips, her eyes alight with excitement. It's like she's a country girl that was accidentally born in the city. She takes such delight in the things that were always just there to me, and it's like she's giving me a renewed appreciation for them. To see the world through her eyes would be a thing of beauty and wonder.

She pushes out from her door when I barely have the truck in park. I shake my head and laugh lightly as she scurries up the front steps while grab her bags out of the back. When I trudge up the steps with her overnight bag in one hand, and her large portfolio-sized art bag slung over the other shoulder, I find her sprawled sideways on the porch swing, legs stretched in front of her. From the giddy smile on her face, you'd never know some monster from her past just popped up in front of her earlier.

"I love this porch," she admits and shakes her head, looking around her immediate surroundings, while I look at her, imagining her living here with me. She looks right at home, and for the first time in my life, I feel something resembling grounded.

"Come on, silly girl," I say, fiddling with my ring of keys and finding the one to the front door. She pops off the swing, leaving it gliding behind her, and is at my side as I open the door. I give her a quick tour of the main living area off the entry way and the kitchen on the other side, before showing her down the hall. She gets sidetracked in the bathroom when she sees the deep, clawfoot tub, and fangirls over it for several minutes – which includes actually climbing in and sitting in it.

In less than five minutes, this house has been brought to life by her being in it, and while I thought it would be overwhelming, it feels exactly how it should… and I just never knew it.

At the end of the hall, we reach the two bedrooms and I open the door to the right, the one that used to be my room growing up. After Pops died, I took over the master and made this a spare room of sorts, not that I ever have any company.

"Is this where you want me?" Luna asks as she trails in behind me. I lay her art bag down on the double bed that still sports the old blue and white quilt from when I was a kid.

"Nope," I respond and back out of the doorway, taking her overnight bag with me, and turning towards the master bedroom and opening the door. I walk into the room, dim from the drawn curtains, and set her bag down on the floor. "I want you with me," I tell her as I turn to find her stepping through the threshold and taking in the rumpled grey comforter.

"Aren't I supposed to be able to bounce a quarter off this bed, solider?" she teases as she points at it, giving me a cocky eyebrow, but I'm quick with my rebuttal.

"No, but I know something else I can bounce off it!" I playfully growl before scooping her up and tossing her on the mattress while she lets out a delighted shriek before bouncing – thank you – and falling back to her elbows. She squeals again when I dive on top of her, careful to catch myself with my hands, caging her in as I hover over her.

14

KALEB

*B*ringing my mouth down to tease her lips with mine, her wanton sigh makes my dick grow hard at an almost painful rate. It starts to throb hard as she teases back, feathering her tongue over the seam of my lips, and it ignites my need to dominate this kiss. My mouth presses down on hers and the whimper that hums between them is my reward. I grunt shamelessly into her mouth before tearing away to ravish down her neck, bringing both my lips and my tongue into the fray, kissing hungrily between hits of her orange blossom scent.

Luna's breath is a sequence of shallow gasps with mewls of pleasure in between, and I've never felt the need to come so bad in all my life.

"Lu," her nickname drags from my throat on the tail of a ragged breath. "I need to get inside you," I convey, and she nods frantically as I rear up to rid myself of yesterday's shirt as I'm already feeling a flash of heat spreading across my back. She takes the same second to pull her white tank top over her head, leaving me with an overhead view of her lilac lace bra when she drops back down to the bed.

Fuck, who knew I had a thing for lace? Something about the delicate material against her light olive skin and cupping her perfect fucking tits just makes my head spin, and I can't resist bringing my mouth down over one, sucking at her nipple through the lace. Luna moans and keens into my mouth, arching back and elongating the arch of her throat. It's an invitation I can't pass up as my lips journey up her chest, and dance with my tongue up the smooth skin of her neck as her moans get louder, and her fingers tunnel into my hair.

"Fuck, oh God, Kaleb," she stammers between intakes of breath.

"Can you come, Luna?" I check in, slowing my movements just enough to buy me a few seconds. "If I take you right now, will you be able to come with me?"

"Yes!" she cries out, arching up to grind her pelvis against mine, and I hunker back again and get to work on my fly.

"Undo your jeans," I order as I work my zipper down, and she snaps the button and pulls at her own. "That's my good girl," I grumble down approvingly as I free my cock and shove down at my waistband, getting my jeans and boxer briefs down below my ass at the same time Luna arches up off the mattress, doing the same.

Crashing down on top of her, I grapple with her hands and pinning her wrists together in one hand, slamming them over her head as my dick brushes against her pussy.

"Ah!" The action makes her cry out with a sound of rapt pleasure, and satisfaction floods over me in a wave at the confirmation that she likes the control I'm taking over her. "Fuck yes, Kaleb, take what you want," she rasps, and I don't waste any time taking hold of my dick with my free hand and circling the tip around her slick opening, making her pant frantically with want before I drive it inside of her in one forceful thrust.

"Fuck!" I roar before pulling out and thrusting forward again, and then again, working up my pace. "Ah!" I start rolling my hips, faster with each pass as Luna spurs me on from beneath me, wanting it harder. Beautiful dirty thoughts consume my brain, making my blood pump harder, and I take my chance at voicing them. "You going to come on my cock? You going to come all over it like a good girl?"

"All over it, Kaleb," she assures me with a drawn-out groan. "Come on, harder," she commands and I oblige, pummeling with all my might as I feel her start to clamp around me, squeezing my dick to its climax, Luna's screams heightening the pleasure.

"God! Fuck!" I slam into her, releasing her hands to give me better leverage as I drive us both through our joint orgasm. My dick is drenched inside Luna's pussy as I continue to pump in and out with her nails digging deliciously into my back.

"Yes… K…holy shit!"

It seems to take forever for our explosion to settle, but when it finally does, I collapse on top of my Luna, peppering kisses along her cheek, over to her mouth. She rocked my world, welcoming my rough bedroom style, and now I thank her with sweet gratitude.

I love her… I love her…

Now if I could just face my fear of telling her just how much.

Luna

I DIDN'T KNOW what my sex life was missing before Kaleb. I never knew I liked it rough with dirty talk, which is a huge comment on how lackluster it was with Dipshit. I had no idea my body and soul could twine together in such ecstasy.

I shake my head at his audacity with contacting me this morning as I fluff out my hair and pull my long black cardigan on over my tank top and jeans. I expel a gust of air, releasing the toxic energy as I meander down the hallway to the kitchen, where I find Kaleb with his head in the fridge.

"We're probably going to have to go up to the market," he informs me before straightening up and closing the white fridge door. "I just got back yesterday from Fort Sill, and drove straight out to Indy pretty much right after."

"Wow, you weren't fucking around," I point out as I scooch my butt onto a stool and rest my chin on my hand on the island counter.

"I'd been busting my ass under a strict schedule the last three years," he reasons with an adorable boyish shrug before resting his hands on the counter across from me and locking his elbows. "Beer and a good time were hard to come by. Besides," he leans in closer, "I wouldn't have run into you last night if I'd fucked around."

"True that." I flash him a grin as I reach for the notepad and pen I see resting nearby. "So what do we need at the store, soldier?"

After making a small list of things, we hop back into the truck and drive about sixty seconds to the grocery store that's just a block off the main street. A half hour after that, we're loaded down with plastic bags of sandwich fixings, frozen pizzas, cereal, beers, soft drinks and plenty other snacks to get us through the next couple of days, including the canister of cinnamon rolls with the orange icing I just had to have.

We're just placing the bags in the flatbed when a female voice calls out from across the street.

"Kaleb!" We both turn to see a blonde around our age prancing in our direction.

"Shit," Kaleb mumbles, and I turn to notice a shadow of annoyance cast over his eyes before he puts a faint smile on as she launches herself against him.

Wow. Okay then…

"Oh my God, I can't believe you're back!" Her voice is heavy with emotion as she throws her arms around his neck. A small pang of jealousy rings like a gong inside me but it dissipates quickly when I see Kaleb taking hold of her wrists and smoothly peeling her away. At this point, I have no claim to him, not officially anyway, but a lot has happened in the last twelve hours or so, and this piles on to the things I'm already trying to process.

With this charming girl finally detached from his front, Kaleb releases her wrists but keeps his fake smile in place for her benefit.

"How've you been?" he mutters, while she smiles brightly up at him, forcing herself not to look at me.

"Oh, you know," she gives an eyeroll with a crooked smile. "Still here. Working at the bar." She tilts her head in the direction of Main Street. "We should catch up. Are you free tonight?"

At that proposition, Kaleb takes hold of my left hand and jams his other in his pocket. "No, sorry, I'm pretty busy for the next couple of weeks before I ship out," he informs her as she looks between our joined hands and up at me for the first time.

"Sorry," Kaleb drones before clearing his throat. "Luna, this is Cheyenne."

"Nice to meet you," I hold my hand out. I can tell Kaleb doesn't particularly care for this person, and I'm not sure I like her already. And though my mother is laid back and easygoing, she's classy as fuck and taught me no different.

Cheyenne looks between my hand and my face before saying "Luna," as if it's some sour statement that someone put a gun to her head and forced her to say. I drop my hand but keep my expression unbothered as she adds. "Nice hair," with a thread of sarcasm in her tone.

"Thank you," I smile sweetly at her as she backs away.

"I have to get to work," she mumbles before fixing her face to a flirty smile, eyeballing Kaleb. "Come find me at the bar before you leave town."

She continues backward for a few steps, waiting for a response that doesn't come as Kaleb has already turned away and is leading me to my side of the truck.

"Ex-girlfriend?" I ask softly, wanting to get straight to the point with no games.

"Ex-hookup," Kaleb corrects with a shake of his head and a

roll of his green eyes as he yanks my door open and I climb in. "It was never anything more," he adds, a sincere light coming over his gaze as I buckle in. "Sorry we had to run into her."

"It's okay," I nod truthfully. I believe him, and by the way he brushed her off, she's clearly not a threat. "Looks like we've both got ghosts from Christmas past trying to sour our weekend," I say facetiously, quirking my eyebrows, and he smirks back at me.

"Not a chance," he declares and leans in, stealing a quick kiss before shutting my door.

15

KALEB

It's fucking crazy how Luna and I, up until last night, only knew each other in a couple of isolated contexts: camp in the summers, doing outdoorsy kid shit, and writing letters that only offered each other vague glimpses into the other's home life.

Yet here we are after less than twenty-four hours, carrying our lunch out onto the back porch like we've been doing it for decades. As we set our sandwiches down on the table, Luna looks up to the tree at the back of the yard, and a pleasant smile passes over her face like the light afternoon breeze put it there.

"You still have the tire swing," she observes fondly, and again, I almost can't fathom that this is her first time being here.

"Yeah," I lift a shoulder as we sit. "Didn't see any reason to get rid of it, just because I don't play on it anymore."

"I'm going to get you to play on it," Luna announces, pointing towards it with one hand and holding her other in front of her mouth while she talks around her bite of food.

"No dice," I tell her before biting into my own sandwich, and she gives me a sneaky *just you wait* look before moving onto another subject.

"I can't believe you got to grow up here." There's yearning in her voice as she looks down to scoop a chip into the dip on her plate.

"It's alright," I muse, folding my hands together with my elbows on the table. "I've never seen anyone go apeshit over this old shack before," I quirk an amused eyebrow.

"It's not a shack," she gently argues. "It's a beautiful, charming little house. You just need to bring out all its character," she says matter-of-factly.

"Oh? And how do I do that, Martha Stewart?" I chide before a potato chip bats me in between the eyes.

"Well, you've got a good start leaving the tire swing up," she begins as if she didn't just wing a crispy, fried potato product in my face. "And then you could brighten up the bedroom, maybe add a pop of color to all the grey and white so it's not so dismal looking."

"Oh I don't know, it looked like you were having a pretty good time in there to me." I raise my eyebrows and get biffed with another chip in the face. I try to beam one back at her smug face, but she ducks before it can hit her.

After some more idle chat and the finishing of our lunch, I take our plates inside, and when I come back out, I find her striding purposefully towards the tire swing, her long cardigan flapping in the gentle breeze.

I walk over to catch up, and when she reaches the swing, she takes hold of the rope before turning to me as I venture closer to her. "Will this hold me?" she asks, looking up like she's wondering how old the branch is that it's wrapped around.

"Are you kidding?" I chuckle at her as she pulls off her sandals, and gripping the rope, steps up onto the opening of the tire, her light purple-painted toes curling around the black rubber.

Pulling the swing to an angle, I take hold of the rope and jump onto the other side, letting it swing us both beneath the branches. Luna grins like the kid she once was as her hair breezes into her face. "Can it hold you?" I revisit her question before stepping off the tire and giving her a light push. She pulls her butt onto the top of the tire, wrapping her legs around the rope and crossing them at the calves.

"Told you I'd get you on it," she jeers, sticking her tongue out.

"Yeah, whatever, goof," I tell her, reaching my hand out to push lightly again. She seems relaxed as she sways back and forth, and I wonder if this is really the best time to bring up her ex, but I want to get it out of the way, and she seems to have gotten any heavy feelings out of the way. "Luna…" I say her name in a semi-serious voice and gauge her reaction. Her eyebrows go up in interest, waiting for me to continue. "I want you to please tell me what that Carter guy did to you."

"Come on, Kaleb," she sighs and leans back to swing a little higher. "I told you; he was just really controlling."

"But what was the catalyst?" I persist. "What made you decide you'd had enough and leave him?"

"K, I just really don't want to deal with it anymore…"

"I'm dealing with it," I interject, placing a hand on my chest. "And if I'm going to handle it, I need to know."

"There's nothing to handle." She shrugs as she floats past me again.

"But there could be." I reach forward and grab onto the lip of the tire, slowly bringing her to a jerky stop. "If he continues, which he probably will, I'm handling it, you hear me?"

She stares back at me, her brown eyes searching mine, and I can see the sadness and the struggle. She doesn't want to burden me with this. "Truth or dare?" I pull out my ace in the hole and present it more as a statement, and she sets her jaw, annoyed.

"If I tell you, will you drop it?" She tilts her head, pleading in her eyes.

"You bet your ass I will," I assure her with a firm nod, resting my hands on her thighs as I gaze up at her solemnly. "I just want you to tell me so that I know if anything ever happens again, and then I'll let it go so we can enjoy our time together. Cross my heart." I make an X over my chest with my finger tip.

Luna nibbles at her lip a moment before sucking in a breath and expelling the words like a bad taste. "He hid my acceptance letter to NICA," she reveals, and I feel my jaw drop and my heart stop. "It took a year off my career. No, my life," she corrects herself, her eyes looking up at the oak branches.

He took a year away from her.

I can feel the fire sparking and flickering to life deep in my gut, though I try to keep it in check. I'm going to slam my fist through this fucker's face if I ever meet him.

"If I dared to go out or do anything without him, he'd make my time away from him a living hell by calling and texting and getting upset with me for not answering, or telling me how selfish I was. He'd go days without talking to me after I came back, and then when I'd make plans to move out or something like that, he'd grovel and tell me he was sorry while at the same time making me feel like it was my fault. It was mind games…" she shakes her head as if trying to get the very thought out of her head.

"Did he ever put his hands on you?" I ask, pinning her with my stare and trying not to grind my jaw.

"No," she shakes her head. "He'd hit things and throw things, you know, to emphasize his temper and scare me."

"Son of a bitch," I grind out as I look away. My fury crackles with heat as I picture her standing in a room while he tears her down, scaring her and making her feel like shit.

"I didn't want to believe it until I found my acceptance letter. Oh, after he'd forged a rejection letter and opened my real letter carefully with a knife and replaced it with the one he wrote." She pulls in a deep breath that raises her shoulders and drops them when she exhales. "Can we be done talking about this now?"

"Yeah." I lean in and kiss her and push the swing again. I'm far from done stewing over this, but I promised her I'd drop it.

And the look of happy peace on her face as the swing gracefully arcs in the breeze, it's worth keeping that promise.

Luna

APPARENTLY, Kaleb's friends didn't get their drink on hard enough last night, as we're making a three block walk up the street to his buddy, Ryan's house, who's having a bonfire in his back yard.

With his fingers linked with mine, Kaleb explains there's just little else for young adults our age to do – the downfall to living in a town like this one. It doesn't sully my outlook on the place though. I feel like a person can breathe and think out here; draw inspiration from the beauty and the quiet.

The white noise of chatter gets louder, along with crackles and pops from the fire I can see burning in the backyard of a brown house just about thirty feet away. Kaleb leads me around the side of the house to where a handful of people drink and joke around the orange blaze.

"If you were to fly over this town at night, you'd probably see little orange fires everywhere," Kaleb indulges me with a fun fact. That's how people do it here in CC, Indy," he sighs out, shortening the name of his town and state.

"Corporal Shane!" Some guy with longish blonde hair pops up and snaps off a salute, to which Kaleb rolls his eyes and does a half-assed one back. "Shut up,"

"Jeez, sensitive," the guy mumbles before sitting back down in one of the many folding chairs that surrounds the fire.

"That's Ryan," Kaleb leans in to murmur to me. "All he does is party and talk shit. Don't pay him any attention if you can help it."

I nod up at him, just as we're approached by another guy with hair as dark as Kaleb's, and though I can't see his eye color in the minimal firelight, he's a little shorter than K with softer features.

"I'm Alex," he says and immediately holds out his hand. I'm impressed with his manners.

"Hi, I'm Luna." I shake his hand and I see his lower jaw drop open slowly.

"Luna?" I nod and so does Kaleb as he pulls me in a little closer, and Alex blinks, shaking his head. "But... wait a minute. You were at the club last night. This is Luna?"

"The one and only," Kaleb's voice is affectionate, and I can't tell if I'm feeling warmth from his tone or the fire.

Alex takes a moment to find his voice before finally shaking his head in disbelief. "Camp girl showed up." He tilts his head towards Kaleb as he takes a pull of his beer, and pins him with some kind of knowing stare.

Kaleb stares back, a reluctant smile trying to pull at the corners of his mouth. "Keep chugging that beer, comrade. Whatever keeps words from coming out of your mouth."

Alex swallows while holding both his hands out. "I should've put money on it, that's all I'm going to say."

"Shut it," Kaleb warns, still trying not to smile.

"I'm just saying from here on out you can refer to me as the Prophet. Oh look," he dramatically turns his head and gasps, "Miranda's here!" he announces before dashing off in the direction of an approaching brunette who looks happy to see him.

Just as I tilt my head back to ask Kaleb what that was all about, Ryan, the apparent shit talker pipes up again. "Hey, K, who's the little slice? And since when do you take your game into overtime? Didn't you go home with her last night?"

In about half a second Kaleb is dashing me behind him, and in three strides is right in Ryan's face.

"You looking to get laid out early tonight, fucker?" All chatter ceases as people look to see what's about to go down. Kaleb for sure towers over this guy who thinks he's hilarious. I tuck my hands up under my chin, bracing myself. I always knew

Kaleb had a short fuse due to his unfortunate childhood, but I've never seen it in action before.

I hold my breath as Ryan gets a goofy look on his face and waves Kaleb off like this is an everyday thing. "Come on, bro, you know this is just how I say hello."

Good lord, whatever happened to this poor kid?

Ryan leans around Kaleb's solid frame and waves at me as if to illustrate. "Hi, girl that Kaleb banged last night," he sings out, but before I can even respond with 'that's okay, I'm also the girl he humped in the lake at summer camp, he's in the air. Kaleb has raised him up off the grass by his jacket and is snarling in his face.

"Alright, listen up, asshole. You don't talk to her for the rest of the night. You don't even look at her, you hear me?" Without waiting for any sign of compliance, Kaleb drops Ryan as if he's a sack of potatoes and doesn't even look to see if he landed on his feet before heading to the cooler where he grabs out a beer bottle and a water.

"Need a shot to start off with, K?" some other guy asks him from my right, holding out a familiar looking bottle of whiskey.

"Not tonight." Kaleb shakes his head to my surprise before leading me to a couple of empty seats and handing me the water.

For the next hour and change, I laugh at stories of Kaleb from high school and get to know Alex's girlfriend, Miranda, who works in the salon in town. Ryan obeys Kaleb's orders as I don't hear from him again – well, not directly anyway. He's still running his mouth and drinking however much his stomach can hold, while I intermittently think about whether I want to get to know him in some other setting. Like maybe a church.

In between chatting with Miranda, I catch the occasional wind of more bullshit he spews, and catch him just in time to start in on Kaleb again.

"What did you sign up for anyway?" Ryan sneers, clearly one more sheet to the wind than the last time he opened his mouth.

"You should be sticking around here and making sure your legacy auto shop doesn't go under."

"I can work on bikes but I don't know shit about the business end," Kaleb snaps in defense, his head tilted to the side. "Ever think about how I'd actually run the place? I need to take business courses and the military is going to pay for that. All I have to do is serve my year and get out and that will pay for my schooling. I just need Jackson to hang in there for a couple of years and I'll be helping out as much as I can," he grumbles, bringing his beer to his lips.

"Better hope nothing happens to you over there," Ryan spews out, bringing his joint up to his lips and aiming his conniving glare at me. "Daddy Rick will be the one to notify you if he gets blown to kingdom come."

"Shut your fucking hole!" Kaleb barks, and I can see him getting agitated.

The thoughts Ryan's words put in my head makes me sick. I feel my stomach sink and the rest of my body tense. It's not like it's never crossed my mind, but I choose to not entertain it.

And I thought these guys were supposed to know him better than I do. Why would they goad him like this with such a sensitive subject? I place my hand on the back of his neck and start gently rubbing, hoping to keep at least part of him calm.

"I'm just saying…" Ryan's words sail out of his mouth on a puff of smoke. "He's your next of kin. He'll get notified, and then you know he'll be back here sniffing around the house and seeing what he can get out of your grandpa's business. He'll probably turn it into some kind of sleezy, Podunk gentleman's club." He starts laughing at himself, choking on his own fumes in the process as Kaleb looks down at the grass, the firelight highlighting the pensive set of his eyes. I can see what all this talk is doing to him. I know enough about his father to know he hurt him beyond belief, both physically and emotionally. It makes me hurt somewhat on his behalf, and I feel a protective urge come over me.

"Kaleb?" I say softly, doing the only thing I can think of to get him away from this toxic energy. He doesn't speak, but looks to me with attentiveness in his eyes. "I'm getting tired. Can you take me home?"

He responds by jumping to his feet and taking my hand to pull me up. "Sorry, guys," he announces. "I'm out. My girl's tired and I'm taking her home." He doesn't waste time with small talk; he simply leads me away while giving a few waves and fist bumps as we make our way back to the street.

KALEB WAS quiet on the way home, and I only have a small idea why. His past with his father has always been there, but maybe that ass, Ryan, pushed his buttons in just the right way. Clearly that guy lives for getting a rise out of people.

When we get back to the house, Kaleb excuses himself to take a shower while I go change for bed. Going through my bag, I find the one item I brought along to surprise him, and it might just be the ticket for this moment. Slipping on the old t-shirt, I revel in the feel of the soft cotton falling over my bare skin. It's nothing big, but I'm hoping it will warm his heart and give him something to smile about.

When I hear the shower shut off, I tip-toe down the hardwood hallway towards the bathroom and quietly let myself in. I find my solemn soldier leaning against the sink, droplets of water clinging to the dewy skin of his back, and a seafoam green towel wrapped around his trim waist. His head is dipped downward, water dripping from the front strands of his hair and into the white porcelain basin. His wet lashes are pressed against his cheekbones as he pulls in a deep breath before slowly letting it out.

I don't know whether to ask him what's wrong right now. Our relationship is deep, but it's also very different; only knowing different pieces of each other instead of the whole story from start to finish. All I know is he's hurting, and I want him to know I'm here.

Stepping quietly behind him, I wrap my arms around his waist and press my forehead into the smooth span of skin between his shoulder blades. I nestle my face into his back as if trying to burrow into him, and my heart squeezes when I feel his hands come over mine where they rest against his sternum. He takes hold of them, stroking the back of my hand with his thumb. Turning my head, I press a soft kiss to his back, thanking him for accepting my comfort.

We stand there in the quiet, steamy bathroom for several moments, neither of us saying a word, just breathing together.

I feel his heartbeat finally slow beneath my palm and he slowly turns. When he faces me, the look on his face is priceless. I take a mental snapshot of the way nostalgia dances in those green eyes, and the way his small smile lights up his face.

"No fucking way," he muses tenderly, shaking his head as he recognizes the Shane Auto Repair t-shirt he put on me three years ago.

"Yes fucking way," I throw sweetly back at him.

"It looks just as sexy on you as it did at the lake," he says, skimming his rough hands down my arms until they find purchase on my waist.

"It's nice to sleep in," I inform him, even though I only ever slept in it that one night after we fought. After that, the reminder of him was too much and so I tucked it away – until this morning, that is.

"Is that so?" he retorts, and I nod as he starts to walk me backwards out of the bathroom. "Well, it's now my favorite view – you wearing my shirt," he husks out the last few words before bringing his mouth down on mine while expertly steering me down the hall. This kiss is different from the many he's given me over the last day. There's conviction behind this one. It's like he's trying to tell me an important secret while he claims me.

"I want you to lie down on the bed," he whispers as we cross the threshold of the dark bedroom, "but keep the shirt on," he adds as I sit on the edge of the mattress. The moon filtering through the gauzy curtains is our only light, but he looks like a being from my dreams as he kneels on the floor in front of me. I lie back like he told me to, bringing one foot up to rest on the edge of the bed as I feel his calloused hands pushing the material of the t-shirt up my thighs.

I feel his breath on my inner thigh, along with the brush of his stubble as he nuzzles his face against my skin, and my eyes flutter closed, waiting for the next sensation. I start at the flick of his tongue against my lace panties, followed by a longer, harder stroke before I feel his face dive between my legs, attaching his mouth to my sex and dampening the lace with aggressive licks of his tongue.

"Ohh..." the moan is carried from my lips by an exhale of breath, followed by another sharp inhale when he moans against me, the heat and vibration taking my arousal to a new height. I open my eyes and tilt my head to look down, and find his green eyes penetrating my gaze. Without looking away, Kaleb takes hold of my panties at my hips and starts dragging them down my thighs until they drop to the floor.

My dirty talking soldier is unusually quiet, but I don't say anything. I just follow his lead, letting him take what he wants, whatever he needs right now... and so I let him bury his face between my legs, his arms wrapping around my thighs and squeezing tightly as he devours my pussy. I feel every breath, lick, moan, and the scratch of his stubble, and it's all driving me mad as I reach down and grip onto his brown locks.

"Oh, God," I moan out desperately as he pulls me tighter against his mouth. This feels so good I could cry.

"Let it all out, Luna," he whispers against my folds between strokes of his tongue. "I want to hear it all. Moan for me."

His words take my breath away in a series of pants and gasps as he continues to spear and stroke his tongue. I cry out with abandon, sure I can be heard all over town. "Kaleb!" I scream his name as I get closer.

"Yes," he hisses against my skin. "That's it, my girl."

"Fuck," I whimper on a weak breath as I feel my core start to tighten and coil, and I just barely catch Kaleb whipping his towel off in my peripheral. My hips are rolling, my sex seeking out his tongue as it laps against me faster. I'm chasing my orgasm now, and right when it's just within reach, Kaleb pulls away and rises to come down on top of me. His cock thrusts into me without ceremony, fucking me through the most explosive orgasm that's ever racked my body.

I scream out his name and he groans in approval, letting my moans guide his momentum to bring me down at just the right pace, planting kisses along my neck as he waits patiently for me to catch my breath.

"That was supposed to be for you," I playfully admonish him in a low tone as I look up through my lashes to see his smile come back to his handsome face.

"That was for me, silly girl," he growls down at me before placing a light kiss to my lips.

16

KALEB

I'm about to do something crazy. Crazy, yet so incredibly right on so many levels. After I brought Luna to orgasm last night, I switched places with her and had her ride me, still in my t-shirt. Looking up at her, she seemed to shift from the girl I knew from my summers into some unbelievable young woman that I'd never met, yet had always known. Then after she came again, I laid her underneath me and looked down at her as I made love to her slowly. The gold rings around her irises were alight with all the things I've ever thought or felt about her.

After we both came, I sent her off to sleep, skirting my fingers over her back like I had the night before. And as I almost fell asleep myself right next to her, something clicked, snapping me back to consciousness. I wouldn't call it an epiphany, but it was a crystalizing moment of clarity, where both my head and my heart seemed to come together after a lifetime apart.

She asked me to take her home. And when we got there, she came into the bathroom in nothing but my t-shirt, as if we'd been living together in love all along. And then… she took care of me. Without saying a word or asking me a thing, she somehow knew what I needed and just did it. If that's not a next of kin, I don't know what is.

She may have only come back into my life a couple of days ago, but she's always been a part of it. And now, she's all I have left – and besides that, she's my person. My family. The one I could always depend on, and never do without. This house could burn down while I'm gone, but she'd still be my home to come back to.

If something happens to me, I don't want that piece of shit to know. He doesn't get to know my business or my whereabouts. I will rise from hell if he's the one they give my folded-up flag to, and I will haunt the ever-living shit out of him if Pop's house his and business – my house and business – get left to that motherfucker.

And so, with Luna fast asleep in my bed, I got up and went into the spare bedroom, pulling the big chest-like box out from under the double bed. With a flashlight, I rummaged through all of Pop's old mementos, barely pausing when I found any pictures with my dad in them. If anything, those only stoked the fire within me to find what I was looking for.

And now I hold it in my fingers as I stare out the kitchen window at the backyard, where Luna sits sipping her coffee in the early morning sunshine. The golden rays reflect off her shiny brown hair, making the streaks of purple that lie underneath stand out with a glimmer. Her back is to me as she sits with her bare legs through the tire swing, still in my goddamn shirt. She's doing nothing but enjoying the quiet morning and gazing out at nothing, just content to appreciate the nature around her, and it both kills me and gives me life.

I'm not what I'd consider a spiritual guy, but I swear that this sight… it was made just for me. The time to do this is now.

Opening the back screen door, my heart hammers in my chest as I make my way down the porch steps. It's crazy how what I'm about to face overseas hardly scares me, but what the next moment holds has my adrenaline running rampant through my veins.

"Hey, silly girl." I try to sound warm and casual as I announce my presence, and like the darling she's always been, she tilts her head back to look at me almost upside down, and flashes me a smile, warmer than the sun beating down from the sky.

"Morning," she greets me, before sitting back up and taking another sip of coffee.

Fuck, it makes my heart ache and only enforces the rightness of what I plan to do. The only thing is, I have no idea; no words for segueing into it. Then again, everything about mine and Luna's relationship has been unconventional; never adhering to any traditional format. And so, I just go for it, taking a hold of the swing and turning her gently towards me before I crouch down in the dewy morning grass in front of her.

"What's up?" she asks, leaning her chin on her arm, looking completely nonchalant as if she's just waiting for me to tell her about last night's Pistons game.

I swallow hard, as if trying to get my heart out of my throat and back down in my chest before looking up at her. Here goes.

"Will you marry me?" I ask, my nerves slightly rattling my voice, but I try to keep it steady.

Luna freezes, her smile still in place, but her eyes seem to glaze over, staring right through me. She finally blinks as if snapping out of a trance, and then looks away with an amused giggle. "Shut up," she scoffs, taking another drink of coffee, and I can't help but chuckle a little myself. This is completely out of nowhere, not to mention not at all how most guys go about this sort of thing.

I take a moment to find a way to get her to understand this isn't a joke. "I'm… I'm actually serious," I squint up at her against the sun's bright rays.

Her smile drops slightly, and her brows stitch together like she's trying to figure out a complicated riddle. "What the–" She's cut off by her own dropping of her coffee cup. "Shit!" she hisses under her breath as it lands on the grass with a thud, the rest of the light brown liquid spilling out. "Kaleb…" she looks back to me, pinning me with a serious glare. "What the hell is going on?"

"Well, I'm proposing to you," I chuckle out cynically, trying not to fall deep into any emotional rabbit hole that might open up and try to swallow me.

"But… Kaleb…" he's sputtering like a car engine that's out of gas – only in her case, it's words. "Okay, Kaleb, please back up." She motions with her hands, almost choking on the words she was able to conjure. Her eyes are overshadowed with confusion, and they're starting to get glassy. "Please," she puffs out, her breathing getting shallow, like she's panicking. I don't understand, where is this coming from."

"You're all I have," I explain gently, laying a hand on her leg and sweeping my thumb across her skin. "Ryan's a dumbass who's fucked up in the head, but he wasn't wrong last night. If something happens to me overseas, there's no one that will know about it except maybe my father. Can you understand how wrong that is?" I raise my eyebrows to her and tilt my head to get her to look at me.

Luna nods her head while pulling more crisp morning air into her lungs. "I do, but, Kaleb… get married? We don't even know what this is!" she explains, waving a hand between the two of us. "We just found each other two days ago, we don't know where this will go…"

"We don't have to," I say softly, trying to calm her as I raise my hand to her cheek.

"We're twenty-one, Kaleb. We're practically still kids!" she exclaims, and I can hear her stifle a sob in her throat. "I'm sitting in a tire swing for fuck's sake!"

She's getting more emotional than I anticipated, and I lean up to place a kiss on her forehead, trying to reassure her before I continue.

"I know this is so new between us, but what we have also goes way back. You're the only person that I can count on, that I can trust if anything happens. I want you to be the one that gets information about me, and I know it's like asking for the moon, but I want it to be you that makes sure the house and the shop get taken care of. I don't care what you'd do with it, just so long as my piece of shit father doesn't lay a finger on any of it. That's all."

"So... this would be a favor?" she asks, a disbelieving frown marring her features.

"No," I shake my head adamantly. "That's not all this is. You'd be helping me tremendously, but that's not why I'm doing this," I promise her.

"Well that's what you're leading with," she points out with a huff, climbing out of the tire.

Fuck... she's right. I look like the asshole to end all assholes here.

"You're right, and it's because I'm a fucking idiot." I drop my head back and let out a breath so heavy it threatens to cave my chest. I rub my hand over my face. "I just didn't want to hide anything from you; I wanted to be fully open and honest," I admit and take a step forward, taking her hand. "Stay with me, please, Lu. Don't check out."

"I'm not, it's just this is so surreal. I want to help you, but–"

"If I were just looking at this as an arrangement, I wouldn't bother proposing," I try explaining. "There's more to this than just some favor, and I didn't mean to make it about that."

"Then what else is it about?" She crosses her arms, a woman's signal that they're done fucking around.

Fuck, I'm no good at this. I've never had to put something like this into words before. It's not just about some favor, it's about some kind of love, but I lead with the asking her for her help instead because I didn't want to be deceitful, and I ended up making a huge mess.

"Kaleb." Luna says my name, soft but firm. Gentle, but not

fucking around. That's my Luna. "Truth," she finishes, fixing her eyes on mine.

"Not truth or dare?"

"No," she adamantly clarifies. "Truth is your only option on this one, K."

My heart is slamming in my chest so hard it hurts as I take a few breaths to steady myself. Luna's eyes soften and still hold onto mine, and ever my rock, she takes hold of my hand in hers.

"There's no right or wrong answer, Kaleb. Just the truth."

I press my lips together and steel myself once more. "I love you," I tell her. It's abrupt, but she told me it didn't matter how I said it, so long as it was honest. "I've never loved anyone, ever, in my life, but I love you." I pause a moment, letting my words settle over her, and when I see a sheen of glassy moisture come over her eyes, I take a breath and tell her more of my truth. "This is the first time this house has felt like a home since Pops died, and maybe even before then," I nod at the house and then look down at our joined hands. "You're the one thing in my life that's been unfailing, and the only thing that makes my heart happy. I said all the other shit first because I was afraid if I said it after, you'd think I was trying to play you, but I can't imagine you not being the home I come back to," I finish, not sure of what else to say to convey my true feelings, but feeling good about what I was able to get out.

And then, with the hand still holding the ring I finally found last night, I hold it out to her. A delicate gasp makes her shoulders twitch and her hand to come up over her mouth as she stares in wonder at the princess cut diamond flanked by two triangular amethysts. Pops showed me this ring long ago, and it always made me think of Luna.

"This was my grandmother's," I tell her. "And if you're okay with my truth…" I reach out to wipe a tear away from her eye. "Then I dare you to marry me, Luna Rene."

I barely get her middle name out before she throws her arms around my neck and kisses me senseless with her sweet lips. I lift her off of her feet, bringing her closer and kissing the hell out of her right back. My arms clutch her close to me as we both sink into this moment.

"Does that mean yes?" I ask, taking a quick breath before diving in for more.

"It was a yes the whole time, stupid," she snickers back against my lips.

"What?" I lean my head back and watch her devilish grin turn into a look of sincerity.

"I would've done it," she softly declares, her eyes flitting across mine, "for you, and for Pops. You knocked me on my ass with that one, soldier, but I would've done it. I just wanted more of a reason to so that it could feel good to do it. I guess I needed a little fortitude." She raises a feeble shoulder and I know she probably feels a little unshielded, and I don't blame her. She shouldn't have had to ask for me to tell her my feelings. That's what cost me her last time. If I want to keep her this time, I can't be hiding from my feelings.

"Baby," I take a step back so that we can see each other face to face better. "This is going to be real. Yes, there's some rationale behind you being my next of kin, and this marriage will start off a little out of whack due to my being on the other side of the world, but when I come back, it will be about us," I promise as I slide the ring up her finger.

"It's so beautiful," she whispers, gazing down at it.

"You're beautiful," I correct, as she takes another moment to adore the new decoration on her finger that claims her as mine.

"So," she sighs and smiles brightly up at me. "What do we do now?"

I think for a moment, pursing my lips together. It's Sunday so the courthouse isn't open, but there's one way we could celebrate. "Feel like taking a ride on the bike?"

17

LUNA

Two days ago, I was happily enjoying the single art student life. I was creating challenging art pieces without a care in the world or anyone to answer to. Never in my wildest dreams did I think that in that time I'd find myself flying down a country highway on the back of a Harley with my arms clinging tightly to Kaleb Shane after he put the world's most beautiful ring on my finger.

I know I was just as crazy to say yes as he was to propose… but there was no way in my heart I could say no. While so many of his comrades have whole families and loved ones to be there for them when they come home, Kaleb was asking me to be just that one person for him. No, it's not the way I had always envisioned being proposed to, nor the circumstances, but this is my Kaleb, the exception to all my rules. And besides, we do love each other. Maybe it won't be a 'normal' marriage at first, but I have faith that we'll get there.

After fifteen minutes or so, the lines of trees give way to houses and more farmland, and eventually, opens up to a town that looks to be somewhat bigger than Coyote Creek. After a couple of turns, we roll into the lot of what is obviously a tattoo parlor.

"What are we doing here?" I ask, swinging my leg off and dismounting as Kaleb starts undoing the strap of his helmet. "Are you finally going to get more ink done on your right arm so that your left isn't so weighed down?" I joke while undoing the strap on my own helmet. Although, to his credit, he seemed to be able to squeeze in a couple of military themed tats on that arm while away at training.

"You're hilarious," he deadpans and shakes his head at me as a pickup pulls into the empty lot.

"They don't even look open," I observe, and it makes sense considering it's the middle of a Sunday.

"They're not.," He gives me that mischievous smile as the truck door opens, and a guy not much older looking than us strides in our direction.

"You owe me big, clown," the guy greets with a shake of his head, but there's a mirthful smile on his face as he chides Kaleb.

"Whatever, man," Kaleb returns. "You're the one who still owes me for taking the wrap for that tag job you did on the side of the school gym."

"Yeah, yeah," The guy dismisses him before reaching his hand out. "I'm Travis."

"Luna," I reply and shake back before he turns, and Kaleb leads me to follow him to the parlor's back door.

"Is that something you did a lot?" I ask him as Travis unlocks the door. "Take the wrap for things you didn't do?"

"I was seen as the bad boy around here," he gives an almost proud smirk. "It was expected of me and I never had much to lose," he sticks his tongue out through his teeth, as always, hiding behind that cocky veneer as we head in.

The place has black & and white checkered linoleum flooring, and the red neon signs that Travis flips on, make this the place reminding me of a fifties diner.

"So I know you like your ink, but what made you want to come out here on such a whim and make your poor friend open up on a Sunday?" I ask, placing my hands on my hips.

"I promised you a design," he reminds me, and I think back to the last time at camp as when we were counselors.

"You did," I confirm quietly when the memory morphs from fuzzy to clear.

"And I made one," he adds. "And if you want, we can get it put on you today. And if you're not comfortable, then I'll just find something stupid for Travis to put on me," he shrugs, humor dancing in his eyes.

"'Bout time you got that tramp stamp," Travis jokes, and I bark out a laugh.

"Well, I can't let that happen," I return, before making my decision. Like at the lake, I think about looking back on this day, and the idea of saying I didn't go for it. "Let's do it."

Kaleb's brows actually chase his hairline at my response and he steps in closer to me. "Really, baby?"

"Yeah."

"You're fucking amazing, you know that?" He cups my cheeks and places a kiss to my forehead, before reaching inside his jacket pocket and pulling out a piece of paper. "It's just an industrial stamp that says Property of Kaleb Shane on it, and I thought we could put it on your — ow!"

My slap to his chest cuts off his bright idea to brand my butt, and he gives me a cheeky grin before handing me the paper. I feel a joyous smile take over my face when I look down to see a crescent moon, not quite like the one he drew me that's on his arm. It's gradient, with all the shades of purple you could imagine.

"It's perfect," I say simply, looking up at him with sincerity.

Once I'm settled in the chair, Kaleb helps me with the strap of my tank top, easing it down my arm as if preparing to make love to me. I pull my arm out of it, leaving that side of my chest bare before he cleans the area just below my collarbone.

Travis was okay letting us in off books and off hours, but he about lost his shit when Kaleb told him he wanted to be the one to tattoo me. There was some back and forth before I assured him I was okay with it, much to his chagrin. Now he lingers nearby, watching like a hawk while grabbing his cell phone from his back pocket. He holds it up like he's taking a picture, but when he starts talking, I realize it's actually a video.

"Okay, since our man, Kaleb, is not technically certified, this is you confirming that you're okay with him putting a permanent tattoo on your body?" Travis questions, and I nod, smiling sheepishly at the camera before flitting my eyes back to Kaleb.

"Yeah, I trust him," I say affectionately as Kaleb smiles, shaking his head.

"You won't sue?"

"No, I won't sue," I promise. "If it sucks, I'll just kick his ass," I wink and then stick my tongue out at Kaleb who rolls his eyes.

When he seems satisfied he has everything close to me, he rolls his chair up close and leaning in as he slips on a pair of black rubber gloves. My endorphins are jumping to life and racing through my veins in anticipation – and by his closeness. His posture and the serious look in his eyes has a protective quality that my heart is enjoying.

"Okay, it's going to burn, and what I want you to do is take in a deep breath, hold it, and when you feel the needle, let it out slow, okay?"

"Okay," I whisper, nodding.

"Okay," he acknowledges back, softly. He steps on the pedal and my stomach plummets as the needle buzzes to life. "Okay, deep breath in," he instructs gently and I oblige, pulling in as much air through my nose as my chest can take, and then holding onto it tightly as I feel the needle make contact with my skin, and son of a fucking bitch! It feels like a hot razor is being dragged across my skin. "Let it out," Kaleb cues me, and I release the air, heavily at first, until Kaleb lifts his head. "Slowly," he reminds me and I nod, correcting my exhale. I slowly let my breath out between pursed lips. "Atta girl," he says approvingly, briefly looking up from his task. It's quick, as he has to keep his eye on the needle of course, but that flicker of affectionate encouragement was enough to melt my heart.

Kaleb repeats the process of dipping the needle, coaching me to breathe, and little by little, inking my skin. During the brief respites I get while he wipes the excess ink off my skin, I catch my breath while he looks at me affectionately, so many sentiments in his green eyes. They're a particularly light shade today, and the pain I'm letting him inflict through the needle is worth the look of adoration they're showing me. He's quiet as he works, but it's in a beautiful way.... like he's experiencing a rare moment of Zen. And I won't lie, the confidence is kind of a turn-on.

I hear my cell phone start to ring over on the counter, but Kaleb and I both ignore it, letting it go to voicemail as he continues to concentrate on his creation that I'll wear the rest of my life, occasionally looking up and checking in with me that I'm doing okay. It still hurts like a bitch but I'm getting used to it, and coping well with the meditative breathing, and the look Kaleb keeps giving me that says I've got this.

Just when I'm starting to feel sore and am thinking of asking if we can take a little break, the needle stops and Kaleb sets it down on the metal tray, an air of finality in the action.

"Is it done?"

"All done," he confirms, pulling the gloves off. "You did so good, baby," he smiles approvingly, and I can't help but notice he's got a little bit of his bedroom eyes going on.

I look down at my first tattoo, put there by the man I'll be marrying soon.

"I love it," is all I can think to say, smiling fondly down at it.

"Since I was your first and all," Kaleb says cockily as he leans down in my face, and I scoff at him. "No one else inks you but me."

"Territorial much?" I quirk an eyebrow up at him, but before he can come back with anything, my phone starts ringing again, buzzing obnoxiously on the countertop. This time, Kaleb reaches for it.

"Anonymous," he reads out loud before handing it to me.

"I don't answer numbers I don't recognize," I state, as I tap on the screen to send it to voicemail.

Kaleb puts a dressing on over my tattoo, and I right my top as he cleans up. As I pull my jacket back on, my phone rings again.

"Fuck," I huff in annoyance as Kaleb looks up curiously while I pull my phone back out of my jeans. Anonymous is calling again. "It's got to be some telemarketer," I gripe and shake my head.

"Which means they'll keep calling," Kaleb states and rolls his eyes as he starts shutting cupboards.

"Yeah. I'm just going to take it and tell them to take me off whatever list they have." I shake my head as I swipe to answer, bringing my phone to my ear. "Hello?" I answer.

"Hey, there you are." I hear a dreadfully familiar voice on the other end, and I feel jolt of panic flash through my body. Kaleb must notice it as he halts his movements, staring at me intently, concern etched over his face.

I swallow hard around the lump in my throat before finding my voice. "Sorry, you have the wrong number," I rattle off, trying to keep my voice from sounding shaky before I lower my phone and start stabbing at the screen, desperate to disconnect the call before I hear anymore. When the screen mercifully goes dark, I take a huge breath of relief to look up and find that Kaleb has crossed the room and is right in front of me.

"Was it him?" He stares me down, a controlled anger in his eyes that almost scares me, and all I can do is nod as I keep trying to breathe through parted lips.

Kaleb's jaw clenches as he looks off into space for a moment before back down at me. Taking my left hand, he nudges at my ring with his thumb.

"We're doing this tomorrow," he proclaims in a low and

steady tone that says this isn't up for debate. "We're getting married, and we're changing your name."

His statement drops like a hammer, sending reverberations of every intense feeling I've felt in the last two days.

Yep, territorial indeed.

18

LUNA

"You're insane," Cassidy declares as her fierce eyes follow me around my apartment while she holds one of two pairs of shoes in each hand. "But I say go with the purple pumps." She holds up the hand holding the shoe she indicated.

"Thanks," I toss over my shoulder as I bring yet another dress over from my clothing rack. A very large butterfly beats her wings furiously fast in my chest, and I can't tell if she's excited or having a nervous breakdown as I hold my white and black flowered dress up in front of me in the mirror before laying it on the bed and yanking off the black shirt dress I've decided against. I yank the new selection off the hanger before pulling it over my head. The halter neckline comes down in a low V, but it's not inappropriate, and it feels better for the courthouse than the others I tried on.

I scurry back over to my vanity and have a seat, picking up my curling iron.

"You know," Cassidy muses as she taps the purple heel against her hand thoughtfully. "When I said you should stay and catch up with him, I didn't actually mean run off and marry him and move to Butt-fucking-Nowhere with him."

"We have our reasons," I blow her off as I wrap a strand of my hair around the hot barrel. I really need my mom to touch up my purple coloring next time I see her.

"That you won't even tell me," she adds, sourly.

I let out a sigh. She's my best friend, I should really trust her with something. "We're protecting each other," I clip out quickly, and keep focused on the soft curls I'm putting in my hair.

"From what?" she asks, exacerbation dampening her tone.

Staring at the vanity's surface, I absently unwind my hair from the barrel and set it down before turning to look at her.

"Kaleb's dad is his only living relative and he's… not a good person," I say vaguely, not wanting to expose all of his troubled past. "Kaleb wants to protect his assets from him and keep him from getting any information on him."

Cassidey stares at me straight, her eyes softening as I see all the new information processing in her head.

"I know it's not the way this usually goes, but there's no way I won't help him, Cass." When she presses her lips together and gives the subtlest of nods, I add, "Also… Carter's been trying to get in contact with me."

Her eyes widen and her gasp slices through the air in the room. "What? What the fuck?!"

"It's okay," I hold up a hand before turning and resuming styling my hair. "I mean, it's not okay, but he's not going to pull one over on me again. And getting married to Kaleb will change my last name…" I feel my cheeks warm at the thought, "which will hopefully make it a little harder to harass me."

"Jesus Christ, Luna," Cassidy exclaims on a heavy sigh, dropping her shoulders and tilting her head dubiously at me.

"You know, you could just look at this practically, like me," I suggest, crooking an eyebrow at her in the mirror. "You don't have to make it out to be some tragedy. Kaleb and I do love each other, and signing a piece of paper that says he has one-person back home who gives a shit about him is actually kind of a no-brainer for me," I finish tightly.

"Sorry." Her face falls slightly as she nods, and I feel rotten. The truth is though, I'm still processing all of this myself, and I'm not ready to lay it all out for dissection with someone else yet. Speaking of which…

"Have you told your parents?" she asks, hitting the hot button topic.

"No," I reply, feeling bad about that too. "Not until Kaleb comes back." My parents have always known that Kaleb is special to me, but this is out of nowhere – even to us, let alone them. Out of fear of them intervening, especially my dad, I feel like it's best if I just let them know he's come back into my life and leave it at that. When they get used to the idea of us being together in a more permanent situation, I'll tell them.

After Cass helps me with my makeup, I slip into the shoes in time for a heavy knock to sound through my door. Clacking over to the barn-style metal door, I yank it open to reveal Kaleb like I've never seen him before. The bad boy that put his tattoo on me just yesterday is clean shaven, and completely neat and polished in his Army greens. He's an absolute conundrum as he stands completely straight, yet takes me in with an amorous smile.

"Hey, silly girl," he greets as he steps inside, and I think I hear a swoony gasp come from somewhere behind me, but I'm too distracted at how debonair Kaleb looks. It's like seeing some surreal, alternate version of him, and it's doing something strange to my insides. The perfectly tailored slacks, the buttoned green jacket… I love my rough and edgy Kaleb, but I can see this being a treat on special occasions.

"Hello, soldier." I give him an exaggerated, approving look, and he lets out a quiet chuckle while looking away for a beat and then turning back to me, pulling me into him.

"Don't get used to it," he whispers cheekily in my ear.

"Don't worry," I wave him off. "At the end of the day, I prefer your ripped jeans."

"Yes," he celebrates under his breath with a heavy nod before adding, "you look beautiful."

"Thanks."

"Got everything?" he asks, his voice a soft croon, and I nod, stooping to retrieve my duffel full of some clothes, and he scoops up a box of art supplies that was sitting next to it. Cassidy trails behind us out the door, her reservations seemingly forgotten for the moment as she emits a subtle glow. It must be the uniform.

We had agreed that we would get married here in the city in front of the Justice of the Peace, and then move some more of my things back to his house. And then while he's gone, I'll be dividing my time between here and Kaleb's home – *our* home, technically – depending on my classes and work. Maybe I can see if some ladies in Coyote Creek want to throw a Corks and Canvas painting party.

As Kaleb treks down the long flight of stairs to the ground floor, I hang back a little bit with Cassidy.

"Thank you again for doing this," I say softly, linking my arm through hers. I'm sincerely grateful that she agreed to be our witness, despite not knowing all the details.

She shrugs with a quirky smile. "Everyone at camp thought you and Kaleb would get married one day anyway. I just don't think this is what anyone pictured."

I see dazzling stars in my mind for a moment at the mention of other people noticing back then. I always thought it was only Kaleb and I that saw it. "Me neither," I lift a shoulder. "But who knows, maybe it's better."

Kaleb

My thumb fiddles with the ring on Luna's finger as I hold her hands in mine. I can easily see this becoming my own nervous tick, or a habit I'll start doing when I'm on edge.

Looking around the room, it doesn't seem very romantic. It's very official and clinical with harsh lighting. But Luna makes it beautiful with her brown and purple hair falling over her shoulders in soft waves, and her almond brown eyes smiling serenely up at me. Her dress is pretty. And when I look down, I smirk at the smudge of white paint I see cemented to the pointer finger on her right hand.

"It wouldn't come off," she mouths looking playfully annoyed, and I give her a wink, letting her know I get it. In fact, I find it as part of her charm.

We both speak steadily through our instructed vows, though occasionally, Luna hunches her shoulders with a giddy grin, giving her confident words a hint of I can't believe we're doing this vibe. I raise her hand to lay a kiss to her knuckles for reassurance, and when the Justice orders me, I pull out the wedding bands I found this morning after a more thorough search through my grandfather's things. With such short notice, his and grandma's plain bands will have to do. I inwardly vow to get Luna the ring of her dreams when I come home, and when I'm told I may kiss her, I make it count. This may not be the wedding most people dream of, but I'm going to make sure she never forgets this kiss. I take hold of her face as if she's delicate China, and lay my lips deliberately on hers, letting them linger before making them move in undulation. The best part about it is that I can feel her smiling, and it makes my heart pound out a few beats of elation, beaming that it's now in the safest place it's ever been.

"Whoa, what the hell are you doing?" I exclaim over my shoulder as I carry her box of art supplies through the front door.

"What?" she asks, holding her hand out in question as the other grips the duffel strap slung over her shoulder.

I quickly set the box down inside the door and then gently place a hand on her shoulder, making her back up a ways before relieving her of her duffel. Once I sling the bag inside the door, I turn to find her standing with her head tilted in a dubious expression.

"Kaleb Shane, are you seriously doing the – ah!" she yelps as I throw her over my shoulder. Yes, I love doing that.

"Yes, Luna Shane, I'm really doing the threshold thing." I answer the question she didn't get to finish asking.

"You're supposed to do it cradle-hold!" she protests from somewhere down by my ass, and she gives it an impressive smack.

"Not my style," I fire back teasingly as I smack her ass right back, before turning down the hallway in the direction of the bedroom. After setting her down on her feet at the foot of the bed, I turn towards the dresser and strike a match to light the one lousy ocean breeze scented candle I had in the house. Hopefully Luna can give this place more of a girly touch.

Turning back to her, she looks from the tiny flame to me, her lips closed in a beautiful smile as I start unbuttoning my jacket. She reaches for the bottom of her dress before I stop her.

"Don't," I whisper gently. "I want to do that job."

Draping my jacket over the nearby chair, I reach down and slowly pull the flowery material up and over her head as she steps out of her shoes, leaving her in nothing but her lacey bra and panties. One thing I've learned in the three days since we've reunited is that all of Luna's underwear is one shade of purple or another. She'll mix it up with a white or black bra that I've seen so far, but all her panties are purple, and I never knew I'd find that sexy as fuck.

Hooking a couple of fingers around her bra strap, I pull it aside to check in on my work from yesterday. Her little purple moon looks fucking decadent against her beautiful skin, and I wonder if she's noticed the word Mine in slanted letters beneath all the shades of her favorite color.

Marking her was a euphoric experience yesterday, and it brought my already burning desire for her to a new Fahrenheit.

The way she trusted me to do something that was painful, knowing I was taking care of her at the same time made my dick hard, but also did something to me deep inside. It was like... in that moment, she became a fixture in my life as permanent as the ink I was imbedding in her skin. Don't get me wrong, she's always been important, and even during those three years of radio silence, she was still here; right here in my heart. But she let me put my brand on her, trusting me fully to mark her with a product of my imagination. It was almost like yesterday was our wedding... where she became my person... my life. We're forever.

Her hand comes up to the one I'm using to pull her strap down, her finger gliding over my grandpa's band that she slid on my finger earlier. For some reason, it prompts me to bring my knuckles up to her face and glide them down her cheek. While the sadistic fetish in me that she so sweetly indulges is revved from yesterday's inking, I'm determined to take this slow. Just like our kiss at the courthouse, I want her to have this beautiful wedding night where her husband makes love to her tenderly, making it last.

With my other hand, I reach behind her and unsnap her bra, and we let it fall to the plush carpet at our feet. Backing her up to lay down on the bed, I crawl over on top of her, taking in her delicate features in the flicker of the meager candle light.

"Luna," I voice in a low rasp. "My wife."

19

KALEB

"I know it's crazy," I hear Luna's voice through the open door of the spare room, aka her new art studio. "We just ran into each other after three years," she says to her phone screen that's propped up on her easel before looking away to squirt some blue paint onto her pallet that sits on the nightstand that's been draped in a drop cloth. We might have to move that bed out of there so she can have more room.

"That's amazing," her mother says from the screen. "When was this?"

"Um…" Luna's dark brows pull together as she concentrates on the math as well as the white she's now squeezing a healthy glob of onto her palette. "A week ago." Those eyebrows shoot up as she stares at the task. Unbeknownst to her mom, I'm pretty sure she's inwardly reacting to how quickly we got married.

She sets the white tube of paint down as I continue to stare, taking extra-long to wipe the grease from my hands with an old cloth. I had just done all the necessary maintenance on my Harley before putting it back to bed in the garage for the duration of my deployment, and walked in to find a vision of a girl, sitting on a stool in dark blue paint-splattered overalls, and it stopped my heart. Luna has taken one of the least sexy articles of clothing and given me a boner with how she wears them over nothing but a sports bra, and her hair is pulled up in a knot with purple strands floating down to cling to the back of her neck.

"By the way, I can see how brightly you're glowing," her mom says in a knowing tone. "Did you guys start dating or something?"

Luna does indeed light up in the prettiest way with a shy smile as she looks away from her mom again to apply some black paint to her setup. "Something," she answers, again hiding the real meaning from her mother before noticing me eavesdropping out of the corner of her eye. "You want to say hi?" She tilts her head in the direction of her propped phone. Her tone is light and holds no pressure, but I feel an odd pull to this part of her life I haven't gotten to see much of. My interactions to her family have been short, meeting at the drop offs and pickups at camp, but they're nice people.

Shifting my weight forward, I stuff the old rag in the back pocket of my jeans and walk into the sunlit room to hover just behind Luna, dipping my head so her mom – the older version of Luna – can see me.

"Hey, Mrs. Isaak," I greet warmly with a friendly wave.

"Kaleb!" she responds cheerfully with her bright white smile. "How are you, honey? The last I knew you were headed to boot camp," she begins and leans in like she's settling in to catch up.

I take a moment to quickly sum up my time in training, my promotion, and my interest in starting my own tattoo studio once I pay my dues overseas and get some education out of it – and hopefully a business loan.

"Good for you, honey," she gives me an approving nod. "Life is too short not to do what you love."

I know her sentiment comes from experience as she herself is a hair stylist, which is what she'd always wanted, according to Luna.

"So you're shipping out soon?" She tilts her head with a what

I can only assume is a caring mom look that makes me wonder what it would've been like to grow up seeing more of those.

"Yeah, in about a week," I nod.

"Oh boy," she sighs. "You come back to us in one piece, you hear me?" She gives me a stern look, and it does something funny to the organ in my chest. My mind flashes forward to coming back to Luna. I didn't even think of it until now that her family could... maybe become mine. The feeling is a confusingly exciting one, but as per habit, I quickly dismiss it. One thing that's been ingrained in me by living this particular life is to not hope for too much, and right now, I'm just thankful to have one person to come back to.

"Mom, who are you talking – Luna!" A young kid's voice can be heard before a blue-eyed boy with brown hair commandeers the screen, leaning completely in front of his mother.

"Hi, buddy." Luna's eyes crinkle at the sides as she waves at him, and he gasps when he sees me.

"Hi, Kaleb!" he shouts, and I wave back at him.

"How are you doing, man?" I ask him.

"Good, bored," he responds with a huff before looking back at his sister. "When are you coming home?" he implores urgently – and loudly.

"Probably in a few weeks when the semester ends," she tells him gently with a head tilt.

"Will you be home all summer?" he asks hopefully, and she regretfully shakes her head.

"I have more classes, Matty. I've got some catching up to do."

And now my newfound nostalgia has been thrown in a blender with my rage at the memory of what her shitball ex cost her. While I have a sudden urge to rush out to the garage and bench press my weight and then some, I allow myself to be centered by the solidarity I'm feeling with her mother at this moment. Mrs. Isaak sighs heavily with a frown that could set a glacier on fire. She only lets it linger about a second before her eyes dart to Matthew, and that seems to shake out of her stewing for his benefit.

"Well, come home for a visit anyhow," she suggests, and Luna nods. "Your dad is getting twitchy, your grandmother wants to go shopping, and you should probably take your cat back with you. Buster's been hardly doing anything but hanging out in your room for the last year," she grouses and rolls her eyes.

Luna wraps up her FaceTime visit in the next couple of minutes and signs off before shooting me a smile and reaching for her pallet with her left hand and that's when I notice something missing.

"Hey, where's your ring?" I ask her, feeling trepidation pull at my brow.

"Right here," she quickly assures me, pulling a necklace out from beneath the bib of her overalls with both her engagement and wedding rings looped on it. I must not look totally placated because her voice raises a little with her continued explanation. "Kaleb, look at my hands. I don't want to wear them when I'm working because I don't want them to get damaged, but I'm never going to lose them."

I take in all the paint smudges and stains on her hands and slowly start nodding. It makes sense, and I'm surprised at myself for worrying about such a thing as her sporting her wedding bands... as if my tattoo isn't enough, now I want the world to know she's Mine with a capital M, especially while I'm away.

After giving the band on my own hand a quick worry around my finger, I lean in and place a kiss to her forehead.

"I'm sorry," I whisper affectionately. "I should've known better than that." The last word is barely out of my mouth when something cold and wet and awful-smelling gets dabbed on my jaw. Perplexed, I straighten up and touch my fingertips to it to find they come away blue.

"What?" I look at her disbelievingly as she giggles like a little devil.

"Let that teach you never to doubt me," she says righteously as she turns back to her easel and picks up a brush like she didn't just smear me with blue paint, and she's getting down to business as usual.

"Well," I blow out on a cleansing breath as I swipe my fingers through the white paint and flick them at her. She gasps as white paint sprinkles her face, and she looks at me in horror while I grin back. "Let that be a lesson to not mess with the bull, silly girl."

Clearly I've opened a can of worms, because Luna's face morphs into a frightening mix of irritation, mischief, and excitement. Her lips curl in together as her eyes widen and she dips her brush in the blue.

Fuck.

I go to reach for her arm but she's too quick, even for my reflexes. With a flick of her wrist, I'm splattered all over my t-shirt, arm, and half my face with blue paint. I look down with an amused smirk, surveying the damage before looking up at her with my arms wide.

"Well, now you're in trouble, baby…" I advance towards her as she shrinks back, giggling. "And you owe me a hug!"

She squeals as I tackle her around the middle, jostling her pallet, and I'm thankful she had the brains to drape everything in here first because paint is flying everywhere as we wrestle and laugh, making memories that I have no idea will pull me through my darkest times.

Luna

Kaleb puts the truck in park in front of one-story establishment built from solid grey bricks and black side paneling. There are three bay doors, all of which are open to display what's going on inside.

As I step out and shut my door, I can see that a car of some kind occupies the first and third bay, while the skeleton of a Harley sits in the middle one with a man on a stool nearby tinkering with its engine.

I hear drills and zip guns adding to their own melody to the classic rock blaring through the sound system as Kaleb leads me through the door with Shane Automotive displayed in electric orange above it. The smell of must and grease fills my nostrils as we walk through a small vestibule that shows us to an even smaller office, with harsh fluorescent lighting and a steel desk that you can't see the top of as it's littered with things like invoices, inventory lists, owner's manuals to various vehicles, as well as unopened mail and folders.

Standing behind the desk is a man with overgrown black hair, several days' stubble, and bags under his eyes. He looks like the state of the desk might very well represent that of his mind. But what's really curious about him is the infant strapped to his chest. The little angel gnaws away happily on his pacifier, seemingly oblivious to his dad having a nervous breakdown.

"Jackson," Kaleb greets as we stroll in, and the guy looks up and reaches his hand out.

"Kaleb," he sighs in return as if he's in a vice that's squeezing the life right out of him. "Thanks for coming down."

"Yeah, sorry it took so long," Kaleb says and places a hand on my back. "This is my wife, Luna." The guy gets an amused grin on his face as he shakes my hand.

"Since when are you married?" he asks, raising a questioning eyebrow.

"Don't worry about it," Kaleb replies, dismissing his question, not wanting to get into it – and I get it. Time is precious at the moment and he leaves in a few days, knowing the business is already starting to flounder. Kaleb knows that whatever he can do before he leaves will be a Hail Mary, and I hate the idea of one of the few things he has in this world going under. "What's going on, man?" he asks attentively.

Jackson gingerly takes a seat in the chair behind the desk, careful not to disturb the baby he's wearing. "About one good thing, and the rest is shit," he conveys honestly. I can tell the guy is weary.

"Jax, I'm sorry," Kaleb laments sincerely as he takes a seat on the edge of the desk, a few papers crunching underneath him. "I don't know the first thing about running this place, and I don't know what to do, but I'll do what I can before I deploy. I can see you're drowning, but what's the one ray of hope you just mentioned?"

"I've got an interview with a new mechanic in a little while," he slumps back, and it disturbs the child who drops his pacifier and starts fussing. Jackson's eyes close and he looks like he's praying for a meteor to take him out.

In the last few days, Kaleb's told me little bits here and there about how Pops had this shop running like a well-tuned Harley, but since he passed, his head mechanic has had to step up, doing both the bulk of the work as well as trying to handle the business end. By the looks of things, he can barely keep his head above water, not to mention he looks deliriously tired. Even not knowing him, I feel for him, and I step forward, holding my arms out.

"Need a break?" I offer. "I love babies."

"Oh my God, you freaking angel," Jackson exhales, and I can already see relief written all over his face. I bend to retrieve the pacifier from the floor before taking hold of the baby boy who looks to be around six months and pull him from his carrier. Kaleb gives me a small smile, gratitude radiating from it as I carry the baby towards the office door. There's a utility sink just outside the office door, and I take the little guy to go clean his pacifier as the two guys talk.

"Tell me about this mechanic," Kaleb begins as he settles in, wanting to hear more, and Jackson leans forward, resting his elbows on the messy desk and starts ticking off qualifications on his fingers.

"Third generation mechanic, grew up in an auto shop and knows his shit from Acura to Z cars. He's looking for full time, and has taken college business courses."

Kaleb's eyes dart around like he's looking for the catch. "That all seems great," he shrugs. "If the interview goes well you could hire him on as lead, and he can be your right hand in the office," he suggests, already looking relieved as I look on from across the small space where I'm swaying the baby on my hip. The little guy has his pacifier back in his mouth and so all is right in his world again.

"He took said business courses from jail," Jackson huffs and sweeps both hands outward as if he's laying this bombshell neatly on the disaster of a desk, as Kaleb's mouth drops open slightly and his gaze wanders off somewhere towards the back ceiling.

"So... what was he in the clink for?" he asks. He's probably like me, hoping it was for parking tickets or bootlegging DVDs or something.

"Get this – street racing and grand theft auto."

"What the fuck?" Kaleb practically laughs. "Okay, he's clearly not from here," he says and rolls his eyes.

"What, you never raced your motorcycle or your truck around here?" I chide him as the baby starts grabbing at pieces of my hair.

"Sure, I did," he admits and gives me a pleased smirk. "But cops around here don't give a shit, and there sure as hell aren't cars nice enough to steal."

"He's from somewhere outside St. Louis," Jackson explains. "Just moved here – or will move here if he gets the job."

"What's his story?" Kaleb asks, perhaps trying to dig a little deeper.

"I ran a background check, and all that came up were the exact things he oddly came right out with in his cover letter, and anything else, I frankly don't care," Jackson admits and waves his hands again, defeatedly. "The only way we were going to get any help around this godforsaken town was if someone applied that didn't already live in it."

"And you're not worried you'll open up one morning and find the place cleaned out?" Kaleb calmly challenges, and Jackson stands to meet his height.

"Kaleb, I know this place means a lot to you, but we started with a goddamn empty barrel, and this is what I was able to scrape up off the bottom. It's been six months, and I'm fucking wrecked. I don't have much longer before this place goes belly up. With me in the office, we've had to cut back on services, and you know what that means." He levels Kaleb with a formidable glare that speaks a hard truth. "Look," he tries again, face softening. "I don't want to lose this place or Pop's memory any more than you do. That's why I've stuck it out this long, but I don't have child care, Marcie is picking up extra shifts at the diner, and I'm about to break," he concludes his case to a silent Kaleb who simply nods at the floor.

"Alright..." he finally breathes out, relenting. "You're right." He looks up and makes eye contact as the baby starts fussing in my arms, looking across the room, searching out his daddy. I cross the space and hand him back just in time for a new presence in the form of a rugged, biker-looking man to take up the doorway. The guy seriously looks like he could run with Kaleb if he were a few years younger.

"Hey, I'm looking for Jackson," his voice grumbles by way of greeting.

Jackson peeks over the top of his son's head. "That's me. Are you Weston Bradford?"

"I am," he nods and walks on in as one of the other mechanics appears, looking all macho and hardcore, save for the bottle he's carrying in one hand and the goofy face he's giving the baby with the other.

"Let's go, buddy," he coos at the little guy, and it's almost laughably in contrast to his appearance. "Time for your next lesson in motorcycle transmissions," he informs him in a gentle voice as he takes him from Jackson and replaces his pacifier with the bottle which he happily accepts.

Kaleb gives an endearing smile at the sight before announcing our leave. "Alright, I guess we're going to leave you to it," he pushes off the desk and comes over to escort me out of the office. We don't make it all the way to the truck however before we're stopped by Jackson calling out to him.

"Kaleb!" He jogs over and stops just feet away, resting his hands on his hips. "There's one more thing I forgot to tell you that I think you should know."

20

KALEB

The look on Jackson's face is twisting my insides and making my heart beat overtime.

"What is it?" I impatiently prod, as he sucks in a breath.

"Your old man called up here a couple of days ago," he reveals, making me feel a wave of shock and anger flash over me.

"You're shitting me," I bark out as I slam my truck door and march forward a few paces, and Jax regretfully shakes his head. "What the fuck did he want?"

"Well, first he asked for Pops…"

"Tell me you didn't tell him," I practically demand, desperation ratcheting up my breathing rate.

"Of course not," he assures me with a hand up. "I told him Pops was up in Indy buying some parts."

"Thank fuck," I let out on a heavy breath, but my blood is still pumping furiously through my veins at the knowledge the bastard even called. I'd led myself into a false sense of security, hoping he was either in jail or dead. Ignorance truly is bliss.

"And then he asked how business was going," Jackson adds cynically.

"Fucking – A." I grab at the back of my neck and squeeze, trying to slow my breathing. In my peripheral I can see Luna watching me, and I let my gaze lock with hers like I'm taking just a tiny dose of sanity from the exchange. Her eyes speak the message of concern, but also reassurance that I've got this… and if I don't, she'll jump in front of me and fight my demons for me. I tilt my chin in her direction, letting her know I'm good before looking back to Jax. "Please tell me you told him to fuck off."

"Those exact words, actually," he guffaws, running a hand through his hair. "I told him he has no business asking questions like that, and that I didn't have time to answer them even if he did. And then, yeah, I said fuck off. I hung up and blocked the number, not that that will do any good. I'm sure the guy just buys burner phones with God knows what money he's able to scrounge."

I take as steady a breath I can manage and blow it out before telling him, "Thank you."

He nods in response before backing up a few feet and turning to retreat back into the shop while I find a crumpled oil can on the ground and send it sailing into the grassy embankment that edges the lot off the toe of my boot. Then, cursing under my breath, I wrench open my truck door and haul myself into the cab while Luna does the same, not saying a word.

In the few minutes it takes to get home, I grip the wheel as if it's the lifeline, keeping from flying off the proverbial handle while Luna rides next to me, her body slightly turned towards me, but her eyes on the road ahead of us. A thought breaks through my mental storm clouds that I'm thankful for her particular brand of silent support.

When we get in the house, I make strides straight back to the bedroom. Gripping the bill of my hat, I yank if off and toss it towards the chair in the corner before reaching behind me and grabbing a fistful of my shirt and pulling it off.

As I start undoing the fly of my pants, I feel Luna before I see her, and allow her soft, warm hands to glide around the sides of my waist until they come close to meeting against the front of my torso. As I push my jeans down my hips, the faint tickle of her lashes and her sweet breath along the skin of my back make my dick spring to life in my boxer briefs.

"Have you seen the shorts I was wearing earlier, babe?" I ask, looking around as I step out of the jeans.

"Mm-mmm," she denies with a hum against my back before placing a kiss to the skin. "But it's okay, you don't need them right now," she announces in a sultry voice before one of her hands travels south to grip my hard shaft through my briefs.

Fuuuck...

"Damn," I huff out with barely any voice to the word. "Baby, what are you doing? I'm all sorts of fucked up right now."

"I know," she whispers between the kisses she's trailing across my back to my shoulder. "I thought I'd take your mind off it for a little while."

"No, babe, I can't right now," I try to tell her gently as I turn to face her. I've got one hell of a fucking temper when it comes to Rick Shane, and I learned some valuable lessons in Basic on how to channel it. "I need to go out to the garage for a while... lift weights or hit the bag or something."

Her pretty brown eyes innocently look me up and down as her pretty lips part, as if in thought. And then, she goes up on her toes and not-so-innocently kisses me.

"Mmmm," I moan out involuntarily when she licks at my lips before pressing hers against them. "Luna," I protest in a whisper, "I appreciate it, but I can't right now. I've got to work this anger out."

"I know," she whispers again between her mouth's assault on mine, "and I want to help." She goes in again, plunging her tongue into my mouth with one hand gripping the back of my neck while the other glides down the front of my abs to find my cock again.

"Fuck," I husk out, because thirty seconds of her magic and

it's about to explode. "Babe, really... I don't want to get carried away, or get too rough with you..."

She's let me be rough with her a number of times, but this is different. Those other times I wasn't harboring any serious rage beneath my skin. That said, I'm hanging by a goddamn thread here...

"I'll be the judge of what I can handle," she purrs against my lips as she lightly rakes her nails up the ridge of my shaft and then back down to give it another squeeze.

"Goddammit, Luna," I exclaim in a hoarse whisper, and little does she know it's what she just said that's doing me in – almost more than her actions.

My hands take purchase on her hips and give them a firm squeeze, just a bit harder than how I normally grab her. Pulling her away just enough to pin her with the most serious glare I have in my arsenal, I pin her with it while flexing my fingers in a borderline bruising grip on her. She takes a sharp intake of breath – but not in the way I expect. Her eyes flutter to a half-closed position, yet I keep our gazes locked as I take hold of her chin.

"Please," she whispers as I bring my lips a hair's-breadth from hers.

"You know what to say… if I take it too far. You say stop."

Her brown pools shine a lighter shade, the gold rings around her pupils practically glowing as she nods. "Take what you want so I can take it all away."

The last syllable is barely out of her mouth before I place a sweet, light kiss to her lips – a promise that her Kaleb will be coming back without a second to spare – before swiftly shifting gears and whirling her around and pushing her against the wall.

"Oh," she gasps out as I take hold of her hands and pin her wrists together above her head. Pulling her hair to the side with my other hand, I latch my mouth onto the side of her neck, sucking ferociously on the skin a moment before clamping down just enough to make her yelp. Ripping my mouth away, I look to her, making sure she's not in any pain or distress.

I release her wrists, yet she still holds them in place above her head.

"Good fucking girl," I praise before reaching around to snap the clasp on her jeans before jerking them harshly down her hips and giving her ass a hard smack.

"Ah!" she cries out but I keep going, slapping the other side before crouching down and moving the violet lace of her panties out of the way just enough so that I have room to sink my teeth into her right ass cheek. "Ooh," she breathes out, her breathing becoming labored, and she barely has time to catch her next breath before I take a better hold of the panties, and with a brutally sharp yank of my arm, they tear away from her body.

She gasps again as I toss the lacey scraps to the floor and whirl her body towards the bed, throwing her down on the mattress. She only has the time it takes me to shuck my briefs down to find her bearings before I'm on top of her, pinning her wrists above her once again.

"Ohhh..." she moans – actually moans – and the approving sound both surprises me and fuels me to take it farther. I reach beneath her to find her pussy hot and throbbing for my invasion, and waste no time lining my cock up with her entrance.

"Sure you want this?" I growl between clenched teeth right in her ear as my left hand leaves her wrists to take a fistful of her hair.

"Fuck me, soldier," she barely puffs out from beneath my weight, and I oblige by driving forward, entering her with a deep, sharp thrust that makes her cry out, the sound prompting me to do it again. But it's her next words that really make me let go. "Is that all you've got?" she pants out, and I rear back and barrel forward again and again, pounding into her with fierce, punishing strokes.

A beast has taken over as I completely abandon any inhibitions I had. My anger at Rick Shane and his fucking nerve to walk this earth, let alone stick his nose in my business, take the form of blazing hot flames behind my squeezed eyelids. With every pass, I visualize some of the flames abating, albeit minimally, but enough to spur me on, drilling Luna as hard as I can. With every thrust, I shift my body forward as much as hers will allow, putting all my strength behind it, just to see those flames die just a little more.

My hand grips her hair harder and I pull hard enough for her head to tilt back towards mine, her feral whimper dousing the flames a little more. Releasing her hair, my hand travels down her neck and snakes around to the front of her throat. The vibration of her moans and cries are like a rainy mist over the fire, just like when Luna came to me that night in the bathroom after that asshole, Ryan, shot his mouth off, it settles the fire in a beautiful, calming way.

I love Luna for what she's doing for me right now; trying to give me a channel, an outlet for my temper… but now, I want the mist.

Slowing my strokes and releasing her throat, I gently pull out of her.

"Kaleb?" she pants, trying to look at me over her shoulder.

"Shhh," I assure her. "Turn over."

She obeys, flipping onto her back, and I take hold of her jeans and work them carefully the rest of the way down her legs before just as carefully laying back down on top of her.

"What's the matter?" Concern furrows her forehead and clouds her eyes.

"Nothing," I whisper, shaking my head. "I just want you a different way.

I definitely still want her, as my cock is still painfully hard and wet with her arousal as it brushes against her sex, but I want her gentle softness to dull the flames like no one but her can do.

Rolling to my back, I take her with me, gazing up at her sweet face hovering over mine. Taking hold of the hem of her clingy t-shirt, I raise it up her torso and she raises her arms, helping me to get it off of her before reaching behind her back to unclasp her bra.

Placing my palm over the tattoo I marked on her skin, I put my other hand on her hip and start guiding her to rock against me. I groan out in ecstasy as I look up at the pink flush that branches out across her skin, likely from the frenzy our bodies were tangled in moments ago. Her head drops back as she gets lost in the waves while her sex caresses my cock over and over in a warm embrace.

I can feel her walls closing in, her wetness getting tighter and tighter, and she suddenly opens her eyes and leans forward, her brown and purple hair providing a curtain on either side of my face. "What do you need?" she breathlessly asks down at me as I take her face between my hands.

"I want you to come for me," I grunt up at her; the pleasure falling down over me like the gentle rain I was craving. "And then I need to hold you." She concedes by pressing her lips to mine as her hips continue to roll and rock against mine in a steady, perfectly measured rhythm that takes me higher and higher up to the peak. Luna cries helplessly into my mouth as she comes with a thunder at the same time I find my release inside of her. My groans are dragged over gravel as they are pulled long and satisfyingly from my throat as I pump up into her, jets of my cum spurting out, taking the last of my anger with them.

The flames are now a pile of charred embers, flaking apart into ash when I pull Luna down on top of me and hold her body tightly against mine. Her weight on my chest dulls the ache and any last repercussions of my earlier rage. Just like the gentle rain doesn't get mad at the fire for burning, it just simply soothes it into waning down.

With no words, Luna turns her head to the side, resting her face on my chest as we breathe together, each breath longer and slower than the last. I peer down to see her dark lashes fanned over her cheekbones, and her features completely relaxed as she drifts off to sleep.

Resting my own head back against the pillow, I reach over to grab the nearby blanket and drape it over the two of us. And then, never feeling more secure and protected from my demons, I join her in our blissful bubble of sleep.

21

LUNA

My cheek is pressed against Kaleb's chest, trying to take in one last whiff of his musky scent through his fatigues. So much has happened in the three weeks since we found each other again, and yet not nearly enough. His warm breath in the top of my hair sends a delightful shiver down my spine.

"It's just a year, my girl," Kaleb reminds me. "It will go by before you know it."

"I know," I murmur, still not letting go of his waist. With his arms locked around me, I chance opening my eyes to see all the other soldiers with multiple family members crowding them before they get on the bus. All Kaleb has is me. If we hadn't run into each other in that club, he'd be going off to fight in a war with no one to see him off; to tell him to be safe and take care of himself, or tell him they can't wait for him to come home. He'll have Alex with him of course, but I'm happy to give him something that reminds him he's got someone to stay alive for. I'll forever be thankful for that night we reconnected, because married or not, I'd be right here seeing him off; being his person.

When the last call is announced for Kaleb's platoon to board the bus that will take them to the airfield, I reach into the pocket of my hoodie and pull out the clear plastic baggy I brought for him. He takes it from me and looks at it curiously for a minute before his green eyes light up with the realization of what it is.

"Oh my God, are you serious?" He cracks open the Ziploc and takes out the small, curled strand of braided purple hair.

"Too creepy?" I raise an eyebrow, my eyes squinting against the afternoon sun.

"So creepy," he chuckles shaking his head. "But I couldn't ask for a better memento. I love it," he tells me tenderly, placing a small kiss on my lips as he tucks it into one of the button pockets of his uniform as I reach in my pocket again, this time producing a pen.

"My turn for a present," I inform him, and he takes the pen, giving me a cheeky smile that reminds me of us being kids again.

"I'll never get tired of this," he grins, taking hold of my left hand. It's always the left, which I think was a fluke the first time, but after that, we both realized that the picture would stay on my palm longer if it's on my less dominant hand.

The ball point tickles as always, in the most calming way. Watching Kaleb draw has the same effect as letting a summer breeze settle over me. I feel peace, wonder... serenity. When he finishes, he closes my hand.

"No peeking until I leave," he says softly, and out of nowhere, I feel the prickle behind my eyes forcing tears to the front, and I blink hard against them.

"Then don't leave," I barely choke out as I bring my unmarked hand to wipe at the emotion streaming down my cheek.

"Lu," Kaleb's voice is husky as he reaches for me, pulling me to him, threading a hand in my hair as if he's protecting me from our reality. "I'm coming back, you know that. But I tell you what, it's some kind of incredible having something make it so damn hard to leave."

"What if something happens to you?" I sniff. "Now that you're back in my life, I don't want to live without—"

"You won't," he cuts me off gently, taking my face in his hands. "And neither will I. But, baby, you've always been the strong one, and I know you can be strong now. Please do that for me."

Pulling in a breath and releasing it, I finally nod, though my heart sits in agony in my chest. But my concession brings a small smile to Kaleb's face, and I take that as my microscopic consolation.

"Hey," he says softly. "Truth?" I nod, sucking my bottom lip in while I try to keep it together. "Do you love me?"

"Yes," I say on a gust of air that I'd been holding tightly in my chest. "I love you," the words tremble out of me.

"And that's all I need to get me through this year, baby," he promises, laying another kiss on my lips.

"I dare you to come back," I tell him, words getting more and more difficult as I try to tamp down the sobs, and he brings his forehead to mine.

"And you know I never turn down a dare." His words come out in a low voice, full of conviction and determination. "Okay?"

"Okay," I nod, and this time can't help the whimpering in my voice.

He gives me one last kiss, and makes it count. Fierce, passionate and full, as if he's pouring every part of himself into it. Even as his feet start to shift backwards, his mouth is still on mine until the last possible second as he gets ushered toward the bus as a superior relieves him of his ruck sack. With one foot on board, he leans back and blows one last kiss as the engine starts.

I continue to watch as the bus rolls out of the parking lot towards the street while I take more deep breaths in an effort to calm my body from being rattled with emotion. And when the bus is out of sight, I finally look down at my left hand to find a heart with lines and cuts to make it look as though it's made of diamond. But it's not nearly as beautiful as the messaged scrawled beneath it.

I love you, Luna Shane
Kaleb

"Loverboy!" Alex teases from next to me on the musty-smelling bus.

"Please…" I scoff. "Like you didn't have your tongue down Miranda's throat out there." I tip my head towards the window. "Did you lock that down, by the way?"

He shakes his head. "No, I'm testing Miranda's loyalty."

"What do you mean?"

"I mean we haven't been serious for that long. I need to see what this relationship is made of first, and then we'll talk about a ring."

I nod, because he's making sense. He wants to see if his girl can hold steady while he's gone; to see if she cannot cheat, or fall out of love with him.

I don't need to test Luna's loyalty. Every summer, she was there without fail – and that was when we were two dumb kids. Now we've survived a three-year estrangement, and she's my wife. She'll still be here when I get back.

The last two weeks went by way too fast, but were beautiful nevertheless. Even when we were stuck at the DMV for three hours getting the name on her ID changed. We spent that time in the waiting room with me giving her another drawing lesson. With her on my lap and her hand in mine, we might as well have been sitting under an oak tree instead of a stuffy, windowless room.

Her artwork hangs in the living room, including a couple of pieces we worked on together. There are several shades of purple towels in our bathroom, and vanilla candles everywhere. Nothing could feel more right in my house – and my life. Now if

I could just get that last wall to come down, the one that stands between me and giving in to my feelings all the way.

I still harbor an epic amount of anger at my father. It's been concentrated and compressed to fit in a small box deep down in my soul, but it's still there, burning hot as magma, along with the anger at the unfairness of the way Pops died alone. After everything he did for me, the universe couldn't even give me the small consolation of being with him in his last moments.

All my life has taught me to do is keep my guard high and my expectations low; to acknowledge my feelings but not give them any control. Luna coming back into my life made me knock down several of those walls just to let her in, knowing I'd be a fool to shut her out. And now, I'm just hoping with all I have that this next year will give me a place to put my fury, or better yet, release it and vanquish it. I don't know what I'm expecting. Maybe I'm hoping the adrenaline and gratification of helping people will make me stronger; build my character or endurance... that being up in a helicopter will give me a sense of perspective. Or maybe just doing something with my life other than waiting around for something to happen will make me feel accomplished – despite my piece of shit father. If nothing else, I'll go home after a year and make something of Pop's business, and that will be enough. And if that last damn wall can come down, maybe Luna and I can truly join forces and build something amazing together.

22

LUNA

June

From: Moongirl621@xmail.com
To: Cpl.K.Shane@army.gov

To my sexy soldier. After you left, I drove back to Detroit for a visit and I'm glad I did. Being with my family helped that initial shock of you leaving. I played a lot of one-on-one with Matthew in the driveway, went shopping with my mom and Granna, and while dad was busy at work a lot, I hung out at his practice a little bit and we squeezed in a couple of movie marathons. My mom touched up my purple coloring, and... we now have a cat. Welcome to the old 'what's mine is yours' adage. I brought my tabby cat, Buster, back to your house... our house? It feels so weird to think of it that way. Anyway,

my classes are only Mondays and Thursdays this summer. I clustered them together to make it easier to go between the city and Coyote Creek, so I've settled Buster in at the house since I'm there more. Not much else to say except I miss you and hope you're staying safe.
 I love you.
 Lu.

From: Cpl.K.Shane@army.gov
To: Moongirl621@xmail.com

 Hey, goof,
 So far, pretty boring here. I'm working long-ass night shifts just doing patrol. Other than tired and uncomfortable as fuck, and missing the shit out of you, I'm doing fine. I'll keep you posted as to when I can get on the webcam so I can see your pretty face. In the meantime, I look forward to these messages. Being away from you is harder than I could've ever imagined. And I'd ask what color underwear you're wearing, but I already know ;)
 And it's our house. Definitely. I know everything happened fast and totally ass-backwards, but this is the real deal, baby. We're married. Everything's ours. Except the cat, you're going to have to get rid of him. I'm allergic. In fact, I can feel my throat closing up from here...

> Baby, if I don't get my hands on an epi pen... please know, that I love you.
> -K

FROM: Moongirl621@xmail.com
To: Cpl.K.Shane@army.gov

> Very funny, asshole. You're lucky you're kind of cute and somewhat satisfactory in bed.
> Anyway, I just want you to know that I dropped by the shop and the new guy, West, seems to be working out pretty well so far. If nothing else, everyone seems more on top of things, and there's definitely kind of a flow. I think I even found half of Jackson's desk.
> Xo, Lu

FROM: Cpl.K.Shane@army.gov
To: Moongirl621@xmail.com

> Ah, but I'm your asshole. But what's this satisfactory shit? You're paying for that one when I get home, that's a promise.
> And that's amazing to hear about the shop. It almost sounds like it's being run the same way Pops did it. Thank you for checking in on it, babe, you're the best.

Xoxo K

July

From: Moongirl621@xmail.com
To: Cpl.K.Shane@army.gov

Hi, baby,
So... pottery class sucks. I really thought I'd be into it. I'm starting to get frustrated. I wanted there to be more to me as an artist than just a painter. Like all I can do is throw color on a canvas. Anyway... sorry... just had to get that out. I know it's all relative compared to how you're having to spend your time over there. Are things still going okay? It's been a couple days since I've heard from you.
Loving and missing you hard today.
Xo
Lu

From: Cpl.K.Shane@army.gov
To: Moongirl621@xmail.com

Hey, baby,

Natalie Parker

Sorry it's been a few days. As you know, for security purposes I'm not allowed to talk about what-all goes down, but I'll just say things went sideways on my last shift. It was rough and a little scary, but I'm okay.

And don't be such a silly girl, silly girl. You're a brilliant artist, and so what if you only paint? You're up there with Monet. And who knows, maybe you'll come up with your own form of art expression.

And if none of this helps, then how about when I get home, we throw a bunch of paint on a canvas and have sex on it? Bet you anything it will sell ;)

I love you, Lu. And even though I tell you not to worry about me, I'm thankful I have you love me that much.

Xo,
Your soldier.

FROM: Moongirl621@xmail.com
To: Cpl.K.Shane@army.gov

Oh my God, babe...I'm so unbelievably thankful you're alright. And I'm so damn proud of you.

Ugh, I feel so fucking foolish now for complaining about pottery, I knew I shouldn't have brought that up.

Knowing what you're doing over there makes me realize how much I take for granted.

Again, I'm so proud of you, babe. You're so getting laid when you get back ;)

Love you, my hero. And you should be getting an envelope soon with something for your eyes only.

Xo

Luna

FROM: Cpl.K.Shane@army.gov
To: Moongirl621@xmail.com

I got your delivery and... Wow... baby... okay, you need to send me more of those. You just had to go with the all-lace corset, didn't you? Holy fuck, you look like a dessert, and the way your boobs are pushed up... damn. I have to be honest. I had to beat off twice before I fell asleep yesterday.

If my commanding officer wasn't lurking around, I'd have you wear that on our next webcam date.

And you don't have to worry about venting to me, goof. It gives me a sense of normalcy. It's nice to talk to you about regular things.

I'll be dreaming of you like always.

Xo,

K

⛺

August

Luna

MY VIDEO CHAT notification starts going crazy about ten seconds after I pull into the parking spot. I have no earthly idea why Kaleb insisted today's webcam visit take place here at our old stomping grounds, but here I am, feeling like a complete idiot as the only person arriving at Mystic Hills Camp while everyone else is leaving.

I grab my phone as I push the door open, and swipe the screen after it shuts.

"Hey, goof," Kaleb greets and gives me his charming grin when his face populates the screen.

"Hey, soldier," I flirt back, but give him look of mock admonishment. "Want to tell me what I'm doing here?"

"Well," he looks down coyly for a beat, and then back up at me. "As you know, it's the day camp closes down for the summer."

"Uh huh…" I prod him to keep going as I take moseying steps from the lot toward the cabin-like buildings. My goal in this conversation is to not bring up the last closing day I was present for.

"Well… happy stupid, fight that almost ruined everything -aversary," he quips, and I stop in my tracks, my shoes scraping against the dirt.

I tilt my head and gape at him for a moment before finally saying. "You're so fucking weird," which earns me a smug grin. "So you thought you'd bring me back here so we could wallow in our teenage angst?"

"Not exactly," he says low and sweet, and it gets my attention. "But I do want to show you something."

"I'm not climbing up the ropes course," I forewarn him.

"Don't worry, it's not on the ropes course, you chicken" he huffs. "Just keep walking towards the main counselor's cabin.

I purse my lips together in thought. The only nostalgic thing about that place I can think of is my name carved into the side of the building in teeny tiny letters.

"Kaleb Shane, if you brought me here just to glance down memory lane, we could have saved me the drive," I huff at him as I start trekking the dirt path.

"No, there's something for you to actually see that I've been wanting to show you, but... kind of didn't have time before I left, so this will have to do."

It's true that the couple of weeks we had were busy between moving me partly into his house, taking care of the shop, my classes, and lots of sex, there wasn't really any time for anything like this. I just can't fathom what he could possibly show me, until I round the corner and actually see it.

My heart swells in my chest and my throat goes dry. I feel my lips part and my pulse thrumming through my extremities.

On the side of the cabin, in letters so big I can see them from thirty paces, are the words Kaleb + Luna inside a perfectly carved and whittled heart.

Where the four letters of my name had been dug into the dark wood panel too small for anyone to know of its existence, this proclamation is loud and clear, for any visitor to see.

"Oh my God," my voice is a breathy squeak and my eyes dart away from the masterpiece only long enough to catch the warmth in his green eyes before being drawn back to it again.

"Does that mean it's still there?" Kaleb's brows are raised as I quicken my pace up to the cabin.

"Yes, it's here, Kaleb and it's so beautiful," I exclaim as I reach the side wall. I crouch down and hold my phone out at an angle so that Kaleb can see it. His smile is closed-mouth with a warm nostalgia hooding his eyes.

"When did you do this?" I ask, looking between him and the carving. I run my hands over the cuts and grooves to confirm that it's real and not some kind of illusion.

"The morning after the lake." He looks down a moment, and

I can see the regret clouding his features and I feel my own pull in confusion.

"Wh... but you weren't here," I debate his answer. "I didn't see you anywhere, and your bike was gone."

"I'd gone for a ride, Lu, but I hadn't left for good. I took some time to process everything that'd happened, but it turned out I took too long." The words come out of him on a heavy breath. "When I came back you were gone, and I had no way of talking to you again."

His voice from my phone screen breaks my heart as if I just listened to the saddest story told, despite the steadiness of his tone.

"So you did this?" I ask, still smoothing my hands over the marred and weathered wood, noticing a tinier design within the rustically beautiful testament. When I lean in closer, I see that it's the original carving of my name when Kaleb and I were only ten, only it has a tiny crescent moon carved around it. I don't comment, but smile and look back, awaiting his response.

"I had so much to say and no way to say it," he nods humbly. "So, in a way, that was me letting some of it out," he admits and tips his chin at our carved names.

We take a couple moments, just sitting together in the moment, and while I don't know if he actually can, I pretend that he can hear the birds chirping in the distance and the breeze rustling the leaves; a promise that fall is just around the corner. "I don't think you could have brought me anywhere more romantic for our webcam date." My words are solemn but I deliver them with a smirk, and he returns it with a wink.

"So let's stay a while," he leans forward like he's settling in for some idle chat, a carefree veil falling over his face with a small smile that makes me wonder if all this time he's been trying to shield me from what he must be seeing and feeling over there in that grim warzone.

Leaning back against the cabin's siding with the carved heart right next to me for companionship, I take a breath and a beat before asking "Are you doing alright, K?"

He freezes for a moment, his gaze going hard for a moment and then in a blink, relaxes again. "Yeah, babe, I'm fine."

"Kaleb," I prod, trying to get a fragment of truth out of him. The one thing I've learned about Kaleb is not to push, or he'll push back. After making himself vulnerable time and again to the one person who was supposed to protect him, he has a hard time letting anyone else in, even a little bit. Hell, the only time he's actually said I love you was when he proposed. Every other time has been through his own little hidden messages, like the one on my hand the day he left, and this carving on the cabin. Getting him to open up to me has been a process years in the making, one baby step at a time. It's been about finding a balance between encouraging him to trust in me without trying to force it. "Please be real with me," I add gently.

He breathes out a heavy sigh through his nose, gripping his hands together. It's hard, but he's going to give me a little bit. He's going to try. "I mean… it's not fun, Lu." His eyes roll skywards for a second in an obvious effort to downplay it. "It's been scary at times, but nothing I can't handle. And it's not all bad. I love being up in the hawk, you know I love being up high. And I love being a part of something with other people that doesn't involve drinking contraband whiskey and playing XBOX in someone's basement." He wraps it up with a small but playful smile, and I know that's all I'm going to get.

"Okay," I say quietly, smiling back, and we exchange our usual look; the one that says I know he's holding back and he knows that I know, but is thankful I'm not pushing.

"So what about you, silly girl?" he asks, clearly shifting the subject off of him. "How are classes? Talk to your family lately?" He's playfully firing off the questions, but it's that last one that makes my heart freeze to ice and drop into the pit of my stomach. I swallow hard and try to recover as I brighten my eyes for him, but it's too late. He saw it, the look of dread that must've fallen over my face. "Lu?" he asks, cueing me to fill him in. "What's going on? What's that look about?"

Fuck, I don't want to tell him what I found out yesterday when my mom called me. It will just wind him up, especially when he's half a world away where he can't do anything about it. "It's..." I shake my head trying to come up with a way to downplay it and fast. "It's not a big deal, okay?"

The stiffening of his shoulders as he leans in closer and the way his eyes turn into two green lasers tell me he's already decided that this is in fact, a big deal.

"Lu, what's going on?" he demands rather than asks, his jaw as hardened has his voice.

I feel my heart beat faster as he holds a proverbial microscope over me. "Okay," I breathe, "but before you freak out, I want you to know it's been taken care of."

"What's been taken care of, Luna?" He's getting exasperated, and I know now's not the right time to tell him he's sexy when he's mad.

I draw in a dose of air, pulling it deep into my lungs before I let it out with the words as quickly as I can. "Carter sent flowers to my parent's house."

Kaleb goes eerily quiet, his expression stone cold as he stares straight ahead but at nothing. He holds this expression for two to three beats before he explodes.

"Mother fucker!" he roars as he slams his hand down on the tabletop he's been leaning against. I jump at his outburst that makes even my serene setting feel like a panic room about now.

"K, please..." I bring the screen closer to my face, willing my eyes to anchor him. "Look at me," I beckon as his shoulders rise and fall with the heaviness of his breathing, but he obliges, looking at me with a desperate fury.

"Lu, I swear to God, I'm going to come back there and fuck him up!"

"We filed a no-contact order," I cut him off gently, still trying to get him to match my energy.

"What do you mean?" he grumbles out between heaving breaths.

"I mean my parents and I filed an order for him to not contact me again. If he tries anymore shit, he'll be arrested. Don't worry."

Kaleb holds a clenched fist in front of his mouth, trying to calm down. "Luna," he grinds out, my name muffled by his hand.

"K, I don't know why he's popped up after a year with all these crazy ideas," I shake my head as the words come out serrated by my raucous heartbeat. "But I've been doing the right thing by not engaging, and now I'm shutting him down. I've sent the message that if he keeps this up, there's going to be consequences." My tone has mounted in firmness, ensuring that I get through to Kaleb loud and clear. Sometimes he needs just what he gives, and right now, I know he needs firm reassurance that everything is under control.

He stares downward at nothing for a moment, but the set of his eyes gives away the depth of his thought. "I hate not being there, Lu," he finally says around his tightened fist. "I hate not being able to protect what's mine."

A thrill shoots up my back and tickles at my neck at the possessive quality in his statement, but I try to stay focused on calming him down. "I know," I murmur quietly, "but you're protecting thousands of innocents instead," I remind him. "I'm taking care of what's yours right now. I promise. Okay?" I raise my eyebrows, trying to get him to unclench and let go.

I see his fingers flex and a weighted sigh release from his body before he gives a reluctant nod.

"Now..." I proceed, feeling partial relief as I try to move us forward. "Can we get back to this beautiful moment please?" I raise my eyebrows giving him a hopeful look, and he shakes his head.

"For now," he grunts, still grumpy, but it's good enough for me as I settle back against the cabin wall.

23

KALEB

I'm seething. The explosions happening in my mind right now rival those that are happening over on the front lines.

So... Luna's ex ran into a wall when she changed her last name, and so he's trying the last bit of contact information he had. While I wanted to hunt him down and deliver an in-person message to fuck off, I listened to my girl and allowed her to just shut him down.

Seems it only made him all the more persistent, like he's enjoying the game, or he knows if he just keeps pushing, he'll get what he wants. I get the feeling he's not used to not getting his way. And now here I am... in the eye of this war, seeing things I'd give my soul to unsee, and some sociopathic piece of shit is fucking with my girl. Back home, where things are simple with only my own shit to deal with, I'd be able to protect her with no problem. One visit from me would fix the whole thing. There's one person in this world that I love. Just one. But instead, I'm over here, futilely defending thousands of nameless people – innocent people who didn't ask to have their homes invaded, or their lives terrorized. Not being part of the front-line infantry, there's not much I can do but pick up the pieces. Never in my life have I felt so ineffective, and in Luna's case, helpless.

My palms sweat as my fists clench, though I try to hide it from Luna. I try to focus on her, sitting back against the cabin with a light breeze ruffling the strands of her honey-brown hair, but my mind is millions of miles farther away than my actual body.

"Baby," she says so softly, yet it breaks through my thoughts like a nuclear blast. I feel the muscles in my back and my arms immediately unclench as if by involuntary reflex, and my vision refocuses. Seems I was looking at her without actually seeing her now that her beautiful face is clear on the screen with her eyes searching mine, willing me to feel calm. "I'm never going to tell you not to feel things," her soft voice continues as she looks thoughtfully down at her lap, "but please don't let them rule you. Not the bad ones anyway."

I pull in a deep breath through my nose. If she only knew how hard it is not to let bad feelings rule you when you're stepping over the dead bodies of helpless people that were defenseless against their plight. Pulling brothers that I'd just had breakfast with that morning onto the hawk as they cling to life; barely breathing. These are things she can't understand, even if I told her about them. You simply can't if you're not the one living it. Instead, I'll protect her in the one way I can right now. I'll protect her heart.

"Okay, baby," I begin and exhale the fortifying breath I was building, "I'll try," I concede, winking at her and letting my heart release at the smiling relief in those brown eyes.

⛺

"Uggghhh!" Alex grunts as my fist connects with his jaw, but he recovers quickly, whipping his head back in my direction. "That's it," he nods approvingly, wiping sweat from his brow with the back of his taped hand. "Now I've gotta tell you, I wasn't too happy when I couldn't get a hold of your wife," he quirks an eyebrow at me, goading me to release my pent-up rage all over his fucking face. "She's just playing hard to get, but there's no way she doesn't want me – oof!" I hear the air whoosh out of him as I deliver a blow to his gut.

We continue to circle and spar as a few of our brothers sit around the perimeter of the tent, heckling in amusement. It was Alex's idea to role play as that fuck, Carter, and help me get out some of my aggression. I'd held it together for the rest of my conversation with Luna, but I was ready to blow when our video date ended.

I don't know how long we go for, but I let myself zone out, thinking of every woman and child I've found among the shambles as I throw each punch, occasionally coming back to reality in time for Alex to make a jab about Carter going after my woman. She's mine, and he clearly thinks he can still have her at his will. The horror I've seen… and the conniving shit that I can't cyclone together as I lash out at it. Every flash of pain it sends through my nervous system I give back full force, knowing that after all our training together, Alex can take it.

When I've used up every last ounce of strength, fury, sweat, and breath, I sit on a folding chair with my arms resting on my legs, thoroughly depleted. An occasional bead of sweat drops from my hairline to the dirt floor, and I stare at it like it's some oasis. I sometimes wonder what I'm doing all this for. I wanted to do something with my life, but was this really the only option?

I was a bad boy going nowhere, and I wanted to be good enough. Good enough for my good girl. Good enough for the world. I wanted to do something significant in my life; something heroic, and then maybe spend the rest of it giving back to Pops' legacy. With no money or education to get started, serving seemed like my only option.

I see Alex plop his ass down in the chair next to me, the stink of sweat wafting off him, and before I can look up at him, a can is held out in front of my line of vision.

"What's this?" I ask quietly, all the rage and energy gone for the night.

"Some piss water the locals call beer," he scoffs out with a half-smile. He looks like shit, but also like he couldn't be bothered in the least.

"Thanks," I mumble, cracking it open. When you're deployed, things like beer are hard to come by. Tipping it back I take a hearty glug, and he's right. It tastes terrible, but at least it's cold. After a few swallows I lower the can, holding it between my hands and look up at him again, taking in his battered, and sweaty appearance. "Thank you," I say sincerely. Not every friend will take a beating just to help you manage your emotions. And with Luna letting me get aggressive during sex, the two of them are like peas in a pod.

He waves a hand, taking a slug of his beer before swallowing. "I'm at war, I have to come home with some kind of battle scars," he jokes. "People won't believe where I was when I come back."

"Like I left any marks," I huff, shaking my head. I stuck to mainly body blows – except when he dug at me about Luna. Then I had to go for the face, pretending it was that shithead, Carter's, not that I know what he looks like. I've been reluctant to look him up for fear that I'll blow a fuse.

I'm not sure when I became such an angry person. I was a happy kid at one point, despite getting knocked around by my dad.

Hell, maybe I thought being in a world full of carnage and demons would help me expel my own, that the brotherhood would provide the camaraderie that would give me a sense of belonging.

"Besides," he adds, ignoring my remark, "I owed you a solid after you took the heat for us when we snuck that bottle of Jack into prom.

I stand, ready for a shower, a jerk-off session to thoughts of Luna, and a few hours of sleep. "Hey," I shrug, "you'd been trying to hit that with Colette Jeffries for a year. I'm there for you, man." I reach my fist out and he bumps his against it.

"Debt finally repaid," he says and sits back, shaking his head.

"Night, man."

"G'night."

Luna

I HAND my cash over to Colleen, the barista that hosts a tiny espresso stand in the parking lot of the Gas & Grocery and tell her to keep the change as I take my latte from her in return. I cross the lot that's damp with dew from the night before, and find the gas tank still fueling my car.

Leaning my back against it, I wait for it to click off, taking a sip of my hot coffee as the sun starts creeping up over the brick buildings of main street. It's not quite fall yet, but the nip in the morning air heralds its impending arrival.

Once again, for the fall semester, I was able to lump my classes together two days a week, but I've realized the downfall of living in a small town – and that is you can only get so many people to book a paint and sip party, so I've had to put in an extra evening or two a week in the city, trying to make some money.

"Well aren't you just settling in?" A slithery voice breaks me from my morning thoughts, and I look over to see Cheyenne approaching, hands in the pockets of her jacket as the glass door to the gas station closes behind her. Her blonde curls are down and around her shoulders today, and I'm almost envious. My hair has some waves, but it was curlier when I was younger.

I lift a shoulder, taking another sip. "It's been almost five months," I hint. This isn't the first time our paths have crossed since I met her. She has an affinity for sneering at me at the supermarket, the bakery, and the post office. This is just the first time she's bothered to speak, and the obvious is what she goes with?

Her eyes roll as she tips her head to the side, snorting. "Please. Does Kaleb even know you're skulking around his hometown while he's gone? It's pretty pathetic, by the way, playing make believe in his house while he's deployed."

Alright. I'm not a morning person to begin with, and this bitch is chapping my ass before I'm even three sips into my coffee. Not what I would call a good idea. I draw in a long breath and let it out in an exaggerated sigh, making sure my exasperation gets across loud and clear.

"Being that I'm married to him, no, not that pathetic." I keep my face neutral as possible as she tries to catch herself from letting the shock show on her face. Too late. I saw those eyes widen and her skin go pale. "Not as pathetic as say, trolling me at the farmers market to make sure I see you scowling at me, and driving by the house each night, really slow, to see if I'm there?" I raise my eyebrows, searching her face to see if she'd like to comment. She does the fish out of water thing for a moment before straightening her spine and backing away slowly in the direction of her car.

"Headed out for the day?" she asks cooly, as if I didn't light her ass up a minute ago. "I wonder what Kaleb would have to say to you disappearing two days a week. Every soldier just loves to hear that their 'wife' has a side piece." She gives me finger quotes before shoving her hands back in her pockets.

I busy myself with replacing the pump and my gas cap. "He'd tell you to stop stalking me and that he knows I go to school in the city," I say incredulously with widened eyes, and it dawns on me how not-mature I am and it blows my mind that I'm a married person.

Cheyenne's mouth falls open and she blinks at me before turning around with a huff and retreating to her car.

"Have the day you deserve," I mumble to myself in dismissal of the conversation before I climb behind the wheel and secure my to-go cup in the cup holder.

My Thursday only gets better from there. Some jackass stole the last parking spot in the lot closest to the campus when I got to school, leaving me no choice but to park six blocks away. I don't mind walking, but it's awkward and exhausting when you're schlepping a large portfolio bag on a time constraint. From there, my classes were only okay which is sad and disappointing. Normally, learning new ways to create beautiful pieces is where I come to life… but my mind has been with Kaleb lately. When we talk, he acts so easygoing, as if trudging around deadly terrain is just another day at the office for him, which in a sense, it is, I guess. But he's holding back, I know he is.

I feel like I've been back at that night at the lake for the last couple of weeks. Kaleb is once again trying to protect me from his truths for fear of what it would do to me. I know better than to push, because he's shown me in the past that he'll push back, but I'm a double-sided coin flipping through the air right now. The man I married is someone I know better than anyone else, yet in some ways he's a stranger. I guess I should feel good about being the one person he's at least let partway in and not shut out completely, but some greedy, entitled part of me wants to be the one he lets in all the way.

I kept my promise to him. I told him when Carter tried something, but it was different than when he was still home. He felt some semblance of control when he was near me. But what benefit did it have telling him when he's a million miles away? It was like pouring gasoline on a barely contained fire. He's already in what has got to feel like some kind of alternate plain; a realm of terror and danger, and it gave him one more thing to feel powerless against.

The brush strokes on my canvas were nothing more than colorful blobs in watercolor class today, refusing to take on any kind of life, and I know it's because my inspiration is clouded out of worry for Kaleb. I can feel it in the tone of his emails, and every time we get the chance to video chat, his eyes look a shade darker and his face more hardened. We're both still so young, yet his eyes look like they've seen several lifetimes. And though he's affectionate as ever and tries to keep our interactions light, I can see the undercurrent of frustration and uneasiness flowing just beneath the surface.

This annoying black cloud follows me around the rest of the day, through every class, and sure enough, my pottery project that I was already struggling with goes to shit, and I have to scrap it. Clearly, molding clay is not my niche in the art world, but I want to get a damn passing grade, and after some pleading with my professor, she agrees to let me have use of the studio after hours to try and construct something that will at least accomplish that.

With no one else around, I'm able to employ my go-to method and put on some music. Before I start, I grasp onto my wedding rings that dangle from the chain around my neck and take a few breaths, trying to expel the toxic energy and reset my mind before tucking them back inside my shirt. With a chill indie mix droning in the background with a few hits from my uncle's band thrown in, I'm able to somewhat zone out and create a vase – I know, how basic can I get? While the object itself is pretty plain, I'm able to use my real talent and etch an intricate design wrapping around it. I'm hoping the alternating rows of looping ivy and swirling paisleys will be impressive enough to pass me on this project, and that I can hopefully get my shit together for the next one.

It's late when I put my completed project carefully on the shelf with the other submissions, and after the long trek back to my car, I'm just not feeling the hour drive back to Coyote Creek. While I yearn to get back so that I can wake up already there tomorrow, I'm exhausted and decide to head to my apartment for the night.

The sixteen stairs feel like Mt. Everest as I trudge slowly up them, and I dig through my bag for my key when I reach the summit. I think I hear something as I stick the key in the lock and I still, listening hard. The door at the bottom of the door slams closed, confirming I'm not delirious enough to be hearing things. I feel a quick pang of anxiety and it eases slightly when I remember there's three other studio apartments down this hallway, and it's likely one of the other occupants. My relief is short-live however, when I see who's steadily approaching up the stairs; a casual smile in place, and eyes fixed on me.

24

LUNA

"Carter?" His name falls from my lips in a shudder. "Hey," he says sweetly with a slow blink as if we've just been innocently missing each other all this time and he finally caught up to me. I, on the other hand, feel every bit of me cringing against my racing pulse. My face warms over as I try to keep it neutral while I inwardly panic.

I want to ask him why he's here, but the words won't come. Besides, I don't need an answer. I need to get away from him as fast as possible. I anxiously deliberate if I can turn the key in my lock and throw myself inside fast enough to shut the door on him, or if I can dial 9-1-1 on my phone quicker. I grip the strap of my backpack harder as I turn slightly towards my door, trying to conceal my other hand reaching for my phone in my back pocket.

"Surprise," he holds his hands out, a smile of relief on his face, again, like he hadn't controlled me with mental abuse for the better part of a year, and forged my rejection letter from my school. Like we just got in a little tiff and he was being the bigger person, generously giving me space. "I've had the hardest time getting a hold of you," he relays softly with a small smile like we've been playing a little game of cat and mouse.

I still have no response as I grip my phone in my hand, still trying to figure out a way to discreetly dial for help as I swallow around the lump in my throat. Who would've ever thought that those puppy dog eyes that once made me swoon would terrify me now as he gives them a light-hearted roll. "Okay, I knew you'd be surprised to see me, but I didn't think you'd be speechless," he laughs as he takes a few steps closer.

"You shouldn't be here," the words come out hoarse and quivery.

His shoulders drop with a sigh and he halts his advancement. "Luna," he begins and I can hear the effort it's taking for him to keep his voice steady. "I know I messed up big time with you, and I backed off and gave you what you wanted. You're at your fancy art school, and I gave you more than enough time to cool down, but I didn't think we were done forever or that we'd never talk again." He shakes his head incredulously, and I feel an appalling sense of disbelief pull and twist my facial features.

"There's no reason we can't reconnect," he states, stunning me further. "It was a mistake. I can be forgiven for a mistake, Luna."

My fear is slowly but surely starting to give way to anger at his audacity. "It... was a vile form of betrayal, Carter," I manage to get more words out by using the sheer force of my diaphragm, "on top of the ways you were already controlling and manipulating me."

He huffs out another sigh as if I'm exasperating him, and he blinks hard. "I know it looked that way, but I was giving our relationship my all, and I'd occasionally get a little pissed off when you wouldn't put in the same effort. But I get it now, and if you'll give it another chance, I'll show you."

"No," I vigorously shake my head. "No, Carter. After what you did, you don't get to be in my life anymore. I didn't even go to the cops, you should be thankful that leaving was all I–"

"No, you should be thankful!" he cuts me off, leaning into my space, his voice tight and laced with acid. "You should be thankful that you had someone who loved you like I did, who gave up his nights out with his friends to be with you. Who would buy you flowers and gifts just to show you how much you were adored, and all the thanks you could show was talking about going away to pursue your little hobby!"

I lean away from his angry face and hold up a finger. "Carter, please, this is why I don't want you near me." I hate the tremble in my voice, and right now, I'm thinking about how angry Kaleb was when I told him Carter sent me flowers. I can't even imagine how livid he would be right now, and I want it. I want him here to protect me.

"I'm sorry." Carter's shoulders rise and fall with his heavy breathing as he shakes his head like he doesn't know what just came over him. "Luna, I'm sorry…" he pushes a hand through his hair and turns his back, pacing. I take that moment to bring my phone in front of me and unlock the screen with my face before he turns back around and I turn back to the lock at my door. "Luna, no… please." He hurries the few steps back over to me, holding his hand out. "Please don't go, I didn't mean to get like that. It's just… don't you see what you do to me? That's how much I love you, and I even loved you enough to let you go! Why can't you just stay and listen to me? Give me a chance?"

He's losing stability, his control slipping away. This is how he would get in the past before he'd really start yelling; throwing things or backing me into a corner while he punched the wall beside me.

"I did what I did because I didn't want you to leave me," he grumbles out, trying to stay calm, but I can hear the slight tremor in his voice, and see it in his fingertips as he curls them into a fist at his side. "Doesn't that mean something?" he beckons, a small waver of desperation in his tone.

I stare back at him, willing my eyes not to mist over with fear. I know telling him the truth would be a mistake in this moment; that his so-called devotion meant something alright. It meant how selfish he was.

"And then, just like the saying goes…" he continues, this time taking on a snide tenor, "I loved you so I let you go, just like you wanted, but you didn't come back did you? You were supposed to come back!" He snaps through clenched teeth.

"Carter, I want you to leave." I give my phone another squeeze in my hand behind me and grip my shoulder strap again, trying to ward off the terror coursing through my veins.

"But why, honey?" His shoulders drop, and he's back to harmless Carter again. "I don't get why you're looking at me like I'm some monster."

"Because you put me through a lot of mental abuse, and I don't want you interacting with me anymore," I explain, clenching every muscle in my body in an effort to keep my voice from quaking. "And you shouldn't be here because you're violating a court order not to–"

"Oh yeah…" he rolls his eyes cynically. Mean Carter is back, taunting me with venom in his voice. "The no contact order. That was really fun to get by the way. Made me feel like even more of an idiot than the day you left me, holding your grandmother's hand," he nods, before straightening his back. "Let me ask you something… do you remember the times you used to love when I would do this? When I would just show up at your dorm or surprise you after class? You'd always smile so beautifully when you saw me because you thought it was sweet. That's the kind of love I showed you, and you threw it back in my face!" he practically spits out. "You never appreciated the little things or the big things, or the monumental things like giving you the time and space from me you so desperately craved!" His fury rises another level with each word that passes his lips, and he takes several swift strides towards me.

"Stay away!" The words come out grated with fear as I hold my hand out. This is what finally makes a shadow fall over those eyes, one I'm eerily familiar with.

"I've stayed away long enough, I think." He takes hold of my face in both hands and his touch is surprisingly gentle which makes me panicky and sick. Not that I want him to hurt me, but the confusion of his scathing words with his tender touch are messing with my mind and making my stomach turn over.

I want to scream at him that I'm married to a man that will beat the shit out of him for even touching me, but I'm terrified to even speak, let alone say something that will stoke the flames of his rage. Tears spring to the corners of my eyes and leak out down my cheeks, betraying the brave front I was trying to put on.

"Luna," he whispers calmly, and it petrifies me as he attentively smooths the tears from my face with his thumbs. "Please don't do this... don't push me away. Try to see this as a good thing. Look how much you're loved."

"Stop it," I squeak out in a whisper.

"If you would just quit acting so stubborn and realize a good thing when you have it, this would be so much easier," he continues. "We can go back to being happy."

I want Kaleb. I'm happy with Kaleb, and I want him here this second. I want him to hold me and keep me safe from all of this. But he's not here... so I need to protect myself.

"Get away!" I release a strangled scream as I shove as hard as I can, but he comes right back at me like a pendulum, this time taking hold of my arm and slinging me around to slam my back against my door. My eyes fly open at the shock of the impact – as well as the line he just crossed. When we were together before, he would always act aggressive but he never actually got physical.

"What do I have to do to get through to you?!" he shouts in my face and I let out a whimper, as I can no longer care about feeling mortified. "There's got to be something wrong with you that you don't want me, you ungrateful little bitch!" he hisses at me.

"You're hurting me!" I yell and continue to struggle against him. With one hand still clutching my phone, I press them both against his chest, pushing with all my might to get him away from me.

"Good!" he shouts in my face again. "Maybe something will finally sink in!"

"Get off me, you're scaring me! Help!" I scream, now desperate for anyone in the building or walking by on the street to hear me.

His hand catches mine as I slap at his chest, and a wicked smile pulls at the corners of his mouth. "Finally, look at you, giving a shit." With that, he squeezes my hand and bends, causing a sharp, shattering pain to shoot from my fingers and up my arm.

An ear-splitting shriek tears from my throat at the pain.

Releasing my hand and leaving my last two fingers throbbing, he takes hold of both of my arms. The shock of the pain has made me slightly dizzy, but I keep fighting, only pushing and hitting at him with one hand now as I baby the other close to my chest. I want to do what I'd learned once on a YouTube video – to drop my weight – but with the way he has me pinned it's virtually impossible.

Running out of ideas, I raise my leg and dig my boot into his stomach and shove him away. It's only a foot or two, and only for a second, but it's enough time and space for me to squirm away from the door in the hopes of being able to whirl around and turn the lock over, but Carter is back on me in a blink.

"Good idea," he snarls. "Let's take this inside." He belts one arm around me and reaches for the key to turn it himself.

"No!" I cry out, but this time, I am able to lower my center of gravity, lifting my feet out from under me and letting myself drop. Not expecting that, Carter loses his hold on me and I slip from his arm. Crouched down, I scramble for the steps, seeing it as my only way out, despite how many there are of them.

With my good hand, I pull myself up by the banister but lose my grip on my phone, which goes clattering down a few stairs.

I don't even make it two steps down before Carters hands are on me again, but I don't stop struggling and fighting.

"No you don't," he growls, turning me to face him again. We're facing each other sideways on the stairs. "You're not leaving. You're not leaving again! You're mine!"

In the midst of this frightening chaos, a vision of Kaleb on the video chat flickers through my mind.

I hate not being able to protect what's mine.

It's crazy how after everything that's happened in the last five minutes that what gets under my skin and embeds itself in my being is Carter calling me his.

I'm Kaleb's. I belong to him.

"I am not yours!" I scream as loud as I can. "I've always belonged to someone else you fucking piece of shit!"

I watch the fire ignite in his eyes as he clenches his jaw, staring daggers at me as if with my outburst a decision has been made. The look of malice in those hard-set eyes portrays a sense of finality as he gives my arms one more hard squeeze and swings ninety degrees, putting himself uphill from me and my back facing the descent of stairs.

"Then you don't belong to anybody," he grits out between his teeth as he gives a violent shove forward, releasing my arms.

25

LUNA

Flashing, bright white lights is all I see. That's all my senses pick up on before anything else. I feel nothing and can't hear anything. I don't think I'd even see this light if it wasn't so bright, it's as if it's a right in my face. Where am I? Have I fallen into some state of nothingness?

But then I hear something. I can't tell what it is, some kind of muffling sound. I try with all I have in me to grab onto it, to make sense of it. There's more than one sound, there's several mufflings, taking turns and sounding over each other at the same time.

I feel pain now... it starts simmering in my core, right near my diaphragm, and gets sharper and stronger as it spreads wider throughout my body at an unbearable speed. My mouth falls open and I cry out... but I have no voice. I still can't see, but the muffles are getting louder, almost as fast as the pain is spreading. I don't like it. I don't like the muffling, I want it to stop. As if the owners of the sounds hear me, they get clearer as they get louder. Then there's a pop in my ears, and the muffles become clear voices.

"Driver's License and Military ID in her purse," I hear a female voice say clinically. "Name is Luna Shane."

"Luna?" I hear a deep male voice say cautiously, though loud and clear as a bright light shines in one eye and then the other. It hurts, though I barely feel it in comparison to everything else. My entire body feels like it's threatening to shatter if I try and move the littlest bit.

My hearing seems to go in and out, either that, or I'm going in and out of consciousness.

"Luna?" I hear the man's voice again.

Someone raises my shirt.

"Ow," the miniscule word comes out on a sob as a warm tear slips out of the corner of my eye and down my jawline.

"She's conscious. Receptive to pain," another voice says.

"Severe bruising across ribcage and abdomen," someone says with a hint of urgency underneath their voice.

"Cut it off."

What?! What are they cutting? I panic for a moment before I feel light tugging moving gradually up the front of my shirt.

"She's in bad shape," another female voice utters, sounding regretful. "We should probably get the Red Cross to get ahold of her spouse so he can—"

"No..." the word escapes my lips in a drawn-out groan.

The only thing keeping me going is that you're back there, safe. That my girl is back there thriving and waiting for me.

I hate that I can't be there to protect what's mine.

This will sink Kaleb. He's barely treading water over there with all the things he's going through. I need to be his beacon right now. He'll go mad if he knew something happened to me without him here.

"She's trying to speak. Luna? Luna? Do you know where you are?"

No... not really, but I don't know anyone here... but obviously something horrible happened to me as I can't see and don't feel like I can move. My head hurts and my recollection is hazy but Carters' name is strong at the forefront. He did this.

The pain is dominating every cell in my body, and these people are acting urgent around me...

"E- emer... emerge,"

"Yes, Luna, you're in the ER at St. Andrews," the deep, authoritative voice chimes back in. "You've been through some trauma, but you're safe now and we're here to help you okay?"

"I... ohhh..." I wince again with more tears.

"She can barely speak, let's get some morphine on board."

"No," I say, this time more firmly though it hurts my throat like hell. "No drugs," is all I can choke out. "AA," I add on feebly before letting out a breath I didn't realize I was holding just to get those few words out. I'm not in AA, but letting them go ahead and think I am an addict that's trying to stay clean is the best way to ensure they don't pump me full of narcotics.

"No drugs, she's AA," someone interprets more clearly for me.

"Luna, are you sure?" Deep voice is back. "You've got some bad bruising and broken bones. Will you let us give you something for pain?"

"No," this time I mouth the word and try to shake my head but feel my face scrunch up with another flash of pain and realize I have a neck brace on.

Second time in my life, some weird inner voice jokes in the back of my head. I was put in one when I slipped on the dock and almost drowned as a kid.

"Get me some topical anesthetic and a suture kit," deep voice orders. I'm going to go ahead and guess he's a doctor now. *Just like my dad. Shit. My dad is going to flip a nut when he finds this out. And what the fuck, I need stitches?*

"Luna, we're going to put you under conscious sedation while we reset your bones. It doesn't involve opioids."

I feel my body give up and give in, having used its last ounce of strength. I begin to feel every sensation dissolve and melt into the gurney as I attempt one last protest before the darkness takes me. "Don't call Kaleb... please don't call Kaleb."

LAVENDER MOON

Kaleb

I LOG on to find nothing new in my inbox from Luna. We normally message each other twice a day, every twelve hours or so unless I'm out on a rescue mission, and I always let her know. But my morning email still sits there unanswered.

I let out a heavy sigh, shaking my head and mumbling fuck under my breath. This isn't like her. I know things happen all day every day to keep people from getting to their emails, but I have a bad feeling.

"What's wrong with you?" Alex asks from the seat next to me.

"Haven't heard from Luna since last night," I raise a shoulder.

"Fuck are you pussy whipped," one of my other comrades, Jenkins, clips out from my other side, and it makes my jaw clench. He's good at having his brother's backs while on duty, but when we're at ease, he's one flippant motherfucker.

"Fuck off," I return in a grumble as I open a message draft and start typing.

> *Hey, baby,*
> *It's been a while. I just want to check in and make sure you're okay. I'm sure you had a busy day of classes, just know your man misses you. Write back when you can so I can have my peace of mind.*
> *Xo,*
> *K*

"Clingy much?" he digs again as I close out my email. "She'll get back to you whenever she's gets off of whatever guy she's riding—" He doesn't get to finish his hilarious jab as I'm up out of my seat so fast it topples out from under me.

I grab onto the lapels of his fatigues and haul him up, and his lazy smile as I do so enrages me further.

"Dude, sorry," he holds his hands up casually, completely unfazed by my sudden assault as Alex braces in arm in front of me and reaches past me with the other to literally pry my hands off of Jenkins.

"Calm the fuck down, K," he grumbles before jutting his chin at Jenkins over my shoulder. "And Jenkins, what's your fucking problem, man?"

The asshole shrugs. "Military wives cheat. It's practically a fact of life. Just trying to help you accept it."

"Luna is not like that," I bite out with gnashed teeth. She isn't. The idea of her sneaking around never even crossed my mind because that's how well I know her. There's not a deceitful cell in her beautiful heart, and I'll be damned if I don't lay out anyone who tries to put that thought in my mind.

"Neither was my wife," he confesses, shrugging again with a remorseful headshake. "She was the last person I thought would. But army wives... they get lonely and insecure, followed by impatient." His face falls as he imparts this knowledge from personal experience.

I get ahold of myself too, gently shaking Alex off, letting him know I'm cool. "I'm sorry your wife cheated, but don't you ever question mine's character," I say in a controlled growl, piercing him with a glare.

He takes a moment, looking like he's thinking of saying more before clamping his lips together. "I'm sorry," he murmurs out quickly instead before turning and striding out of the room.

"She's alright, K," Alex quietly reassures from behind me. "She probably just got caught up in something."

I give a barely there nod as I consider this, and will it to be true. She has to be okay or I might as well walk right out onto the front lines right now. And the thing is, I'm not just worried about her. I fucking miss her so bad it causes a tightness in my chest. I had no idea those twice a day emails and occasional video chats were getting me by like regular doses of medicine. I just want to hear from her; hear about how much she hates her pottery class, and how she's making friends around Coyote Creek. How she drenched herself trying to fix the leaky pipe under the bathroom sink. All of it soothes the cold, rock-heaviness I carry around here every day.

I'm not mad, but until I know she's okay, I won't be either.

26

LUNA

Stiff, all-over pain is what my body registers before my eyes even open. My body feels like cold, rusted metal, but I'll take this kind of pain over the kind from when I was in the E.R., the kind that made me feel like I was being ripped apart by a pack of wolves.

I blink and roll my head to the side and reach up to rub at my eyes when I realize there's an annoyingly awkward splint on my right hand – my dominant hand of course. Sighing, I drop it on the mattress beside me with my left hand.

At least I can still wear my wedding rings, I think, which triggers a jolt of panic to strike me in the middle of my chest as I place my hand to my chest, feeling around for my necklace with my rings, hoping they're resting against my skin under my hospital gown. No dice. Where are they?

With a shaky left hand, I reach for the remote that lies in the bed next to me, attached to a long, thick cord and hit the call button that summons a nurse.

Within a minute, an older woman in navy scrubs is in the doorway. "Hey, you're awake," she cheerfully congratulates me as she moseys in. "How are you feeling?"

"Do you know where my things are?" I ask, dodging her question. I don't mean to be rude but I'm inwardly panicking, and its worse torture than the pain. "My necklace? With my wedding rings?" My voice is serrated by my erratic breathing, and the nurse holds a calming hand up.

"Yes, honey, we have all your things right here." She opens a cupboard to the left of my bed. "We have a personal safe in every room for patient belongings. Your rings and your cell phone are right in here, do you want them?"

"Yes, please." I nod vigorously in relief and she hands me a clear baggy with my rings on the chain, and another that contains my cell phone that has a cracked, lifeless screen.

Shit. I was hoping to turn it on and message Kaleb ASAP. I haven't messaged him since... when? Was it yesterday morning? The night before?

"What day is it?" I ask the nurse as I slide my wedding band onto my left ring finger. Fortunately, it's only the last two fingers of my hand that are broken, so I still have some dexterity.

"It's Friday afternoon," she tells me, watching me slide my engagement ring down over the top of the band. "Are you sure you don't want me to call your husband?"

That word still seems so foreign. We've been married for over five months, but we've hardly been together during that time. It doesn't change how I feel though. I love him. I love him so much and I miss him desperately right now. How I wish he were here and could crawl in this bed with me and hold me.

"I'm sure," I breathe out, wincing as I shift in the bed and take my phone out of the baggy and try to power it on. Dead as a doornail. "But I'll get ahold of him if I can get a phone charger?" I lift my phone up to indicate.

She nods warmly. "Actually, when I called your father earlier, I told him that's one of the best things to bring in. Nobody expects to be here, and therefore don't have those kinds of things with them. But I guess he knew that, being a doctor himself."

I nod. I can just barely remember one of the times they woke me up last night to do neuro checks. It's fuzzy, but I'd been asked for the umpteenth time if I wanted anyone to call Kaleb. Finally, I decided I wanted someone. I'm going to tell Kaleb this one day, when he's not going through hell, but even then he's going to be horrified – and it will be even worse if he found out I went through this completely alone.

I was almost as hesitant to call for my dad, afraid this would bring back memories for him. A certain tragedy from his life before me and my mom, and I don't want to give him another similar experience in his life. But on the opposite side of that same coin, he knows a lot about trauma.

So I finally conceded to the staff calling him, but with specific instructions.

"Did you use my maiden name when you called him?" I ask, and she nods again.

"Yes, sweetheart, I said Isaak."

"Thank you." I wince again. My ribcage feels like it's going to break open if I so much as sneeze. When I was taken off sedation last night, the doctor surveyed the damage with me. Three broken ribs on the left side, a slight concussion, a bruised kidney, and the broken fingers. As for the nurse using my maiden name with my dad… I know I'm going to have to tell him now, even though I really wanted to wait until Kaleb came home, but I really didn't want him to find out through some stranger over the phone. "Is he coming?"

"Yes, he is," she assures me. "He should be here soon."

In the next half hour, Bonnie – my nurse, helps me go to the bathroom. I can't tell you how glamorous it is to pee on a bedside commode with someone standing by, but she wanted to start with baby steps to see what I could handle. My legs are surprisingly okay, save for some bruising and a sprained knee, but it's crazy what little movements hurt my ribs.

She attentively changes my gown and my bandages when

she helps me get back into bed, and she's just pulling the covers back over me when my dad, looking disheveled as all hell in a wrinkled button-down over his joggers and his brown hair completely mussed arrives in the door.

The relief that washes over me like a tsunami immediately brings tears to my eyes, and I let go of every shred of strength I've been carrying.

"Dad," I sob as he rushes over to me. I grip onto his shoulder with my good hand as he cradles my head and drops a kiss to the top of it. I don't know which one of us is more relieved to see the other as he rocks me slightly.

"It's okay, kiddo… I'm here, it's going to be okay."

"Carter fucking Lange," my dad grinds out between clenched teeth as he paces my hospital room in front of the uniformed cop that's jotting things down on his pocket-sized notepad. "He's been harassing her for over a year, and he violated a court order showing up at her apartment! He did this," he continues growling, resting his hands on his hips as he continues to pace.

I sit back in my bed, trying my best to stay calm, but also leave my dad to let loose. In a way, I feel like I'm doing something for Kaleb by proxy. When I do tell him all of what happened, I'm hoping he'll take a small piece of solace knowing I let my father go apeshit in his stead.

"This kid went so far as to forge a rejection letter from NIA to get her to stay with him in Detroit. He's obsessed!"

"Can you confirm all this, Ms. Shane?" the cop asks as he looks up from his notepad, his eyebrows raised at me.

I feel a cold sensation shoot down my throat to the pit of my stomach as my mouth falls open.

"It's Isaak," my dad puffs out, still continuing to speak for me, and carrying on with his pacing.

"Her license says Shane," the officer points out.

Just as dad tilts his head up with his brow pinched at the officer, I intervene before he can say anymore.

"Officer? Could you give us a couple of moments, please?" I ask, my eyes pleading. I know he has to finish getting my statement, but I need just a moment for dad to hear this from me.

The cop stares at me a moment before hesitantly nodding. "Okay, but not too long," he concedes, shifting his weight backward before turning and ambling out the door and my dad turns his face to mine, his expression unreadable.

"Dad..." I start, while a hummingbird furiously beats his wings in my ribcage. There's no easy way to say this, and it's torture on my already battered spirit to draw it out, so I just say it. "I married Kaleb."

He stares hard at me for a moment, and it makes me flash back briefly to the few times I got in trouble as a kid. I feel scrutinized under that stare as he searches my face for signs of what, I don't know. "What do you mean? What are you talking about, Luna?" He fires off both questions, blinking rapidly.

I let out a shuddery sigh, trying not to let my hands shake. "Before he deployed, Kaleb and I got married."

"Before he deployed?" Dad leans his head forward as if he didn't hear me right. "That was several months ago and you had just started dating, what do you mean you married him?" There's no surprise to him that Kaleb and I found each other again and fell in love, as we chat often, but I'm giving him the story in small pieces so that he can wrap his head around each one.

"He needed someone the Army could contact in case something happened to him, Dad," I explain gently, "otherwise they were going to contact his father, and I've told you what a bad person he is. He just wanted his home to be okay in case something happened."

"Luna," my dad sighs, and I can see his hands clenching on

his hips as he shakes his head. "I can't believe you'd do this – marry someone so quickly when you're both so young..." he trails off as he stares off towards the far wall. He clearly doesn't know what to make of this. It hasn't sunk in deep enough for him to process.

"I love him," I say quietly, "and I'd do anything for him. He had no one, Dad."

My father lets out a rattling breath before bringing his hands to scrub up and down his face before pulling them into prayer position.

"We also thought my having a different last name would help with the Carter situation." I inwardly cringe at the asshole's name.

"And you've been married all this time," he grumbles out. Not once during this bombshell has he raised his voice. I actually wish he would lay into me instead of the disappointment his low tone is conveying. "My twenty-one-year-old daughter has been married this whole time. You didn't tell me or your mother," he finishes with a solemn look at me.

"We wanted to give you guys some time to get used to us being together," I mumble while staring down at my lap. "We thought that would be easier on everyone," I finish and lift an uncomfortable shoulder.

And fat lot of good the name change did me when my studio's lease is in my maiden name. I'm sure that's how that despicable shit found me. If I'd just gone home instead of there...

Fortunately, a tap of knuckles on the open door keeps me from falling too far down that rabbit hole.

"I'm afraid I need to finish getting your statement, Ms. Shane," the officer's voice rumbles, but he gives me a tenderly regretful look before I look to my dad to check in.

His hands have found his hips again, and his shoulders rise with the deep breath he pulls in. "We're going to talk about that at another time," he informs me, referring to my eloping with

Kaleb. "I'm going to need some time to get my head around it anyway." His lips press together as I nod like an obedient kid. "Right now, let's focus on getting you better and making sure Carter gets his ass tossed in a jail cell," he sighs before coming over to sit in the chair by my bed. It's like his way of stating he's shoved this conversation in its own compartment and is focusing on the matter at hand, leaning in close with his arm on the bed rail. My dad is giving me one hundred percent of his support right now as I confirm and clarify everything for the officer.

Dad lays a hand on my shoulder and gives it a squeeze as I recount every excruciating detail. When he's confident he got everything, the officer gives me his card, as well as that of the detective assigned to the case.

"Is mom okay?" I ask my dad after the cop takes his leave.

He takes in a breath to answer, just as I hear his phone ping and he reaches in his pocket, pulling it out and looking at the screen. "Your mother is a damn wreck," he reports, holding the phone up to indicate this isn't the first text he's gotten from her. "You don't know what it took to convince her to stay home. You're her baby girl, and she doesn't like that you worry about what this would do to her. In the end, I explained that Matthew shouldn't see you like this, and since I'm the one with the medical license, I should be the one to be here." He exhales, gripping the bridge of his nose and then scrubbing his palm over his forehead.

I drop my head, feeling immense shame. Noticing my phone that's charging in the bed next to me, I distract myself by picking it up to examine it, and though the screen has a nasty crack in it, it seems to be charging and functioning okay. I look back up at him. "Dad, I know you have to tell Mom everything, but I was wondering if maybe you guys could… not tell Matty?" I ask cautiously. My brother's so young and I feel the need to shield him from the evils of the world, futile as it may be. "At the very least, I just don't want him worrying about me. He should just get to be a kid."

My dad's eyes dart around slightly as he turns the thought over his head, and then he nods. "Yeah... we can do that."

"Thank you." The words seep out on the breath I was holding just as my phone rings next to me, startling me. I pick it up and squint at the screen. It's hard to decipher who's calling as it's a number I don't recognize, and the big-ass crack doesn't help.

"That better not be that piece of shit trying to call you!" My dad's words come out between teeth clenched so hard, you'd think his jaw has been wired shut.

The number is longer than the ten digits the States use. "It's foreign," I observe as it rings a second time and a possibility lights up and explodes in my chest, making me gasp as I frantically swipe to answer.

"Hello?" My voice wavers with the hope of who it could be.

"Lu? Baby?" I hear Kaleb's gorgeous voice like comforting velvet, and I feel the concrete barrier inside me crack and give way, a damn of emotions flooding out.

"Kaleb..." my voice is barely there as I choke on a sob and tears prick at the backs of my eyes.

"Oh, baby, thank God." His voice comes through the line on a heavy breath, and I smile through my tears as I look up at my dad. He's taking me in, his brown eyes looking like they're taking several pieces of a puzzle and putting them together. Finally, he gives me a somber smile that's hard to decode until he strolls a few steps forward and leans down to place a kiss to the top of my head. I look up at him gratefully as he straightens up before turning towards the door, looking down at his own phone before he moseys out the door, no doubt to return my mother's persistent messages.

"Are you okay?" Kaleb's voice sounds mildly distressed in my ear, and I feel the rest of my resolve breaking apart. I had no idea that I'd even been trying to hold myself together all this time until Kaleb's voice signaled that it was okay for me to let go. I start sobbing uncontrollably into the phone.

"Oh, Kaleb…" I barely manage to get out between sniffs and hiccups.

"Hey, hey…" he coos soothingly like he's trying to urgently make me better as quickly as possible. "Shhh… babe, it's okay. What's going on?"

I sniffle as my voice quakes. "I just miss you so much…"

27

KALEB

I've never seen or heard Luna cry. Ever.

Even when we fell out years ago, she didn't cry because she was too busy tearing me a new asshole. She's always been my happy, silly girl that's always kept me up whenever the universe tries to drag me down. Even all these miles away, in this grim underworld of darkness and gunfire, her messages and seeing her smiling face on video chat are what have kept me from getting buried.

"I miss you too, my girl..." I tell her quietly into the phone.

Phone calls home are hard to make here, hence the use of the internet, and even that isn't secure. I had to plead my case to my commanding officer that I had reason to believe something was wrong at home, and without her saying anything, I know that I was right. The way she's crying like this proves it.

"Luna, what happened?" I ask, my voice letting out a trace of the desperation that I'm trying to keep in. "Are you alright, baby?"

"I just miss you," she tells me between gasps. "I've been fine for the last few months, but yesterday, I just... had the day from hell," she stammers. "And it all just boiled over I guess, and it just made me wish you were here."

"I wish I was there too," the words rush out of me without hesitating. Thrusting a hand in my hair, I turn and slump against the wall, dipping my chin to my chest. She's made me feel a myriad of things all the years I've known her; amazingly beautiful things. Never has she made me feel like this. Needed. Wanted so badly it hurts my heart in both the best and worst of ways. "What happened, baby? I knew something was up when I didn't hear from you when I usually do. I even had to sit out last night's patrol. /my captain said I was too unfocused, which is too much of a risk."

That had pissed me off too. Of all the times I needed something to do, to be useful, I got pulled to basically sit on my ass and worry about both Luna and my brothers. Drove me half insane.

I hear a sniffle, then a pause, followed by a deep breath on her end. "Really?"

"Yeah, it puts you and your brothers in danger, they preach it to us all the time." Drilled into us is more like it. We have to be mentally checked out from our home lives, otherwise our guard is down and our reflexes go to shit. "All vigilance goes out the window if we're too preoccupied," I add.

"That makes sense." Her words come out on a shuddery breath that makes me close my eyes with the pain I feel of not being there. "I'm so sorry."

"Shhh...no," I say with a gentle firmness. "It's not your fault, baby. Not at all. I just want to help. Can you tell me what happened?"

"Well... it started with a run-in with your lovely ex and went downhill from there," she sniffs, and my head snaps up.

"What did she say to you?" My voice is weighted with the threat of anger. Even after three years Cheyenne's been petty as fuck, as she proved when she met Luna. Makes me wonder if I'm going to have to make wild love to my woman right on her bar for her to get the picture.

"Just some feeble shit, and I gave it right back to her," she responds.

"Good girl," I murmur my firm approval into the phone.

"It just got my day off to a shitty start and it was one thing after another. I even lost my phone for a while and... and that was the worst part because I just wanted to read any messages from you and talk to you."

Hearing her like this is ripping me apart while humbling me at the same time. I hate that she's hurting, and I feel like I would burn down the world to make it stop. But it makes my heart soar to know that she's also yearning for me too. "If I were there right now, I would take you to bed and hold you tightly against me all night long."

"I need that so bad right now," her voice still wobbles on a ragged sigh.

"I want you to sleep in one of my shirts tonight, alright?"

"I will."

"Lu..." I falter, as I know I'm not good at this. "You know how much I love you, right? I know I don't say it out loud a whole lot, but I do. So much."

"I know," she whispers. "I know it because you show it. And when you do say it, it's extra special."

I drop my head back against the wall, closing my eyes at the relief and the peace that came with that. The warmth they just brought to my soul washes over me and I'm grateful. I'm so grateful that she knows how much I love her and understands the way I show it. And while I would never ever wish any kind of pain on Luna, I can't deny that having a purpose in someone else's life; to fulfill a deep need within them, means more to me than I can say. I've never been that to anyone before her.

"We're almost halfway done with this baby," I tell her, unable to think of anything else to say. And because it feels so right in this moment, I add, "Then I come home to you."

"Where you belong," she tacks on, her voice steadier now.

How about that... I belong to someone. "Damn right."

Luna

FOR THE FIRST time in my life, I lied to Kaleb. Maybe I didn't tell him a made-up story, but I gave him an explanation full of half-truths and omissions, and I hate myself for it. I as good as lied.

And I lie to him still when we video chat, by keeping my splinted right hand out of sight and trying not to show I'm in pain or have trouble breathing because of my broken ribs. I lie simply by smiling at him through my phone screen and keeping my text light-hearted in my emails.

As much as it cuts at my heart, what he told me on the phone when I was in the hospital really got to me. That having his mind on personal issues, or worrying about loved ones, can get him killed. If he's not one hundred and ten percent focused and vigilant while out on patrol, a one second delay in response can cause epic destruction and cost lives – including his.

The way he blew up when I told him about the flowers Carter sent to my parent's house also flashed back to my mind. If he knew what he did... he'd go mad.

I'm going to tell him when he comes back, and I've made my peace with the fact that he's going to be multiple levels of furious – not just about what happened, but at me for keeping it from him. He'll be livid... but he'll be alive, which is the only outcome I can live with.

The last three weeks have been a spiral of shame, fear, and anger, to say the least. My conversation with my parents about how Kaleb and I hadn't seen each other in three years and then got married after three days went about as well as you'd expect. Combine that with the terror of what happened to me, and I'm frankly surprised it didn't send my mother over the edge. Actually, I'm not surprised. She's held it together and been more solid than an oak against her addiction the last fifteen years, but I'm still glad it didn't send her running for the pills.

Her shock and disappointment at the marriage made me feel like I'd failed her and my dad. Combine that with my trauma and injuries, and I suddenly felt like a burden, no matter how much they preached and professed how much they love me and this wasn't my fault.

The hindering feelings only got worse, of course, when Carter was found and taken in for questioning, but later released by his lovely lawyer cousin, who's basically his blood brother. He was able to argue that Carter didn't lay a finger on me. He couldn't deny he was there, and breaking his court order, but that only worked in his favor. By pleading guilty to that, he was given credibility that I was just trying to get away from him in a haste and clumsily tripped down the stairs. He just wanted to talk and I lost my shit, screamed at him to get away, and tried to call the police while fleeing down the stairs, and oops… that's his story, and it's his word against mine.

So while Carter is forbidden to leave the city of Detroit, he's not in jail either. He, so far, seems to be taking his cousin's advice to have no contact with me seriously, but I'm terrified, as it's the one part of my life it seems he wasn't able to find anything out about. He doesn't know I'm married, as the idea of me being with anyone but him has never entered his puny brain, and so to him, Kaleb, our house, this town – they don't exist.

Coyote Creek is the only place I feel safe. My parents agreed, despite their misgivings about my hasty marriage, and though they wanted me to come and stay with them, I was able to talk them out of it. As much as they could argue that who could I be safer with than with my parents whose purpose in life is to do just that, I could argue that I didn't want to be in the same city as Carter. His whole restriction on not being able to leave the vicinity is a lot less effective when I'm in it with him, not to mention I just plain don't want to be on the same planet, let alone the same state.

It took a lot of debating and convincing, but I wouldn't allow either of them to come stay with me either, and I know how miraculous it is that I won out. For the first time in I don't know when, I actually got a little agitated with them both and I think that might have sent some kind of message not to push the issue. I told them that feeling like a hindrance was making my healing process worse, and that it would be better for my recovery to have some peace. What I didn't come right out with is that I'm in a weird paradox of wanting to be alone yet close to Kaleb in some way.

The ending compromise was that I have to check in twice a day, and not just by phone or text, but FaceTime so that my parents aren't wondering if Carter found me and is messaging them from my phone. Given the circumstances, I forgive them for being neurotically overprotective, and even if it does make me feel like I'm back in middle school, I'll take it. Having them around while I recoup would be a true blessing, but it would also make me feel compelled at some point to talk about things I'm not ready to talk about, and my mental bandwidth has diminished significantly to where staying strong for Kaleb is all I have enough for.

I sit here now, at my easel, a blank canvas in front of me, and no music now. What used to inspire me and get me flowing is now too much stimuli. My mind just can't handle any noise right now, and I revel in the quiet as I nibble on my left thumbnail, trying to get something – anything – to materialize in my head.

Painting used to clear my head, and I mentally beg for it to do that now. With everything that's fallen apart and gone to shit, my head is so noisy and full. While I took the first week off classes, I'm now playing catch up, and when I do go into the city, it's for school only, and I carry my keys at my side, constantly looking over my shoulder when I'm not in the safety of a class-room. I've since ordered a can of pepper spray to hang on my keyring and a taser to keep in my purse, and once my injuries have fully healed, I intend to sign up for a self-defense class. If

I'm truly going to press on with giving Kaleb nothing to worry about, I have to work on it.

God, why won't my head clear? Why is there not a drop of paint on my canvas? I look down to my variety of paints in their case – every shade of every color of the rainbow… and none of them are speaking to me. No scene or design is calling to me to be put into a beautiful visual.

As the anxiety and stress twist and tangle together with the anger and fear inside me, I reach for the black. Holding it up, I wonder if there's a color darker, one that would represent the torment that's happening inside me right now. The shade I hold in my hand is pitch, and I hate feeling this way, like it's just not dark enough to express how I feel.

I've never been one to give into feelings like these… and I can't now. I give in, and then I'm lost down that rabbit hole forever, useless to Kaleb.

Black is for mixing, Luna, I lecture myself. You don't use the color on its own, it's not your style.

Placing the black paint back down in the bin I take in a restless breath, and just as I'm letting it out is when my phone goes off with a video chat request. Grabbing it up, I swipe the screen to accept, and it populates with my handsome soldier, looking ragged and tired, but otherwise happy to see me.

"Hey, silly girl," he smiles with hooded eyes, and he looks relieved, like it's been a hell of a day, and this is the only good thing about it. This… this is what I'm fighting for. This is what keeps me pressing on.

Tilting my head, I smile back at him. "Hey, soldier."

28

KALEB

For the last two months, Luna's been acting… well, herself… but it's like she's turned it up a notch and it's got me confused. The idea that I'm confusing myself is just one of the many swirling around in the tornado of turmoil in my brain at the moment.

Between the fucked-up hours I'm keeping, the sullen and apathetic attitudes my brothers have taken on – and rubbed off on me some – and just the plain uncertainty all have me not knowing which way is up. Finding some of my brothers drenched in their own blood as their body slowly dies next to a civilian they were trying to save, has jaded some of the rest of my platoon to the point where it's just like another day at the office for them, whereas I seem to be using all my mental energy on holding onto my sense of humanity. What little bandwidth I have leftover tries to make sense of everything else, but ends up just tying me into knots.

Just like I try not to turn to the dark side and lose my empathy for the lives injured and lost over here, I try to hold onto the notion that my Luna is doing nothing more than trying to give me one less thing to worry about. And then that begs the question of what it is she's not telling me in the interest of that.

Whatever it is, it can't be about Pops' shop and the new hire, West. Just like last time she updated me, she's had nothing but positive things to say about the guy and his work ethic.

"He works hard and gets the job done right, at least according to Jackson." She lifts the shoulder that's keeping Jackson's young son hoisted on her hip, the very same one that she relieved him of when we met in the office just before my deployment. She's been babysitting for him and his wife; her way of contributing, as she put it.

"That's so good to hear," I sigh in relief, shaking my head at the news as I watch her carry the small boy towards the shop via the video screen. Talk about the pot calling the kettle black; I've been doing the same thing I'm recently suspecting her of: acting like everything is a-okay so that she doesn't worry. She flashes me another smile as she turns her head to watch her step as she maneuvers through one of the garage bays, and I notice one of the back strands of her hair hanging down from her messy bun. The purple she normally keeps hidden back there has faded some.

"And look!" She raises her brows before I can even comment on it. Her brown eyes dazzle behind her lashes with the smile she's maintaining as she shifts the phone away to showcase her entrance into the office. As she pans her phone across the desk, I find it in tidy, clean, and dare I say, orderly condition. It's completely clear of clutter, and when she shifts the camera up, I see Jackson sitting behind it, lounged back in his chair while he plays around on his phone. He looks laid back and relaxed in comparison to the nervous wreck he was when I left.

"Hey, look at that," I marvel at the mess-free desk as she hands the now one year-old boy off to his father.

After Jackson thanks her, she makes her way back out the way she came, and I catch a glimpse of West in the background, confidently focusing on twisting a cap in place beneath someone's hood before glancing at his watch. The shop seriously looks like it's running just as smooth as when it did with Pops at the helm.

"So," Luna breathes out, and I can see a puff of white vapor escape her mouth. It's February and it shows as her cheeks get pink from the cold air, and I can hear the crunch of gravel mixed with snow beneath her feet as she walks back to her car. "This is the part where I go back home and miss the shit out of you while I try to paint." She rolls her eyes and quirks a half smile at herself.

"What do you mean try to paint?" I guffaw at her choice of words. She seems to falter, her lips falling open as her eyes downcast momentarily but she quickly blinks out of it.

"Eh, you know… just not a lot of inspiration. It's the weather." She lifts a casual shoulder as she reaches her car and slouches back against it. "It's like that in the winter sometimes."

Being that she and I have never spent time together in the cold months, this is new to me. "Huh…" I lift an eyebrow in thought. "Alright then, well, I have faith you'll be able to tonight."

"Why?" She tucks a wayward strand of hair behind her ear.

"Because one of us has to," I say simply. "And you're not you if you're not creating something beautiful."

Her smile is small, her lips taking on a blue hue as she nods, shifting her eyes off camera.

Yeah… she's definitely stressed or tired but doesn't want to tell me. She doesn't want me to worry, and she's right to feel that way. I seem to spiral so easy when things go sideways, especially when it's things that are thousands of miles away that I have no control over. It gives me one of those rare moments where I don't inwardly question what's behind her happy-go-lucky demeanor. It's a peaceful feeling, like everything is as it should be, and I savor it, knowing it will be gone in a matter of moments.

"Speaking of beautiful…" I raise an eyebrow at her, waiting for her to look back at me, and she does, giving me a coy smile. "Watch the mail. It's almost Valentine's Day, you know."

That does it. She may be tough, but my girl is a sucker for romance and she lights right up.

"Shane!" My C.O.'s booming voice makes my shoulders jerk as it rattles the room. "Report for duty!"

"I've got to go, baby," I tell her regretfully, but I'm pleased the smile is back on her face.

"Okay, I love you," she tells me.

"You too," I return, before raising a commanding finger at her. "And you hit that canvas."

She chuckles, rolling her bright brown eyes as I blow her a kiss before signing off.

Luna

UGHH… I feel so clammy after sweating my ass off during my kickboxing workout and then leaving the facility in West Bridge to make the freezing cold walk to my car. I've been at it for months now, taking classes alternating between basic self-defense, kickboxing, and jiujitsu.

I feel gross and I should've showered there at the gym, but I'm eager to get home and see if the gift Kaleb teased me about has arrived, because so far, this Valentines isn't shaping up to be the best one for my books. It started with no morning email from Kaleb, which was a bummer. I know sometimes his patrols go overtime and so he can't always get to the office on his post, it's happened plenty during his deployment. But still, I was looking forward to a sweet, mushy message to start my day off – especially after the hell this week has been.

Two days ago, I had to go to a hearing and testify against Carter. Both my mom and dad were there, and it thankfully didn't proceed any longer than it had to. But it was still sickening being in the room with that monster. I answered every question and refused to look at him the entire time, even though

I could feel the burn of his gaze while he stared at me from my periphery. When it was over, I pushed away from the table and hightailed it out as fast as I could with my parents hot on my heels, and I've been trying to forget it ever since. I've been hitting it hard at the gym ever since, even today, the day of love or not.

Now, as I park my car in the driveway, I can think of nothing else but curling up in front of Netflix with Buster and hopefully finding that surprise from Kaleb. If nothing else, I hope I at least get a message from him.

I'm just stomping up the front porch steps when a beautiful sight stops me in my tracks momentarily. I can't believe it. In a pale, pearlescent vase, stands a dozen roses, each in a different shade of purple, adorned with curly strips of purple ribbon. The assortment is breathtaking. I mean it, I can't take a breath because it's lodged in my chest where my hand rests, trying to calm the exhilarated rhythm of my heart.

Absently, I set my keys down on the little table to fully take in the beautiful display, caressing a fingertip over the smooth and silky petals. My eyes dart around, taking in each one, and I realize what has been planted sporadically in between the stems - paintbrushes. Brand new paint brushes with beautiful bristles in all different sizes, hide like sweet little secrets between the mass of stems and petals.

Finally, I take hold of the card from its plastic folder and unfold the tiny envelope.

> *To my wife on our first Valentines Day*
> *Sorry we're spending it apart.*
> *But I love you, silly girl.*
> *Love, your soldier.*
> *Xoxo*

This bouquet couldn't be any more perfect. It's everything.

Letting out an elated sigh, I snatch my keys back up and unlock the door. Scooping up the roses, I scramble through the threshold, eager to message Kaleb about how much I love his beautiful gift. I drop my bag just inside the small foyer and kick off my boots before continuing further into the house.

Once in the kitchen, I rush the vase over to the island counter and carefully set it down before hastily whipping off my coat. God, if I could only call him or FaceTime him, or obviously have him here so that I can jump on him. Emailing him will have to do, and I want to do it now, while I'm still giddy and glowing so that it at least comes out in my text. And shit, my phone is... it's in my bag by the door.

As if to summon me to its whereabouts, I hear my phone start ringing from the foyer and I frolic through the house towards my bag. When I retrieve it from the side pocket, I find an unknown number flashing across the screen, much like the one Kaleb called me from when I was in the hospital.

Oh my God, I wonder if they let him call me today because of Valentines.

I fumble with excitement and almost drop the phone as I swipe the screen and bring the phone to my ear, my smile so wide it's hurting my face.

"I got your gift, babe, and it's sooo beautiful," I swoon into the phone.

"Is this Luna Shane?" I hear a serious and gruff voice on the other end, and immediately I feel dizzy.

"Y-yes?" I stammer, gripping onto the back of a nearby chair. I swear I'm seeing black spots in my vision and the room is tilting sideways as the man continues to talk. I only pick up on certain words as if they're flying through the air, and I'm only able to grab onto and process select ones.

The is Second Lieutenant Guitierez... the commanding officer of Corporal Shane's unit...he's been severely injured...

Severely injured.

Oh my God he's hurt...Kaleb's hurt...but sweet Jesus, he's not dead...or wait... how bad is he hurt? Could he die?

My breath is coming in raw gasps as I try to keep up.

"Wh-what happened, is he okay?"

"He's stable," is all I hear before take another sharp breath and let it out, closing my eyes to keep the world from spinning. I only pick up more pieces of what the Lieutenant tells me as I hold a hand over my mouth, trying not to sob in his ear.

Unit was doing a sweep of a nearby town... unexpected explosion... burns... shrapnel... surgery...

My brain finally rejoins the conversation when I hear the man say "... will be transferred stateside in the next two weeks. I will be in touch with updates."

He's coming home, oh God, he's coming home.

"Thank you," I barely whisper out as we disconnect the call. I only just now realize that I've been gripping onto the threshold between the foyer and living room all this time. I let go, allowing myself to slump to the floor. I can feel the flush creeping up my neck and my head still feels disconnected from my body. Shit.

I scramble to my feet and hustle through the living room, staggering through the lightheadedness until I make it to the kitchen and retch over the sink. My stomach cramps and caves as I empty its contents in a series of heaves. When I feel I can trust there's no more coming, I turn on the faucet, simultaneously rinsing out my mouth and the sink, before patting my face dry with a nearby dish towel.

My breathing deep and rhythmic, I try to reel in my calm while at the same time trying to sort through the whirlwind of thoughts in my head.

He's coming home, but... it shouldn't have been this way. It's four months early, but I would give those four months back just to have him come back unharmed, not to mention his spirit still intact. What happened must've been terrible... horrifying... painful. Even for the toughest of the tough like Kaleb, this had to be so frightening and traumatic.

Folding my arms on the counter and resting my head on them, I try to sift through my conversation with the official that called me, but everything is mud. There's only one thing that I've taken away clear, and it's the very obvious.

Kaleb's coming back… and he's going to need me more than ever.

29

KALEB

*P*ain sears through me as something jagged and hot scrapes across the flesh of my shoulder, making me see white-hot light behind my eyes. I barely have time to register the sharp pierce of the lead before another hit tears through my side, bouncing along my rib cage. I feel every cell react to the agony as another bullet whizzes by my ear, the sound like a mosquito from hell – which is where I am.

Then, as if those two hits were gearing up for the grand finale, the ultimate pain blasts through the meat of my thigh. It's like some beastly creature with hot steel for teeth is sinking them in and mangling my leg.

I feel my body fall with a thud against the dirt, my head slamming hard against something, ringing my bell louder than shit. That, and the other various points of pain on my body are lighting me up, the rest of my senses picking up everything and nothing all at once. It's hot, like all around me is fire, yet the pain drowns it out. The noise… gunshots and explosions and… some kind of sputtering, gurgling sound beside me. Someone choking on something. What the fuck? I almost want to laugh to myself because some bastard has the nerve to just lie here and choke while the world is quite literally exploding around them.

Risking burning my eyes in the hot smokey air, I crack them open just enough to see a blur of snow falling in slow motion. How the fuck can that be? It's so damn hot here, yet I'm certain those are fat, grey snowflakes. And rain? It's hard to tell against the night sky and the glare of the fire all blurring together in my burning eyes.

I smell everything burning, and it makes my stomach turn over. Rubber, metal, dirt, and what I don't want to believe is human flesh; it's all burning and making my gut revolt.

I feel the heat creeping around me, closing in, and I'm boiling. And then just as quickly, I feel cold. Merciful cold is enveloping me in frost, chasing the flames away.

And the visions flash through my head. Luna, laughing as she flings her paintbrush at me, splattering blue paint across my shirt and face. Cut to another flash where she runs from me, squealing with laughter before I catch her in my arms and smear my face all over hers while she hollers in delighted protest. Her smile is brighter than any light I've ever seen as she laughs loud and hard, blue paint clinging to the strands of hair that have come loose from her messy bun.

My vision tries to blur back to life, and when I hold my hand up in front of my face, I find it coated in liquid that turns from dark blood red to bright blue paint and back again.

Returning my hand to press down over the oozing raw wound on my leg, I bring my mind to that moment with Luna. I will myself to be there with her instead of this filthy hell; fighting the blackness that tries to burn it away from the edges in like an old photograph.

Death can take me, but he can't choose what I see when I go with him. Keeping my eyes closed, I hold Luna from behind, both of us covered in paint splatters on the hallway floor. I breathe her in and smile into her neck as the blackness takes over.

My own panicked shouts and heavy breathing are what bring me back to wakefulness once again. It was like this in Germany, where I was first sent, and continues here stateside. And, cue the medical staff that comes rushing in, trying to talk me down while shining their annoying fucking penlights in my eyes and quizzing me on my orientation to self, time, and place.

"Corporal Shane, try to relax. Do you know where you are?" one of the nurse-bots asks me, and I wish she'd just fuck off and leave me alone. I can calm myself down, I don't need these people checking to see if I'm crazy.

Because no such luck. Going insane would be a godsend right now, but I'm completely alert and oriented, and my miserable reality couldn't be clearer. Slipping into some oblivious state would be a merciful experience. Or better yet, if the alternative had happened like I thought it was going to… like it was supposed to.

I bat them away and growl as I throw an arm over my eyes to block them out. "Corporal Kaleb Shane, Second class. My birthday is January 22nd, and I'm this damn military hospital in Maryland," I gripe out before cynically adding, "anything else you need to know? My middle school locker combination maybe?"

Content that I know where the fuck I am and what's happening, most of the staff turn to leave the room, ignoring my snark, leaving only one nurse at my bedside. Millie, or as I call her, the sigher.

"Corporal Shane," she sighs, dropping her shoulders and looking despondent.

"Just Kaleb," I correct her, with my arm still over my face. "We can drop the formalities." I don't add that I don't want to be addressed by my rank as I'm sure my military career is pretty much done.

At this point I know I have muscle and nerve damage from a piece of shrapnel the size of a damn dinner plate piercing my left thigh.

"Kaleb," she concedes, with, you guessed it, a sigh. "You know you hit your head pretty hard. We have to do neuro checks every few hours, especially when we hear you screaming from your bed."

"You go get yourself blown up, shot at a few times, and stabbed in the thigh while the rest of your family dies all around you. I bet you don't scream once," I blow out on a heavy breath. I'd roll my eyes too if my arm weren't laying on them.

"You're wrong about that," she shoots back firmly, "which is why you should be taking advantage of the resources we've been offering you endlessly since you got here."

"Your designated hospital shrink who's never met me can see inside my fucked up brain and make me all better? I don't think so," I snap. There's only one person I want to talk to about all this, and since Alex choked to death on his own blood right next to me while I was sliding in and out of consciousness, I'm shit out of luck. "Look," I try to collect myself and take a calmer approach. "If you're not going to get me anything for this rip-roaring pain in my leg," I gesture with my free hand at my left leg that's been mummified in gauze, "could you please just shut off the light and let me attempt to sleep again?"

Because Lord knows that's all I want to do – just sleep, and maybe not wake up.

"Millie?" I say her name when she doesn't respond to my apathetic request. Chancing the harsh fluorescents blinding me, I remove my arm and squint an eye open to find I'm alone in the dark hospital room. Guess she got fed up with my bullshit. On a normal day I wouldn't be able to blame her, but right now... I've been hurt so bad I don't seem to give a shit how I make anyone else feel.

Something's different... and I still don't know what as I drift back off into my own personal hell.

The most soothing sensation brings me slowly and gently out of my sleep this time, like an angel is rescuing me and pulling me out of the darkness with her touch like delicate feathers sweeping against the side of my cheek. Just that gesture alone seems to ease the stiffness that's trying to keep my body on lockdown, and while it doesn't dissolve the storm clouds in my mind, it breaks them up a bit. It's like a high better than the pain meds I'm on.

"K," a familiar voice coaxes me further out of the fog. Cracking an eyelid open, I tilt my face in the direction of the voice and see a blurry view of light olive skin and brown hair come into focus.

"Lu," my voice is hoarse, but she gives me a faint smile when I acknowledge her.

Fuck, I've thought of nothing but coming home to her for the last eight months. Stayed strong and positive for her, just to have my resolve literally blown away. In the blink of an eye, I'm not the man that left her all those months ago. I'm nothing but his charred and hardened remains. I'm wondering if she's seeing that too right now with the way she's looking at me. It's like she doesn't know what to do with the man in front of her.

"Hey," she whispers back at me, and while her sweet voice still soothes my inner fire, something feels off. Is there a darkness in her eyes? She almost looks afraid, though not of me. I know it, even as I reach for her. I love her, God, how I love her… but something's different.

Nevertheless, I take hold of the side of her neck and pull her in until her forehead is resting against mine, and she lets me. Without me needing to say a word, she allows me this moment of peace where we simply connect in a way we haven't been able to for the better part of the last year. For just this moment, any uncertainty I feel disappears, and we're the us I remember.

When we finally pull away, I feel a little more awake as I take her in. She's trying so hard to light up for me, but something is missing in those brown eyes. A certain radiant light I remember, that gold ring that has always surround her pupils is gone, or it's slimmed down so much I can't see it. My heart slams in my chest as hard as it ever has for her... and I know this is Luna, but... it's like it's someone else. Like a different soul has come along and assumed her human form. Someone reserved, quiet, and a little scared.

"I told you I never turn down a dare," I mumble, reminding her of the day I left.

"You came home," she affirms in a whisper, nodding sweetly.

I reach for one of the back strands of her hair and run it between my fingers to examine it. The purple flare is all but gone, barely detectable.

As if to detract me from what I'm noticing, she takes my hand from her hair and threads it with her own, just as our moment of privacy comes to an end.

"Corporal Shane," the doctor says as he walks in, looking way too cheerful and casual for my taste. "Let's get your discharge paperwork going so we can send you home with your wife."

My home.

My wife.

The two things I've been fantasizing about all this time. So why the fuck does it feel so awkward now? Why on God's earth do I want to crawl back into nothingness?

Luna

WHILE I WAITED to hear more updates on Kaleb's return, I drove myself crazy by doing internet searches, joining online forums for Army wives with spouses in active duty, and pacing the floors. I admit I fell down a God-awful rabbit hole, reading horror stories of husbands coming home and never being the same again. Wives have walked on eggshells to keep a new level of anger at bay, managing PTSD episodes, and panic attacks.

By the time I reached the point of feeling my brain threatening to implode, I had a truckful of information, yet I learned nothing.

It's been so long since I'd seen Kaleb, and so much has happened in that length of time. I didn't know what to expect – besides the obvious injured leg and him being physically weak and sore. Would he look different? Would he be happy to see me?

And now, even that I have seen him, I don't know what I'm actually seeing, or how to act. It's still Kaleb behind those eyes, but so much else resides in them now, blocking my ability to see what I remember of him. I wonder if he'll try to push through all those new, overbearing memories and experiences and come back to me, or if he'll succumb to them, letting it be all he sees for the rest of his life.

Fuck, now's not the time to be selfish, I remind myself for the umpteenth time as I pull the rented caravan up to the curb.

Kaleb's commander had told me in updates leading up to today that it hurts Kaleb to sit and have his leg bent for extended periods of time. Neither my car nor his truck was conducive to that, and plus I wanted to save time, so I flew to Maryland and rented a van once I had a better idea what I was dealing with.

Our reunion went better than I thought. From all the insane things I read, I wasn't sure if I'd be a welcome sight or if he'd be cold and unfeeling towards me. I just did my best to act natural, the way I remembered things between us, and let him take the rest of the lead. It wasn't how I'd been fantasizing over the last year – obviously – but there were notes of sweetness and love in there, and they weren't forced.

It's not long after I put the van in park that I catch movement in my peripheral and see Kaleb in a wheelchair, being pushed by a nurse in blue scrubs. His left leg is extended in front of him by one of the pedals, and he holds a pair of crutches over his shoulder. I scurry around to the front to meet him as he stands, getting situated on the crutches.

"I wanted something with options," I tell him when I see him curiously eyeballing my vehicle choice.

He huffs through his nose, shaking his head. "So I need special transport, now. Wonderful."

"Babe, it's just a long drive back home," I try to reason. Normally I'd toss something snarky back in his face, but I'm still feeling this situation out. "I want you to be able to recline if you want."

He closes his eyes briefly as if inwardly scolding himself. "Sorry... that's sweet of you. Thank you."

"It's okay," I murmur back and he lifts his chin in the direction of the front passenger door, indicating to the nurse to pull that door open. Looks like he at least wants to start off up front. As he shifts and scooches into the seat – which takes a small eternity given he has to put his left leg in first – I think I hear him mumble something about how he doesn't want his wife to be his chauffeur, but again, I ignore it. He can have his frustrations, at least for right now.

Not much is said on the ten-hour drive back home. Kaleb mostly sleeps, and when he's not asleep, he just stares out the window. Sometimes it looks like he's in a trance. I check in with him every now and then, but he just gives me a faint smile and squeezes my leg affectionately before signing off again. He's so distant, but I know that's something I just have to be patient with, and I hold onto the hope that once he's in his home again, things will look up.

30

KALEB

*O*h, sweet Jesus, I've found Heaven, I think as I flop back onto the bed I haven't seen for the last year.

Luna gives an easy smile as she props my leg up on several pillows. "Feel good?"

Never mind, I guess I actually said it out loud.

"After a one-man cot for the last eight months, are you kidding?" I quip, attempting a smile of my own.

After assessing the position of my beat-to-shit leg, I look up at Luna to see her looking at it as well, seemingly satisfied that it's secure before tucking a strand of hair behind her ear and turning to pull open a dresser drawer.

She must be tired after the long drive and hefting me up those front steps. That was fun, although she managed me and herself miles better than I expected. And all that time on the road, I know I wasn't the best company. I had little to say as my mind seems to have become my worst enemy, torturing me relentlessly with visions of Alex being lifted from beside me and carried away by what was left of our platoon. It's bad enough she has to see me injured like this, I don't need her seeing me mentally weak too. Hell, I was supposed to be vertical for our reunion, not flat on my back in a flimsy hospital gown.

As I watch her undo her jeans, I realized I haven't even kissed her yet. There just hasn't seemed to be a right time as our reunion was a flurry of paperwork, physical therapists, and nurses.

"Lu," I beckon from the bed just at the right moment that's she's pushing her jeans down her legs. My dick springs to life behind my ranger shorts, surprising even me. One would think this wouldn't be the best time, but here I am, having a physical reaction to being home with her.

"Yeah?" Her hair flips as she turns her head to look at me.

"Come here," I hold my hand out, and I fucking hate how helpless I feel. I want to be her man and get up off this bed and go to her, taking her in the fiercest kiss she's ever had.

Kicking her jeans off and away from her feet she comes over to me, sitting on the edge of the bed and leans in as I reach for her. "You haven't kissed me yet, silly girl," I point out to her.

"You haven't kissed me yet," she returns with a playful quirk of her lips.

There she is.

That glimpse of the girl I left behind is all I need to pull her to me the rest of the way and touch my lips to hers, brushing them gently at first before crushing them together in a kiss so powerful and hard I will it to make up for the last few months absence.

"Mmm..." she whimpers against my mouth, and I don't know if it's from pleasure or from the force, but I find myself not caring either way. Some carnal need is taking over, and that little noise from her made my cock pound out a hard throb, signaling to me what it is I need right now.

With my other hand, I take hold of her hip and pull her closer, lifting her leg to help her straddle me but she falters. "Kaleb, wait," she utters breathlessly between our lips. "Your leg... we shouldn't do this."

"My leg is injured but my dick still works," I growl against her lips before forcefully jamming my tongue between them.

This earns me another delectable moan that gets my blood flowing hot through my veins. "Come on, baby, he misses you," I whisper wantonly between my tongues undulations.

"You need rest, and I don't want to hurt you," she pants, but she's not fooling me. She speaks the truth, but she wants me as much as I want her, and I know it's only going to take little more convincing.

"You're not going to hurt me, you're going to help me," I reassure her. Because what I need is to be in control of something; to not feel fucking weak. I need to connect with my wife, I need to fuck her. "Lu, I promise. It will be okay, just please get on top of me, I need this. I need you."

"Ohh…" she moans out again as she gingerly lifts her leg and brings it over me to straddle my hips. "Oh, Kaleb, I want this, I've missed you so much," she confesses as she takes my face in her hands and re-engages our kiss while I move my hands up one of my long t-shirts she's had on all this time and take hold of her hips, relishing the feel of the lace that meets my hands there.

"Baby girl," I breathe against her mouth as I break our kiss just long enough to pull the t-shirt up and over her, leaving her beautiful tits pushed together in her lilac lace bra in my face. "Fuck," I muse in a gruff whisper as I push them together, squeezing and kneading before ducking my head to let my tongue slip between her cleavage. I hear a gasp escape her throat in response and her hands find my hair, holding me tightly to where she wants me as I drive my erection upwards between her legs.

As my hands continue to grope and explore her body, I feel a certain firmness in her back I don't remember. She's always been a knockout and in damn good shape, but this is a different level of muscle tone. I feel it in her thighs too as she squeezes against me. Unhooking her bra with one hand, I peel it away from her, freeing her beautiful breasts that I immediately grab onto and my mouth lavishes each one with attention in turn.

Fucking damn, my thigh is starting to burn with my erratic

heart rate pumping my blood through my body at a hard and fast rate, but I don't give a fuck, I ignore it. Reaching between her legs, I find Luna's panties absolutely drenched, and it floors me. "Holy fuck, baby. Do you know how wet you are?"

"Yes," she nods frantically as she scoots back just a bit to work my shorts down. I help the best I can, lifting my hips despite the screaming protest from my leg as I yank the wet scrap of lace to the side.

"Wrap your beautiful pussy around my cock, baby, and I'll do the rest," I growl up at her, and I'm rewarded with her enthusiastically obliging.

"Oh my God, K," her head falls back as she sinks down on my shaft, her warm wetness enveloping me beautifully, each inch better than the last. Once she's fully seated in my lap, I move slowly at first, just a couple of pumps to acclimate us, but after that, I go all in. With how fucking wet she is, she slides up and down so fucking easily as I jack my hips upwards, pummeling her sweet cunt. Luna bounces with my movements and takes hold of the headboard above me to steady herself. "Oh, Kaleb, oh God yes, baby," she cries out, and it brings my confidence almost back up to its baseline.

I'm getting one fuck of glute workout as I'm doing my best to lay off my leg and let my ass do all the work, but it's worth it to feel Luna's pussy begin to quiver around my dick. My balls are tight and painful with the need to come and so I pull her down closer, licking my tongue into her mouth to help her along as my thumb finds the hood of her clit and rubs in small circles.

The vice-like squeeze of her pussy and the scream she releases into my mouth are my go-ahead to let go and pound into her. Fuck, I can feel her coming on my cock, coating it with her arousal as my cum streams into her in spurts that rack my body.

"Fuck! Baby!" I roar out as I empty into her, and the staccato sound of her shallow panting is the soundtrack bringing me down. I slow my thrusts little by little until the aftershocks of our joint orgasms dissipate enough that I feel safe to move again.

Still trying to catch her breath, Luna presses her palms against my chest and eases herself off me, I can tell, trying to be extra careful. My hands come over the top of hers however, keeping her from getting completely off me. Something about the way they feel on me makes me feel grounded, and I'm enjoying it more than I ever thought possible.

Reading my signal like only she can, Luna shifts only partially off me so that her body is free and clear of my leg and snuggles into my side, keeping one hand on my chest over my rapidly beating heart.

My leg feels like it's going to explode, and once again, me being my stubborn-ass self, I'm doing my best to not show my discomfort, but Luna can see me shifting and wincing next to her.

"Do you want an ice pack?" she asks, sitting up and grabbing the nearest t-shirt, and fuck, I can't turn that down.

"That'd be great," I grumble affectionately, trying to show appreciation in my best, casual this is no big deal, it's just a little pain tone.

She stands from the bed and pulls open a drawer. "No problem," she says softly, pulling out a frilly pair of bed shorts and stepping into them. "Need anything else while I'm in the kitchen?"

"Uh… yeah, I guess I could do with some pain meds."

"Okay," she says sweetly, sashaying out of the room and returning less than three minutes later with a bottle of water, an ice pack wrapped in a towel, and holds her hand out to me to receive some pills. When she drops them in my hand, I recognize them as ibuprofen.

"Hey, do you mind getting me the stuff the doctor

prescribed?" I ask looking up at her, and she stalls in her task of positioning the ice pack over my leg.

"Um... those are..."

I fucking know their oxycodone, but I try not to snap at her through the pain that's starting to radiate down my calf. "I know, babe, but this really hurts. Do you mind?"

"I know," she straightens up and lightly waves her hands with her words. "It's just that those can be habit forming and –"

"I know, I know everything you're about to say." I blow out on a heavy sigh, cutting off her rant as I drop my head back on the pillow. The pain is starting to take over, and a vision of the explosion flickers in the back of my mind, reminding me of its origin. "But fuck, I need some sleep tonight, Luna, so would you get them for me please?" I ask yet again, trying to be nice.

She lets out a sigh as her eyes wander the room in thought before biting her bottom lip and suggesting, "Can't you just give the ibuprofen a chance and if it doesn't help you can –"

"Dammit, Luna!" I bark, cutting her off once again and making her shoulders jump with the loud boom of my voice. "You have no idea what kind of pain I'm in – no idea!" I say, finally showing all my cards and revealing how desperate I am for relief. "Now please go grab the prescription meds or I'll get them my damn self!" I yell, shifting in the bed like I'm making to get up so she knows I'm serious.

Luna's mouth drops open slightly as if she's about to throw something back at me, but quickly closes her mouth and whirls around. She strides out the bedroom door and her footsteps echo down the hallway and back when she returns with the clear orange bottle. She tosses it at me and the pills rattle as it lands on the bed next to me.

Fuck, I messed up. I still can't pinpoint the change I've seen in her in the hours since first seeing each other again, but for a minute there we were us again, and my little outburst didn't help things.

"Look, babe..." I tell her as I unscrew the cap and take just two of the tablets out. "I'm sorry, I've just never felt pain like this. I just need these tonight and I'll start to ween myself off tomorrow, I promise."

"Mmm hmm," she responds without looking at me before crawling into the bed and shutting off the light. As I slug down the pills with some water, she turns on her side, her back to me, and I hate it. After setting the pills and water down on my side of the bed, I try to turn towards her but my fucking leg won't let me. Instead, I turn my face towards her in the darkened room and reach my hand out, letting it rest on her back.

31

LUNA

*K*aleb ambles past me through our front door that I'm holding open. Handsome as ever in his dress blues, his face is the stoney expression he's been opting to sport for the last two weeks. I shut our front door against the crispy March chill, and shrug out of my peacoat before hanging it in the hallway closet.

More than ready to get out of this black dress and tights, I eagerly make my way down the hall and find Kaleb in our bedroom, a few steps ahead of me, leaning on his cane while he yanks at his neck tie, his face twisted with the frustration.

His physical therapy has been going better than expected, although the therapist is still encouraging him to stay on the crutches. But Kaleb being Kaleb ditched them days ago and has only been mildly struggling with the cane. He finally tosses it down to the floor so that he can tackle his tie with both hands.

"That was a beautiful service," I say softly, testing the waters as I reach behind my neck to undo the button at the back of my dress.

"Yeah, putting Alex in the ground was just fucking peachy," he snarls under his breath.

"That's not what I meant and you know it," I sigh as I lift up my skirt to wrestle with the itchy as hell black tights, working them down my hips.

"No, you're right," he says facetiously as he whips his jacket down his shoulders as if it's covered in cold slime. "It was really beautiful seeing his mom get handed a folded-up flag instead of her son back. All the while the rest of his family fawns over me like I'm some kind of hero."

The way he's talking right now is enough to make me sick, and sadly, it's not the first time. I've been getting a steady diet of this the last couple weeks. Not only has he not laid off the pain pills, but I swear they make him surly as fuck. Don't get me wrong, he's been no prince in the first place, but I definitely notice a difference when he has a hefty dose on board. And then when they wear off, he seems lost and restless. He's hooked.

"Kaleb, I know you don't feel much like a –"

"I accomplished nothing over there, Luna," he gripes out, furiously going to work on the buttons of his shirt. "Story of my fucking life. Couldn't afford college so thought I'd make something of myself in the military, and what do I have to show for it? A dead best friend whose body I couldn't even bring home myself because I was too busy getting my damn leg babied in a hospital." He concludes his rant by shucking his shirt down his bare, tatted shoulders.

I, in the meantime, take off my necklace and watch while schooling my emotions, keeping them in check.

"Okay," I say so quietly I practically mouth it. "I don't want to fight. But I do hope one day you won't feel that way," I say before padding over to him and turning my back. "Unzip me?" I request, signaling that I'm letting this go. He seems to go still behind me and I hear nothing but a couple of his breaths being let in and out before I feel his fingers graze the back of my neck, taking hold of the zipper. He trails it down slowly at first, the material yawning open, revealing the bare skin of my back. It feels sensual and almost sweet, until he reaches dead center and gives the zipper a voracious yank the rest of the way down, making me gasp lightly in surprise. In my next breath, he's shoving the dress down my arms before drawing me back against him, one arm crossed over my chest.

His teeth nip at my earring while he palms one of my breasts, squeezing harder than his usual pressure. I know what's happening. I've always let him take out his aggressions through sex with me, and that's clearly what he's instigating now.

With his free hand, Kaleb works my dress the rest of the way down my hips, along with my panties, before letting his fingers dive between my legs, stroking my clit.

"Come on, babe, get wet for me," he growls in my ear and I close my eyes, trying to get in the mood. I'm normally happy to let him do this, but this moment feels different than the others. I've let him be rough, but there's still always some kind of tender concern behind his actions. I'm torn between shutting him down due to lack of arousal or giving him what he needs.

Slowly, I start riding his fingers back and forth, trying to get my body and mind to tune in with each other

"I need you to get wet for me and take your soldier's cock," he grunts again, releasing his crushing grip on my breast and using that hand to work on his belt while continuing to rub me. "Need you to take it like a good girl."

"Mm-hmm," I nod, letting his dirty words take me there as I feel the warm skin of his dick brush against my ass, free from its confines. He keeps rubbing my clit and it's a little too much pressure for my liking, but I'm starting to finally get a little wet – just in time for him to grip my neck, way too hard, and thrust me down on the bed.

The front of my body connects with the mattress hard enough to make the breath whoosh out of me, and before I can even react, Kaleb is crawling on top of me. He takes hold of my hips, his grip bruising as he straddles my legs, putting all his weight on his right knee.

After taking barely a second to position himself, Kaleb slams into me without ceremony and takes right off, thrusting into me fast and hard. He grunts and growls between brutal, punishing strokes.

"Oh yeah," he rasps through his ramming. "Fuck..."

I swear this is different from all the other times I've let him have angry sex with me. There's a coldness behind it this time, and I don't like it. It feels like he's somewhere else and I can't get into it with him, and it's even scaring me a little.

"Fuck..." Kaleb's voice has turned to a whisper. "Fucking stop... stop!" He grits out.

"K?" I check in with him but it's like he doesn't hear me.

"Fucking stop! No!" He grunts, pummeling me harder and taking me by the throat and pulling back.

Oh my God, he's not Kaleb right now, this needs to stop. I frantically bring my hand up, clawing at his, and thankfully get my fingers beneath his before he can squeeze, giving me just enough leeway in my windpipe to scream.

"Stop!" I shriek. The word is a drawn-out shrill that echoes off the walls and I feel Kaleb jolt on top of me before throwing himself off me as if my skin were burning his.

I cough only a couple of times and after gasping just once, the breath flows through my airway normally.

I swallow hard and lift my head to find Kaleb right in my face as his hands roam over my body, my face, as if checking me for injuries.

"Lu? Babe?" His voice is panicked but his eyes are a beautiful light green, harboring regret and concern. "Are you okay? I'm so sorry." Those eyes practically plead for forgiveness.

"I'm okay." The words are betrayed by my trembling body. I'm shaking and I can't suppress it.

"Fuck, what did I do to you?" He cups my face in his hands and brings his lips to my forehead. "I don't know what happened," he murmurs painfully against my skin.

"It's okay, it's okay," I whisper just as frantically as I take hold of his wrists, stroking his skin up in down, trying to calm him.

"I didn't mean to," he continues, practically groveling, and I take him in a hug, my arms wrapping around his head. "I just... I was back there. I don't know how I believed I was back there and not in bed with you, but I blinked and then that's all I saw."

"I know, baby. I know you didn't, it's okay."

I'm not sure how much time I spend reassuring him... I just know it goes on until we both fall asleep.

⛺

I WAKE up after I don't know how much time asleep and reach over to the space beside me to find nothing but rumpled sheets. It's dark outside, but it can't be too late as it was still light out when we came home.

My stomach lets go of a deep growl, and I'm reminded we didn't eat since the funeral. That's probably what Kaleb is up doing, making something for dinner. My starving appetite pulls me from between the covers, and I go over to the dresser to pull out some pajama pants and a t-shirt to go help him.

Only after making my way down the hall to the kitchen, I don't find what I expect. No lights are on except the one above the stove, and Kaleb sits at the center island, his leg propped up on a stool and an open bottle of whiskey and a glass beside him.

Dammit no... not this.

"K?" I try to get his attention as he brings the half full glass to his mouth and sips. "What's going on, are you okay?" I ask with concern, knowing that ripping into him about drinking with his pain meds is only going to push him away further.

"I'm fine," he barely grumbles staring into the glass as he sets it down. "Just been doing some thinking."

"Yeah?" I ask cautiously as I casually slink over to the island and grab up the bottle, twisting the cap back on but leaving the glass with him. By the looks of things, he's not too deep into the bottle, and I want to keep it that way. Fortunately he doesn't protest and just nods at my retort. I place the bottle back up in the cabinet above the fridge and come to lean my arms across the island from him. "K, if this is about earlier, I told you there's nothing to be sorry for. You didn't mean to get carried away; I know that one hundred percent. You'd never hurt me."

"It's not about that," he shakes his head sadly down at his drink. "I mean, it's going to be a while before I forgive myself for that, but... no. It's not that, it's about... us. Me."

I bow my head, examining the tiles of the counter top while I collect my thoughts. "It's only been a couple of weeks, Kaleb. We spent a long time apart and we – you – went through a lot during that time. It's going to take a while for us to reintegrate." I shake my head, willing him to see my reasoning.

It's no secret that we haven't been the same since he came home, but it also hasn't been very long. "These are growing pains, and if we see it through, everything will level out again."

He lets out a sigh heavier than the world before shaking his head and finally looking up at me.

"I think we should get divorced."

32

KALEB

*L*una's face goes stone still and those brown eyes seem to zone out. She swallows hard and sets her jaw, and it's hard to tell in this dim light, but I think she goes a little pale for a moment.

I knew this wouldn't be easy, but it's for the best. I can't go on like this, the way we've been. I'm going to be beating myself up for the rest of my life over what happened in the bedroom. I didn't think I was capable of such a thing; letting some monster take over me and scare her like that. But I wasn't lying when I said it wasn't about that – at least not all about that.

Since I came back, she's been looking at me like some poor loser she's stuck taking care of. I may be a bit off-kilter from all the pain meds, but I'm sure that's what I'm seeing. And why shouldn't she? That's all I am anymore.

And she's changed, too. She's not the sassy, free spirit I found my way back to in that bar in Indianapolis. The one that rooted for herself as much as she did me. What drew me most to her was the way she was living life for herself and was making herself happy before I even came along.

Now, it's like the life has gone out of her eyes, and she's resigned herself to a sentence of taking care of a broken-down excuse of a man just because she married him. I didn't stop to think that becoming an Army wife, waiting for her man, only to have him dumped on her at not even half of what he was, but I no longer see the cheerful, radiant girl with the purple in her hair. Just like she probably doesn't see the hardcore, aspiring tattoo artist that bravely went off to war.

I stay silent, letting her process what I've said, but what happens before my eyes is not what I expected. She squares her shoulders before the color returns to her face – no, more than returns to her face. It's almost taken on a radiance, but not the kind I've seen before.

"No," she finally speaks, her voice low and deliberate. I expected a little denial in rebuttal, but as her eyes refocus on mine, she looks dead serious… So I try again.

"Luna, this isn't turning out how either of us thought. I think we should cut ties and move on," I say huskily. Or at least she should.

But she straightens up to her full height and levels me with another hard glare. "Yeah, no, I don't think so," she says plainly before turning and stalking towards one of the cupboards and pulling out a mixing bowl and an egg beater.

What the fuck is going on here? I instigate a conversation with divorce and she blows me off?

"What are you doing?" I crinkle my forehead at her and shift forward to ease my leg down off the stool.

"I'm starving," she informs me before turning to the other cupboard and retrieving the pancake mix.

"Luna," I whoosh out a stress-rattled breath. "I'm serious about this. You can't just pretend this isn't happening."

"I'm not pretending, Kaleb," she retorts as she takes out the measuring cups. "It's not happening. It's been two lousy fucking weeks, and you want to give up? I don't fucking think so, you do not get to pull this."

Dammit, I was trying to approach this sensitively, but her denial and avoidance tactics are chapping my ass.

I had poured just a couple fingers of Jack to take the edge off, as I was expecting a little pushback, but this is just jacked.

"Luna, come on," I huff as I gingerly stand. "You're being unreasonable."

"No," she returns as she measures a cup of the powdery mix. "You're being an unreasonable fucking idiot, suggesting divorce after two not-so-blissful weeks. You're going against your vows, you moron."

"Look," I say firmly, "I'm not the guy you knew before I left."

"Bullshit." She turns around and runs the water in the sink, narrowing her eyes at me as she looks between me and the measuring cup she's filling. "One month ago, you sent me the most beautiful, loving bouquet of flowers and paintbrushes with a note telling me how much you missed me. One fucking month!"

"I was just barely holding onto that guy before I got my ass blown up, Luna. And in that moment, it all crumbled and I crawled out of the rubble... this," I gesture up and down at myself. "I've changed, Luna. We've changed."

"No!" She slams the water off and looks at me, setting the filled cup aside and resting her hands on the counter to look at me. She glares at me hard, and it's now I notice that the gold ring around her pupil has returned and it is ablaze, burning brighter than ever as she lays in to me. "You crawled out of the rubble, period, Kaleb. You're the one who sees you as weak, not me! You're projecting and you're scrambling to do away with the last good thing in your life before you lose that too!" she shouts.

"I am not your Kaleb anymore!" I shout back, grasping at straws.

"No, my Kaleb is still in there," she snaps back, pointing at me. "He just got spooked and he's hiding out. Hiding behind this rock solid I don't give a fuck about anything veneer."

I fall silent a moment, not knowing how to respond, because I can't deny she may be on to something there... But it's too hard to hope for.

"Well he's not coming back out again," I finally sigh out as she picks up the water and turns to dump it in the bowl with the mix. "Luna…" I try to speak again but I'm cut off by the egg-beater running loudly, combining the pancake mix. Shithead.

I rub my hands down my face in exasperation until she finally shuts it off, seemingly satisfied with the consistency of the mix. Finally, she turns around to face me again.

"So this was fraud?" she challenges in more of a statement than a question.

"No, it wasn't fucking fraud, it–" I try to argue with a slice of my hand through the air, but she keeps rolling.

"Because it sure feels like it, Kaleb. Asking me to marry you so that your assets would be safe, and now that you're back, you want to scrap the marriage? Like I was basically just a place holder?!"

"No!" I holler back. It doesn't even occur to me to let her believe that to make this easier. I just can't. I want what we used to be. I don't want any more of what we've become, but I don't want her to hurt or think that she was ever nothing to me, yet I can't bring myself to say that either. I'm more vulnerable than I've ever been in my fucking life, and laying that out is sure to eviscerate what's left of me.

"Are you saying you don't love me?" Her voice is ominously low as she crosses her arms, and her eyes, while glassing over a little bit, are challenging me.

Words fail me. Breath catches in my throat where they should be, and at my silent response, she rounds the island. Taking a few charging steps closer to me, there's a look of determined fury on her face I haven't seen in years. "Are you saying you don't love me?" she demands this time, her clenched jaw biting the words out hard. "Tell me! Is that what you're saying?!"

"No," the word comes out soft but swift, because no matter what favors that would do me in this moment, I can't admit to it.

Pulling the collar of her t-shirt to the side, she reveals the moon I tattooed on her. "You fucking branded me if you'll recall!

You love me so much you permanently marked me, and I let you, because I love you, too!" she yells, her voice getting throaty with the passionate effort.

I inwardly wince at both her choice of words and her delivery. She's handed me my ass before, but never like this. With how unhappy she's seemed, I didn't think I'd get this much of a fight, but I can hear the pain in her voice – feel it.

"Now," she sighs, her voice coming back to the gentle lilt I'm used to. "I will move into the other bedroom. If you need space, I can understand that. I know we've been in each other's face very suddenly and nonstop and it's hard for us to reintegrate, but I'm not going anywhere, Kaleb Dominic. You may be willing to puss out on your vows, but I'm not. I'm here for better or worse."

I glower down at her, refusing to admit I don't have a good rebuttal for that, so I finally settle on something petulant. "I'm going to fucking break you, Luna. You're either going to reach your boiling point or I'll crush your spirit before that. That monster in there?" I point in the direction of the bedroom, "that's who's here in your Kaleb's place," I remind her, hoping that will do the trick. She can't deny I scared the hell out of her when I saw bombs going off behind my eyelids like firecrackers, rapidly firing all around me. Screams, gunshots, and flashes of lights took me somewhere else in that moment, oblivious of what I was about to do to her. It scared the shit out of me, and I want her to think about that. Little do I know about the curveball I'm in for.

Her shoulders rise and fall with her deep breaths, but the passion in her eyes doesn't falter.

"I dare you to give it two months."

"What?" I feel my eyebrows go up.

"Our anniversary. You don't turn down dares, Kaleb," she says quietly, tunneling both hands through her hair, pushing it out of her face. She's running out of steam, but this last blow is the clincher. "I dare you to make it to the one-year mark, but if you truly want this game to be over, then fold, right now, and I'll give you your divorce."

Son of a fucking bitch. She turned the tables and is now offering to do the very thing she's been protesting. And she got me, I can't fucking do it, because I can't turn down a dare… at least that's what I tell myself right now, pretending that I won't learn later on that it's fucking bullshit.

33

LUNA

It's not that Kaleb's revelation didn't devastate me. It did. In that moment, however, it pissed me off even more. He's holding back, and while that might be a reasonable prerogative for him, I can do the same. He doesn't get to know how much I hurt. But he did do me a favor that night… he lit a fire under my ass.

Kaleb's recent behavior is solely on him, but he accidentally showed one of his cards the other night. He said that we're not the same people we were before, not just him. There's been a change in me since Carter's attack, and though I've been trying to protect Kaleb from it, it's showing through on the outside, and I can't help but wonder if I got back to myself he wouldn't feel like things are so different; he could see that this era of our lives can be surmountable.

I need to take care of Kaleb, but I also need to take care of myself. I feel like he'd trust me more and lean on me if I did.

As much as I miss sleeping with him, I think my moving into the spare bedroom is for the best for right now. I truly believe that he didn't mean to hurt me the last time we had sex. His trauma took him to a scary place in his mind, but I can't risk it again, and I can't be falling into some toxic rinse and repeat cycle where he loses his shit and I console him. We need to work on ourselves – both separately and together – it's just that I think I'm the only one who knows it.

But that doesn't matter. One thing I need to do is get into painting, no matter how much of a struggle it's been since last year. With my overalls on, I sit on the stool in front of my easel, playing with a stray hair that's come loose from my ponytail and noting it's lack of purple. Only if I twist it a certain way in the light can I see it. Guess I haven't felt very expressive lately, not enough to keep up with it. Releasing it, I put a slow, girly station on my music app, and while my choice isn't very upbeat, it can be emotional and moving and I'm desperate.

Grabbing hold of my brush in my left hand, I examine the fingers on my right. They've obviously heeled, and it was only the last two, the ones I use the least. But still, they always have a stiffness to them now that only I notice, and I feel the need to flex them a few times before settling in with a task.

A creek in the hallway floorboards gets my attention, and my head swiftly turns to find Kaleb on the other side of the doorway, looking at me curiously. We hold our stare for just a few beats, saying nothing; just taking each other in, before I turn back to my blank canvas. A couple of seconds later, I hear him retreat down the hall and I take a look at all my paints. I sigh, still feeling no inspiration or colors calling to me but I push through, selecting a few shades before rising to close the door. For the next while, I dab, swipe, brush, blot, and blend, not sure exactly what it is I'm constructing, but going with it – even if it's not my signature style, I need to do something to get me back at it. This is just a phase I tell myself.

When I finally hit a wall, I change back into clean clothes and sit down on the bed and pick up my phone for something to do while my progress dries. My heart takes a swan dive into the pit of my stomach when I see a missed call from both my mother and our family lawyer, Mike Harris. I chew on the inside of my cheek and press my eyes tightly closed, trying to ward off the incoming flood of sickening nerves. I can only guess the two calls go hand in hand with each other.

I bypass the voicemails, wanting to get straight to the root of the phone calls and dial Mike's number. I do want to talk to my mom, but I want to have some kind of handle on things when I do; some semblance of control.

"Luna," My name is a sigh on the other end when Mike picks up, already signaling that this is bad.

"Mike, what is it?" I ask eagerly, wasting no time.

There's a pause, followed by more air being blown out before he answers, "Sixteen months' probation and a thousand dollar fine."

I go dizzy for half a second before swallowing hard. "That's it?" I ask incredulously. "Mike, I did everything. I recounted my story dozens of times, I testified in that hearing in the same room as that fucking monster. His lawyer is sleezy and clever but you're a fucking shark, how did this happen?" I rattle every confusing, heated sentiment in quick succession while simultaneously tamping down the sobs trying to inch their way up my throat.

"It was the plea deal, Luna," he says regretfully. "Confessing to half the crime is what saved his ass from going to prison."

"This is bullshit," I protest in a venomous whisper as I scrub a hand across my forehead.

"I know, Luna. I'm so sorry," he consoles before his tone goes up, trying to instill some shred of hope. "We can try again. We could start a whole new case if you still have that forged letter and –"

He doesn't get to finish as I disconnect the call, not wanting to hear anymore. Another action that's not like me. I guess pre-deployment Luna is going to be harder to get back to than I thought.

"Lu?" I jump at Kaleb's voice accompanied by a tap at the door.

"Yeah?" I call back, rising and striding across the room, smoothing my hair and schooling my features on the way. I whip open the door to find Kaleb in his joggers and his bomber jacket. In the last few weeks he's let his hair grow back long in the front, and despite my inner turmoil, my insides warm a little bit when he tosses it out of his eyes. "Time for PT," he says softly.

"Okay," I nod and quickly turn to throw a cloth over my art piece and follow him down the hallway.

Once in the car and headed to the VA in West Bridge, as always, I try to act cheerful and make small talk. Today is extra challenging however, what with the lame-ass sentence Carter got for beating the shit out of me.

"You've been working really hard... maybe today they'll clear you to drive. You could drive us home?" I give a hopeful smile as I watch the road, but catch Kaleb's nod in my peripheral. Since I told him to give our marriage a chance, he hasn't been mean, but hasn't been outwardly nice or affectionate either. "You know, after physical therapy, we could head upstairs to the counseling offices..."

"I'm not seeing a shrink, Luna," he cuts me off, firmly.

"You need to talk to somebody," I say softly, "even if it's not me."

"What the hell difference does it make?" he asks, incredulously. "It's just talking."

"Talking can help you work through it, believe it or not. It can help you expel some of that toxicity, and those people there can relate to you, what you've been through, far better than I could ever try to. Besides, you agreed to give this a try, and you haven't done shit." I raise my eyebrows facetiously, being mockingly perky as I turn into the center's parking lot.

"I said I'd give the marriage a chance, I didn't say anything about going to therapy," he points out.

"And you don't think that might play a part in working on

the marriage?" I counter as I slide the car into a space. "Merely tolerating my presence doesn't count," I say, annoyed, throwing the car into park, perfectly in sync with that last word.

I cut the engine and look up to find Kaleb regarding me with a thoughtful expression.

"What?" I ask impatiently as I crank my door open.

He shakes his head slightly, as if amused. "Nothing, just… you've got that fire. Kind of like you did that night in the kitchen – and that night at the lake."

I blow out a frustrated sigh as I'm not in the mood for riddles, but I want to know where he's going with this. "Is that a good thing or bad?"

"I don't know," he sighs back, before opening his own door. "I've never been able to figure that out."

Kaleb

W<small>HEN</small> I <small>SAY</small> I can't tell if Luna's fire is a good or bad thing, what I held back is that it's because it's a damn good thing… a good thing that pisses me off because it dares to challenge me. It pushes me out of my comfort zone and challenges me to lay off the stubbornness and try thinking in ways other than my own.

It's not that I don't love Luna, because I fucking do. And I think that's what makes it harder. There's no one on this planet whose view of me I give a shit about but hers. Fuck, I thought I'd come home to her the man she deserves, someone who'd accomplished something great and would put that greatness towards our future. Instead, I came home wounded, weak, and vulnerable. This was not how my future with her was supposed to be, and the idea that I will be less than my part of what's always made us, us, makes me sick.

Today I tried walking without a cane, like a toddler learning to take wobbly steps for the first time, while Luna watched from a nearby window seat, and though she seemed rigid throughout the session, she beamed at me when I got the all clear to drive.

It did feel good, however, to drive us to the auto shop afterwards, though my pride wouldn't let me admit it. It felt like I'd been handed back a scrap of control. Hopefully I can get back on my bike when summer comes.

When we get to the shop, my already slow gait comes to a stop as I take in what I see all around me in the garage bays. A handful of confident mechanics are working on several vehicles, including two motorcycles in a swift and smooth manner I haven't seen before. They've got a rhythm to their work flow, accompanied by classic rock music and easy conversation. Not one person falters as they pass tools to each other, and rather than focusing on one project, I see them moving around all the different vehicles, contributing to each one. Not to mention all the tools, equipment, and machines are arranged and orderly. It's got the smooth, laidback disposition as it did when Pops was here, but with the efficiency brought up to a new level.

Previous conversations with Luna while I was away flash through my brain, and I'm reminded that the change correlates with the arrival of West.

The ex-con mechanic with a head for business. I scan the garage and find him sitting on a rollaway chair, nodding his head to the music as he as he works on the drive chain of someones Harley.

"Hey, walking wounded!" Jackson shouts from the office doorway, yanking my attention away from West.

I look down at my leg as if Jackson's greeting would make a piece of jagged metal emerge out of a gaping flesh wound before looking back up to him. "Hey," I tip my head as he approaches, surprisingly with no small children attached anywhere on his person. "Things look like they're going good," I say and look back to all the employees, nodding at all the hard work I see.

"Things are going so great," he shakes his head, an air of contentment wafting off of him as he rests his hands on his hips.

"Business is back in full swing and then some. Get this, West is the son of some racecar driver. He worked on his old man's pit crew for a long time, and it's brought this whole new dynamic to the work environment. He won't say who it is though, so you know it's got to me someone famous," he reports wistfully.

"No shit?" I ask, looking back to the rough and rugged man again as he tosses a zip gun to one of the other employees in exchange for a drill. I feel a wave of something I can't put my finger on. I don't want to say it's jealousy, but it's some kind of confused form of it. Getting this auto shop taken care of is everything I've strived for, from enlisting in the army to coming home with a torn-to-shit leg, and some newcomer slides in and gets the place turned around with a snap of his fingers. It stirs something in my gut – along with a dose of relief that things are going so well, and a dash of guilt for feeling that relief.

I'm Pops' next of kin... I should be taking care of his place like he took care of me.

In my peripheral, I see Luna looking up at me from beside me, offering silent support.

I draw in a long breath and exhale hard and slow, trying to expel the negative energy trying to fuck with this good thing before gripping the bill of my ball cap, acting like I'm just adjusting it when really its serving as a stress ball at the moment. "That's good," I finally say. "That's really good to hear."

"Yeah, we've even got people coming in from West Bridge because word's gotten around that this place is high quality and fast with reasonable fees," he shrugs. "It's the best it's ever been."

High quality without breaking the bank is what Pops always stood for, and hearing this actually lightens the smog that was trying to settle over my brain, making my heart pound out a few beats of appreciation. It's a good way to feel, but having it swirling with all these other sudden thoughts and emotions, it's overwhelming me.

"Well shit," I tell Jackson with a quirky smile, "this made my day." I'm not lying, at least I don't think I am. All I know is that my head's hurting and I'm tired as fuck after PT as I turn to Luna. "Think I'm ready to get home, babe."

She nods, and with a quiet wave to Jackson, falls into annoyingly slow step with me back to the car. She's too tough to walk on eggshells around me but she does choose her battles, and right now, she's choosing to keep any thoughts to herself. I hate what we've become, and I don't know how the hell we're supposed to fix it with only a little bit of time.

***

FUCK, why am I here again? Just once was one time too many, so why do I need to relive it almost every night of the damn week? I know this is a dream because I've been through it too many damn times not to recognize it. I just don't know how the hell to get out of it.

I've stepped over that poor dead kid's body before, only this time, I close his eyes for him. I continue kicking and trekking my way through the ash and rubble. I look ahead towards Alex, just in time for him to look back at me. He shakes his head and we exchange a look as if to say this is our life right now. And then a ball of orange and red explodes behind him, and we're hit with a blast of heat that sends us both flying back.

"No! Fuck! No!" I scream in terror as one wave of heat and fire after another washes over me. "Goddammit, no!" More screams of protest rip from my throat, and I can feel it getting sore.

I feel myself panting rapidly between screams before something presses against my back. It's soft and warm like a blanket, and I don't know where the hell in this war zone it came from, but it seems to be slowing my erratic heart rate. Something is squeezing me tight, like a soft vice or safety harness too, like it's keeping the warm blanket strapped to my back.

It moves against my back slowly, and I feel this unconscious desire to slow my breathing to match it. In and out, the blanket moves with me. I breathe in with it and blow out with it, slower and slower. And then it starts raining… just a mist, and then a gentle sprinkle. The air cools, the flames dissipate. And for the first time in this recurring dream, it fades out with a sense of peace.

34

KALEB

"Where you headed?" I grumbly ask Luna over the rim of my coffee cup as I push my hair off my face to take in her get up of yoga pants and sporty tank top.

"To the gym in West Bridge," she tosses over her shoulder as she fills her water bottle. "Do you want to come with me?" She asks, her back to me again.

"What would I do there?"

She raises a bare shoulder. "You could do some weight conditioning. Your PT said you're ready for that now. Maybe go on the bike or the treadmill. The endorphins might feel good."

"Hey, since when do you work out?" I ask curiously, leaning my head against my fist.

"I..." she shakes her head, her ponytail swaying with the movement as she twists the top on the bottle. "Just got turned on to this fun kickboxing class," she explains before turning around to face me.

"That's cool, I guess," I note before draining what's in my mug.

"So do you want to come along?" she asks, grabbing her hoodie off one of the kitchen chairs and slinging it around her shoulders.

"I don't know…" I release a breath out through my nose as I get up gingerly to rinse out my cup.

"You don't have to do anything, K," Luna softly prods as she zips up her hoodie. "Just come for the sake of getting off your ass and out of the house then." She sweetly tilts her head to the side, and for a split second, looked like the ten-year-old version of herself I fell in love with.

I look around for a minute, trying to figure out what the fuck else I'd do with my day, and when I come up with nothing, finally concede with a reluctant nod. "Alright, fine," I moan as I start ambling behind her when she grabs her gym bag.

⛺

THE GYM LUNA apparently attends now is situated in an outdoor galleria of sorts. I've driven by it plenty of times, but never checked out what it had to offer. The white brick buildings are lined up in a horseshoe formation.

The air is a bit crisp as summer is still a few weeks off, and I lower the bill of my head against the breeze as I slide out from behind the wheel. Looking around, I see a couple of boutiques, a juice bar, several cafes, and of course, the token coffee shop. There's even a bar right next to a law office, and I can't decide if it's hilarious irony or just smart marketing on the bar's part.

I glance over at Luna who's preoccupied with her phone, subconsciously minding the curb as she steps up on it.

"You know, I think I'm going to check out what's around here for a bit and then I'll be in."

"Okay," she looks up and nods before looking back down to her phone and strolling in the direction of the gym.

⛺

MY PILGRIMAGE TOOK a lot longer than I thought it would, but when I make my way back to the gym, I don't see Luna anywhere. She must still be in her class. It's probably too late to get into anything, but I might as well stop at the desk and see about memberships.

"Shane?" The guy in the bright yellow polo looks up from his computer to verify the last name I just gave him.

"Yeah," I nod, leaning an arm on the counter.

"Your wife got a family membership when she signed up. You're all set," he says and tips his head with friendly affirmation.

"Oh," I raise my chin, surprised. "By the way, do you know what class she's in? I'm just curious when it lets out."

"Uh, yeah she's in…" he squints his eyes like he's going through a mental catalog. "Power strike," he finally settles on. "It's just got a few more minutes."

"Alright then, thanks." I tap my knuckles on the counter and wander away, unsure what to do with basically no time left. I find a hallway that looks like it hosts a row of classrooms, so I venture down it to see if I can find Luna. By the time I reach the third door on the right, my thigh is screaming in protest and I can feel it turning my demeanor sour. The one thing I hate more than the pain is not having the means to quell it, as my prescription ran out last night.

I let myself lean against the open doorway and scan the group of women and a few men jabbing and kicking at the air around them. I spot Luna towards the front and barely recognize her with the look of determination and… absolute hatred on her face. I have no idea what put that look on her face, but I can only imagine it's me she's imagining punching in the face and kicking in the balls.

I continue to watch her lithe body, sheened in sweat, do things I didn't know it could. Loose hairs from her ponytail cling to her face as she twists and contracts, and per my new usual, I have no fucking idea what's going on in my own head right now. I don't know if I'm impressed to the point of being turned on, or unnerved that here's one more reason to believe we aren't the same people anymore.

When the class wraps, Luna grabs up her things from the floor against the far wall and makes her way over to me while taking a healthy chug from her water bottle.

"Hey," she huffs, still a little out of breath. "Did you get to do anything?" she asks before taking in another breath and scrunching her nose. "Oh my God, K, have you been drinking?"

"Fuck, Luna, I had one shot at the bar across the way," I close my eyes with a scoff as I turn away from her, and she meanders behind me down the crowded hallway.

"In the middle of the day?"

"My leg is killing me, and I'm out of the meds," I defend myself exasperatedly. "I had one shot to take the edge off. What do you want from me?" I hold my hands out as she quickens her pace and darts around to get in front of me.

"I want you to try, Kaleb," she supplies. "You're not trying."

"I got out of the house, and if I recall correctly, you said just that would be enough. I'll go out to the garage when we get home and lift a few dumbbells if it will make you happy," I fire off sarcastically.

"Just forget it," she sighs as we get into the truck, and once again, my fucked up traitorous mind torments me. She's relented. She's off my back like I was demanding, and as the engine turns over, I can't help but be angry as fuck that she has.

⛺

Luna

ANOTHER ARGUMENT with Kaleb is in the books, and after my first time back at the gym since he got back, Carter seems to have waltzed back into my mind and made himself comfortable.

I took up these classes to prepare myself for if it happens again, because let's face it, he's proven relentless with no regard for court orders, but also to work off the aggression. I'm not feeling like the poor little victim he beat up on. I'm mad as hell after all of these months, and being back in the class just seemed to bring him to the forefront of my mind.

I've always allowed him in during those sessions because I thought it was a healthy outlet; to let it fuel my energy. But today, I was left wondering if it was really the best idea. Having my mind clouded with my own issues is not what my marriage needs right now.

For the last couple of days, I've left Kaleb alone. He's griped about being out of his pain pills, the very ones he swore he was going to only take as needed, and that he'd ween himself off of. He's been standoffish, and when we do interact, I can expect either caveman grunts or sarcasm.

It's been a rough couple of days since the gym and I've hardly slept. I'm so tired and so mentally exhausted that I feel like I would do anything to sleep, which both scares and angers the hell out of me. I'm afraid if I took any kind of sleeping aid one would never be enough, and my genetic predisposition to addiction would never let me be unaffected. So here I am, lying here in bed, with Buster curled up on my pillow while I try with nothing but my own volition. Willing his purr motor to lull me, I shut my eyes and try to fall into a meditative state.

I CAN FEEL MYSELF SPIRALING; swirling down into some kind of dark haze.

This feeling of terror is killing me, and I can think of nothing but blasting it away.

All of a sudden, I'm craving… cold. I want something cold to zap me out of it; to blast away the evil fog trying to overtake me. To wake me up. Despite the fact I'm awake, I don't feel lucid. I still feel the terror as if I'm right back there on that dark staircase.

I struggle from my bed, trying to untangle myself from my mess of sweaty covers, stumbling through the dark. My pulse in my ears and the deep wheeze of my breaths are my ominous soundtrack as I gingerly pad down the hallway. I feel like even my shaking body has a sound.

When I reach the bathroom, I grip onto the door frame for support as I throw on the light. My eyes squint against the bright fluorescents, but I welcome it. Anything to make me feel like I'm right here, and in the present.

I wrench the cold-water faucet and run my hands under the cool water, splashing it haphazardly up onto my face. Each hit of the cold water seems to chip away at the haze, but it's not enough.

Reaching over into the shower, I turn the cold knob all the way to the left. Hurriedly, I pull off my shirt and step out of my shorts before stepping in, not bothering to let myself acclimate. I let out a gasp with small yelp as the chill penetrates my skin tissue and racks my body, but I don't care. I sit down in the tub and tuck my arms around my knees, tilting my face up to allow the ice-cold water to pelt down upon it.

I visualize the cold water like rain coming down over a wildfire, gradually extinguishing the flames. The residual smoke is like the dark panic rising from my body and evaporating.

"Luna?"

I jolt at the sound of Kaleb's voice, my heart giving a few hard thrashes against my chest wall as if scolding him for interrupting its peaceful deceleration.

Shit. In my haste to snap out of my attack, I didn't even think to close the door. The light and the noise likely woke him. I look up to see that I also didn't have the damn curtain wrapped all the way around the tub and he can see me huddled here like a pathetic baby animal cowering from a storm.

"Kaleb," I try to keep my voice calm. This is not my time; this is his time. As much as I need him right now, he needs me to be the strong, stable one, and he's not going to think he can stay and depend on me if all he sees is a broken-down wreck.

I slam the cold water off and search around for a towel.

Kaleb, bleary-eyed and squinting against the harsh lights,

reaches for the laundry basket by the door and grabs one of the fresh, folded towels.

"What the fuck is going on?" he grumbles, making me even less inclined to appear vulnerable around him.

"Nothing," I try to convince him as I reach for the towel and feel confusion pull at my features when he doesn't hand it over and instead steps closer to me, opening the fuzzy, lavender terry-cloth. "I…" I stammer as I realize he's reaching over me, slinging the towel over my shoulders.

"You're freezing," he observes, his brow softening, and for a second, I think I see concern in those green eyes of his. "Were you taking a cold shower? In the middle of the night?"

"I…" I trail off again, as his sudden tender attentiveness has made my brain fail to synapse and form a sentence. He closes the towel tightly around me, and I automatically grab onto the front ends. When he starts rubbing his hands up and down my arms, I seriously scramble to keep my head. "It's nothing," I say softly, lowering my head, the cold, wet strands of my hair hanging forward, dripping little dewdrops of water onto the bathmat.

As much as I want to look up into his eyes and see if some of that old tenderness might be swimming somewhere within, I'm afraid if I do, I'll fall in. Right now is about proving that I can be strong for him. I can't get all lovesick on him now.

"It was just this crazy dream." I shake my head at the floor and give out a self-deprecating guffaw. "It just shook me up a little, and you know how my mom does those ice soaks, I thought I'd try something similar," I rattle it all off, hoping it will make me sound more cavalier as Kaleb takes another towel and starts softly blotting at the drenched strands of my hair.

"Well, are you alright?" his voice is a tender murmur and seems to come out of him so naturally. Maybe he's just not awake enough to be holding up his cold, hard front he's determined to show me. Whatever it is, I can't fall into submission. This is my season of sacrifice, not his, and I need to be the caretaker.

"Yeah," I nod, lifting my head, but only just shy of meeting his eyes. "I'm totally fine. You should get some sleep," I absently advise as I reluctantly sidestep out of this loving bubble he's formed around us, and pad out of the bathroom towards my room.

35

KALEB

"Ow, son of a bitch!" I gripe up at Jason, my physical therapist as he bends my bad leg, trying to work out its sore as fuck muscles.

"Sorry, Corporal," he murmurs, letting up a little before lowering it back down. "Have you been following all the exercises and tips in your treatment summary?" he inquires as he sits back on his stool and rests his hands on his waist.

I push out a heavy breath, trying to quickly come up with an answer that's at least half-true and believable. "You sound like my wife," is the best I come up with.

"Your wife speaks the truth," he says with a tilt of his head. "Healing is more about coming here and having your leg worked around. You need to be taking care of it at home – ice, soaking in the tub with Epsom salts, letting the pain be your guide…"

"Yeah, yeah, I know." I wave him off, trying to sourly placate him just so he'll stop talking.

"So have you been doing all that?" he pushes, "Or do you just try to go about your business until your leg is screaming at you because you pushed it too far?"

I scrub my hands down my face in frustration. I don't answer because he called me the fuck out. I haven't been doing any of that because I've had no motivation. It's hard when every time you try to get some sleep, all you see are bombs going off behind your eyelids, so you spend the next day like a zombie. Half my mental energy is spent warding off those awful memories while I wander the house, the backyard, and sometimes the garage where I just stare at my motorcycle with no desire to pull the sheet off it. All I want to do is to go to sleep, dream of absolutely nothing, and then wake up to the way things were before I deployed.

Luna's been driving me fucking crazy this last month. That night in the bathroom I felt a quick flash of desire, but not in the sexual way. For about thirty seconds I felt a yearning; a want. Like I wanted to do something with myself and spend some time with Luna. It was like a soothing balm to the ache I've been feeling inside and out. But before I could try to piece together what was stirring up that feeling, back to her bedroom she went.

Since then, I've gone back to being cranky while I try to solve that lovely riddle all the while she keeps on my ass to do my exercises, lay off the alcohol, and God almighty will she ever not let up on me going to therapy. The truth is, I don't want to face the truth. I want to keep my head buried in the sand and not bring up the traumatic and depressing as fuck reel that is my life for a stranger's viewing and assessment. Why the hell should I relive all the shit I've been through? What could it possibly do but make it all worse?

"I know it seems daunting, but that's because you haven't started the process," Jason continues his preaching. "If you can just get yourself rolling, even slowly, you could..."

He trails off and when I look up at him, I follow his line of vision over to who just walked through the door of the small gym.

Ah. Speaking of my annoying wife, here she comes. But when I look from her and back to the man who's supposed to be my physical therapist, a small fire sparks to life inside of me when I see the borderline obsessive element in his stare.

"Something I can help you with?" I ask cynically through a hardened jaw.

I won't say I blame the guy. Luna's still the knockout she always was, even in a baggy hoodie and track pants. I don't hate the double French braids either. In fact, if it weren't for the tired look on her face, they'd be kind of badass.

"Huh?" Jason does a double take between me and Luna before snapping out of his stupor. "No, not at all. Good work today," he finishes, looking away and nervously clearing his throat.

That's what I thought.

After rising from my seat, I stand in front of Jason a second, letting him take in my full height before grabbing my jacket and marching over to where Luna stands, waiting.

"All set?" she asks, and I see her eyebrows raise faintly as I zealously take her hand in mine and escort us towards the door.

"Yeah," I answer curtly and push through the door.

"Do you want to stop and make an appointment before—"

"No, Luna." I cut her off with my ready-made answer. "Get off my ass about therapy," I grumble as we stride briskly down the hall, only for me to slow our pace as we get halfway to the exit because my leg is fucking killing me.

"You know I'm going to keep asking." She shrugs a shoulder with a sigh, acclimating to our slower speed without a hitch.

"And I'm going to keep shutting you down."

"Why?" she asks, this time with a locked jaw, and I know I've gotten under her skin with that one.

"You tell me why," I rebuff as I push through the exit door where a cool, overcast April afternoon greets us. "Tell me why you want me to talk about all the shitty things in my life to someone?" I stop and turn to her, releasing her hand when we reach the truck.

"Because talking can help," she holds her hands out, making

the same argument she does on a daily basis. "Especially with a professional who can guide you through–"

"And you know this because you've gone to therapy so many times?" I challenge her, leaning in with my eyebrows raised.

"No, but my–,"

"Then save it, Luna!" I bark, cutting her off again as I turn away and wrench open the driver's side door. She doesn't respond except to whip around in the other direction and make her way to the passenger side. She gets in beside me, her brown eyes displaying a quiet fury as they stare straight ahead.

We drive home in the loudest silence I've ever endured. It makes my blood run hotter and my grip on the wheel has a hum traveling up my arm. We make it about halfway down the eight-mile country road before I can't take it anymore.

"Are you going to let this go?" I ask.

Luna is quiet for a moment and I see her worry her wedding ring around her finger in my peripheral as she blinks out the front windshield.

"The therapy or the marriage?" she asks quietly, and I admit, that was a curveball answer I didn't see coming. The state of our marriage is something I'd gotten comfortable not thinking about, just like the other issues in my life. I don't even know how many days have passed since she gave me that dare.

I huff out a long breath through my nose, squeezing the wheel again before releasing. "Look, Luna, I…" I don't even know what to say. "Just… I already go to physical therapy like I'm supposed to. And by the way, I can obviously drive myself now like a big boy," I gesture at myself doing just that. "You don't have to come with me to make sure I don't crash the truck," I snip out, irritated.

"I come with you to make sure you go," she mumbles.

"Well, you don't have to," I stress to her. "You have my word; I'll go without you having to hover.

"Fine," she bites out hard, and the low growl in her voice almost scares me. We put another mile or so behind us before she finally speaks again. "Jackson wanted you to come by the shop. Could you just drop me off at home please?"

I give a stiff nod on the outside as I turn off the main drag, but on the inside, I'm feeling a small but welcome twinge at the way she said home.

I pull into our driveway and keep the engine running as Luna pushes open her door and slides out. Turning around, she places a hand on the door but before shutting it, looks at me with a stone-cold stare.

"Just one question... How has not talking about your issues with someone been working for you?"

That unexpected blow hit me square in the diaphragm and knocked me so off kilter I'm too dumfounded to give a response. Instead, I just return her glare, engaging in some strange standoff before she seems to take my silence as the answer she wants and unceremoniously slams the truck door closed.

I SWING the truck into the auto shop's small lot and throw it in park. I sit stewing for a few beats before angrily beating my fist against the wheel several times in a row. Letting out a brisk growl, I run a hand through my hair and over my face before taking a couple of breaths and exiting the truck.

Stuffing my hands into the pockets of my jacket, I amble through the garage and into the office doorway where I find Jackson standing behind the desk and straightening a few papers.

"What's up?" I mutter in greeting, and he looks up.

"Hey, Kaleb," he acknowledges one more time before putting the papers in a folder.

"Luna said you wanted to see me?" I ask, and I inwardly bristle at how awkward this feels. I own this small business, yet I feel like I'm being called to the principal's office.

"Yeah," he straightens up and comes around the desk.

"Right, so West is up in Indy, finding a part for the Callaway's Dodge 4x4, but this was his idea…" he pauses and I actually feel my brows go up.

"He's outsourcing parts?" I ask, having never thought of having to do things like that. I wonder what Pops did when he had to do that.

"Yeah, the guy has actually really turned this place around." He has a seat on the edge of the desk. "Anyway, he wanted to know what you'd think of him buying the place from you."

I feel my chin dip low as I try to process what I just heard. "Buy Shane Auto?" I ask for clarification, and he nods, thoughtfully. "Honestly, I think you should consider it. He has the expertise, he's brought in more customers, our service is higher quality and more efficient than ever…" he counts off all the benefits on his fingers, nodding at me to get me on board.

"And that is all great, but, Jackson, what do you think I joined the military for? So I could go to school and be able to take over this place myself," I remind him, holding my pocketed hands out.

"I know, and the nobility behind that is invaluable, but it's at least a three-year plan. The shop is already doing so much better, and that has nothing to do with what you did or didn't do. It just happened, and it's been a godsend. Now if you don't sell to West, I don't think he'll walk or anything, but–"

"So you're asking me to sell to him and then do exactly what with my life?" I ask, pulling my hands from my pockets and crossing my arms as I lean back against the opposite wall.

"Anything you want," he says with conviction as he pushes off the desk, holding his hands out. "You take the money and instead of taking over for Pops, you do what you want to do. You could open that tattoo parlor and pursue your passion!"

"Pops was all I had in this world, and now you want me to give up his shop?" My voice elevates as my emotions push my brain out of the way, taking the wheel on this one.

"He may be gone, but you have a wife now Kaleb. You two could do something great with that money together."

The mention of Luna makes my argument with her earlier come roaring back to the front of my mind, cuing me to get something else off my chest. "Yeah, speaking of her, next time you need me for anything you can call me. You don't have to go through her. I'm stateside and I've got my own damn phone."

Jackson blinks at the change of subjects but goes with it. "Hey, I'm sorry, it's just habit. She was here a lot while you were gone. She took care of Jacob so I could get more work done, and that made a huge difference."

Too much is happening too fast on very little sleep and the screaming pain in my leg. My logic has left the fucking building, leaving nothing but a few petty emotions in charge. "Great, well it sounds like everyone has this under control," I huff out spitefully as I push off the wall and head for the door.

"Kaleb, come on," Jackson holds his hand out, trying to stop me. "You know damn well it's not like that."

"Glad I could help. Lemme know if you need me to go to war for nothing again," I mock salute on my way out the door.

"Kaleb!" Jackson shouts after me, I keep walking back out towards my truck.

The thing is, I do know better. I know that no one is trying to box me out. I just feel so damn useless in every aspect of my life, and here Jackson threw one more at me. With the frustrations I've had reintegrating and how damn tired I am, my self-control has diminished. I need to blow off some steam and bad.

After sliding behind the wheel, my cell phone goes off in the console, and for a minute I ignore it. When it continues to ring while I turn the engine over, I finally snatch it up, intent on getting rid of whoever it is.

Imagine my befuddlement when I see the name Ryan on my screen.

What the… hell… does this motherfucker want?

He's always been one of my "friends", but he's an uncouth

asshole with no filter as we saw at the bonfire the night before I proposed to Luna.

I connect the call and bring the phone to my ear.

"Yeah?" I grumble.

"Welcome back, Private Shane," he jeers into the phone before a fit of childish laughter like he took a hot minute to come up with that one.

"It's Corporal, dipshit. What do you want?"

"Jeez, sensitive. Anyway, you haven't been over since you got home. I've got a few of the high school clan over. Let's knock a few back."

I let out a heavy breath as I ponder this prospect but don't take long as it feels like the fucking planets just aligned. "Ryan… your timing is fucking impeccable."

36

LUNA

"What if I... just left?" I say my thoughts out loud into the phone as my eyes burn with the tears that have had enough of being told to hold off.

"I don't know, sweetie," Cassidy tries to comfort me from the other end. "I'd like to tell you to just do that, I mean we both know I had my reservations about this the day you got married. I guess I've just been hoping all this time that you'd prove me wrong."

"I really tried." I sigh hard as the hot wind of defeat blows over my body that lies supine on my bed. "Kaleb doesn't want to do this anyway, and my spirit has taken quite the beating this past year."

"Have you talked to your parents?" Cass asks, interrupting my thoughts as Buster hops up on the bed next to me. I scratch his ears as he tries to comfort me with his loveable purr motor. Warm moisture trickles down my cheek and my head hurts as I try to figure out what to do.

"No," I admit quietly, and I know I need to follow that up with an explanation even though I to taste the words. "I got caught up with a controlling, abusive, narcissist for a year before I wised up. "Then I ran off and married Kaleb after two days of knowing him again." I feel my face crumple with the pain of my reality. "And now that marriage is falling apart after less than a year. He's turned into this cold, hard shell of what he was before, and I'm just not ready to tell them, Cass." I sniff as a sob I'd been trying to hold back escapes. "I'm ashamed, and I'm just not ready to face them with this. I'm not ready to tell them that every time they turn around, I dig my whole deeper and make a bigger mess of my life."

"Lu," she says soft but deliberate. "You didn't do any of this. And there'd be no shame in throwing in the towel after everything you've done. You've more than tried, and I'd be behind you one hundred percent if you did."

It's true. I've been putting in all the effort, and the only reason I'm still here is because I dared him. In that moment I truly believed he was just messed up from his trauma and the pills and that my Kaleb was still in there somewhere and needed me.

But with each passing day, the more I think maybe he did change over there. Everything was so wonderful and solid between us so I didn't want to believe it, but maybe he was just barely holding on… and that explosion made him lose his grip. Maybe he's gone, and this angry and bitter man in his place is here to stay and really doesn't want me.

But what will happen to him if I leave? Will he keep withering away without me here to push him?

Cassidy consoles me a few more minutes before we end the call. I continue to lie here, deliberating, never feeling at such a loss.

Kaleb's been gone for hours with no contact. I'd like to reach out to find where he is, but part of me thinks it would just make it worse… so I've just been sitting here in the empty house, waiting and thinking while I, myself, fall deeper.

This is doing neither of us any good. Maybe I really should cut my losses and leave. Maybe Kaleb really will be okay on his own, finding his own way without me hovering.

I feel hollow, yet heavier than a tank at the same time. Flipping on the soft light of my bedroom, I look around aimlessly for a minute before walking over to the bed and crouching down to retrieve one of my bags from under my bed. Setting the purple weekender with white polka dots on the bed, I unzip and pull it open.

All I have to do now is put my things inside it, I tell myself, but the words make my heart sink, splitting open as it descends.

In the quiet of the house I pick up a sudden but soft melody coming from the living room. My phone. Maybe it's Kaleb…

I hustle back to the recliner and find my screen lighting up with Kaleb's name on the side table, and relief floods through me as I pick it up. "Hey," I breathe out shakily.

"Hey, is this Luna?" an only vaguely familiar voice comes through the line instead of Kaleb's.

"Yes?" I respond cautiously, feeling my brow furrow. "Is Kaleb okay? What's going on?"

"Hey, this is Hunt," he answers. Hunt… the contractor. I think I've seen him around town. "I think we've passed each other in the market a couple times," he continues, answering that question. "I graduated a couple years ahead of Kaleb, but anyway, Kaleb's alright, he's just… well he's a bit tossed and needs to be taken home. We're at Ryan Farley's – are you able to come get him?"

Ryan the asshole, as I remember him. His house is only three blocks, but if Kaleb is loaded, I better take the car.

"Yeah," I sigh, feeling my nerves rattle to life and disperse through my body. "No problem, I'll be there in a few minutes."

⛺

"Hey!" Kaleb finally notices me through the fire light. "There she is." His voice wavers out slowly as I turn and reluctantly amble over to him. He's being held up by Hunt, an arm slung around his shoulder and grasping a beer bottle in his hand. I definitely recognize him now. The splatters of plaster on his jeans and the sawdust on his work boots bring me back to the times I've seen him around town. The expression on his face is a cross between relieved to see me and regretful sympathy for what he's about to dump on me. I'm not liking it either, but vows and all that. "My wife, everybody," Kaleb slurs in presentation, dropping the half full bottle to the ground as Hunt removes his arm from around him and substitutes me as the new crutch.

"Okay, let's go home," I say gently, trying to turn me and my burley soldier in the direction of the car. My suggestion is rebuffed, however, when Kaleb takes hold of my chin with his free hand and nuzzles the side of my face.

"Isn't she something, fellas?" He rhetorically addresses no one in particular before laying a kiss to my cheek. My insides claw at each other at the affection; blissful excitement duking it out with disappointment that it's not the Kaleb I want showing me this kind of attention.

"You've got a good woman there," Hunt responds. "Go on home with her," he firmly advises with a warm tone.

"She is a good woman," Kaleb agrees, halting us in our slow gait towards the car to take my face in both hands. "She's so good to me," he whispers and it's almost like he's saying it more to me than anyone else before trying to bring his mouth down on mine. I want so badly to welcome it, but the stench of whiskey and beer emanating off him remind me that it's not right. Not like this.

"Kaleb, come on," I softly blow the words out, so reluctant to say them as I try to pull his hands away from my face and resume our previous position so I can get him to the car. That's all I need to do – get him to the car. Remove him from this setting, and then it's downhill from there.

"S'matter?" he mumbles. "Too good to kiss me now?" He tries to arch an eyebrow, but those green depths are darker than the night, as if the alcohol has them under some kind of evil spell.

"If you still want to when you're sober, I'm all for it," I shoot back as I take one arm from around his middle and reach out to wrench open the passenger door. "But right now, you're drunk and you need to sleep."

Too drunk to argue further, Kaleb finally turns in the direction of the passenger seat, bracing a hand on either side of the frame as I help him lower himself into the car. He lazily drags his legs inside one by one, dropping his head back on the headrest.

Thankfully, it's a quiet ride to the house. With Kaleb's eyes shut, and his head slightly lulling against the headrest, I can't tell if he fell asleep or is just resting. Either way, I'm thankful he's not rowdy-drunk while I'm trying to drive us home.

Getting him out of the car is my next challenge. Holding on to both his hands with mine, I try to put my hours at the gym to good use, trying to pull back using my legs. Kaleb is trying to help by leaning forward but he's dead weight, and it feels like a miracle when he finally straightens his legs and stands.

We make it up the steps with Kaleb leaning on me for support the whole way. Once we're inside the door, I lock it behind us with a sigh of relief. As much as I would like to get Kaleb to bed properly, if he passes out right here on our kitchen floor, at least he's safe.

Pushing off the door, I strut passed him to the cupboards and pull out a glass before dispensing it with water from the fridge. When I turn, I find Kaleb eyeing me while he partially leans against the wall. His eyes are half-lidded in a sleepy yet sexy way as they scan me up and down. Slowly, he starts to peel off his jacket, one shoulder at a time before dropping it sloppily on one of the kitchen chairs.

In his black t-shirt, his tattoos blaze against the skin of his biceps, igniting my core against my inner protestations.

Schooling my expression, I clear my throat and approach him with the glass.

"Here, you should drink this and then go get some sleep," I implore him, holding it out.

Without even looking at the glass, he takes it from my hand and jerkily sets it on the table, never taking those hooded eyes off mine.

If I really wanted to, I could block out the smell of the alcohol and only focus on his signature scent as he steps closer to me. I could pretend that desire for me in his eyes is genuine and unfiltered. I could imagine that he's putting his hands on my hips and drawing me closer because he really wants to, and not because he's trying to scratch an itch that his intoxicated state is telling him to.

I could have Kaleb back for a night. I could let myself believe that his body for one night is better than not having him at all, possibly ever again.

"Kaleb, please," I whisper. "Don't…"

"I'm not doing anything wrong," he grumbles back, leaning down to plant soft kisses along the side of my neck. I melt into him slightly. "You want this," he ascertains, and it almost sounds like a caution.

"Not like this," I reply in another quiet gust of breath, feeling helpless to my yearning for him. "I can't do this."

"Can't get naked for your husband?" His warm breath teases against my skin and I feel the tenderness between my legs betray me. "Come on, baby, it's been a long time since we've rocked each other's world." His tone turns mischievous as his hands slide up under my shirt. They are warm and possessive against my ribcage, making me want to give in so badly. I need to get away from him.

"Kaleb, stop…" I begin to struggle, pushing against his chest, and alternating with trying to pull his arms from around me, but it makes him pull me harder against him, his crotch pushing against my abdomen.

"Feel that?" he teases in my ear. "That's for you, baby."

The idea that it's really for whoever happens to be conveniently in his presence at this moment is the last push I need.

"Kaleb, enough," I grit out, trying to push at him again, but he continues to hold me fast.

"Calm down," he pants, his breathing picking up. "Let me make my wife moan on our kitchen table."

The next three moments seem to slow down as I feel the earth shift and my emotions snap. Because Kaleb puts his hands on my arms. He doesn't grip hard, as he tries to turn me in the direction of the table. It's not threatening or controlling either, but with my emotions and efforts to get away from him already simmering, that's all it takes. I feel myself rapidly bubble over and erupt and without thinking, I knee jerk. Literally. My knee swiftly swings upward to meet his groin with a good wham, and I shove him back with the strength of my arms against his shoulders. When time snaps back, my asshole husband is crouched over, holding his junk and wheezing.

Shit.

"Oh my God," I gasp out, looking down in horror at what I've done to him.

"What the–" he pants out between coughs, "–fuck, Luna?!"

"I'm sorry, I..." I try to explain but I catch myself. I can't tell him about Carter. He's not ready to know that my fuck-wad ex put his hands on my arms before throwing me down a flight of stairs. "I'm sorry." I swallow hard before trying to come up with something better than apologizing over and over. "I didn't mean to do that, it just... I have never seen you like this, and I panicked."

"Makes me wonder," he wheezes as he tries gingerly to straighten up, "why you want this marriage to work out so bad when you'd rather put me out of commission than make love with me," he grumbles, making my head snap up.

"If you were sober and sincere," I grit out, my frustration rising, "and if I really felt that that was what you wanted, I'd let you make love to me all fucking night. I'd let you do whatever you wanted to me, and I would do everything to you."

Kaleb's eyebrows raise slightly as his shoulders lift and fall with a heavy breath.

"But right now, you're plowed and temporarily forgetting that you don't want me. And what I can't take is you waking up and remembering that in the morning!" I confess, when suddenly, a drop of moisture leaks out of the corner of my eye, quickly followed by another on the other side.

I was determined to make none of this about me until Kaleb was better, but it felt good to let a small drop of my emotions leak out in a moment I don't expect him to remember anyway.

Taking a cleansing breath, I shake my head as if trying to snap myself out of it before walking past him and towards my bedroom.

Kaleb

"You don't want me."

I don't know if those words were actually spoken or a dream, but in Luna's voice, they play on a loop in my mind before I even open my eyes.

I don't remember much from last night; just glimpses.

Luna approaching me, looking breathtakingly beautiful in the light of the bonfire.

Street lights flashing in the car window.

But the most vivid memory is holding her close to me while hearing her say those words.

Forcing my eyes open, I blink blearily in the morning light at my surroundings. I'm on the couch in my jeans while my t-shirt hangs on the lampshade. Awesome. I bet I was just a picture of distinguished self-control last night.

Draping an arm over my head, my other hand comes to rest

on my stomach where I feel an unsettling feeling. I want to say it's the stale alcohol swimming in the cesspool that is my hangover, but it feels different than that; colder.

Closing my eyes again, I will more of last night to break through my mental fog.

"Come on, baby..." I'd droned in a low voice while my hands groped along her body.

God, I remember how bad I wanted her last night, and the ache in my balls is telling me I still do. Or could that be...

A flash of myself crouched over and holding my crotch while I try not to black out from pain flickers behind my eyes.

My wife pummeled my balls last night.

I find myself smirking at the thought before my mind goes back to the memory in progress. The kitchen was dark but enough moonlight shone through the window to reveal the glassiness of her eyes. I was too stupid drunk to take note of it then, but my mind is playing a reel for me now, and pointing out the things I missed.

She misses me. She misses us, the same way I do. She's hurting and lonely and I did that to her.

I hear movement at the end of the hall.

Slowly blinking, I catch a blurry glimpse of Luna crossing the hall from her bedroom to the bathroom. She's hard to make out, but I swear to God she's in her cutoff overalls with only a sports bra underneath. She's clearly intent on a day of painting. When she comes out of the bathroom, my focus sharpens slightly and I see that her hair is in a bun with brown strands falling down. The loose whisps make me just want to kiss her neck, and now I know the ache in my groin is one hundred percent from my want for her.

"Hey," she says softly, and I appreciate her keeping her voice quiet.

"Hey," I croak back.

"What are you doing on the couch?" She stops a few feet away, a look of mild concern on her face.

I didn't want to go to bed without you.

I remember that. I remember her leaving the kitchen with those unshed tears in her eyes. I let her go, before dropping into one of the kitchen chairs and downing the water she had put there. I sat there, trying to see if the throb in my balls or my head would give out first, and when neither did, I hauled myself up and headed down the hallway, only bumping against the wall a couple of times as I went.

The spare bedroom where Luna's been living was open just a little, and I remember peering into the moonlit room, seeing her alone in that bed with her hair splayed over her pillow and her back turned to me. My disinhibited self wanted to say fuck it and crawl in to bed with her, but she'd made her stance on that idea painfully clear. I had then turned and stood in the doorway of my own room, and the empty bed had never looked less inviting. It looked cold and lonely and I didn't want to be in it without Luna.

"Bedroom was too far," I mumble instead, and she dismissively nods before heading in the direction of the kitchen.

Dammit, just once I want to give in to the love I still have for her. It's an urge I'm too tired, weary, and hungover to fight. I haul myself into a sitting position, despite my head's roaring protest. Then I stand stiffly, and without even grabbing my shirt, start taking one stride and then another towards the kitchen to where she works at the stove. The rest of my journey is easy as I glide right over to her, and placing one hand on either side of her on the counter, I cage her in. Not in a way that is dominating, but rather protective, like I'm giving her a small, loving space to be wrapped in.

She stills but doesn't resist as I press my lips to the back of her head.

Please, I inwardly request, let me love you, just for a minute.

"I'm sorry," I whisper into the back of her hair, feeling the warmth of my own breath against the strands of her hair while breathing in the sweet musk of its scent.

Luna's head turns slightly to the side as if she's looking for something before softly closing her eyes, as if accepting there's nothing but this moment, and she's locking it away in her mind. So am I. And then it's over, with the turn of her head back to the griddle where she's monitoring what looks like French toast. The buttery smell and that of the coffee confuses my senses, until a whiff of her orange blossom scent joins in and brings me a nostalgic flash of memories from before I deployed.

Home. This is home.

I realize I'm still hovering and back away, pushing a hand through my hair. Luna turns and brushes past me to pull the milk out of the fridge, and while I enjoy the soft warmth, this time her beautiful scent raises a flag.

I must seriously reek.

Shaking out of my haze, I grab a mug from the cabinet and pour myself some of the coffee from the carafe and shuffle towards the bathroom, taking a swig as I go. The black liquid burns as it goes down, but the smell and the taste definitely helps zap away some of the fog.

I take my time in the shower, letting the steam engulf me, and letting all the thoughts and memories of last night come to me in more flashes.

Back when I asked Luna for the divorce, I was both messed up by my trauma and the drugs, and also completely selfish. I had wanted to hide from all the turmoil by coming back to the way things were before I left. I wanted my life and my Luna back, and what laid out before me wasn't it. So I wanted out, and convinced myself she probably did too. I expected a fight of course, because Luna's a stand-up, noble woman, but what I did not expect was what I saw in her eyes last night.

Hurt. Loneliness. Love. Yearning.

I didn't think for a minute that the idea of me ending things hurt her like that.

Fuck, I've created some kind of monster in my mind – that monster being a conjured-up idea that having her Kaleb come back to her as less than what he was caused the change I saw in her. That it was disappointment, obligation, and resentment that I was seeing.

I'm so fucking confused. I don't know what's real and what I've made up in my head. For once, the idea of seeing a shrink sounds appealing. Let someone else figure this out. The only clear thoughts I'm having is that I want what I gave into in the kitchen moments ago. I want Luna to not have last night's look in her eyes ever again.

After shutting off the water, I wrap a plum-colored towel around my waist and go to the sink. After wiping the steam from the mirror, I take a good look at myself, resting my hands on the vanity.

I thought almost choking my wife during sex and then asking her for a divorce while jacked up on pain meds was my rock bottom. But after last night, I realize I was wrong. Seeing that look in Luna's misty eyes while she said "you don't want me" was.

All our lives, she's never let me hurt her. Our fight at the lake, she flipped me off as she walked away. When I asked for the divorce, she essentially told me to eat shit. But last night, the idea of me not wanting her made her voice tremble and tears shine her beautiful brown eyes, and this morning's realization of it fucking broke me. Just like that night on the phone when I was able to call her and heard her crying for the first time ever. Her voice wobbled so much I could barely make out that she was telling me how much she missed me. That had gutted me.

I stand here now, dizzy, and I don't know if it's residual intoxication or the heat of the shower, but I grip onto the sink, closing my eyes as more thoughts come; fragments of memories. Luna's voice.

My Kaleb is still in there somewhere.
You love me.

She wants us back, too. That's why she's been fighting – not just to do the right thing or because she's a good, caring person.

When the humidity of the bathroom gets to be too much, I push away from the sink and open the door, welcoming the clear, cool air of the hallway, and I stand, glancing down towards the kitchen where I still hear dishes clanking. I don't even know what to do with all these sudden epiphanies, but I feel like I want to go to Luna. I don't want to come on too strong after the way I acted last night, but if I could just hug her, or give her a kiss…

I look down and realize if I'm going to tread carefully, I probably shouldn't be wet and naked when I do it and head towards my room, intent on finding some clean clothes.

The door of Luna's room is ajar and something dark but shiny catches my eye, making me stop and change course.

Pushing the door open a little wider, I'm stunned still at what I see.

37

KALEB

The painting glistens in some places where it hasn't dried yet, especially the parts that are extra saturated with black that reflects the daylight trying to seep through the gauzy curtains. This tells me that Luna wasn't intent on painting today like I'd thought. She already had. And this…

It's got some kind of a shattered effect to it, and it never ceases to blow my mind how she can create looks like this.

I don't even know how she made all the cracks and wrinkles to give off the broken look, but I don't doubt it was by some means clever.

What has my body locked up and my heart feeling cold is the color, or lack thereof.

I've always known Luna to paint in vibrant colors; shades of purple I'd never even heard of, along with a varying array of yellows, blues, and greens.

This piece is predominantly black with grey accents in varying shades.

As my eyes peruse up and down this dance of dark hues, they pick up an occasional dab or smear of light purple. It's almost like she didn't want the painting to go completely dark and dismal, and the little flecks of violet and lilac represent glimmers of hope.

But still... this isn't my Luna.

A sudden flash of Luna in the bathtub under the cold shower assaults me before I blink back to the moment and am once again studying this dark and shattered expressionistic product of my wife's inner thoughts and feelings, before another flash hits me... Luna in her power strike class, looking furious with her forceful punches and kicks, as if she were fighting off Satan himself. Luna's eyes looking puffy when she showed up to the bonfire last night, and then again with the tears in her eyes in the kitchen.

I did this.

This whole time, she's been suffering on the inside while trying to be brave on the outside. For me... She's been donning her tough-as-nails armor for me, trying to get me back on my feet, all the while I've been tearing her down on the inside.

I was wrong both those other times.

This is rock bottom.

Unable to look at this anymore, I back out of the bedroom and turn to retreat into my own. The excessive heat I felt from the shower is gone, replaced by a damp chill that's only partly courtesy of my wet hair and cooled water droplets clinging to my skin.

I have to do something, I think as I reach in the dresser and pull out a Henley.

How can I make this right? My heart pummels rapidly in my chest as I pull the shirt on over my head, the material clinging to my dewy skin.

She was meant to light up the whole world, not just mine, and it would be a crime to waste that light on a broken-down lost cause: a wounded veteran who couldn't come home to her whole. I wonder for just a split second if setting her free would be a gift to the rest of the world... But too bad for them, because it turns out I'm still as selfish as ever when it comes to her.

Besides, I saw in her eyes last night how much she doesn't want that, and I know now neither do I.

Consider me fucking awake. Time to find a way to salvage this so that I can keep Luna with me.

After pulling on jeans, one of my earlier conversations with Luna bubbles to the surface of my percolating psyche.

I want you to try, Kaleb. You're not trying.

I remember not knowing exactly what she meant in that moment and blowing it off, not caring to, but it's so damn easy now to realize she meant trying at everything. My marriage with her, and getting myself back.

I'm going to try, Luna. I can tell her I've woken up and seen the error of my ways all I want, but that doesn't mean shit unless I do it. Besides, expressing myself verbally has never been my forte and she knows it.

I wish I knew what the fuck to do, and start stressing out over it for the next few minutes. When I realize it's taking me in the wrong direction, I take some deep breaths. I need to try, but that doesn't mean conquer the world immediately. Small steps is fine. Just go with it, I nod to myself.

After lacing up my boots, I wander out into the hallway and down towards the kitchen.

I find Luna at the very table, playing with the design app on her phone. There's about two bites taken out of her French toast that's been pushed aside, and her hand absently scratches Busters ears, whose curled up in her lap. She looks up when she hears me approaching and her eyebrows go up.

I stand like an idiot for a minute, not saying anything as I take her in. My brave girl who currently hides the dark pain that she's released onto a canvas in her room.

"You look nice," she tells me, her eyes panning me up and down.

"Thanks," I murmur, feeling stupid and sheepish as I should be saying that to her every day.

"Something going on today?" she asks with gentle curiosity.

"No," I answer, twisting my wedding ring around my finger as I keep looking at her, looking for the words to say. "Just... trying."

Her facial expression doesn't change except for her eyes. I see a light spark to life in them though she tries to keep her face neutral as she nods.

"Thought I'd run up to the market," I say, hiking my thumb over my shoulder in the direction of the front door. "You know," I shrug, "get out of the house and all that. We need anything?"

"Um..." those bright eyes blink as she tries to think of something, and I already feel like I'm on top of the world for the change I'm seeing in her, no matter how faint. "Coffee creamer?" she finally says.

"You got it," I promise before turning and heading for the door.

Luna

He's trying.

At least that's what he said, and as I stand here under the warm water, I try not to get my hopes up. This is just one morning. As happy as I am to see the absence of anger and bitterness, it can't be gone just like that. Even if he had dropped to his knees in the kitchen and professed to be a changed man, I wouldn't believe no matter how badly I'd want to.

But the simple act of apologizing for being a slobbering idiot last night? And putting on his old ripped jeans and a clean shirt that made him look like the Kaleb I remember? Those little things give me hope that he's taken a step. It's a small hope, and I'm going to hold it very delicately. But still... it was good to see.

Just take it for what it is, I tell myself as I frown at the black paint that's stuck to the heel of my hand, trying to work it out with some suds from my bodywash and the strength of my thumb.

After the events of last night and the shitty sleep I got thereafter, I gave up when I saw the first trace of daylight and got up.

The pain of yesterday had me on the verge of giving up. Thoughts of packing my things and heading back to the city alone were so dark and dismal and were eating me up from the inside. If I didn't get it out, it felt like I was going to implode into a cloud of black ash. Instead, I let it all out onto my canvas like I have in the weeks since Kaleb came home.

Over the din of the shower, I hear the muted sound of the front door slamming closed, jarring me from my little trance. Rinsing the rest of the conditioner out of my hair, I shut off the water. Pulling the curtain aside, I go to reach for the towel I keep on the nearby rack to find nothing.

Oh my God, Kaleb took the last towel with his shower this morning, and I'll bet you anything it's laying in a damp heap on his bedroom floor. Fabulous.

Clutching the curtain close to my body, I call out. "K, is that you?"

"Yeah," he shouts back from the kitchen.

"Could you bring me a towel, please?"

"Yeah..." he bellows back after a short pause. "Yeah, just a sec."

I'm starting to shiver when the bathroom door swings open and Kaleb walks in, carrying the basket of clean linens that'd I'd forgotten in the dryer. He glances at the empty towel rack and blinks, shaking his head as if his morning shower is just coming back to him.

"Sorry," he murmurs, setting down the basket and lifting a fluffy lilac-colored towel and walking it over to me.

"It's okay. Thanks," I say taking it from him and ducking behind the curtain to wrap it around me. When I have it secured around my boobs, I pull the curtain back again and step out to find him hanging a couple more towels on the rack. I pick up another one and start patting my hair dry, and a little tiny light glows to life inside me when he starts folding the rest and putting them in the wooden cupboard next to the door. But again, I try not to make too much of it and step out of the room and head to my own to finish drying off.

Dressed in my favorite baggy jeans and Turn it Up baby tee, I come out into the kitchen and my attention is immediately pulled to a brand-new sketchpad laying on the surface. I feel my eyebrows bend curiously at it before opening the fridge and finding something else unexpected. Right on the center rack sits a full six pack of root beer. I haven't even thought about my favorite beverage in so long, and now my mouth is watering for it.

"Thought you could use a beer." Kaleb's voice grabs my attention from the hallway entrance and I look up, feeling my face lighten in a grateful expression.

"Thank you," I exhale through my nose, feeling a whisper of a smile pull at the corners of my mouth as I look back down and reach in to grab one of the inviting brown bottles. When I look back up, shutting the fridge door, I see what looks like a warm look in his eyes, and the rest of his face is relaxed. For once it's not pulled into a rough landscape of hard planes and rigid lines. It's like my pleasant reaction to his thoughtful gesture brought him a modicum of peace.

He finally nods, his eyes half-lidded – again, in a way that suggests relaxed and not broody.

From there, I shuffle gingerly out of the kitchen towards the living room, not sure what I intend to do there besides enjoy my root beer.

So far, this day has been the best in a long time, but still, I tread lightly, giving this dynamic time and space to breathe and hopefully grow.

38

KALEB

I want to go to Luna.

For those first few weeks I was home, I missed her and I wanted her, but it was endurable as I had my anger and my traumatic memories to keep me company, making me only vaguely aware of how I was hurting her. But seeing her tears that night... it gave me a feeling bigger and worse than all the other turbulence going on inside me. It overshadowed it, making it seem smaller and less significant.

I haven't been perfect since that awakening, as my demons still try like hell to follow me around. I still have my bad days where I'm not motivated to do anything but lay on my bed and stare at the ceiling... but I'm nice to Luna. Even when she comes to my room and gives me shit for missing a PT appointment or not getting up and showering, I make a conscious effort not to indulge those demons that are floating around overhead. I don't snap at her like they want me to.

And when I'm having an okay day, I try to put in a little effort, like asking her about her classes, or putting a bunch of violets in a mason jar for her on the table when I saw them in the nearby field.

What I haven't done much of is physically touching her.

I've been afraid to for fear that the monsters will overtake me again, and I don't want to give either of us false hope – especially with those bad days still coming around, even if they are rarer.

In the last couple of weeks, I've been gradually finding pieces of my old self and snapping them carefully back into place. Finding that sketchpad near the checkout in the market was like a small omen, and I picked it up on impulse. It's been a good thing as it's gotten me back into drawing. Sometimes I hole up in the garage, tinkering on the bike. Sometimes I sit in the living room with Luna and draw while she reads or looks up art projects on YouTube. She's more relaxed, I've noticed, which is a good thing, but we're still missing something. It's been a while since I've seen her be my silly girl, and that's on me. Like I said, I've been too afraid to try and make things all better and blissfully happy when I'm not there yet.

But still, I think as I sit here taking a stupid salt bath... I have to admit though, it really helps draw the pain out when I'm sore after a PT session, or when I've done too much around the house.

I push a hand through the wet strands of my hair, slicking them away from my face as I think about how to carefully move forward a bit more with Luna. These small steps we've been taking have felt just right, but the last couple of days I've been a little restless, wanting more. I lean my head against my fist, pondering if it's a sign that I'm ready to be more affectionate; that I wouldn't be taking two steps back afterward. Earlier, in the kitchen, I actually gave her side a quick tickle as I walked by her, making her jump and let out a shrieking laugh that gave me some kind of endorphin hit that I didn't know I was missing, and now I'm craving more.

Fuck it, I decide, sitting forward and looking around for a towel. I want to be close to her, and I need to do something. Only problem is besides the bathmat, there's not a scrap of terry cloth to be seen in here.

"Lu?" I call out loudly so she can hear me from wherever she is in the house.

"Yeah?" I faintly hear her voice coming from the laundry room.

"Can you bring me a towel?" I beckon, and now I realize how she feels when I take the last towel and she's had to call to me to bring her one several times in the last couple of weeks. Okay, one time I did it on purpose, just to see her naked, and I can neither confirm nor deny if I rubbed one out later that night.

The white, wooden door swings open, and in walks Luna with the laundry basket full of purple towels on her hip. She gives me a smart look, like, gee what's it like to get stranded in the bathroom with no towel, but it's the way her hair is up in a messy ponytail with strands hanging down around her neck that's waking up my pheromones. And when she turns to hang a couple of towels up, I notice that she's got nothing on but a long with tank top that can only make me wonder if she's wearing panties underneath it. The racerback shows off her defined and delicate shoulder blades.

She's to die for right now, and I feel myself rapidly growing below the water's surface. But it's more than just that. My need to touch her just went through the fucking roof. I want to hold her close and breathe her in for hours.

I watch from my front row seat in the tub as her lithe body moves and bends as she folds towels and goes up on her toes to stash some in the cupboard.

"Here," she smirks, tossing the last one over the back of the chair by the tub we moved in here to help me get in and out.

She tucks one of those loose strands behind her ear as she moves past me and opens the door, but before she can exit, I snap out of my stupor.

"Hey," I stop her, watching her stop at the door and turning to look at me with her eyebrows raised, waiting to hear what's next. "Wanna join me?" I ask after a few seconds of looking her up and down.

She stares back at me for a moment, looking as if she's struggling with something. She goes rigid but twitches and it only takes another second before her almond eyes crinkle at the corners and her mouth wins the fight she was putting up against a smile. A small laugh bursts out between pursed lips as her upper body drops forward, her hands finding her knees.

I feel myself frown at her response as she tries to straighten up, full-on laughing now.

"Oh - my - gaw-aw-awd!" she barely gets out as she wipes at one of her eyes.

I want to get mad and indignant, but even I can admit that came out lame. And besides, that laughter? I'm getting a huge dose of the aforementioned drug I got earlier, and it's making it impossible. It feels too fucking good.

"Shut up," I mumble out anyway, dropping my head back against the porcelain. Can't even ask my wife to get in the tub with me. I had no idea I was that off my game.

"Come on," she takes a deep breath trying to restore the oxygen in her lungs. "What are you, in middle school?" she teases.

"Yeah, yeah, yuk it up, goon," I volley back, shaking my head. I give her a minute to get ahold of herself while secretly basking in her smile, but as soon as it looks like she's composing herself, I jump at another chance. "Lu… come on," I look up at her, trying to gauge what she's thinking.

"You're serious?" she asks, her eyes searching as she still catches her breath.

"Yes," I reach out for her hand and squeeze it to demonstrate. "Please get in here with me."

We're both still a moment, looking at each other, like we have several times since I came home. Like we're trying to see each other; know each other again. And then Luna slips her hand from mine and reaches for the bottom hem of the dress-like tank top. Pulling it up, she gives me a slow reveal of lacey boy shorts in a shade of pale lilac, followed by the gorgeous, smooth plane of her stomach. Then she pulls it over her head, revealing the absence of a bra.

After she's bent to pull down her panties, I brace both hands on the edges of the tub and pull myself up to make room for her, but before I can slide backwards, she surprises me by getting in behind me.

"Wait, what are you doing?" I ask, trying to look at her over my shoulder. "I'm pretty sure this is not how couples are supposed to sit in the tub together," I chuckle out.

"Deal with it, soldier," she chides, her voice sounding a relaxed kind of sultry as she brings her knees around either side of me. "Just give me a minute," she sighs out and presses her bare chest against my back, and dammit... I thought I knew how badly my skin was craving the feel of hers against it, but it turns out, I had no idea. Luna hooks her arms undermine, wrapping them around my chest and leans her head against me, her cheek resting on the back of my shoulder.

I close my eyes as she lets out a sigh. I melt into this moment, not just because it feels good to me, but because of the realization that it feels good to her too.

Placing my hand over hers on my chest, I let go and give into the bliss of this long-awaited connection. There's a raw but pure quality to it, and it heightens the tenderness.

My thumb finds her wedding ring and nudges it absently, just like I did a lot when we first got married.

Luna's holding me... she's infusing me with her peaceful comfort, her quiet support, her steadfast love... Just like she did on countless occasions before I deployed, and I'm pretty sure she's the blanket I've felt that stifles my nightmares. She's been holding me together this whole time. She's been holding us together. She's the hero in our love story.

But taking care of her gives me life. From the ropes course when we were little, to that night on the phone, and I definitely noticed how good it felt that night I found her in the shower.

I just want to give back; to balance us out. Not because I need to feel more adequate, but because it seriously uplifts me, making me feel like the kind of person I want to be.

Reaching behind me, I wrap an arm behind her neck, trying to pull her closer against me, but it's not enough. To hell with small steps. I need us to wrap up in each other so fully that we disappear inside one another.

"Lu..." I husk out, my need for her making my breathing labored. "Please come closer, baby, I need you."

Luna abruptly stands, the water sloshing around her as she moves and steps over me and I slide back so she can take the place in front of me. The tub is deep but not very wide, and so her long legs bend and scrunch up as she faces me. I take hold of her calves and pull her even closer, wrapping her legs around me and pull her into my arms, wrapping her up completely as hers go around my neck.

"K," is all she says against my bare shoulder and I pull away only enough to take her face in my hands. I search her eyes, looking for any sign that taking the next step is okay; that she feels safe letting me in. When her eyes close halfway, I bring my lips to hers, kissing her for the first time in weeks. Her lips are moist from the steam of the tub and as soft as ever.

The kiss deepens, the brush of our lips getting more languid with each pass. Our heads tilt in different directions as if trying to taste each other in all possible ways.

When the need for air makes itself unavoidable, we pull back, resting our foreheads together as we catch our breath. My eyes flicker open to catch a glimpse of the light purple moon I etched into her skin almost a year ago. Leaning in, I press my lips to it as her hands find my hair. She lets out a low sigh as I breathe against her.

"You've been taking care of me all this time, my girl," I lament. "I want to take care of you now."

Luna

"Wʜ–" I breathe out. "What do you mean?" I ask, searching his green eyes for any sign that this isn't real; that it's too good to be true, but they're as clear as ever... Without the angry cloud or drunken haze, they remind me of the color of sea glass. Like the eyes I remember.

"I mean..." he looks down at the water between us for a moment, presumably searching for the right words before looking back up. "I mean, whatever will make you feel whole right now, I want to do it. Whatever will make you feel loved. Safe."

I let out a shuddery sigh as he touches his forehead to mine, and I try to keep the burning moisture in my eyes from falling.

"K..." I whisper, "is it really you? Please tell me you're coming back. That's what would make me feel safe. It would make me happy." A maverick tear spills from the corner of my eye without my permission and Kaleb must sense it because he pulls away just enough to look at me. When he sees the tear, he brushes it away with his thumb and then leans in to kiss the track it left, his lips lingering on my cheek.

"I'm sure as hell trying, baby," he assures me. "I'm not all the way there, and I don't know if I'll ever be, but I can promise you that I'm no longer the guy who won't try."

I let out a heavy breath, feeling it expel so much pain and worry. So many scary and sad feelings get pushed out and another tear leaks out, running down my cheek as if to make sure they leave.

"Baby that's all I need," I tell him, giving him a small smile as I rest my hands on his bare shoulders.

His eyes close briefly as if the same relief just came over him too, but when he opens them, there's a yearning shining bright in them. "But I need to do something. I want to give to you."

Of course, when he says this he shifts us, and I notice his hard-as-steel erection brushing against my sex.

"Hey," he murmurs, getting my attention when I suck in a breath. "I don't mean that. I'm not saying and doing all this to get laid," he says and shakes his head gently.

"I know," I murmur down at him as I sweep a wet strand of his hair away from his face. "But um... for the record?" I raise an eyebrow at him.

"I want to," he nods adamantly at me, and it makes me giggle. "But really," he straightens his face and reaches down to scoop up some bath water and let it stream down my back to keep me warm. "I'd be happy to just hold you the rest of the day and into the night, or help you draw something, watch a movie – anything you want. I just... want to be all about you right now."

While it's my first instinct to circle back to my original request, I can tell how much he wants this; that it would make him feel good to do it.

"Okay," I finally agree with a hesitant smile. "All of it?" I ask, raising my eyebrows hopefully.

"Of course," he nods, before closing his eyes and leaning in to place another kiss on my lips, and it feels like heaven after so long with barely any affection between us.

"Water's getting cold," I whisper against his lips and he nods, reaching around me to pull the drain plug.

I stand as the water gurgles down the drain, its level lowering as it goes. When I'm safely out on the bath mat, I turn and let Kaleb lean on me as he steps out. Pulling the towel I brought him off the chair back, he wraps it around me and the gesture is so tender, it warms me all over and I glance up into those greens again. It's there. The love is surely there.

"Kiss me again," I request up at him, and as if he was hoping that would be my next request, he eagerly cradles my face and presses his lips to mine again. This time, I can't help a moan as it takes my breath away, along with the feel of his hard length brushing between us. It awakens a hunger in me, and all of a sudden, kissing isn't enough. Wanting to touch more of him, I skim my hands up his torso, and taking hold of the towel, he pulls me closer.

"Lu, baby..." he husks out between brushes of our lips. "I'm serious, we don't–"

"I need you, Kaleb," I cut him off breathlessly, my mind made up. It's been too long, and I don't think in this instance that there is such a thing as connecting too much.

The towel drops and I'm up on my toes, my arms looping around his neck, and his strong arms pulled tightly around me. Kaleb pushes his tongue into my mouth, immersing me in his kiss and making me moan into his mouth again.

"I need you too, my girl," he says urgently between kisses, and with one arm around me, he grips the edge of the tub with his other hand. Without breaking our kiss, he lowers us to the plush bath mat.

39

KALEB

Supporting myself with an arm on either side of her head, I hover over Luna, so ready to lose myself in her. The thought of it is already healing more of the pain inside me as I feather my lips over hers, lightly teasing. My cock is brushing against her, straining and aching for her, but I swear to God I won't make her regret this.

"I might not last long," I warn her with a half-smile.

"Neither will I." She gives me the same smile back and my face dives into the nook between her neck and shoulder, a frenzy released. I need to breathe her in, taste her. I want to make her feel so good, loved, and grounded, that stars explode behind her eyes.

Her fingers find my hair again as I worship every inch of her skin I can get to. Our bodies are warm and wet, pressing together, rubbing and gliding as I cherish her.

Reaching down between us, I find her clit dripping and slick, and a hard gasp escapes her lips when my fingers glide through it.

I want this to last, but she already assured me she won't, and my balls are aching so bad with the need to come. Maybe the actual act won't last, but I can make sure the afterglow does. After all, all I wanted from her today was to simply be with her.

Using my hips to nudge her legs open wider, I settle between her thighs, my dick notched at her opening, and I'm rewarded with the most beautiful moan as her mouth falls open. Desperate to hear it again, I nibble gently at her earlobe and I'm not disappointed. Gripping her thigh, I work my mouth down her throat start pushing forward, my dick gliding into her warm pussy.

It's fucking heaven, and I groan out loud at the sudden wave of pleasure.

"Luna," I rasp, rolling my hips against hers. "Oh God, Luna."

After three passes I'm buried to the hilt, and my thrusts stay deep and tight, not wanting to pull out of her even an inch.

Reaching beneath her, I'm able to get my arms wrapped completely around her as I continue to pump steadily inside her. I thrust hard and deep, reveling in her cries of arousal, my cock swelling inside her each time. And just when I'm about to tell her I can't last any longer, I feel the beginning tremors of her orgasm fluttering around me.

"K..." she cries out on a drawn-out moan as it builds, and when I feel it crest, I let go. I pound us through the most powerful climax as the earth shakes around us. I feel myself sweating and getting a little dizzy as my cum shoots into her.

"Lu...Lu... baby!" I grunt into her neck as I slam into her several more times, making sure we both get the longest ride we can out of it.

I slow my pace as we both wane out before I shift to my right so I don't put too much weight on her or my bad leg.

Luna lays sated beneath me, trying to catch her breath, and I gaze down at her, pulling a damp strand of hair off her forehead.

"I love you," I pant down at her and her eyes flutter open, showing me that amber ring glowing brilliantly around the irises.

"I love you too," she returns, still breathless.

I roll to my side, bringing her along and cradling her close to me.

⛺

ONLY A FEW MINUTES pass by as we lay in silence and Luna draws little hearts on my chest with her fingertip. In this moment, we're exactly how we were when we first got married, and it's perfect. I know all moments fade as the world spins on, but I'm dedicating every move I make to her from this point on. And I still want to give her all the things I promised her, but I also want to hold her on this hard-ass, uncomfortable as shit bathroom floor for as long as she'll let me.

"What do you want to do?" I ask softly into her hair. "Do you want to get off this bathmat and go to bed for the rest of the day?"

"Mmm..." she hums and I can feel her smile against my neck. "That'd be nice I guess..." her finger pauses the hearts she's drawing and starts trailing down my chest, and it sends a flash of excitement up my spine.

I'm trying to think of all the things I want to do with her, like get in some sweats and cuddle up with her on the couch with a dumb movie in front of us... ordering take out and taking it to bed with us... rolling naked in paint and making a masterpiece on canvas.

Speaking of paint, I also want to find a way to talk to her about the painting of hers I saw, but as per usual, words aren't my strong suit, and as I feel her soft lips and her sweet breath sweeping against my chest, I decide this is definitely not the right moment.

Despite coming like there was no tomorrow mere minutes ago, I'm still hard between her legs and she's making every fluid inside me run hot with what she's doing.

"What are you doing, silly girl?" I groan out on a raspy breath. Another small hum is the only response I get, and it drives me out of my mind. Reaching between us I palm her breast and brush my thumb around her areola, eliciting a full moan from her. "You like that?" I whisper and she nods, licking her lips. "You want more?" I ask, grinding my hardness against her and pulling her leg up over mine.

"Yes," she whispers nodding before another mewl comes out of her when I start trailing my mouth down her neck and give her breast a squeeze.

"You want to come again?"

"Yes," she pants and then cries out at the sudden invasion of my cock.

Grabbing hold of her ass, I pull her down further on me before I start pumping inside her again.

"I'll make you come as many times as you want," I tell her between ragged breaths. "Whatever my beautiful wife wants."

"God, Kaleb," she groans, winding her arms around my neck and holding me close as I fuck her, facing each other on our bathmat.

I feel her start to quake around me and everything in my groin tightens up.

"Come for me, Lu," I coax her and she squeezes hard around me, moaning and crying out against my shoulder. "That's a good fucking girl," I growl approvingly as I feel my own arousal build further.

"K… K…" she gasps as she peaks and I pummel into her, chasing my own release.

Holy fucking shit.

We explode together for a second time, her scream mingling with my roar as we shudder against each other.

This time we pull away from each other, the heat and the sweat getting to be a little much, but I take hold of her hand as we lay panting side by side.

"Do you want another one?" I ask looking over at her, and a laugh bursts from between her lips.

"Um...maybe later," she laughs. "That was like six crammed into two."

"Thank God, because that about killed me," I quip, making her laugh harder.

"But it was hot to say in the moment," she says once she recovers before looking over at me. "My dirty talking soldier," she recalls sweetly, and I look back at her.

"My silly, spitfire wife."

Luna

YESTERDAY WAS OUR WEDDING ANNIVERSARY. Kaleb met his deadline, his dare fulfilled, so to speak. If he realizes it, he hasn't spoken about it, and today we made love. The unfolding events of the last couple of months would indicate that things are going to be okay. I'm a little nervous, though. I'm afraid of it being too good to be true, or at the very least, too much too fast. It's not that I have any intention of looking back, it's just that I don't know about Kaleb. I don't know if he's here to stay permanently, or if another setback is imminent.

Nevertheless, I shower off with Kaleb and with a towel wrapped around me, head in the direction of my bedroom to put on some clean clothes.

I'm just stepping into a pair of clean panties when I hear a heavy sigh behind me. I look over my shoulder to see my husband leaning against the doorframe, toweling off his hair with the ends of the towel draped around his neck.

"What?" I smile over my shoulder at him before turning back to open a drawer and grabbing out the first old t-shirt I find.

"Nothing," he says innocently. "Just watching you... get dressed."

"And?" I smirk, pulling the t-shirt over my arms and letting it drop down my body.

"It looks wrong in here," he sighs out his nose.

"Why?" I grab my nearest pair of sweatpants and sit down on the bed to pull them on.

He lifts his shoulder and shakes his head and it gives me trepidation. We took a really big step less than a half hour ago, but neither one of us can seem to just say it; that we're going to be okay, that we want this marriage to work out.

I make no further comment as I stand to pull my sweats the rest of the way up. The stoney silence is just starting to cross over into awkward territory when Kaleb speaks.

"Will you sleep with me tonight?" he asks, gently, yet it surprises me, my head snapping up to regard him. I don't know what to say, and I push a strand of damp hair behind my ear, hoping he'll continue, which he fortunately does. "I have dreams… nightmares," he corrects himself, and I can tell what he's trying to say is hard for him. "And um… I think you've been taking them away. Have you been getting in bed with me?" he asks, unsure if what he's felt at night when the terror dissipates is real or not.

I press my lips in a line and finally nod, which makes his half-lidded eyes seem to glimmer behind his lashes as he gives me a faint but warm smile.

"It felt like maybe you had," he comments before hi expression tightens slightly. "Have I… I haven't ever hurt you, have I? When I'm in the throes of a nightmare?"

"No," I'm quick to assure him. "No, you've never hurt me."

He nods thoughtfully, looking down for a moment, and as much as I'd love for him to just tell me what's going on in his heart, I know he's been compromising a lot of vulnerability in the last couple of months.

"I have dreams too," I confide, stepping closer to him, "and I'd like to have someone there to take them away."

This makes him smile, and those green eyes dance behind his lashes some more. He looks away coyly before back at me. He knows what I'm doing. We both know what's going on here, but we're good with it.

The heaviness of the moment seeming to have lifted, K holds his hand out to me, his relaxed smile back on his face.

"Let's go have some dinner."

40

KALEB

"*K*!" I just barely hear Luna shout from the front porch just after I fire up the Harley. I look up to see her hustling down the steps, pulling on one of my hoodies over her tank top and sweatpants that she must've thrown on in haste because I'm damn sure left her naked in that bed a few minutes ago. She looks troubled, the space between her brows pinched and her eyes wide.

"Baby, what's wrong?" I ask, genuinely concerned as I cut the engine. I set my helmet down on the tank and hold my arm out to pull her towards me.

"You didn't kiss me goodbye," she supplies, her voice soft and her expression still a mix of disappointment and worry... and it gives me life – not my tough girl having an insecure moment, but being needed and wanted like this. The way she came rushing out here because she's missing a simple show of affection.

"Aww, baby..." my voice goes tender as my heart turns to absolute mush. I reach out to thread a hand in her hair and pull her closer. "You were sleeping," I explain as I lean in and give her a sweet kiss that I hope makes up for it. "I didn't want to wake you."

I give her another kiss before asking if she's okay now and she nods, looking somewhat placated. Meanwhile, my heart is fucking dancing.

"Where are you going? This is early for you," she comments, wrapping her arms around herself, the sleeves of my hoodie hiding her hands.

"I'm just headed out to West Bridge for a while," I explain, taking hold of her hand. "I've got one more PT appointment, and then I was going to run some errands. West had a rare Harley come into the shop that needs an archaic exhaust, and I think someone on craigslist might have what he needs, so I was going to check it out."

"Okay," she nods, a faint smile starting to relax her features.

"What have you got going on today?"

"Pottery," she rolls her eyes disgustedly but it makes me chuckle. I'm proud of her. It's the one art class that's been kicking her ass but she's stuck with it, determined to make it her bitch.

"Give 'em hell, baby," I snicker, leaning in for one last kiss, and this time, she full-on beams as she turns away, leaving me to fire up the Harley once again. Helmet secure, I knock the kickstand up with my boot and head on out of the driveway in the direction of West Bridge.

That simple, short little exchange filled me with the extra vigor I needed to go do what's on my agenda today... the one thing I left out of the plans I told her about. I've actually made a therapy appointment, but I don't want to tell her that just yet. I want to see how it goes before I get her hopes up that I'm talking out my issues with someone. Lord knows this is something I still don't want to do, and I don't foresee it helping one iota. But I'm finally in a place where I feel ready to try. On the off chance it goes well, then maybe I'll make a recurring appointment, maybe bi-monthly, and then I'll let her in on it.

When I reach the VA, I take the elevator to the second floor, not quite ready for that amount of stairs yet. When the doors open, I follow the sign around the corner and approach the reception desk where a woman, I'm guessing somewhere in her fifties, sits behind a computer in a wheelchair. She looks tough as nails despite that, and I'm presuming she, herself, is a veteran.

"Morning," I announce my presence, and she looks up with a tight smile.

"Name?"

"Kaleb Shane to see Dr. Jeffries," I supply.

"He's actually all ready for you. Just power off your cell phone and you can go on back," she instructs and jerks her head in the direction of a hallway to her left.

"Thank you," I nod at her before reaching in my jacket pocket and turning off my phone as I walk around her desk and down the hallway she indicated.

My arms and chest are tight and my heartbeat has picked up a rapid rate as I walk down the fluorescent-lit hallway, looking for the man's name plate on one of the many doors.

Just an hour, I tell myself. That's all you have to get through.

I suck in a breath and will my heart to settle the fuck down as I tap on the appropriate door.

Here goes…

Luna

I DON'T KNOW why the hell I got in such a tizzy over Kaleb leaving without kissing me. Things have been mostly good the last couple of weeks since we fucked each other senseless on the bathroom floor – and several other surfaces of the house since then.

They haven't been perfect by any means, as he's still grouchy as fuck half the time – especially if he doesn't get a good night's sleep. While he tries to be my big, tough man, he's given in and allowed me to be the big spoon so I can rub his back at night as we're falling asleep. I love the give and take to it as I usually wake up to our positions being reversed, and him waking me up the same way in the mornings.

This morning, however, I must've been dead asleep because I don't remember him trying to do that. Maybe that's what cued me to get a little upset when he tried to leave. I didn't wake up in that usual, comforting way, and it threw me off. My eyes opened to an immediate, uneasy feeling, and I just reacted. It happens.

And the difference is, these days he's more vigilant; self-aware. His demons are still hanging around, but he's not blindly letting them drive anymore.

After showering and dressing, I lock up the house and get in the car to make the drive to the city for classes. I don't need gas, but stopping at Colleens little Espresso Hut in the Gas and Grocery lot has become a routine for my class days. I've taken comfort in ordering a supersized latte to keep me company on the drive.

I'm just receiving my hot drink and telling Colleen to keep the change when I notice a woman approaching in my peripheral. I tip my head in her direction with a polite smile before heading towards my car.

"Luna Shane?" she calls, and I stop and turn to acknowledge her again.

"Yes?" I look her up and down, confused. I don't think we've met before. She's in her late thirties, I'm guessing, and dressed business-casual in simple black slacks and a green blouse. But the most curious thing about her is the large manila envelope clutched in her manicured hands.

She gives me an oddly pleasant smile as she holds it out towards me, and without thinking, I hold my free hand out to receive it.

"You've been served," she informs me, pulling her purse strap higher up on her shoulder. "Have a nice day." And then she turns and retreats towards a black sedan with its engine still running.

I feel like my heart has just been hit like a gong, stunning me frozen to this spot in the middle of the Gas and Grocery weathered parking lot.

Served.

As in, court papers. Legal papers that contain some kind of order or summons.

This is unreal and I feel dizzy a moment; as if my surroundings on this sunlit morning aren't even real.

I'm not here. I'm not this girl who just got served legal documents – they must have the wrong girl. I'm… a good girl. Who would want to send me something like this?

I wonder if this is how Carter felt when I filed the no contact order. I hope so, because this feels all kinds of horrible… Carter.

Oh my God, this has Carter all over it.

I shake out of my stunned state and hustle towards my car before I accumulate any spectators. Now this is making sense.

After sliding behind the wheel and slamming my car door shut, I pull my phone out, ready to call Kaleb and let him know immediately what's in this damn envelope when I open it. He'll jump on the war path and I'm ready to let him. I know this means telling him what happened while he was gone, and while I'd rather not do it like this, I think we're both ready to handle it. He needs to know if he's going to help me through the rest of it.

After placing my latte in the cupholder, I hastily undo the clasp of the envelope and yank out its contents. My eyes frantically dart back and forth over the front page of the stack, looking for any words to jump out at me that will answer my questions as soon as possible. But my confusion torments me further when the top heading reads:

Petition for Dissolution of Marriage

What?

I read it again, a migraine threatening to erupt behind my eyes, possibly from my heart urgently pumping all my blood to my head as I try to comprehend this. But as I skim down the document, I swear my vision blurs in and out of focus.

Petitioner: Kaleb Dominic Shane

Respondent: Luna Rene Shane

That's my husband's name. Next to petitioner, he… he filed these papers?

This has to be a mistake. Kaleb had said he wanted – no – he said he thought we should get a divorce a couple of months ago, but he was in a bad place then. He did and said whatever the trauma and stress told him to. Now, he's turned a corner, or at least… I thought he had.

He never did say he'd changed his mind about it; I just figured we were out of the woods. We aren't how we were before he left, but I thought we were on our way to something resembling that. I mean, he moved me back into his room.

But then this morning…

This morning he got up early, and told me he'd be gone for a few hours.

Oh my God…

I break out of those thoughts and look back down at the papers, and this time, I can read everything clearly.

He's still divorcing me. After everything.

After goddamn everything.

Without thinking, I start the engine while grabbing up my phone. I've kept my cool all this time, and now I don't care how dramatic I'm being. Kaleb has earned this. My hand shakes as my thumb takes a couple of tries to swipe the screen to his contact.

My heart is threatening to explode from being overworked, and the pit of my stomach feels dark and cold.

After a little more fumbling, I turn on my phone's Bluetooth and put the car in gear.

My classes in the city all but forgotten, I turn the wheel and burn out of the gas station lot. My anxiety is leading my movements as I drive in the opposite direction of where I was going.

The call goes straight to voicemail without ringing. It's turned off.

He leaves for the day and turns off his phone while I get served divorce papers...

My insides tighten and twist as I speak into the interior of the car, being extra deliberate in keeping the tears out of my voice as I speak to him – to his voicemail – for the last time.

He doesn't get any more of my tears.

41

KALEB

"So how are things now?" Dr. Jeffries – who is not at all like I expected – asks as he thoughtfully leans his head on his fist in his armchair.

We've only got ten minutes left in this session, and I didn't even see the first forty fly by. Unlike the slacks with a sweater over a button down I was expecting, this guy is wearing worn jeans and a flannel open over a t-shirt. His laidback demeanor immediately made me relax, if only a little. It was still hard work getting me to divulge the pain of my childhood, but it led to me talking about how I met Luna on that ropes course, and how that was the first time I felt needed or depended on by somebody. That moment had given me new life, and I never wanted to be anything different to her. I never wanted her to see me as weak.

"They've been... really good actually," I say quietly on a heavy breath.

"So do you still think she sees you as a burden?"

"No," I let out quickly, shaking my head. "I don't know why I even did before," I shrug uncomfortably. "She's not like that, she knows me."

"May I share a theory?" he asks carefully as he straightens up, giving me a cautious look.

"Have at it." I wave my hands out before dropping them in my lap.

He leans forward, resting his elbows on his knees. "Severe stress… can often have certain delusional effects on our way of thinking."

"Are you saying I'm delusional?" I cock my head at him, hoping to God he isn't.

"Actually, no," he reassures me with a light chuckle. "But severe stress can cause some of our mind's natural defense mechanisms to kick in. One of those is projecting."

"Are you serious?" I ask, feeling my head tip forward, and he nods. "I remember now that's what Luna said, that I was projecting."

"Kaleb, do you think it's possible that you were? That you were seeing yourself a certain way and were afraid of what would happen if she thought the same way, and so to protect yourself from the fallout, you convinced yourself that was indeed how she saw you?"

I think on that for a moment, feeling the space between my brows furrow. Instead of pressuring me to answer on that, he continues.

"You know, losing your mother before you could even remember her, followed by your father as you knew him… then meeting Luna who didn't care about what you'd been through, and saw you as brave and tough… then later in life losing your grandfather and one of your best friends… I could see where that would leave you feeling raw and vulnerable, not a way you like to feel when you're with her."

"Pffft…" I blow out a stress-riddled breath between my lips. "That definitely clicks together. And thanks for piling all that on by the way," I snark.

"No problem," he quirks a joking eyebrow at me. But he is right. Since we were kids, doing anything for Luna was like medicine for me. It made me feel alive and competent, and I liked how she looked at me. I'd have rather died than have her see me any other way. I know now that she would've seen me that way no matter what. She gave me that puzzle piece long ago, I just never snapped it into the big picture until now. "Our time's up, I'm afraid," he notes, shifting forward in his seat.

I don't stand right away, feeling like I need a moment to process everything I just learned.

"These are just things to think about Kaleb," he reminds me as I nod. "We can pick up on this again next time, if you're interested in doing that that is."

I end up stopping by reception and making another appointment. I made it through this one, and obviously I'm still alive. Still, I decide to take it one step at a time, and I don't book anything continuous. But even so, this is worth telling Luna, and I know she's going to be thrilled which will make me happy.

I head down to the main floor and do an hour of light PT, and then, hopping on the Harley, I head over to the local department store parking lot to buy that motorcycle exhaust I found for West. After storing it as securely as I can to the back seat of my bike, I dig in my pocket, wanting to hear Luna's voice and find out how her class is going.

When I look at the screen I remember that I had to turn it off for my therapy session. "Shit," I mumble to myself and press the button to turn it on, hoping I didn't miss any important calls. Sure enough, my notifications alert me of a voicemail, and I immediately tap the screen to listen to it.

Kaleb... Luna's voice plays on the line and I immediately detect a difference in it. Just in my name, I can tell that it's thick with some kind of heavy emotion, making a chill run up my spine. Something's wrong, and my hackles immediately go up.

I really thought we were going to make it, her heady voice continues. *We just made love last night – literally hours ago. But apparently, you didn't. You stuck it out through our anniversary. You achieved your dare, so good for you. And you still want a divorce...*

My heart jumps up into my throat and starts pounding like a sledgehammer when I hear that word.

Then you can have your fucking divorce, Luna's message continues with an edge of conviction that stabs right through to my core.

No. No, no, no, no...

I'm signing these papers, and I'll even do you one better, she adds, and though I'm not sure what that means, my mind is racing in so many different directions and at an impossible speed.

And by the way, she adds, *ducking out of the house to supposedly run errands and turning your phone off while you have me served? You're a fucking coward!*

My heart is shattering and I think I'm hyperventilating as I anxiously wait for her to say more, but there is no more. The automated voice comes on to inform me that's the end of my messages.

"No, fuck!" I belt out loud to no one as I push a hand through my hair. How the fuck did this happen? I filed the papers but I never processed them. I never sent them. How does she have them?

I don't even have the number of the law office I went to that day. I do a frantic Google search to find them and dial their number as I feel my heart still sputtering in my chest.

"Good afternoon, Mr. Shane," the secretary greets me after I identify myself and I want to reach through the phone and throttle her for being so damn perky while my marriage is falling apart as we speak. "Yes, the papers you drew up were served at 10:05 this morning, as per our sixty-day waiting policy upon filing." She sounds like she's cheerfully reading from a fucking script.

Sixty-day policy...

I feel my heart start to cave in on itself as I frantically start flipping through my memories.

Luna and I arriving at the gym.

Me wanting to walk around the galleria first, or at least that's what I told her.

I walked over to where those two establishments stood fatefully next to each other. The law office and the fucking bar.

With the pain in my leg and my memories tormenting me, a shot sounded like a damn good idea at the time, seeing as how I'd run out of my prescription meds.

The guilt, the anxiety, the anger, the withdrawals, and the pain were all eating me from the inside, and I just needed something to dull the anguish, if even just a little.

That one shot did nothing but take me to a place one level darker, my thoughts racing even faster.

Did I really want to divorce Luna? Or was I just fucked up at that moment?

There was one way to find out, and it was right next door. I could go in and just ask about the process.

I remember just wanting to see how it would feel to go through with it.

Initiating the paperwork was surprisingly easy until I failed to answer a gauntlet of questions to their satisfaction.

You've been married less than a year?

Have you tried counseling?

Is there a chance she can counter-file for annulment based on fraud, coercion, or duress?

It was all so confusing, but I remember them telling me:

This county has a sixty-day waiting period before we can file or serve. If, by the end of this period, you have not made motions to withdraw, the process will move forward.

I remember feeling frustrated as I stalked out of that office – not about the damn waiting period, but because it didn't give me any kind of answer I was looking for. It sparked nothing, pointing me in neither direction. From that day, I surged forward with my vexations, leaving that infernal law office behind me for the first and last time.

And then it seems it faded into the back recesses of my mind. Forgetting was a blessing… until this moment.

How is it that only three hours ago, I was kissing Luna in our driveway, and now there's no sign in this house that she ever lived here? Just a menacing painting and her lingering orange blossom scent, haunting me like a heady apparition. Now I sit here in the hallway with my head in my hands, trying to calm the fuck down and figure out what to do, when all I want to do is tear this fucking place apart and burn it to the ground. But then I try to imagine her seeing that spectacle, and know she'd never return to that.

The idea of Luna not in my life, not living here, not being married to her, just doesn't seem possible. I know I need to see her. While I know talking to her on the phone is just not going to do it, I tried anyway – multiple times. I'm blocked. She said her last words and completely cut the cord, with no hopes of even a whisper or a glimpse.

And the papers...

She said in her message she signed them... and that she'd do me one better. They're nowhere to be found, and I feel like if she were serious, she would've left them out in the open for me to see them and her signature.

Think, Kaleb... I can't, I need to calm down – and not with the whiskey calling to me from the cabinet. That helped me into this boat in the first place; there's no way it's going to help me out of it. If Luna were here, she'd hold me until my heart rate slowed, not saying one word.

Closing my eyes, I picture her doing just that. I imagine myself slowing my breathing to match hers, and before I know it, all I see is her face.

It takes a little while, maybe ten minutes or so, but I do feel myself even out. Neither my heart nor my brain is racing anymore, and I can feel the difference. My thoughts are clearer now, and I can sort through what I need to do first.

She filed the papers. That's why I can't find them. She's taken them to file them or she's mailing them in.

Luna is most likely driving, or is already back in Indianapolis. Either that, or she went to her family in Detroit. That's two likely locations; I can work with that.

Keeping Luna's face in my mind as my focal point, I finally struggle to stand, using the edge of the desk for leverage. While I didn't overturn it like my rage wanted me to, it's still a mess from me rifling around, looking for the divorce papers.

The main drawer is still open with a multitude of papers haphazardly sticking out of it. I pick up a few of them, wanting to check just one more time that they aren't the ones I'm looking for, so I can set them on fire.

I leaf through them, only to find myself disappointed when something catches my eye on the last one. I pause, setting the other papers down, and peruse what looks to be a bank statement. It's Luna's account, so she clearly didn't take everything, but that's not what's pulling me in.

One of the payments she made was to a hospital in Indianapolis.

Why in the fuck was my wife in a hospital?

42

LUNA

The door whips open, and there stands what feels like my only friend in the world. While the majority of my belongings are still stashed in my car, I clutch the strap of my weekend bag that's slung over my shoulder with one hand, and Buster's cat carrier in the other.

Cassidy doesn't say a word as she steps forward and wraps her arms around me, giving me the tightest hug I've ever received, yet it's still not tight enough. The entire drive here I yearned to put myself in a vice that would hold my shattering pieces of my soul together.

Pursing my lips, I let her squeeze the air out of me.

"Get in here," she says gently after releasing me, and stands aside so that I can shuffle in, schlepping my belongings. After setting them down by the door, I open the door to the cat carrier so that Buster can come out when he feels ready. Standing, I take a glance around Cassidy's apartment – more traditional and civilized than my studio, which I wasn't going back to. Not after the Carter debacle.

"Thanks, Cass," I murmur, tucking my hands in my back pockets.

"Forget it." She waves a hand, and thankfully, bypasses the I told you so that she could very righteously use in the moment. "Listen, you're sleeping with me tonight, and tomorrow, we can take our time, moving some of my things to the studio."

"Cass are you sure?" I tilt my head and furrow my brow. When I called her from the car, she not only agreed to let me crash with her for a few days, but had the idea to swap homes until my lease at the studio is up.

"Of course, I'm sure." She eyeballs me, holding her hand out. "You're not going to stay in that studio and be reminded of what your fuck-rag ex did to you every time you climb those stairs. Besides, that place doesn't allow pets, and you need Buster right now," she points out, and I turn to look over my shoulder to see my little striped baby curiously sniffing around the edges of the carrier opening.

"Okay ... thanks" I sigh, exhaustedly. "I'm just going to run down to the car and grab a few things then." I hike my thumb towards the door and turn without even looking for a response.

The hour drive drained every cell in my body, simply by replaying every meaningful moment of my brief marriage, right up to being handed papers that stated Kaleb wanted to end it. I feel hollow, and everything hurts, which is why I can't wallow in the aftermath of this last year. I won't make it out alive. I need to get back to myself, and I know I need to do that by completely separating myself from all of it. That's why I signed the damn divorce papers and immediately put them in the mail with the provided envelope. Kaleb had to have filed somewhere nearby so they should be getting them tomorrow and can start the proceedings.

When I get outside the building and onto the sidewalk, I walk over to my car that's parked on the street. After opening the door, I grab two more bags and my phone from the console. After locking the car back up, I set the bags down and slump against it with my phone and pull up my camera roll.

Don't think, just do it.

Swiping through all my pictures, I don't even take a second to look at each one that has Kaleb or the two of us in it before deleting. I can't have those on here, or I'll be too tempted. I need to eliminate everything to do with my life with him. I know nothing can be done about my memories, but those will ease with the time and lack of reminders. I force myself to drive forward, swipe – delete – repeat, no matter how much I feel tears sting at certain snapshots of us in bed making goofy faces. I bite my lip hard, trying to ward off tears when I come across one where I'm smiling for the camera while Kaleb presses a kiss to my cheek. His eyes are closed in a way that makes him look so peaceful, and I just don't understand. Before the tears break through, I quickly delete it and move on.

With all the sentimental photos and Kaleb's phone number deleted, I've only one thing left to do for tonight. Swiping and tapping the screen a couple more times, I bring up my mother's contact and hit the FaceTime option. Crossing my arms and holding my phone out, I wait for her to pick up, and when she does, I bite down on the corner of my lip.

"Hi, sweetheart," she greets, smiling brightly at first before confusion pulls at the space between her eyes when she takes in my face. "What's wrong?"

"Hey, Mom," I sigh shakily. "I'm okay, it's just… well actually I'm not…"

Kaleb

I NEED to get Luna back, that goes without saying, and the only reason I'm not barreling my way down the freeway towards Indianapolis is staring up at me from one of her bank statements. I can't go to her without finding this out. Something obviously happened to her while I was gone.

Shuffling through more papers that were originally in neat piles, I move onto the side drawers, finding some old junk of mine, photographs, and address books. When I try the bottom left drawer, that's where I find a few of Luna's things. There are a few discarded sketches she attempted but never finished by the looks of them. There's a bag full of colored beads, a few photos of herself with her brother, and some with her friends. Beneath it all, however, is a manila envelope lying flat on the bottom, and I immediately snatch it up.

My heart gives several resounding thuds when I see one word written across the tab: Carter.

Son of a fucking bitch…

The bombs won't stop dropping, and without the safe haven of Luna here, I can feel my breathing pick up and my nerves going haywire.

I'm about to go off the rails. I can't seem to calm down for more than a few minutes at a time before I get amped again. I'm headed straight for a heart attack, and I don't know what to do or who to go to. Everyone I love is officially gone.

Fuck, I don't have time for more panic attacks.

Luna… be strong for Luna… breathe…

I need to stay grounded while I get through this. I can't … I have an idea.

Digging my phone out of my back pocket again, I unlock it and go to my camera roll and find a video of Luna and me goofing around. She sits on the tire swing, sticking her tongue out at me as I push her and we joke. I let her smiling eyes and the sound of her laughter remind me that I'm not on the battlefield as I proceed to open the folder.

Inside are more official looking papers. The top two are from NICA where Luna goes to school. I scan the first one to see that it's a rejection letter – the one the asshole forged to keep her with him, and the second is her actual acceptance letter. Both have the same date.

After shuffling them to the back, I see the next couple of papers are hospital bills. Bingo.

My eyes quickly scan over the bill, looking for anything that might tell me why Luna was there.

"What in the actual..." I trail off to myself as I scan the document up and down again. From top to bottom, I re-read, the words fading in and out of a blur.

2 view X-ray of chest
1 view X-ray of right hand
CT of head and neck
Ultrasound of kidneys
Splints, IV fluids, stitches...

"Luna, what the fuck happened to you?" The pounding of my heart in my ears drowns out the question that falls from my lips. "When..." I feel my rate pick up again, banging out a few hard beats when I think to look for the date.

Date of service: November 9th, 2023.

I look up to the ceiling, wracking my brain... was that the time I couldn't get a hold of her? She told me she'd lost her phone... she was crying so hard. The memory grabs hold of my heartstrings in an iron grip and pulls agonizingly hard.

Goddammit, my head is so messed up. It's spinning just knowing that this is my wife's hospital bill, and can't wrap itself around the fact that it was a visit I had no clue about.

There's no summary of the visit, just an itemized list of charges that are all covered by my insurance. There's probably no way I could get my hands on one either, even as her husband.

She's going to have to tell me, which I'm not sure she will, seeing as how this is the first I'm finding anything out about it in the first place, and not even from her. The fact that Luna has her hospital bills in a folder with his name on it – along with the bogus rejection letter he drafted – says he's behind everything that's happened to her.

But for now, the contents of this folder tell me all I need to be certain of one thing.

Carter is a fucking dead piece of shit.

The blood in my veins has been replaced by hot acid and a sweat has broken out on the back of my neck.

My need to find Luna has multiplied exponentially and I need to move; to do something now.

I'm still her husband. We're not divorced yet. We need to talk and–

"K!" Luna's exasperated but good-humored lilt breaks through my thoughts and I return my attention to my phone screen where videos of her are still playing. This one displays her tucked behind the shower curtain with her face peeking out. Her hair hangs in dripping wet strands, and her eyes are smiling as bright as ever as she tries to give me a look of mock annoyance. "Put your damn phone down and hand me a towel!"

This was just last week. I'd made a game out of taking the towels out of the bathroom while she showered so I'd have to bring her one, which would lead to a good look at her wet, naked body, sometimes followed by a loving kiss or a blissfully passionate fuck.

This is us… we'd gotten back to an even better version than we were before, and it just can't be over in the blink of an eye.

Scrambling up from the desk, I book it to the bedroom and pull my duffle out of the closet. If I know Luna, I'm not going to be able to come back home in one day. I'm going to need some necessities which I tear around the room grabbing and carelessly throwing in the bag.

When I think I've got everything, I sling it over my shoulder and start to head out of the room when something catches my eye.

On top of the dresser near the door lie her wedding rings, side by side. I pause for a moment, letting the reality that they're here and not on her finger settle over me. I feel hot and somewhat lightheaded for a few seconds before I mentally shake out of it. Setting the duffel down, I unhook my chain and grab up the rings, letting them zipline down to join my dog tags.

There's no time to fall apart right now, I tell myself. You have to go get your girl and you need to be level headed when you do it.

With that, I continue on my way out of the room and down the hall. I have no business going after her and trying to get her back, or even deserve for her to hear me out after all I've put her through, but I will not be on my death bed ruminating over how I didn't try. I'm going to try with everything I have.

I'VE ONLY EVER BEEN to Luna's studio twice before, and I don't remember the address to plug into my phone. Fortunately, I'm able to remember the general area, and it only took a couple of wrong turns from there until I ended up in front of the building I know it's in.

After scaling the long staircase, taking two at a time, I pound on the sliding metal door and am met with no answer.

I pace… I sit on the stairs a while… I pound again… repeat. I do this for close to an hour before I finally entertain the idea that she's really not here and not just avoiding me.

The late afternoon is shifting into early evening, but I don't want to go far in case I miss her. Fortunately, the small donut shop across the street is still open, and I duck in just long enough to grab a large coffee and take it back to my parked truck on the street.

I want badly to look up Carter so I know what he looks like and where I might find him, but now's not the time. It will get me in a worse headspace than I already am, and that's not what Luna needs if I get the chance to talk to her. I'll save those feelings for my own time, but she gets everything else, and I'll grovel every day for the rest of our lives just so long as she comes home with me.

It's a good thing I've slept on a hard-as-shit cot for most of my eight months overseas, and some of it even in a ranger hole. Otherwise, more parts of my body than just my leg would be pissed off at me right now. Stiff pain flashes up and down my thigh, protesting at me to get out of the cab of the truck and stretch it a bit. I had a feeling I'd be doing something like spending the night in my damn truck, given how late in the day it was when I made it out here, but I couldn't just stay home while I waited for an appropriate time. Besides, it's not like I would've gotten better sleep in my bed without my girl.

After taking a short walk up the street and back, I duck back into the donut shop for more coffee, and to make a call to the law office in West Bridge. Sure enough, I get the paralegal sunshine bot again.

"I'm sorry, Mr. Shane, but if you want to stop the proceedings, you have to come in and file a voluntary dismissal with the court, and that's if your wife hasn't responded to the petition yet."

"Well, I think she might have," I exhale in frustration. "I don't have them; I think she might've mailed them in."

"If that's the case, both parties have to sign the voluntary dismissal, which means she has to agree that she also wants to stay married. If she doesn't, she has the option to counter-petition."

Shit. That means putting a stop to the divorce is going to mean more than making a phone call. I drove out here prepared for Luna to shoot me down, at least at first, but I was hoping for more time where the divorce is concerned. If we're still married, we're at least still tied to each other in some way, and this is me holding on to whatever small, shattered piece of us I can.

"Okay, well, uh… I'm going to be filing that dismissal as soon as I can, and I'll go from there I guess," I answer hesitantly before ending the call. I polish off my coffee and that's when I see a silver Malibu pull up on the opposite side of the street. The girl who gets out is familiar, and it takes at least half a minute of scrutinizing to place her. The fact that she has colorful streaks in her blonde hair thankfully pulls me back to visions of her laughing with Luna at camp, and ... under the club lights the night I found Luna again.

Cassidy.

I jump into action, wrenching my door open and climbing out of my truck as she opens the back passenger door to retrieve something from the back seat.

"Cassidy!" I shout, briskly crossing the street to her.

She straightens up, holding a laundry basket full of neatly piled fabrics in both hands as she looks around for whoever called her name. When her line of vision falls on me, her mouth parts open and the set of her eyes goes from momentarily stunned to downright irate.

"What in the actual fuck?" She draws out each sentence fragment with a dip of her chin.

"Where's Luna? Have you seen her?" I ask urgently as I approach her side.

"Like I'm going to tell you," she responds with a serious bite in her voice. "You're done with her, remember?"

"No, I'm not done with her!" I hold my hands up and shake my head, pleading my case.

"Nothing says done like divorce papers," she spits cynically and widens her eyes as she moves to walk around me.

"She was never supposed to get those," I explain, following her to the building's front door.

"Oh well, that makes it okay then," she fires back sarcastically as she turns and pushes her back side out to push through the door. "You still filed, Kaleb. You wanted to leave her."

"I was fucked up, Cassidy," I continue as I follow her up the tall staircase that she's marching angrily up. "I'd been through the worst hell you can imagine, then I came home to the only person left in my life to find out things had somehow changed between us," I argue gruffly as she sets the basket down to dig in her purse. "What's going on, where is she?" I ask, bending my brows as she produces a key and fits it in the lock.

"She doesn't live here anymore. I do," she supplies, pulling the door to the side. And after she bends down to retrieve her basket of fabrics, she adds, "by the way, get out," before turning and carrying it through the threshold. Only I don't follow her instructions. Instead, I take a tentative step inside and glance around to see the place unchanged from the one night I spent here. It's like I'm back there again, only the euphoria is gone. "I mean it, Kaleb." Cassidy's brash voice snaps me back to the moment. "You've done enough. The least you can do for her now is to leave her alone and let her heal from the damage."

I have no argument for that, as it's truly what I should do for Luna. But I'm selfish, and can't let her go without a fight. Instead, I follow Cassidy back down the stairs when she passes me. "Why isn't she staying here?" I ask. "And where is she?" I ask again.

"I'm not answering either of those questions."

"Cassidy, please." I soften my tone as I follow her back out to the street as she uses her key fob to pop the trunk of her car. "This was nothing more than a colossal mistake I made when I was in the worst place of my life. She's the most important thing in the world, and I would move heaven and earth to make it up to her," I convey as she reaches in her trunk and pulls out what looks like a sewing machine under a protective cover. It looks heavy, and absentmindedly, I take it from her as I stand there, still waiting.

Cassidy looks at her sewing machine in my hands and up at my eyes a moment, her expression softening just minutely. "She doesn't want to come back here," she sighs, reaching in and grabbing a quilted duffle bag, as well as an empty tote before slamming the trunk lid shut. "It… bothers her."

I follow her again as she marches up the stairs and continue on into Luna's studio. I set the sewing machine down on the small kitchen table as she drops her bag and heads over to what used to be Luna's art corner. Luna had most of her supplies with her in our home, but there appears to be a few items left over that Cassidy starts carefully setting into the tote.

"Why does it bother her?" I ask, strutting slowly over to her.

She closes her eyes and shakes her head with a sigh. "Forget it. I shouldn't've even said that."

I want to push on that issue, but know it's probably best to pick my battles and play my cards right here if I want the chance to see Luna.

"Alright, but, Cassidy, I meant everything I said downstairs. I want to stay married to Luna more than I want my heart to keep beating. I don't deserve a chance to talk to her, but I will do anything if you'll give me one anyway. I will do anything on this earth to have her back so I can love and protect her for the rest of my life. I will make sure nothing hurts her again. Not even me." I place a hand on my chest as if to emphasize my plight.

Cassidy stands there for a moment, looking around the space while she agonizes over my words before her eyes roll skyward with another heavy sigh.

"You're such an asshole, Kaleb."

"I know."

43

KALEB

I originally wanted to keep a cool head in the best interest of getting Luna to listen to me, but now that seeing her is finally imminent, my eagerness is getting away from me.

As opposed to Luna's downtown studio, Cassidy lives in a more traditional apartment complex in a quieter part of town across from a nice, tree-shaded park.

After giving me the address, Cassidy only agreed to give me a ten-minute head start before she came back to intervene, and hopefully I don't have to spend too much of that looking for the right building.

As luck would have it, the sound of some kind of heel clacking on the sidewalk draws my attention to one of the buildings on the far right, and when I look, I see a leggy brunette in ripped jeans, ankle boots, and a loose white t-shirt with paint splatters. Luna pulls the strap of her bag higher up on her shoulder as she walks briskly and deliberately toward the street, and I waste no precious time. Once my brain confirms it's her, I bolt.

"Lu!" I call out to her, and when her head turns in my direction, the look on her face is an iron fist to the gut. Her beautiful features darken, pulling together in a blended collage of heartbreak, anger, and pain. Her body starts with the shock of seeing me, and her lips squeeze together as if she's just walked into a nightmare.

I did this, but I can rectify it.

"Kaleb," her voice is low and broken before she sucks in a fortifying breath. Her shoulders rise and fall with several more of them as she slowly walks towards me. She shakes her head, her body stiff, as if she's warding off some kind of force that's trying to take over her.

"Hi, baby," I breathe out, so relieved to find her, yet so anxious to fix what I broke.

She pauses, staring up at me before asking, "Why?"

The deep tone of her voice is cold, and pierces through to my heart.

She could be referring to a number of different things here, so I just cut to the chase. "I don't want a divorce," I spew out quickly, and it does make her eyes squint slightly.

"Wh... what?" She tilts her head. "You filed papers, Kaleb," she reminds me.

"I didn't file them, I just had them drawn up. They were never supposed to get filed or sent to you."

Blinking, she shakes her head incredulously. "You know, I have no idea what you're talking about, but it doesn't matter. You sought out divorce, Kaleb, because you didn't want to be married to me anymore. You didn't want me any-"

"No!" I shake my head, desperate for her to believe me. "I know this is a convenient argument to make, but I swear to God, that wasn't me. That wasn't your Kaleb. I was so fucking messed up Luna–"

"No, don't you dare pull the pity card, Kaleb!" She cuts me off, her voice thick with pain. "You don't get to use your pain as an excuse to cause it for someone else!"

"You're right, but that's the truth, Luna." I reach to touch her arm and she slaps me away. The action drives the ice pick deeper into my gut but I press on, holding my hand away to show her I won't touch her again. "Between the scary as fuck eight months I went through and the damn drugs, I was all kinds of fucked up. And when I came home, things didn't feel the same between us. It scared the shit out of me and pulled me further down into that hell I was already living."

"Kaleb… I was there. Things were different because you were different, but I was there! I was there loving you every second, trying to help you heal and trying to bring you back!"

"I know, baby, I know. I was feeling sorry for myself like a pathetic bastard while you were doing all the heroism. It was a vile mistake. After everything I went through overseas, you were the one thing I was clinging to. I was holding onto the idea that I'd come home to the Luna I always remembered and we'd be that blissfully happy couple of friends that fell flat on our asses in love with each other. I lost my grip on that when I got blown up and expected our marriage to be the magic cure. When I came back, we were different and I hated it. We went from best friends in love to helpless loser and his caretaker, and I couldn't take it." I feel my throat getting choked up as I press on. "I thought I wanted it to end, but I didn't want to feel that way… so I had the papers drawn up to see how that would make me feel. I wanted to see if having the prospect staring me in the face would tell me whether what I was feeling was real or not."

"And you didn't care what it would do to me, just so long as you wouldn't have to deal with it anymore." She juts her chin up at me, her eyes narrowed.

There she is.

"Luna, you're the fucking toughest woman I've ever known – you're tougher than I am. I knew you'd be unhappy, but I didn't think it was possible to hurt you, not deeply, but once I realized I could, I never, ever wanted to again."

"That worked out just great, didn't it?" Luna's voice is steady again as she raises an eyebrow and turns, walking in the direction of the park.

"Where are you going?" I ask rhetorically, trying to keep up with her furious pace.

"You don't get to know that anymore," she snipes.

Ouch… but I'll take it.

"I deserve that, baby, have at it," I tell her encouragingly as we venture across the street. The sidewalk then leads into the park, and I follow Luna under a canopy of deciduous trees. I take only half a second to marvel at the irony of how angrily she's walking through such a pretty and peaceful place.

"Come on, Luna, lay it on me," I stoke further, wanting her to unleash that fire that I know lies within. If she can just rain that hellfire down on me, we can get back to where we were. I'll even let her smack me for making such a stupid mistake.

"I don't want to do this," she sighs. "I just want to heal myself, and you coming here is making me worse." Her head swivels towards me before facing forward again, continuing her vehement pace.

Heal myself.

For some reason, those words grab onto the other burning matter that's been eating me alive and yank it towards the front of my mind.

She was there trying to heal me after my trauma, but who was there for her through hers? How did she heal herself? The answer is she didn't. She couldn't.

"I want to talk about what happened to you," I spew out with less ceremony than I intended. When I envisioned this earlier, I wasn't trying to cause a scene while trying to keep up with her power walking through a public place.

Fortunately, it makes her stride falter slightly and she slows down a little, giving me a chance to reach for the envelope from the inside pocket of my jacket.

"What do you mean what happened to me?" she throws back sardonically. I got married, and then my husband came back a wounded martyr and kicked me to the curb…" she trails off and slows down even farther as she sees what I'm holding up. "What is that?" she asks, coming to a complete stop and facing me.

"Medical bills from November, Luna," I inform her curtly before tucking it away again. "I'm not the only one who went through something while we were apart. I know that much, and now I want you to tell me the rest."

Luna goes quiet, looking around the park like some random sycamore is going to bail her out of this. "It doesn't even matter," she sighs, shaking her head. "We're not married anymore, so it's nothing you need to be concerned about. I got through it on my own."

"Bullshit," I state and tilt my chin.

"No, it's not bullshit. It truly doesn't matter anymore. Hell, it didn't even matter then. It was–"

"Luna, I swear to God, if you don't tell me what the fuck happened to you while I was gone, I will find out some other way," I warn gruffly. "I know I came back some bruised, pathetic version of myself, but I knew you had in some way changed too, and now I want you to tell me! Tell me I'm not fucking crazy, Luna." I lean in, not trying to scare her, but to convey how badly I want her to let me in on this.

"Carter found me," she finally blurts as her face pales slightly.

There it is. I already knew this, yet I feel every muscle fiber tighten around the bones in my chest, my shoulders, and my back when she confirms it. My heart is screaming from inside my chest wall as I bring my fist up to my mouth. "Why the fuck didn't you tell me, Luna?" I ask feebly against my hand.

A tender compassion veils her eyes as she answers. "And how was I supposed to?" she implores. "I know you were overseas for eight months seeing things people only catch glimpses of in their nightmares, not to mention you lost your best friend, and almost died, too, but could I get a little sympathy from you because I had my crazy ex smack me around? Come on, K, there was no place for that, and that's okay." She waves a hand outward in dismissal. "It's not a competition, but with what happened to you, it wasn't the time for my hardships, and there was the very real possibility it would've made things worse for you," she points out.

I stand there, staring at her, taking in everything from the set of her eyes, the way she rubs at the spot between them, to her breathing. I try to imagine what it was like for her then, how she would go about approaching that subject, and I can't come up with anything that would've resulted in anything good or constructive. But despite not having any good reason to fault her, I still do, unfair as they may seem.

"You should've told me," I whisper. "Do you know what taking care of you would've done for me? How much it could've changed things?"

"Do you not recall how you acted when I told you he'd sent me flowers when we were on that video chat?" she challenges with a head tilt. Shit. Lifting a shoulder and shaking her head, she adds, "Maybe I should've. But like I said, I just didn't know how. I did know at that time that you didn't have anything to give, so I knew I had to be the one. So I gave, Kaleb, thinking if I just did that for a while, it would help you to come back to yourself. And when that didn't work, I gave more. And then when that didn't help, I gave everything. And now... I have nothing left. I can't give anymore, it's all gone... I'm gone."

I've just been stabbed in the heart with a hot knife, but despite how damaging it is, I fight it. I rage against it, hurrying after her when she turns and starts walking away again. "No," I insist, and I don't recognize the depth of desperation in my voice. "No, that's not true, Luna. You love me, and I know you can keep fighting for us."

"I can't!" She finally whirls around on me and stops our progression on the middle of the path. There's a wrought iron bench nearby, along with a few dogwoods in full bloom dispersed around a tiny pond, and again, I can't believe something of this manner is happening in this setting.

"What do you mean, you can't?" I ask incredulously, holding my hands out. "I made a huge fuckup when I myself was fucked up. Now jump all over me and put me in my damn place!" I urge her, starting to feel my voice waver. There's no question I'm desperate here, but I'm not afraid to show it. "Please," I practically whisper. "Take me down a few pegs, take me all the way down. Take me down to my knees and I swear to God, Luna, I will beg you to come back to me, fucked up leg and all," I proclaim, and try not to feel discouraged when I see those brown eyes sadden even more.

"I have nothing left, Kaleb," she tells me, her voice laced with defeat and regret. "I used up..." she pauses, swallowing hard while her eyes get glassy. "I used up everything I had, and now I'm empty, Kaleb. You drew up divorce papers–"

"And I'm trying to tell you that was an epic mistake and I don't want that, Luna!" I huff out, trying like hell not to run out of steam. I should've known not to ever go head-to-head with this one in an argument.

"Yeah, well..." She takes a breath like she's trying to revive herself while she looks around our surroundings as if to draw resilience against my words. "You still did it. You did it because you didn't trust what we had to come back around." She nods firmly, not meeting my eyes as a tear slips out from the corner of one of hers. She quickly wipes it away before squaring her shoulders and finally looking back up at me. "And anyway, I sent them in, so it's done." She sucks in a breath and turns to abandon me again, but I take a few long and painful strides to cut her off.

"Yeah, but you didn't take a very good look at them before you did," I throw back at her, and when she tips her head, I elaborate. "I didn't sign them," I announce as I step in front of her, and she looks up at me as she stops, her eyebrows drawing together.

"What?"

"You filed them, but I never signed them, Luna."

"So…" she squints her eyes like she's trying to process this.

"So we're not divorced, and we're not getting divorced," I say firmly. The dismissal is slightly more complicated than that, but she doesn't need to know that right now. Right now, she just needs to see me fight for her.

Luna grips the strap of her bag harder and shakes her head while pressing her lips together so hard they mottle in an effort to fight off more tears.

"Kaleb, I have nothing more to give." The words come out in a trembly whisper. "I can't give any more to this, to us."

She did give everything… and I gave nothing. I took everything; I drained her.

"You initiated those papers for some reason, Kaleb." She shrugs and takes a step back on her heel, away from my touch. "And now, I get to give back to myself so that I don't die of sorrow like some damn Shakespearean tragedy or something." She waves an arm out as two more tears freely fall.

"Please don't cry," I plead in a whisper as I step towards her again, but she backs away before I can touch her.

"Do you remember how you told me that the worst way your dad hurt you wasn't with his fist, but how he tried to start anew? How he'd shape up, get off the drugs and be a loving father, and then on any given day when you'd least expected it, he'd pull the rug out from under you and turn back into a monster?"

I stand there, like an idiot, unaware of the ragged breaths heaving in and out of my body.

"I think I know how you felt now," she sniffs, wiping at another tear, and the revelation destroys me. A war meaner and more horrific than the one I was in is taking place inside me. It gouges deeper when I watch her shoulders jerk inward as she fights back a sob. Tamping it down, she takes a deep breath and then another before saying, "Kaleb… I dare you to sign those papers. End our chapter so that we can both have a chance at making a life for ourselves."

The knowledge of what she's doing with those carefully

selected words twists that knife deeper into my soul. She means what she's saying, and it kills me, making me realize every bit of how I've made her feel, and in true me fashion, I act out instead of listening.

    Stepping closer to her again, I reach out and delicately take hold of her face before bending to touch my lips to hers, the kiss soft and gentle, but I'm making sure it imprints my next words on her heart. "Not a chance in hell," I tell her before releasing her and finally turning to walk away.

44

KALEB

My interaction with Luna didn't go as I'd hoped, but about as well as I expected. But I'm not finished. I haven't done all I can do, and I'm a long way from it.

The next thing I can do is continue northeast on the interstate, as there are things I can do in the Detroit area. I have a good few hours to get my thoughts together on the road, yet I still have no clue how I'm going to go about this next encounter.

The easier thing to do would be to just find Carter and get the gratification of beating him within an inch of his life, like I've been yearning to since Luna first told me about him. But I need to do something else first. While I want to avenge the woman I love, getting her back is more important right now. And besides, there are things I want to know first before any run-in with that fucking piece of shit.

And while she's got her walls up right now, there are other aspects of her life I can try to appeal to… like the people important to her.

Plugging the address into my GPS was no issue for me, as it's one I have memorized, and as I pull up in front of the gorgeous two-story white house with the expansive yard, I finally have a visual to the address I wrote to all those years ago as a kid.

When I get out of the truck and shut the door, I walk up the driveway and glance at the black metal mailbox, trying to imagine Luna checking it for one of my letters.

I can hear the clattering of wood and the occasional blaring buzz of an electrical saw in the back, but I still ascend the porch steps to the front door. This is a situation where I damn well better mind my 'p's and 'q's if I want to get anywhere.

I give a few solid raps on the regal black door and lock my hands at the wrist in front of me while I wait. A minute ticks by and then another, and I knock again, waiting just a few seconds longer before taking my chances to check the backyard.

After trudging down the steps, I bear to the left of the house, coming around the side. There's a tall wooden fence sectioning off the backyard, but it has a fancy gate with a latch that is unlocked. Pushing it open, I enter the well-kept yard to find it sprawling and spacious with a large back deck with bistro lights strung around the canopy. An apple tree with gnarly branches expands in all directions, shading half of the space.

And over by the detached garage stands my father-in-law, leaning over a saw table, carefully sending a plank of wood over its blade. The brash whine is too loud for me to even try to get his attention, so I just wander further into the clearing and place my hands in my pockets, waiting patiently for him to notice me – and preparing to have my ass gift-wrapped and handed to me in some way or another.

When the plywood splits at the end into two perfect half pieces is when Dr. Isaak looks up, taking only a couple of seconds to place me before looking back down to shut off the machine.

In a white t-shirt and blue jeans caked in sawdust, he makes his way around the table, snatching his protective goggles off his face.

"Kaleb," he says, making my name almost sound like a curse.

"Dr. Isaak," I greet back in a mild, non-defensive tone.

"You've got a lot of nerve coming here," he points out plainly as he stops his gait – fortunately a safe distance from me. I may have special hand-to-hand combat training, but if I were a bystander, I'd be more afraid of the one of us that's a father.

"I know," I acknowledge penitently.

"I think my daughter's been through enough, don't you?" He tilts his chin up and raises his eyebrows expectantly. "It ends here." He sweeps a gloved hand through the air in front of him.

"I agree," I nod firmly, "and I know I don't deserve to be heard out, but I was hoping you'd be generous enough to give me a few minutes anyway," I confess truthfully.

"And why should I give you that chance?" he demands, his eyebrows angled downward in chagrin.

"Because if you do, I'll make sure not to waste it. Luna is a gift to everyone she meets, and I'll do anything to get her back," I convey.

"Clearly," he clips out curtly, "seeing as how you're here. You must be desperate if you're coming to the man who doesn't want to let you near her."

"Yes, sir, I am," I confirm. "And Luna loves and thinks the world of you. If you have any insight on how to earn her trust again, it would be invaluable. I've been a miserable excuse of a man since I got home, and I don't expect to be forgiven for the way I've been, but I do want you to know that I've been getting better. I've started therapy, and if I can stay married to Luna, I'll show up for her every day. I will guard her heart with my life. I will never again let my pride or insecurities get in the way of loving her," I profess, my voice rising just slightly with the emotions the words are evoking.

Luna's father continues to glare at me for a few moments as he takes all this in before releasing a heavy load of air through his nose.

"Grab a hammer," he finally responds with a huff.

APPARENTLY, Luna's mom went down to Indianapolis to be with her and took Matty along. Ben stayed behind to let Kasey be there for her in a womanly/motherly way. Matty was allowed to tag along to cheer Luna up, and so that Ben could secretly get some work done on the fort he's going to surprise him with on his birthday.

I've spent almost two hours now, measuring, sawing, and hammering, while I talk and Luna's dad listens, occasionally breaking to direct me in some way. Once in a while, he stops his actions to simply stare down at the grass, hopefully giving serious thought to the things I'm saying. Finally, he calls for a break and heads inside the house, returning a couple of moments later with a couple of beers in hand, and we take a seat on the deck steps.

"Look, I was an ER doctor for years. I've seen a lot – including people struggling with addiction, trauma, addiction because of their trauma," he laments with widened eyes and a heavy sigh. "I've seen war veterans just tortured by their ghosts; their demons. They come home and don't even know who they are anymore, and feel like no one in their private world will understand them ever again, and so they push away," he finishes before lifting his beer to his lips while I nod thoughtfully.

"Yeah, I guess I could say that's part of what happened," I voice, remembering how I'd feel that way on occasion when Luna and I would FaceTime with her safely here at home, and me reaching out from hell.

"All Luna ever seemed to want out of all this was for you to be okay." He voices his thoughts out loud as he looks out over the lawn. "For you to have a chance at what it feels like to be loved, and have someone care about you."

"I know. She gave me that, and I was too much of a stubborn, ill-conceived asshole to accept it, but now–"

"You're focusing on the wrong part of that sentiment, son," Ben cuts me off, his tone easy and neutral, and I try not to feel nostalgic at the way he just referred to me. It was probably just a figure of speech and not an endearment, but he sets his beer down and turns to me, repeating his previous statement, this time a little louder and with clipped words. "All she wanted was for you to be okay... do you understand what I'm saying?"

No.

"Well... yeah. I've always known that, but I don't see how it pertains to earning her love again."

Ben sighs, drawing his knees up and wiping his brow with the back of his gloved hand before folding them over his legs. "When I met Kasey... I was a mess – well, kind of." He furrows his eyebrows while bobbing his head side to side with indecision. "I'd lost my first wife five years prior, and it had been a pretty harrowing experience. I shut down and went on autopilot, traveling like a goddamn nomad for the next few years. After a while the pain eased, but I'd become stagnant. Then I met Kasey and Luna, and they brought me back to life again." He shakes his head nostalgically, and I swear I see stars in his eyes. And I get it. Luna gives me those, too. "They made me happy. But when I looked inside myself, I realized I couldn't just let everything go and just jump into a life with them. I had to be the best version of myself, and while they certainly woke that up in me, I had to do the rest. I had to show them that I could be good for them without it having to fall on them. That I could be strong for them too, and not just the other way around.

"The thing is, Kaleb, we're two very different men with few but very profound things in common. I lost everything – at least, at the time, I felt like I might as well have. When my wife died, it was harrowing and I retreated into myself. I let my medical license lapse and ran to the other side of the world to hide. You lost everything too, only at a much younger age – your mother, and then you basically lost your father as you knew him."

"The thing about that is, what hurt me more wasn't his fist, it was having him turn over a new leaf again and again, giving me love and gaining my trust before he'd turn back into a monster in the blink of an eye."

"So… maybe you thought it was better to not get attached in the first place?"

"Sort of. I attached myself to Luna because at that time, I didn't even have a sliver of a doubt. And then I came home a wounded wreck, and the idea of it became real. I told myself that we'd both changed and our dynamic would never be the same, but I was terrified."

"Sounds like you two need to talk to each other more," he laments thoughtfully. "You're both practically still kids, and you don't get what really makes a marriage work. You're both too busy trying to be each other's hero to share the load with each other."

Something in his words stops my world and makes me contemplate that for a moment, staring down at the grass on the ground.

"You're half right," I voice out loud. "She was trying to be my hero while I pouted, feeling sorry for myself and pushing her away. Just like when she wanted to know about more of my childhood back at camp. I didn't want her to see me as some poor, abused little boy. I just wanted to be her Kaleb. And when I came back stateside, I knew I definitely couldn't be that. I was embracing the damaged, self-loathing, shadow of myself that my demons were trying to make me become, and I didn't want her to see it. I wanted to succumb to that particular animal, but little by little, she brought me back to myself – almost. She did the heavy lifting, made me as close to whole as she could…" And now I need to do the rest, I think to myself. I need to get myself the rest of the way there so I can pull her up with me.

It's like a crystallizing moment, having my father-in-law's words click together perfectly in my mind, and I find myself slowly nodding.

"You don't have to be your father, Kaleb," Ben adds. "You don't have to give into the ugliness he did. You can embrace the love and happiness that's still being offered to you." He tips his beer again, taking a hearty enough swig to polish it off. "Thanks for the help on the fort," he says as he waves his empty bottle at the small, shed-like enclosure. For the most part it's finished; it even has a doorway and a window. There's a fine layer of sawdust to knock off it before he paints it, but I take his observation to mean he's got nothing else to add on the advice front... but I still want to know one more thing.

"Dr. Isaak?"

"Ben," he corrects me.

"Ben," I nod, and proceed with caution. "I know that Carter did something to her."

Ben's body stiffens so suddenly I catch it in my peripheral.

"Did Luna tell you?" he asks, sounding like it's taking extra effort to keep his voice steady, and I shake my head.

"I found the hospital bills," I fill him in. "And when I saw her earlier today, I got it out of her that it was him that put her there, but she wouldn't tell me anything more."

"Then I probably shouldn't either," he responds sternly, and he must see the trepidation on my face because he's quick to add, "I went there, Kaleb. She wasn't there alone," he assures me, and I close my eyes with only partial relief.

"I'm glad you were there when I couldn't be." My voice shakes slightly and I clench my hands between my knees and straighten my spine, trying to feel big against the demons. "But if she'd told me, I would've found a way."

"I know you would've," he nods, this time looking straight at me so I can see his conviction. "And in my opinion, she should've told you, but she was hell-bent on protecting you."

I give an annoyed guffaw as I shake my head, irritated as ever that Luna felt the need to shield me once again. "She's always doing that, and I wish, just once, she'd let me do that for her," I voice out loud, pushing myself up off the steps just because I need to move. When I notice Ben looking curiously from his perch on the steps, I wave a hand in explanation. "I'm not... blaming her, I just... I feel like I could've possibly gotten better a little sooner if she'd just let me in; let me be there for her."

I see his eyes darken as they seem to space out, and he flexes his fists in front of him, locking them together.

"What did he do to her, Ben?" I ask, past the point of caring how I'm being received. I'm pretty sure he and I are officially in the same vessel now.

He just shakes his head, still staring forward as his eyes get glassy. "It's not something she wants you to know, Kaleb. She just wants to move on."

"And you?" I ask him, gripping at the back of my neck. "What do you want? As her father?"

He doesn't answer me as he sets his jaw and then draws in a long breath before looking down at his hands.

"Ben," I level with him, staring hard. "I need to *know*," I slowly grind out, putting stress on that particular word.

"Why, Kaleb?" he asks, lifting his head slowly to regard me. "Tell me why you need to know."

There's an undercurrent in his words; a hidden message. His eyes are connected with mine, willing me to come up with the right answer because he wants to tell me… But I can't tell him why. I won't put my wife's father or his medical license in jeopardy by making him a party to what I intend to do. I, on the other hand, have nothing left to lose.

Instead of supplying him with an answer, I maintain our eye contact and slowly move my head from side to side.

His gaze holds mine right back before he very slowly nods.

We have an understanding…

45

LUNA

I should've gone back to bed after Kaleb's appearance. Because after that, my day was pretty much shot to shit. But because I'm trying not to be that girl, I went to my classes, which he made me late for, couldn't pay attention to save my life, had to scrap two of the projects I was working on and start over…

Kaleb drove out here and fought for me, and it touched my heart in a way I didn't know I could ever feel. But I thought we were good again before, and being handed those papers out of the blue devastated me; the kind of cold, hollowed out, will never love again devastation. I don't even know how I survived it.

Now, I slam my car door shut and lazily drape my bag over my shoulder. I trudge down the sidewalk that winds between the apartment buildings as the evening sun glows orange behind the trees.

Once on the second floor of building C and inside Cassidy's apartment, I make a beeline for the bedroom to change into comfies. I'm just pouring myself a bowl of cereal for dinner when there's an upbeat knock at the door, one I'm familiar with.

No way…

I scurry around the kitchen island, trying not to trip on my baggy plaid pajama pants and fling open the door to find my beautiful mother, dressed not too far off from how I am. She's in damage control mode, and her arms immediately open for me to walk into them. No words need to be spoken, at least for this moment, as I let her just hold me, making me feel safe enough to let out a nice decompressive sigh. I wasn't expecting her, but then again, I'm not surprised, and I don't need to ask what she's doing here.

When she pulls back, she gives me a tight smile that I also know well. It's the one that says *Smile... we're going to smile and get through this.*

Is it the best way to go about things? Maybe not, but it's also not the worst, and I'm all for not falling down the rabbit hole of darkness and despair. Besides, it's just until we get me to a good enough place to talk things out where the risk of that is minimal. I give her a matching smile back that makes us both lightly giggle before I get the ever-living shit startled out of me.

"Tah-dah!" My brother Matty pounces into the hallway, landing in a dance stance with his arms spread wide in presentation. His big, round eyes are wide with the glee that matches his shit-eating grin, that turns to mock fright when I advance on him.

"Oh my God, don't do that, you little shit!" I yell at him, leaning in. I'm glad to see my baby bro, but I hate being startled, and my aggravation is trying to stifle the joy. "What did you have to bring him for?" I ask in faux annoyance that I know my brother can recognize as I turn to my mom. "And why is his hair blue?" I add, nodding at Matty's new spiky do that boasts a bright shade of cobalt.

"For this very reason," she responds calmy to my first question. "You're too flustered and annoyed to be sad. As for his hair color, he came to me and said he wanted to express himself like you..." she reaches for a strand of my hair and presses her lips together when she finds no hint of purple. "... used to. Anyway," she drops my hair and reaches down for the weekend bag I didn't notice at her feet. "It's the weekend, and we're here to spend some quality time with you, baby. Now show us where Cassidy keeps the takeout menus and let's cue up some action movies."

Kaleb

I sit behind the wheel of my truck, a photo from Carter's social media page on display on my phone screen resting on the seat beside me.

Resting my elbow in the window frame, I repeatedly clench and release my fist under my chin as I recall the rest of my conversation with Ben.

Once he gave me that slow nod with that knowing look in his eyes, I knew I had an ally in this. He knows why I wanted so badly to know everything. There's the obvious reason that I want to experience empathy for Luna to the fullest extent possible. I refuse to be her husband that doesn't know what she went through... and then there's the other reason; the one I knew he picked up on by the look in my eye.

"So you're telling me... that fucker threw my wife down a flight of stairs?" I repeat as he grips the railing of the deck, his head hanging between his arms.

"At her studio," he confirms, before raising his head and pushing a hand through his hair with an exhale heavy with anger and grief. "He cornered her there."

I could feel an energy passing between him and I; a mutual fury mixed with pain. And then I asked him to explain the procedures, tests, and treatments I found on the hospital bill. And just like I intended, I felt each injury as if it were happening to me, and I feel it all again right now, as I relive more of the conversation.

"He broke the last two fingers on her right hand, crushed them in his own."

Sharp pain shoots through my pinky and ring finger before lighting up with a throbbing pain.

"Three cracked ribs…"

An imaginary sledgehammer slams into my left side, and I swear I feel the ribs there splinter beneath my skin tissue.

"A bruised kidney…"

A dull, but vicious ache spreads along my middle back.

"And a slight concussion."

My head explodes with pain from all the fucking madness that Luna's had to endure. Her pain is my pain. I know I need to be a better man for her, that part of Ben's message was clear. And I will… starting tomorrow.

I continue waiting in the parking structure of what looks like a large tech company, a lot like the one in Office Space. I spend my time imagining what happened to my girl over and over, each time in a slightly different way, but still feeling the pain of each affliction. I endure this special brand of self torture for just under an hour when I see a few people come out of the elevator. Sadly, not one of them that has a face that matches that of the disgusting dick-fuck on my phone screen. I watch the two men and one woman smile and wave each other off as I let out a stress-riddled breath.

I look again at the placement of security cameras, and while this is a tech company, they don't seem to want to spend much in that department. Their cameras are spaced at least twenty feet apart, giving me a nice pocket of space to have a nice little chat with the fucking cuntface that is Carter.

As if someone rang Satan's gong and summoned him, those elevator doors fatefully part open to reveal the bastard. And the heavens seem to be shining on me yet again, as he's alone. Clad in khakis and an open button-down, the fucker carries his messenger bag over one shoulder into my nice little camera free pocket, signaling the okay for me to abruptly push open my truck door. Pulling the hood of my jacket up just in case, I get out and then slam my door deliberately loud, making his head snap in my direction.

"Carter," I greet him as if we're old friends while I swagger casually up to him. He attempts a nervous smile as he tries to place me.

Tilting his head and narrowing his eyes slightly, he asks. "Hey... sorry, have we met?"

"Nah," I shake my head, willing my scrutinizing gaze to pierce his brown little puppy eyes, and to my delight, he stiffens and his eyes dart away for a second as he tries to compose himself. "But you know someone I love," I finish, making him look back at me again.

I can practically see him tell himself to stand taller and puff out his chest, and it's pathetic. He quirks an eyebrow in mock boredom as he tries to dismiss me. "Okay, well, look... I don't have time for whatever this is." He waves a hand back and forth in front of me.

"Well that's just too bad for you," I reply, my voice a low and cunning growl. "Because you fucked with the wrong man's wife."

"What?" Both his eyebrows and his voice go up a notch before a small veil of relief drops over his face. "Okay, now I know you've got the wrong guy, this is a misunderstanding." He backs up a little as I continue my slow advancement. "Seriously, I've never been with, or done anything with any married women." He lets out a nervous laugh.

"You telling me it's the single ones – or the ones you *think* are single that you throw down the stairs?" I quiz him, and those pupils of his dilate so fast and the color draining from his face is a thing of beauty.

"What?" His voice is barely a whisper as his shoulders shudder slightly. The look on his face can no longer be hidden by any veneer. He's abjectly terrified now. Good.

"I think you know what I'm talking about." I raise my brows

expectantly at him, but he clearly is scared shitless to admit to it. He knows what I'm about to do to him.

"No..." he swallows hard, shaking his head. "No, I don't know what you're talking about." He's clearly starting to panic.

"That's fine" I shrug. "I'm more than happy to jog your memory." I lean in, and Carter looks around for anyone that could possibly be around to help. And that's his first mistake. He opens his mouth to yell and looks back at me just in time for my skull to connect with his forehead.

What comes out of him is a guttural yelp before he drops backward, landing on his ass before rolling to his back, his hand covering the bridge of his nose as I drop to a knee beside him.

"If I were you, I wouldn't try to call for help again," I advise quietly, as we're now hunkered down between cars where someone would be lucky to even notice us.

The pathetic little bitch lets out an agonizing moan from behind his hand, and I try again to quiet him.

"I mean it, Carter," I chide out a warning. "Come on, you can be tougher than that, right? After all, you can beat up on an unsuspecting woman," I remind him.

His moan turns to a slight whimper as he makes no move to get up. "What's the matter? Did that give you a headache?" I taunt. "Really, Carter, it's no worse than what you did to my wife. Man the fuck up."

"Wh- who?" he whines out painfully. "I don't... get what's happening." His words come out between gasps of air as he tries to compose himself.

"You're getting what you deserve," I supply low and adamant. "Since that didn't happen in the court case where you were accused of putting my wife in the hospital – with a concussion." I tap my fingers against his forehead to indicate what I just did to him, and he cries out.

"His cousin's a sleazy lawyer who also happened to play golf with the judge," Ben conveys, looking helpless. They were able to convince everyone it was an accident."

"I didn't do it, she just fell!" Carter stupidly protests. "I was trying to catch her – ugghhh!" he yelps as I grab onto his shirt with both hands and pull him to his feet, his legs scrambling.

"Stop fucking lying!" I bark out before delivering a haymaker to his ribs and feeling them give a satisfying crunch against my fist. Carter lets out a long grunting sound, followed by a couple of gasps and wheezes. "No one's here to save your sorry ass with bullshit probation," I add, taking hold of his wrist in my grip. "And since you wouldn't pay with jail time, you're going to pay with pain, you piece of shit," I inform him while taking ahold of his fingers and clenching them in my fist until I feel them crack. This makes him scream out in agony, and I reflexively snap my other fist forward, hitting him in the windpipe, cutting off his voice.

The impact makes him stumble backward and fall to the ground again, his screams caught in his throat.

"I told you to quiet the fuck down, didn't I?" I spit as I lower myself down to his level again. "You know, I may not have been there, but I already know my beautiful badass wife handled all these things endlessly better than you are."

My eyes squeeze shut briefly, as I painfully remember how my Luna never made a sound... ever.

Carter's focus is mainly dedicated to trying to get any kind of breath down his airway, but a good portion of it is still trained on me, as he looks at me with his eyes wide and petrified.

"Now..." I begin, leaning my knee into his chest. "From what I understand, my wife went pretty damn easy on you. You're not going to get that from me. Time to talk about where you and I go from here."

"We were going to try again, and this time get him with that rejection letter he forged," Ben had also informed me. "But Luna just wanted to be done; to not waste any more of her energy on him when she had you coming home to her."

Carter gives a jerk from my ominous words, still trying to pull in air.

"Did you know our family lawyer was ready to take your carefully crafted rejection letter you forged up to the federal level?" I raise my brows. "We still can, actually, and your slimy little cousin won't be any good to you there. You'll be on your own, and with violating a restraining order on your record, I don't think you'd get off so easy this time."

"Wh– whuuu…" Carter tries to get out, but his voice is hoarse.

"What am I going to do?" I try to fill in for him. "That depends on you," I reply and cock my head at him. "When I leave here tonight, you can call the cops and tell them everything that went down, and they'll come and arrest me." I raise a shoulder as if I couldn't care less. "Which is fine, seeing as how it'd be my first offense, I'm a veteran, and have a pretty decent lawyer myself. A couple of them actually." I don't know how much I really have the Isaak's lawyer, or the place I drew up those infernal papers, but he doesn't need to know that. "But the thing is, if you do that, the Isaaks will move forward with pursuing the feds, and I'm pretty sure you don't get another free pass. Federal prison is a whole different animal than local jail, and I'm pretty sure I'll be out before you are."

Carter's given up talking, it looks like. Instead, he just lays there, trying to breathe, eyes still holding mine as if they're afraid to look away.

"Or you can just be a big boy and consider your lesson learned, and you can forget that I and Luna exist." I lean in, pinning him with my fiery gaze, silently warning him to make the right choice. "What's it going to be?" When too much time passes by that he wastes wallowing in his pain, I get impatient. "Look at me, you fucking asshole!" I snarl, wrapping my hand around his jaw and gripping tightly. The action makes him jerk and startle again, and I bring my face within an inch of his. "You touch what's mine again, and one way or another, your life is over. Are we clear?"

After a few moments tick by, Carter finally squeezes his eyes shut and nods before relaxing back on the cold concrete floor. I stare him down another few moments, giving him the look from hell so he knows how serious I am.

When I'm confident he's not going to go back on his word, I finally rise and walk away.

Once my headlights reach the highway, I take the time to mentally prepare for what comes next. The drone of my tires spinning on the asphalt actually calms me as I recall the last thing Ben said to me as I left Luna's childhood home earlier tonight.

"Kaleb," he calls to me as I reach my truck on the other side of the street. I turn and let him catch up to me, eager to hear what he has to say.

"When it comes to Luna, you're going to have to allow it time. The truth is, you guys got married recklessly at a young age, and now you need to get yourselves back in a good place. But if you're able to do that, I want you to know that you have a family with us, Kaleb."

We stand in there in the street a moment as I let that heartening prospect of that settle over me.

"Thank you," I finally say with deep sincerity and he nods back, conveying the same.

"That said," he adds with a lifted eyebrow, that I know is meant to be admonishing. "I know I took an oath to do no harm, and you've had training I can't even fathom. But if you fuck this up, I'll fuck you up."

"Yes, sir," I respond with a firm nod, taking him seriously as a heart attack.

I feel one corner of my mouth quirk into a smile as I recall those last words and tuck them away into a special pocket of my heart.

"I'll be back for you, baby," I say into the void of the cab, hoping Luna hears it somewhere on the wind.

46

LUNA

"How you doing over there, kid?" my mom asks from her perch against the nearby picnic table. Next to her sits a box of donuts we've demolished half of already, and she cradles her to-go coffee cup against her chest.

After dragging me out of bed this morning, she drove us and Matty to get a sugary breakfast and bring it here to the park where she now has me shooting hoops while we dive into my feelings, while Matty tools around on his skateboard.

I look down at the ball as I idly dribble, buying myself a few extra seconds before I answer with a sigh. "I'm twenty-two and I've already fallen in with a guy I didn't even realize was controlling me and who later put me in a hospital bed. Oh, and I'm almost divorced from another guy. I'm a fucking train wreck."

"Trainwreck!" Matty hollers as he zips by on his skateboard while making an explosion sound and mimicking one with his hands.

Ignoring him, my mom lifts an eyebrow as she bounces the ball to me again. "Well… is that what you think of me?"

"What?" I feel my brows pull inward as I catch it in front of my chest. "No, why would I ever?"

"Because when I was your age, honey, I was a single mother in rehab after she met her second druggie boyfriend."

I feel my heart sink like a stone as I look down at the asphalt. "Mom, none of that was your fault. It was just a run of bad luck. No one made me marry Kaleb."

"And no one made me snort pills," she volleys back.

"But, Mom, you've got your shit together, and that doesn't define you." She arches an eyebrow at me and my mouth falls open as I realize my argument holds no weight. Shaking my head, I huff out a breath and turn towards the basket, taking a shot that bounces off the rim.

My mom gives a resigned smile as she picks up her coffee from the picnic table. After taking a sip, she brings up Kaleb's visit yesterday. "Anyway, sounds like Kaleb doesn't want to get divorced anyway."

I shake my head, still not knowing what to do with that as I snag the ball again. Last night, she'd kept her word and we just hung out, and it was a nice distraction. It helped me reset a little bit, and then this morning, my mom plied me with donuts and coffee before moving in for the kill. I seriously wonder sometimes if she's a witch.

"He came here looking for you," she continues, dipping her chin to level me with a serious look. "If he truly wanted to end things, he would've sat back and let you go, but he didn't."

"And?" I sigh petulantly as I start dribbling the ball again. I know I'm being stubborn, but I feel locked in this state of anger and self-doubt.

"And if you don't want to be a young divorcée, as you've expressed your concern, then don't get divorced because you guys went through a shitty time," she quips smartly before taking another sip while Matty yells from across the court.

"Shitty!"

"Language!" Mom fires back before looking back at me. "Anyway, I don't really think you want this, honey. I think you're still reeling from the shock and the hurt."

"He's the one who drew up divorce papers," I argue, turning my back as I continue to dribble, and I can hear a monumental sigh behind me. "What?" I demand, as I whip around to face her. "Why can't you just support me on this? Why does it feel like you're taking his side?"

"I'm not," she holds her hands up defensively. "Never did I say let him off the hook and run back to him like nothing happened. Hell, I raised you better than to be blindly forgiving. I'm saying take it from a former addict, people do unreasonable things when they are in dark places. I don't think it was Kaleb that filed those divorce papers, is all I'm saying. But the guy that was stunned by his own mistake and came rushing after you trying to fight for your love?"

She leaves the question hanging in the air while she looks at me expectantly to pick up what she's dropping.

That was the real Kaleb.

The thought sweeps through my mind against my stubborn will, refusing to be suppressed. The guy that woke up that one morning and bought me a six pack of root beer to apologize for being an ass was my Kaleb. The guy that started putting in work at his physical therapy. The guy that started to draw again. Even the guy who kissed me goodbye in the driveway… I don't want to admit it, but that was him, too.

"He just hurt me so bad," I finally confess quietly, and I look up to see my mom's shoulders drop and her face soften. "I just want to get as far away from that pain as I can and never feel it again."

Mom pushes off the picnic table and comes striding over. I let her envelope me in another comforting mama hug that I can only get from her.

"You still love him, or you wouldn't be hurting like this," she comments gently, "but right now, you've lost some of your faith in him. It's okay to take some time to heal yourself, and let him use that time to earn that faith back again. If he doesn't? Then at least you will have found your own happiness again, and God knows that you guys won't be able to do for each other what you can't do for yourselves."

Her words sink in softly, and it finally feels like I have some kind of clarity; like I don't need to have answers right now. It's like I've been given permission to let go of this whole shitshow; to let go of the pain and just be. I think the answer is that I don't have to have the answer right now. It's to just heal and just be.

We hug another moment before my brother's little voice penetrates the bubble.

"Can we dye her hair now?"

Kaleb

It's been three months since the night I laid out the asshole who hurt Luna – the last thing I allowed myself to do out of anger. I let a hell of a lot of steam out of the pot, and while I don't regret it one iota, I know it's time to reprogram myself. Anger has cast a big shadow over my life long enough, and it's damaged my relationship with Luna. If I have any hope of getting her back, the future I offer her needs to look bright.

And so I've taken Dr. Jeffries advice – whom I've continued to have sessions with – and gotten into a loose routine that's been really good for me so far. He reminded me of the routine I lived by during my time in the military, and suggested I do something similar again, only relax it a bit.

I start each day the same with coffee, breakfast, and a light workout, followed by various tasks around the house, maintaining what needs it. The only alcohol I keep in the house now is beer, that I don't treat myself to until the end of the day, and I limit it to two. I'm even taking an online business class. Just one, as I wanted to get an idea of what I can handle, and it's actually not going too badly.

And then each night, as well as when I feel a flashback or a moment of panic coming on, I put on the videos I have of Luna on my phone. It helps center me and remind me what I'm striving towards.

Dr. Jeffries was quick to advise me however: Do this for you. It's okay to be cautiously optimistic, but first and foremost, make sure you are doing this for yourself. If your solitary goal is to save your marriage, you run the risk of falling apart again if it doesn't pan out how you hoped.

While I'd wanted to resist his sentiment (stubbornness dies hard), I knew I had to acknowledge that possibility and focus on being healthy and stronger to keep going, even if it ends up being on my own. But that doesn't mean I can't still hope and focus on what I want most by keeping her present.

I've only just gotten out of the shower after my morning workout, and with a towel around my waist, I grab a second cup of coffee from the kitchen, intent on enjoying it while I air dry. I'm mid pour when my cell rings on the countertop. I feel my forehead draw in slightly as I see Jackson's name on the caller ID.

Worried that something might be wrong with the shop, I quickly swipe to answer.

"Jax," I greet him, taking a sip of my coffee.

"Hey, K, is this an okay time?"

"Yeah, everything alright?"

"Yeah, it's fine. I just wanted to let you know your dad called up here again." His revelation is followed by a nervous sigh.

I feel my fist start to shake slightly and promptly set down my mug before I drop it.

"Did you blow him off?"

"Of course I did, K. I thought you should know… but there's more. This time he asked for you, and he was calling from jail."

I feel my heart drop down in my stomach and bounce back up in the flash of a second.

The idea of my father lurking around somewhere behind the scenes has always unnerved me. The thought of him contained –

which, I'm sure he has been on and off, but I was never aware of it – does something different to me. I feel an urge... one I don't want to feel.

One thing my therapist occasionally touches on is the power certain aspects of my life lord over me; controlling me in one unique way or another. The worry I've had over Pops' shop and putting my tattoo parlor ambitions on hold. My fear, my trauma... they all dictate my quality of life – but none so much as the tattered loose ends I have with my father that dangle over me like I'm constantly on some old carnival ride.

I notice my breath is coming in and out of my mouth in ragged passes and I swallow, reminding myself to keep my control. "So you said you blew him off, what did you tell him?"

"That you weren't available and to quit calling, then I hung up. Got Metro County Jail off the caller ID," he reports, and I nod to myself.

After ending the call, I push my wet hair out of my face and brace my hands on the countertop's edge.

After stewing for a moment or two, I feel the beginnings of a storm start to brew behind my eyes, and I know what I need to do.

I hate resorting to this, but my therapist gave me his cell phone number for emergencies, and I don't know if I can stop myself from getting amped up from this new information, let alone wind myself down.

"Kaleb?" he answers on the first ring, his voice sounding tentative as I hear papers being shuffled around. "You doing okay?"

"Um, yeah..." I answer, trying to find the words so I don't sound like I'm fighting off what could be a breakdown... maybe. I'm actually not sure. I'm actually surprised I haven't started the spiral process yet. "But I'm having kind of a... moment. Do you have time to guide me through it?"

47

KALEB

After being verified and searched about twenty times, I'm finally let into a room that resembles a school cafeteria, only even more depressing as fuck. Thin, flimsy tables with metal chairs are scattered about the room, and various prisoners meet with their families at a respectfully ordered distance.

After standing for a few awkward moments with my hands in my pockets, I finally stride over to take a seat at a vacant rectangle table. Clasping my hands on the table's surface, I remind myself at least six times to stop bouncing my knee.

The metal door at the far-left corner of the room opens, and a guard steps aside, letting in yet another inmate garbed up in an unflattering khaki jumpsuit. I watch curiously from my seat for a moment as he's escorted further into the room. When I'm sure of who I'm looking at, I slowly rise from my seat. It's been a long time… fifteen years, in fact. The years have not been kind, making him look like he's aged twice that much. His dark hair is completely grey, and deep creases line his face. Clearly he hasn't given up the life of drugs and drinking, judging by how thin he is, along with the rest of his sallow appearance.

His sunken green eyes lock on mine as the guard unlocks his

cuffs and walks away, leaving us to stare across the room at each other.

The man who used to be my father swallows hard, but to my confusion, he then forces a smile.

"Kaleb," he nods subtly, and I can't think of what to do but nod back. We stare at each other another beat before I awkwardly gesture to the table, and he follows suit with me as I take a seat.

"You grew up nicely," he mentions, waving a hand in my direction as he sits. "You're big," he adds with a light chuckle, mocking surprise. "So how've you been? What have you been doing with yourself?" He dives so casually into the small talk, as if we're old coworkers instead of father and son.

"I joined the Army," I answer, releasing my nerves on a heavy breath with the words.

He sits back with raised eyebrows, looking impressed. "Well good for you," he says, his tone light with encouragement. "I'd love to hear more about that when I get out of here. About when do you think? By the way, I'm dying for a smoke," he converses.

"Excuse me?" I relax a wrist on the table and dip my chin in disbelief.

"I called the shop, and a few days later, here you are." He raises his hands at me in presentation. "I didn't get to touch base with you, but you still came. So when am I getting out of here? Do you have some paperwork to sign or something?" he asks brightly, folding his hands on the table like this is a given.

I freeze for a moment, staring at him across the table, trying to come up with the right words that will come across civil when I realize that this motherfucker has absolutely nothing to say for himself after fifteen years of absence, preceded by about six or seven filled with abuse. Nothing except asking what I can do for him. I don't owe him civil.

"I'm not here to bail you out, Rick," I inform him in a low voice, pinning his eyes with my own. And then I watch as his smile stays in place while his eyes dim.

"What?" he scoffs, still trying not to let himself falter. "Kaleb, come on. You drove like, what, three counties to get here? Just to say hi?" His voice is getting more exasperated with each word. "Tell me it was to actually get me out of here, and not just for a drive by."

I shake my head, partly in disbelief at what I'm actually hearing, and partly to tell him hell-fucking-no.

"Kaleb, seriously," he tries again. "I know I wasn't a good father like you deserved, but I was going through some things… and they just snowballed. I'm still your dad. I know it's late in your life, but if we get out of here, we could go have dinner with your grandfather, and … and, uh… we can talk some more."

I can tell by his hesitating stammer, the absent wave of his hand, and the way he broke eye contact he doesn't mean that last part at all.

"Pops died over four years ago," I coldly inform him, and watch as his eyes go cold and his shoulders stiffen.

"He's gone?" His voice wavers and that faux smile's been put away.

"He died alone in his shop," I nod. "You see, the world wasn't just going to stop turning and wait for you to be done getting wasted off your ass. If you gave enough of a fuck to try turning your life around, it maybe wouldn't have gone that way."

"I did try," he snaps back, leaning in. "Don't you fucking remember? I tried; it didn't take."

"And then you quit." I raise a brow at him, leaning in myself. "You gave up, and gave in to a life of drugs and a constant state of fucked up."

"And just what was I supposed to do, huh?" he challenges through gritted teeth. "Nothing was working."

"You were supposed to keep trying," I supply, my tone matching his. "Even if nothing ever came of it, you were supposed to keep trying, and never stop. Even if it was just so that your kid could see you gave enough of a shit about him to not give up."

"I lost my wife," he tries to justify.

"I lost my mother."

"You were too young to remember."

"Exactly!" I counter, holding a finger up at him. "Instead, I grew up without one and spent the majority of my childhood cowering from an abusive, drunk father instead, never knowing if he was going to hug me or hurt me!"

I think I see a flicker of regret in his eyes, but even so, I press on.

"Yeah, you lost your wife, but I lost a hell of a lot more than you did, asshole," I grumble out. "I went to war where I got blasted by a bomb, watched my best friend die, and came home a broken-down wreck. Here's the thing though … I fell in love. I fell so deeply in love with someone that I started to have a sliver of an idea of what you went through when you lost my mother, and I was this close to turning into you," I hold my finger and thumb a half inch apart. "That thought scared the shit out of me so bad I actually tried pushing her away so that I would truly have nothing left to lose."

My father has the decency to actually sit there and take my rant before looking down at his lap. When he looks back up, there's a quiet fury in his eyes, but not the indignant, spiteful kind. He's feeling a passionate anger warm his blood because he knows I'm right. He's finally realizing in this moment what a piece of shit he is.

"So close," I shake my head at him, because I myself am still having trouble believing it. Even if Luna doesn't want to stay married, I will not turn into this disappointment sitting across from me. "This is me forgiving you and saying goodbye once and for all. I wanted you to get a good look at that man I turned into, despite you."

He sits stewing a few more seconds, taking in a few concentrated breaths and letting them out before responding in a voice much weaker than the one he spoke in just moments ago.

"So... you... you really did just come by to unload everything," he states, already knowing the answer as if he'd asked.

"It wasn't something I could do back then," I tell him, referring to when I was just a kid. "You took my childhood, so I figured you could give me ten minutes."

Ten minutes to take back my power is the part I don't tell him.

"Take back your power without pointing out how much he had over you in the first place," Dr. Jeffries had said on the phone. *"But remember, that taking back your power also means not letting your anger at him have control over you. Prove that to him and yourself, but don't be afraid to be real."*

Feeling like I've achieved all I came to do, I tilt my chin up over at the guard. He nods and comes over, pulling the keys off his belt as he walks. I scoot my chair back and stand.

"I forgive you, Rick," I say down to my father, "and I do hope you can make a better life for yourself one day. I'm just not going to have any part of it."

I'm about to say more. I want to add on that I have a wife he'll never meet, and one day we'll have kids he'll never push on the tire swing. But looking down at him, I know I've said enough. He's heard everything loud and clear.

"Goodbye," I finally tell him as I turn and walk out of the room without looking back.

SEVERAL DAYS after that fateful visit with my father, I'm feeling clearer headed than I think I ever have in my life. I'd never considered it before because it never occurred to me, but I think I realize now that I've never learned what it's like to feel level. I've always been full speed ahead or deep down in a rut, but for once, I feel like I'm moving steadily forward. Well... that is after I had a session with my therapist following that visit. Admittedly, I was a bit wired following that grim conversation with my dad, but Dr. Jeffries assured me that what I was experiencing was perfectly normal.

Normal. That's a word I never thought I wanted to describe myself with. But it feels good, though I'm almost afraid to let that feeling get away from me. And while I've been missing Luna every minute of every day since the last time I saw her, I feel like in the last few days, it's amplified. It's as if cutting out that certain cancer in my life; the anger I'd been carrying around for so many years made more room for my love for her to grow even stronger.

As it stands, we're still not divorced. I never did sign those papers, and she never pursued anything further. I'm not sure where that leaves us, but it damn sure gives me some hope.

I sit here at the kitchen island, drawing in my sketchbook with thoughts of her more visceral at the front of my mind than they've ever been. I feel anxious, but not in a nervous way. It's more eager, like I want to see Luna so badly and show her how far I've come. She's the one person I want to be proud of me, and happy for me, even if she decides not to live the rest of her life with me. I just want her to see. I've been biding my time, however, not knowing if rushing to see her is right just yet. I don't know how long is too soon, or too much time.

Setting my pencil down, I sit back and take a sip of coffee while fiddling with the rings that dangle on my chain with my dog tags; the rings that once adorned Luna's finger. Putting my mug down, I flip through the book, taking stock of what I've drawn lately. I've had some good inspiration for possible tattoos that I've marked down in here, and I'm thinking of transferring them to a bigger portfolio that can be sectioned off into themes like music, nature, fantasy, symbolism, and any others out there.

I slowly drop each page until I arrive back at the current one I'd been drawing on. My eyes scan over the lines and shading that make up a mane of dark hair, floating in the night breeze. A few of the strands shine with the reflection of moonlight being cast down by the crescent shape in the sky. My girl has her back to the viewer as she walks down towards the end of a wood planked dock that juts out in the middle of a lake of inky water. With nothing but a t-shirt on, one svelte leg leads in front of the other.

It's beautiful. It's an unexpected work that I'm really proud of, and though I drew it using only my usual dark pencil, I want to add a pop of color to this. Standing, I move over to the other side of the kitchen and shuffle through one of the spare drawers and retrieve a pack of colored pencils that I rarely use. Pulling out the purple, I resume my seat on the stool and get to work on the moon, giving it splotching and shading to give it that mottled look with the purple. After that, I move over to my girl, and with varying strokes, add some purple streaks to her tresses.

Feeling satisfied, I place the pencil down and survey my work, not knowing if I want to keep it private or share it with the world. I wonder for a moment what it would be like if more of the world knew Luna and her work, her expression, and her love of the color purple. That thought turns over in my mind as one gear in the back reminds me to add one more detail to the image. Picking the pencil back up, I etch the word MINE into the curve of the moon. The act immediately flashes back to how I felt finishing the same type of moon on Luna's chest, and the way she smiled up at me. That feeling from that moment twirls together with the other thoughts I was having, and then... wham.

I have an idea. I know what I want to do... I just need to figure out how to do it.

48

KALEB

*I*t goes without question that I've been feeling like the best version of myself, especially since the jail visit, and I'm ready to show it to Luna if she's willing to see it. My therapist verified I didn't have to lose everything about myself, and I wouldn't be me if I weren't a little impulsive. And I'm questioning how impulsive I'm even really being about this.

Ever since that lightbulb moment I had while drawing that epic picture a couple of weeks ago, I've been planning, talking to Jackson and West, looking at listings online, and writing – a fuck-ton of writing – and scribbling out, and crumpling papers to start again.

And then finally, a couple of days ago, everything came together. Everything that could give me a beautifully bright future with Luna, or a decent one for myself if she doesn't join me. Either way, I've learned that life doesn't have to be perfect to be damn good, and neither does a marriage. I put way too much pressure on Luna and our love story to heal me and make me all better when I came back stateside. We should've been healing each other. But we're young and dumb, me more so than her, and we can learn together.

I walk into Donna's Cafe, the breakfast and lunch hotspot on

Main Street, and give the woman herself a cordial smile before ordering a black coffee and having a seat in one of the middle booths.

I'm only a couple sips into the hot liquid when I see West walk in the front door, the attached bells jangling to announce his presence.

He tips his chin up at me in greeting as he saunters over across the checkered linoleum and orders a coffee for himself from Donna as he sits.

We spend only a few seconds on small talk before getting down to it. Looks like neither one of us are bullshitters.

"Are you sure you want to do this?" West asks from across the table.

I nod down at the Formica, taking a moment before letting my eyes meet his. "Yes. All I care about is that you keep the name, and of course, the integrity."

"Done," he assures me, tapping a finger on the stack of papers between us. "It's all right here in the contract.

"Thanks," I murmur, trying not to let the sentiments of this moment get the best of me. I was hyper focused on making sure Pops' shop would be okay, that it would be taken care of. It didn't occur to me until my most recent talk with my therapist that that didn't mean it had to be me who did it. It's enough for me to simply see to it. And I know Pops would be happy with the hands his business is being left in, and how it's being run. "Are you sure you want to do this?" I cock a brow at West, trying to shake off the heavy emotions.

He nods thoughtfully for a moment before speaking. "Yeah. I never thought I'd find myself in a middle of nowhere town like this, but…" he draws in a breath while looking around the rest of the diner and out the windows to the quiet streets, as if seeing it all for the first time. "But I find myself liking this. The people here, and the work, have made me realize I don't need to live large to make something of myself."

The truth of his words settle over me. Pops never left this

little town, and all he did was run his auto shop, raise my miserable ass, and volunteer for the fire station on occasion. Yet the way I saw it, he did everything.

"No truer words," I agree as I take the last cold sip of my coffee and slide out of the booth.

West nods, while following suit. "So… what are you going to do now?" he asks as I fold up his check and secure it in my wallet.

My answer may not be funny, but I can't help a sheepish chuckle to ward off the nerves and the shame. "I'm going to go try and win my wife back with a rather large present," I admit, and his head jerks back a little.

"Wow…" His eyebrows go up in a manner that I can't decide suggests he's impressed or thinks I'm out of my damn mind. "Well, good luck with that."

Luna

A SENSE of pride and satisfaction beams and pulses through me as I finish the last few strokes of paint on my jewelry dish with my detail brush. I can't get over the detail it turned out I was capable of.

For the last three months, I've been hardcore focused, intent on overcoming this particular Everest in my life, and it's been therapeutic. Something about conquering pottery has made me feel some kind of freedom.

Straightening up, I take in my new masterpiece which isn't my first, but I'm just as proud of it as I was the one I handed in last week, where my teacher told me I'd finally gotten it right. This piece is smooth and flawless where it's supposed to be, and imperfect towards the top of the curve where the oceans wave is cresting, creating a jumble of cascading water with an edge of foam.

A tap at the door makes me turn in that direction. I have a feeling I know who it is, but my past experience won't let me leave the door unlocked and just holler to whoever to show themselves in. Looking through the peephole, I scoff out a sigh and smile as I unlock the door.

"You have a key, you don't have to knock," I say to Cassidy as I stand aside to let her in. "Besides, this is your place," I point out.

"Not for the last three months, it hasn't been." She waves a finger over her shoulder as she strolls in with a bounce in her step.

"Yuh huh," I throw back as I return the lock and follow her further inside. "Just because I've been staying here, doesn't mean it's not still yours, plus," I raise a finger to make a point, "it's about to be again in a few short days."

The lease on my old studio – AKA, my personal house of horrors – is finally up, which means Cass can move back in here, but it's a crowded one-bedroom place, so I'm going to have to find somewhere else. The semester concludes on Friday, and while I qualify for an Associate's degree, I want to keep going. I feel like I've hit my niche here, and I feel like I could take it further.

"Okay, fine," she agrees. "But I don't think you should go rushing off to your parents for the summer, just because you don't have another place lined up. It's going to be hard to look for apartments from there. You should just stay with me. I know it will be a tight squeeze, but it will just be until you find somewhere."

"Mmmh," I grunt, knowing I'll probably give in eventually. "I've put you out enough."

"Oooh, what's this?" Cassidy asks with enthusiasm as she finds my new pottery piece, drying on its drop cloth on the table. "Oh my God, you've really harnessed the beast here, Loon." She turns and winks at me.

"Thank you, but please don't call me Tim Dennings nickname for me in middle school. It burns."

"I mean it, you've mastered it. It's the perfect, uh... it's just a beautiful..."

"Jewelry dish," I fill in for her.

"What a beautiful moon," she continues, and I feel my brows stitch inward. "Except what's the bumpy stuff on top of it?"

"It's not a moon, it's a wave," I correct her and I watch her eyes narrow and her lips part as she looks back to examine it again as I start fiddling with my left ring finger. Even though there's no ring to twist around it now, the habit seems to be dying hard.

"Oh..." Cassidy says flatly. "Oh okay, I see it now."

"No, Cass, come on..." I start to whine just a little in dismay. "I worked so hard on this and was so happy with how it came out. Do you really see a moon and not a wave?" I ask desperately.

"Quit worrying your pretty little purple-haired head," she chides, tugging at a piece of my hair that's gone back to being died several variations of the color. "It was just a first glance kind of thing. It's amazing to see you taking so much pride in your art again, and I love how you put your signature purple in it."

"Just a few accents," I shrug.

Cassidy takes another appreciative look at it before her shoulders rise and drop with a long cleansing breath. "Alright, you're taking me out tonight," she announces. "We'll celebrate you kicking this class's ass. Out of the overalls," she orders, waving a hand at my wardrobe.

"Where are we going?" I ask, not feeling like going out at all, but knowing that arguing is useless, especially after blowing off the idea several times already.

She gets an excitedly smug smile and holds her hands out. "It's perfect, actually. I got these exclusive tickets to a new art gallery on the edge of town. It's not even open to the public yet, but we get to go to a private, advanced showing!" She lightly claps her hands.

"Well... that does sound cool," I comment appreciatively. "How did you get the tickets?"

She squints one eye. "The coffee shop. They were having some giveaway with peoples punch cards, and anyway, I won an exclusive tour of this new place!" she finishes with a smile that's exceptionally wide, even for her.

She's being kind of weird, but again, I don't want to call her out on it and get pulled into some push and pull over whether I go out or not nearly as bad as I just want to get it over with so I can say I did and come home to snuggle in my sweats with Buster.

"Okay then." I shoot her an exaggerated look of approval to let her know I'm not buying it, but going with it.

"How long do I have to get ready?"

I'VE NEVER BEEN to this part of town before, but it's quaint, and I like it. It's like a section of the big city was carved out into a charming small town. I love all the hanging baskets outside the businesses; it's so much like Coyote Creek.

Something sinks in my chest at the thought of the town I once called home, and I quickly try to blink it away, much like I do with all memories involving Kaleb. I haven't heard from him, and while I told him to just sign the papers so that we could put all our trials and troubles behind us, I can't deny how much I miss him. I truly did fall so deeply in love with him. I'd been climbing that hill steadily since we were ten, and then last year, we just took the plunge off the edge together.

I haven't heard anything further on our divorce either, and I haven't done anything to reach out or question it. It sounds desperate and pathetic, but I guess I like knowing I'm tied to him in some way still.

I shake out of my nostalgic state once again as Cassidy finds a vacant piece of curb to pull up to.

"What's this place called again?" I ask as we exit the car, even though she didn't tell me in the first place.

"Um," she hesitates, holding up a finger as she starts leading us across the street. "I knew, but I forgot."

"Well, is the name on the tickets?" I ask, noting that she's not even carrying any. Maybe they're in her purse.

"Nope," she answers quickly as we step onto the sidewalk.

There's no question in my mind anymore. She's up to something, but I'm not letting her know that I know just yet. I want to see just how far she's going to take this... except then we cross over a driveway and into a back parking lot. The area still seems friendly enough, but what are we doing behind the pretty brick buildings?

"Whoa, where are we going?" I ask Cass while slowing my pace.

"The front entrance is closed off," she explains, "so as not to confuse people into thinking they're open yet. The invite said to come in through the back."

I nod and nervously push a strand of hair behind my ear, taking one last glance down at myself, wondering if I'm dressed okay for ... whatever this is. I opted for an olive-colored pair of cargo pants and a black top, and made sure my hair was nicely brushed out.

I pull my purse strap higher up on my shoulder as Cassidy stops in front of metal paneled door and pulls on its lever, as if she's been here a hundred times before already. Leading us in, she closes the door behind us as I stop in the vestibule and take in what I can see of the place so far. It's got a trendy but cozy look with exposed brick that's beautifully lit by strategically placed hanging lights. I love the glow and vibe of the place, and the way my chunk heals thunk on the hardwood floor as Cassidy strides past me, leading us in further. The only thing is... it's empty. No people, and no art displays that I can see.

"Cass, what's going on?" I ask pointedly as I look at her. "This clearly is not a gallery, even if it isn't open yet. Tell me," I finish firmly.

My uncharacteristically brash tone is clearly a surprise to her, and I swear I actually hear her gulp. Then her eyes nervously flit to something over my shoulder. I follow her line of sight and turn, my breath getting caught in my throat when I see what she's seeing.

Held to the brick wall by a piece of scotch tape is the drawing of a wolf that's been filled in with a multitude of black and purple shades. The very same that was drawn by a ten-year-old boy, and colored in by a girl of the same age. I reach up to touch it, wanting to feel the paper and crayon beneath my fingertips, and it doesn't fail to take me right back to that moment.

"There's… plenty more art to see," Cassidy whispers and straightens her spine, and I catch a glimmer of moisture in her eyes before she takes a breath and announces. "I just remembered that I have anywhere else to be. I'll see you later." She flashes a heart-warming smile at me before she pulls on the door lever again and swiftly exits through it.

When the door slams, my eyes dart back up to the first drawing Kaleb and I ever did – with and for each other – and my heart floats up to beat higher in my chest. In this moment, I know what I want, what I need more than anything else in this world… and to hell with anything else.

"Kaleb?" I call out, dropping my purse to the floor and hurrying further into the open floor plan that's separated by a couple of stone pillars. One of them has what I'm almost positive is the first sketch Kaleb made of the tattoo he put on me. I come around the side of it to find Kaleb striding out of a back corridor, looking more beautiful than I've ever seen him. In a nice pair of blue jeans, a black Henley, and with his dog tags on full display, he looks like the dream of a guy I married over a year ago, and I don't care what's wrong or right – I rush into his arms.

"Lu," he breathes as he gathers me up tightly, lifting me off the floor. The clean, manly smell that reminds me of summer nights, and the lock of his powerful arms makes me feel more at home than I've ever felt. I feel the rough stubble of his five o' clock shadow burrow affectionately into my neck, and it feels so good I could cry. In fact, I feel the slight burn from my eyes getting watery as he sets me down. His hands cradle my face as he rests his forehead against mine. "Baby, I missed you so much."

"I missed you," I tell him back, no longer caring who was wrong or right all those months ago, or if it was both of us. It doesn't matter compared to how much love and yearning I'm feeling for him in this moment. He looks amazing, and not just his appearance. His stature, his demeanor... there's so much beautiful confidence and strength to it.

"Lu," his voice is a shaky whisper. "Baby, I want to kiss you so badly right now. I want to kiss you and take you home with me right this second, but there's something I need to tell you first. Actually, there's a lot I want to tell you first."

I nod and pull away just slightly, I think, because whatever it is, I want him to get on with it so that we can get on the path to healing together. It's hard to really take it all in, but other drawings and paintings from when we were growing up decorate more of the walls. I glance around at all of it, bewildered, and it's then that a small table catches the corner of my eye, set in the direction he'd walked up to me from. On its surface lies two short stacks of paper – one of which I immediately recognize as our divorce papers. I only saw them once, months ago, and for just a few minutes, but I'd know them anywhere.

I take another step away, my breath quickening as I look between the table and Kaleb's green eyes, swimming in deep emotion. "Kaleb, what is this?" I ask. "What's going on?"

49

LUNA

"*I* have so much to tell you," he whispers, and those words barrel a trail right down to my core. I've never heard him sound like this; the man who never wants to tell anyone anything. "Luna, I know a lot of painful things have happened between us, but I was wondering if you could give me a chance to speak my mind… and my heart. I promise I'm not here to hurt you," he breathes out, closing his eyes.

That's all I needed to hear to put my soul at ease. I'm still feeling a small amount of nerves dancing through my bloodstream, just from the anticipation of what's coming, but this side of him he's showing me, while new… it's him and it's real; and I trust it.

"Okay," I nod, trying to give him a faint smile. He smiles back, taking a strand of my purple hair between his fingers and then placing a kiss to my forehead.

"Do you want to sit down?" he offers, and I shake my head.

"No, I want to stay close to you," I tell him unabashedly, and it earns me another smile before he steps away quickly to grab a couple of the papers that lay on the nearby bistro table.

He steps back in front of me, and it's now that I notice on the chain, along with his dog tags, are both the engagement and wedding rings he once gave me. It makes me automatically look to his left hand, clutching the papers to find the one that I slid on his finger that same day, still in place. Though he leaves a little space between us this time, he reaches his free hand out for mine, threading our fingers through each other's as if quietly asking for strength. He's seeking support from me; showing me a shadow of vulnerability, and it's enchanting.

"I wanted to tell you," he starts, looking at me rather than the notebook papers he's holding between us. "That I've been seeing a therapist," he admits, and my heart squeezes tightly into itself.

"Really?" is all I can think to retort, and he nods.

"I started that day..." he trails off uncomfortably, as if the very words would strike pain into his heart if he dare speak them, and I know what day he must be talking about. "I wanted to make sure it was something I stuck with before I told you about it, and, well, anyway," he swallows nervously. "One of the things we've worked on is how I'm not great at telling you what I'm thinking or feeling. He pointed out how we used to write letters to each other, and suggested I try that, so..." he holds up the papers and I press my lips together, willing the tears to stay where they are so that he can have this moment. He squeezes my hand as he begins.

"My beautiful, silly girl,

"I'm writing to tell you every truth I've held back from you.

The truth is, I've pushed you away at many different points in our lives, and it's because the one thing I've been conditioned to hate feeling is vulnerable. Telling you things, and letting you know the things I've been through made me feel that way, and I avoided it at all costs. And now that I've learned one of those costs is you, I've decided I can't live that way anymore. I want you back in my life, and I want to tell you things.

"The truth is, when I proposed to you, I was in a hurry to marry you because I'd been a hopeless fool for you for eleven years at that point. And after getting you back, I was going to be damned if I waited another fucking second.

"It's true that I needed to protect my assets, I can't lie about that, but it served more as an excuse to get you on board that fast.

"Another truth is, before I left, you and I were this beautiful, powerful force to be reckoned with. We'd just found each other again, and we were stronger than ever together. It felt like we could conquer the world. And then I came back from getting injured. My only other friend in the world had died, and you were all I had left. Rather than cherish that like I should've, I immediately started prepping for you to leave me too. I thought it was a strong possibility with how I seemed to be less than my half of that force that we'd become. I thought I needed to run away from the impending blast, and hide in my proverbial ranger hole the rest of my life.

"I drew up those divorce papers hoping it would test me. That having them in front of me would help me realize if I really felt like I wanted to leave our marriage. I was disappointed and frustrated when it didn't help me find clarity, and then I forgot about them, Luna. The clarity I wanted came when the damn pills left my system. I could clearly see how I was hurting you.

"That leads me to another truth. You've always been so damn tough, you never let anyone hurt you, not even me. Therefore, I didn't think I really could. I was proved wrong that night you kneed me in the balls,"

A giggle bubbles out of me at that, and I'm happy to see him smile too.

"That really hurt, by the way," he smirks before straightening and going back to his letter. "The thing is, that night was the first time I saw tears in your eyes, put there by me. That was when that clarity I wanted came. Up until then, I didn't think getting us back was possible, but in that moment, I refused to accept anything else. I wanted to make you smile for the rest of our lives.

"And you may not want to hear this, but the times I caught glimpses of us again were those few times you let yourself be vulnerable to me. Feeling needed by you gave me life, and made me want to strive for what we had again.

"Which brings me to now, my girl. If you'll allow me the privilege of remaining your husband, the truth is, I promise to always pull you close and not push you away; not ever again.

Love, your Kaleb," he concludes, lowering the letter, and as soon as that last word is out of his mouth, I finally release the tears that had been pushing to leave my eyes.

"Oh my God, Kaleb," I gasp for breath, trying to keep my breath steady as his arms come around me again.

"I hope those are happy tears," he murmurs into my hair, and I nod against his chest as his hand soothingly smooths down the back of my hair. "Even if they're not, I'm happy to be the one to hold you through them."

I don't answer, except to let him do just that. I breathe in his comforting, manly smell, and keep my face buried in his chest until I get a hold of myself and finally pull away just long enough to look at him. "Why then, did you bring our divorce papers?"

He slowly blinks while taking a breath. "I just brought those in case this didn't go how I'd hoped. If you didn't want to take another chance, I wouldn't blame you, and if you wanted me to sign them, then I would. I would *hate* it," he's quick to clarify with raised eyebrows, "but I would do it if you thought it was best for you. But I would always love you, and I would never stop thinking about you."

This makes my heart shatter, but the pieces quickly magnetize back together as I let out a sob, wiping at the tears that are trying to stream down my face. I take a few breaths, still trying to get my emotions under control before finally speaking.

"I dare you to burn them," I choke out.

"Done," he responds before stepping into me and taking me in a beautiful kiss. With his lips pressing gently but deliberately against mine, and his arms wrapped tightly around me, it's one for the ages. We sway together in the middle of the room to no music but the beat of our hearts and the occasional breath we take between kisses. It feels like a small eternity before we come up for air, but when we do, I take a look around this very beautiful, but very empty space.

"Kaleb… where exactly are we?" I chuckle at myself for only now asking, but take delight in the way his face lights up.

"I'll show you." He takes my hand and leads me in the opposite direction from which I came. On our way, we walk past a doorway that has hardwood stairs that match the floors leading upwards. "Those lead up to a private loft," he says as he tilts his chin upwards but continues to lead me to the eastern-most side of the place, where there's another doorway that opens up to another space. I get a quick peek as he walks us by it, but he leads us to what must be the front door that leads out into the street.

Once we're on the sidewalk, he turns me towards the building.

"Look up," he gently beckons, and when I do, I see a beautiful wooden sign hanging down over the door antique chains with the words Lavender Moon burned into the wood, and painted with shades of purple and gold.

My breath catches and my hand immediately goes the spot on my chest, just below my collarbone, where a tattoo I've been trying to ignore for the last few months now beams brightly through the material of my shirt.

"Kaleb, I love this, but what is it?" I ask and shake my head in wonder.

"It can be whatever you want it to be," he supplies. "It can be an art gallery that features all your work, or you can conduct art classes here…" he trails off, leaving my imagination to soar without limits.

"How did you do this?" The question comes out hoarse as all the breath has left my lungs.

"I sold the auto shop." His revelation comes out on a heavy

breath, and his face is not one of regret but of mild fear as I start to go off.

"Kaleb Shane!" I exclaim, giving him a shove. "Why would you do that?" I demand.

"Because it was the best thing for it," he fires back, but with an easy grin. "West bought it and is going to take very good care of it. To be honest, I think I did Pops proud."

I bite my lip as I turn that over in my head. He didn't want to give up that shop, or was it that he thought he had to hold onto it? Either way, in the end, he made a healthy decision that speaks volumes of how far he's come. "Okay," I breathe out shakily. It's going to take getting used to of course, but Kaleb looks... free. But wait... "Well, what about you? Your tattoo parlor? You could've used the money to–"

He cuts me off by taking my hand and pointing towards another set of windows. It takes a second, but I realize it's the adjoining space we passed by inside. "Right now, is your time," he explains. "But if all goes well, we can see about expanding and offering tattoos of our work." He drops his hand and wraps his arm around my shoulders. "It can be yours, or it can be ours. Either way, it's going to be about you – at least for a while, and that's not up for debate," he finishes firmly.

"But why?" I shake my head.

"Because you made this last year about me, and you are my beautiful warrior for it, but it's your turn. I refuse to live the rest of our lives without giving back to you."

He steps back enough to level me with a no bullshit look, staring me down hard before a smile finally cracks on my face. "Okay, fine, you stubborn asshole," I finally concede, and he laughs, lifting me off the ground in another hug. "Oh," I begin, a thought occurs to me. "We're in the city. What about Coyote Creek? I love our home there."

"Well, that's why we'll only be open four days a week, and that loft will come in handy for when we don't want to make the drive back home. Our weekends are reserved for home," he explains in finality like that settles it. I raise another questioning eyebrow at him and he gives me a coy smile. "I've also been taking a business class online, and it turns out I don't suck at it. I might keep taking them." This new piece of information exhilarates me so much that I crash my lips down on his. We kiss again for just a moment before he sets me down and releases me to undo the chain around his neck.

"One last thing," he starts, his face takes on a solemn hue. Sliding the beautiful engagement ring off the chain, he asks, "Since I botched it the first time, would it be okay if I proposed to you again?"

"Yes," I nod at him, and without a care as to people walking by, he drops to a knee.

"Luna Shane, the truth is that I've loved you since we were kids, and it's never stopped growing. It never will. I'm a better man because of you, and I will never be able to thank you enough for that, but I'll spend the rest of our lives trying if you'll let me. Will you please stay married to me?"

"Yes!" I joyfully shout out for everyone to hear, and we're serenaded by a lot of hoots and hollers from random strangers as Kaleb slides the beautiful ring back home where it belongs. Once it's in place, Kaleb is back on his feet kissing the hell out of me again, as more cheers and clapping, as well as a few honking car horns, offer their accompaniment.

This time when our mouths detach, Kaleb suggests, "Let's go christen our new business," tilting his head towards the pretty brick building and giving me a mischievous grin that takes me back to the day we met at camp. And then I squeak out a joyful yelp when my soldier throws me over his shoulder; both of us laughing as he carries me inside.

EPILOGUE
KALEB

I can't think of a time I've cried in my life. I think I stopped showing tears and weakness towards my father at some point, and when Pops died, I had years of practice, plus the Army's vigorous training had made me a paragon of stoicism. But now, all that is shot to hell because as Luna walks towards me, my eyes are misting over and I'm stifling back a traitorous sob. My tough as nails warrior looks like a princess right now on her father's arm as they walk the path of white rose petals.

Her brown hair is down and elegantly straight, with, of course, some purple strands peeking out from beneath. Her almond brown eyes are sparkling at me from down the aisle, and it looks like she's holding back tears of her own.

I don't know what's come over me – if it's her pale purple gown with sparkling silver flowers over the bodice and lacey skirts, or the culmination of emotions along the journey that brought us here. There's no question that it's both, it has to be.

After I re-proposed to Luna I brought her home, and the last year has been spent loving and growing together. I've still been going to therapy, sometimes on my own, and sometimes with her by my side. We've still hit our share of bumps in the road.

We have the occasional fight, sometimes over something dumb, like me leaving the cap off the toothpaste or her stealing the covers, and sometimes it's more serious than that. But the difference is we both know without a doubt that the other isn't going anywhere.

The hardest part on both our ends has been letting the other care for us during hard times. We've both had a hard time letting the other wear the armor when it's needed, but it's worth it to feel the life you're infused with when it's your turn. Like when she has a nightmare about what happened to her with her ex, I gently wake her and bring her a cold glass of water and sit with her until she's okay. And when the roles are reversed and I'm dreaming about being back on the battlefield, she gets me to turn over and acts as the big spoon, lulling me out of the terror. And then she's kind enough to trade spots in the morning.

Our first year was a rough one but we made it, and today we celebrate another one on our second anniversary, with close family and friends present. We had the idea together to renew our vows and have the ceremony we didn't before, and being that it's warm enough for an outdoor wedding but the schools haven't let out yet, we were able to do this in the place where it all started.

Luna's famous uncle, Matt, has not only helped with some of the costs, but at Luna's persistence, is actually serenading our ceremony from the dock. It's him alone, without the rest of his band, Turn it Up, with him, as he wanted today to be about us. With his acoustic guitar, he sings a cover of "Heart Medicine" by Judah and the Lion, and as Luna gets closer to where I stand waiting in the clearing by the lake, I lose the fight against my emotions.

That damn sob breaks free, and I bring my fist up to my lips trying to stifle it as Luna sniffs and draws in a steadying breath, trying to blink back her own tears. The one minister from our town made the journey to Camp Mystic Hills to conduct our ceremony today, and when he asks who presents Luna, Ben speaks up, stating that he and Kasey do. After doing so, he presses a sweet kiss to Luna's temple, but instead of stepping away to join his wife and son, he comes forward.

As I even myself out with another long breath, I give him a curious look as he comes to stand beside me. Once I realize what he's doing, I have to start all over again trying not to lose my shit. With Pops and Alex both gone, I didn't have anyone to stand beside me today, but Ben found a way to be there for both Luna and me.

Luna hands her bouquet off to Cassidy, who's donned a cream-colored gown, before turning to me and we take each other's hands. Looking into each other's eyes, we give each other a reassuring smile, take a deep, synchronized breath, and give each other's hands a hard squeeze as we vow forever, only better and stronger than before.

I sniff and sigh through our vows like a hopeless idiot, with Luna occasionally reaching up to wipe a drop of moisture from my eyes. And when it's over, I kiss her like it's for the first time.

After family pictures, we moved the gathering onto the covered patio that's been adorned with hanging lights and a plethora of white and purple flowers. I hold Luna close to me as we dance for the first time, not caring that we're not putting on some choreographed ballroom performance for anyone. In fact, for those three minutes, there might as well not even be anyone else here.

When all the fun traditions are out of the way, music blasts as food and champagne circulates, and we catch up with all of our guests.

We've had a busy last year, moving forward with Lavender Moon, and integrating ourselves more into Coyote Creek when we're not in the city for school or developments on the art center, that Luna had the brilliant idea to teach classes in one room, and offer tattoos of our featured artwork in the other. We're only a few weeks from opening, and we're taking that time for the honeymoon we never got to have before – again, financed by her Uncle Matt, who assures us there's a hidden gem in the UK we should check out. While I worry about paying him back for a lavish gift, he's directed us to simply pay it forward.

We've gotten to know the people in our little town well enough that a lot of them made the trip for the wedding.

I'm surprised to see Jace from the fire department made it, as he's not very social, but he'd been a rookie when Pops volunteered and felt a strong enough connection to make the effort. West, on the other hand, has become a good friend. I drop by occasionally to check on Shane Automotive which doesn't bother him in the least. Sometimes I even lend a hand when a mechanic is out sick. I'm glad to have him here, but what's got me baffled is why in the hell he's acting so twitchy. He stands awkwardly against the bar next to me, nursing a whiskey while I sip on one of my allotted beers of the night.

"What's with you, man?" I ask while I lift my chin at him and give him a jokingly scrutinizing look.

"What are you talking about?" he plays off, looking around the dance floor, and I can tell it's not for anything in particular other than to avoid my eyes.

"You've looked all jittery and nervous this whole time," I supply, taking a pull and swallowing. "You would've thought you were the one getting married."

"Pffft," he scoffs. "Hell to the no. And besides, you didn't even really get married today, 'cause you know, you already were."

"Yeah, well, it was fast and clandestine before." I lift a shoulder as I justify today. "And we went through some difficult times after that. We're celebrating a fresh start."

He almost has me distracted with his small talk regarding my nuptials, but when a few people clear off the dance floor, Luna comes into view, dancing with Matty, and West's head immediately snaps in the other direction, before he quickly curbs his movements, trying to act casual as he turns to face the bar. I look back over to Luna and then back to him with a pinched brow and then suddenly, it all clicks together. Anytime Luna's within twenty paces, he looks away.

"Alright, out with it," I demand as I turn to mirror his position, and set my beer down on the bar to let him know I mean business. My attention is solely on him, and he can't avoid that.

"What?" He gives an exasperated shrug as his eyebrows go up.

"You've not looked at my wife once all evening, and that's no small feat considering she's the bride. Cut the shit, what's your problem?"

"I don't have a problem!" he protests indignantly.

"Good, then look at her," I order, waving a hand in Luna's direction.

"Fine," he says calmly but draws in a steadying breath before he turns. What the fuck? He takes a look at Luna as she gives Matty a playful noogie. West's jaw is set hard enough to crack a molar, and he's holding his fucking breath. Then, as if he's been counting the seconds, he lets out his breath and turns. "See, I looked at her," he says and scoops his drink back up.

Son of a fucking bitch...

"You have a thing for my wife," I accuse in a low voice.

"No!" He turns to face me, holding his hands up, drink and all.

I don't give a fuck that this guy is slightly older and was in jail, I'll fuck him up if I find out he was eyeballing my wife all those times at the shop while I was away.

"No?" I raise an eyebrow that says he better explain himself and fast.

"No," he says more calm but unequivocally firm. "No, I swear, I've never felt anything for your wife, it's..."

"What?" I ask, shaking my head with my eyebrows trying to disappear into my hairline.

He looks around uncomfortably, possibly checking to see if anyone else is within hearing distance of us before motioning me to close in a little. "You tell anyone this, I will paint the fucking auto shop pink," he threatens, and I wave my hands in the calm down gesture.

"Not a word, just explain your deal with my wife tonight."

He looks at the ceiling a minute before releasing an extended breath out his nose. "I have a thing for ballgowns," he admits quickly, before grabbing up his drink again. I pause a moment, watching him knock back a swallow as I process this.

"I'm sorry?"

He huffs again. "I get… turned on by ballgowns."

"So…" I feel my forehead scrunch yet again as I try to get my head around this. "You see a pretty ballgown, and you–"

"No! God, you make it sound like I like to just get it on with a dress."

"So… what, do you like to dress up?"

"No, not that either!" West grinds out between clenched teeth.

"Then what?"

"It's a princess fetish, alright?!" West is getting hot under the collar, and he reaches for a nearby glass of ice water.

"A princess fetish?" I repeat, having never heard of this.

"When a girl is dressed up fancy in a gown, you know – looking like a princess."

"Where the fuck did this come from?"

"You don't get to know that part," he spits and pins me with a no-bullshit stare.

"Alright, fine. So instead of leather and lingerie…"

"Fucking ballgowns do it for me," he mutters his affirmation. "Weddings are fucking torture."

"So you're turned on by my wife in her wedding dress?" I look over at Luna's radiant smile again as her dress swishes with the song she's dancing to with her friends.

West takes a little too long to answer for my liking, and when he sees the fire ignite in my eyes, he tries to defend his position once again.

"It's just the fucking dress!"

"Get out," I growl, pointing towards the exit.

"Yep," he clips out, briskly turning and striding out without a backward glance.

Fucker.

When I'm satisfied he's long gone, I make my way back over onto the dance floor to take my wife in my arms.

"Hey, soldier," she coos in a sultry voice, bringing her arms around my neck.

"Hey, silly girl," I return, looking down at her adoringly. "About how much time are the bride and groom supposed to put in at these things?"

"Why?" she smiles charmingly up at me. "You've had enough already?"

"Just ready to be alone with you."

"So you can find out what I might be wearing under my dress?" she asks as she lifts a seductive eyebrow.

"Oh, please say it's lace," I beckon as I smooth a hand down the back of her hair.

"You know," she starts in, with a smug tone, "it's not like we have to actually tell anyone we're leaving."

"Luna Shane, are you suggesting we sneak out to go make love?"

She lifts a shoulder. "Your cabin or mine?" she smirks.

"Fuck that, I've got our own private honeymoon suite set up on the lake front," I inform her.

That prospects makes her nibble on her lower lip before giving me a warm smile I can't help but return. Planting a quick kiss to her lips, I whisper, "Let's go," before taking her hand and leading her out of our reception.

BONUS EPILOGUE
LUNA, FIVE YEARS LATER

A smile of satisfaction settles across my face from where I stand at the front of the room, gathering up used brushes in my bin to take to the sink. It was a small class of twelve tonight, but they're all lit up and proud of themselves for completing the painting of a misty forest I instructed them through with the sun shining through the trees as they take turns posing for pictures with their respective pieces. I let them all hang out and carry on, despite the fact that we're closing shortly.

I set the bin of brushes in the sink and grab up the laundry basket to collect aprons and drop cloths next as one of the customers approaches me. She's a petite woman looking to be around my age, and she adjusts her glasses as she asks, "Excuse me, is it true we can actually have our own work that we did here turned into a tattoo?"

"Uh-huh," I nod warmly. "Did you see the parlor on the other side of the hall?" she nods in answer. "Kaleb can easily have your project put on the transfer paper. Do you want to come with me up front to schedule a consult?"

"Sure!" She lights up and I smile back at her as I set the basket down and wave lightly for her to follow me up to the front desk so I can hop on the computer to look at our calendar.

When we reach the desk, I catch a glimpse of my husband through the entry way that opens up into the parlor. He looks up at me as he's placing the plastic wrap over a man's bicep that he just finished work on, and gives me a wink.

I take my place behind the desk, carefully lowering myself into the chair which makes the corner of my customers mouth pull up.

"When are you due?" she asks cordially, nodding to my boulder of a belly that protrudes from under my stretchy black top.

"About four more weeks," I smile coyly as I wake up my computer. I don't tell her that it could actually be any day now, seeing as how twins tend to arrive early.

"That's exciting," she muses before we get to work scheduling her for a consult with Kaleb, as well as a first session in a couple of weeks.

A couple more patrons have gathered behind her, their eyes scanning the wall behind me as they wait their turn. There, they get to be assured they're in good hands with Kaleb as his certification is displayed, as well as his business degree, boasting from a beautiful frame. On the other side resides my Bachelor's degree from NICA, and between them, is a wonderfully fun photo of the two of us posing with Leo Mills, who owns Wishbone Tattoo in the UK. My Uncle Matt thought it would be a great way to spend our honeymoon, visiting another country while learning a thing or two from him. He's a Jason Momoa-looking dude with an astounding talent and incomparable wit.

"Thank you so much for the class," the next person in line says as he steps up to the desk.

"You're so welcome." I flash him a smile as I take his debit card.

"Just asking for some friends," he begins as he leans his forearms on the desk as I process his payment. "For tattoos, do we have to choose from your portfolios?" He nods to the coffee table by the cozy couch in the waiting area, where a collection of binders sit, containing works from both Kaleb and me.

"Nope. If you schedule a consultation with Kaleb, he can draw up anything you want. It just costs an additional fee if you want him to come up with something." I glint up at the man in question as he strides in, ushering out his last customer of the day. His sleeves are pushed up, revealing more tats than ever that he's accumulated over the last few years.

"Bragging about me again?" he smirks as he comes behind me and starts massaging my shoulders.

"Never," I snark at him with an eye roll as I peruse our calendar for the next open time slot.

Once everyone has been taken care of, we close up for the evening. We're open again tomorrow and I'm exhausted, so we've opted to stay the night here tonight up in our loft.

"Food's on its way," Kaleb updates me as I settle down on the couch in the corner where we have a living area set up with a TV.

"Good," I sigh with relief as he sets a root beer down in front of me, and a regular beer for himself on the coffee table.

"So who's craving the root beer and who's craving the pineapple?" he asks with a grin, sitting down next to me and pulling my feet into his lap.

"Well, normally I'd say that I'm the one craving the root beer, but I'm thinking Amanda's caught onto it," I theorize, simply because she's the girl that we're naming after Kaleb's mother.

Kaleb leans over and presses his mouth to the right side of my belly where she sits. "Amanda Violet," he addresses her with a mock sternness in his voice. "Your mother does not need more root beer, you hear me? And that must mean Mr. Alex Benjamin is craving the pineapple that had to cover half the pizza I just ordered," he snickers. I smirk and roll my eyes again as I brush the strands of his hair out of his face while he places a kiss to my belly and sits back up. He starts massaging my foot which makes my head drop back on the cushions in ecstasy and I let out a moan I'm helpless to hold in.

"Hey, watch it with that," Kaleb chuckles. "You're going to make me tent these jeans with sounds like that."

"Hey, not in front of the kids," I joke. "And you're going to hear a lot more than that when that pizza gets here. I'm starving."

"Please," he scoffs. "I said and did worse things to you last night."

After driving my poor husband insane while I moan around countless bites of pineapple pizza while we watch reruns of Sons of Anarchy, he's had enough and decides to take me to bed. After gingerly helping me up off the couch, leads me over to the bed where we get undressed and he lays me down.

"Truth or dare?" he whispers down at me in the dark.

"Truth," I say easily, as I trace a fingertip down the contours of his chest.

"Is there anything about our life that you would change?" he asks, though his features in the dark tell me he doesn't have a single worry; he just wants to hear it.

"Not a thing," I tell him truthfully. "Your turn."

"Dare," he smirks and tips his chin up at me cockily which makes a smile pull at the sides of my mouth.

"I dare you to show me how much you love me."

"I said dare you goof, that's the easiest thing in the world," he chides down at me. "But anything for my silly girl," he adds, bringing his mouth down on mine.

WANT to find out how Luna's parents got their start? You can meet them in book 4 of my Turn It Up series in Where You Are, and then watch them fall in love in book 5 of my Turn It Up series in Read Between the Stars.

. . .

ARE YOU CURIOUS ABOUT WEST, the fugitive mechanic? He just might have a story coming as well as some friends! To keep up on future books as well as my rockstar series Turn it Up, be sure to sign up for my newsletter, join my Facebook reader group, or join my street team!

ALSO BY NATALIE PARKER

TURN IT UP SERIES

SEE HER 2ND EDITION
Jack and Mayzie Book 1

STILL HER
Jack and Mayzie Book 2

PICTURE US
Tyler and Annie (A Turn it Up spinoff) – Surprise Pregnancy Book 3

WHERE YOU ARE
Matt and Melanie – Brother's Best Friend/Second Chance Book 4

READ BETWEEN THE STARS
Ben and Kasey (A Turn it Up Spinoff)
Widower/Single Mother Book 5

FOR HER
A Jack and Mayzie novella Book 6

SOMEWHERE IN BETWEEN
Josh and Bobbi – Slight Age Gap, virgin heroine Book 7

STANDALONE'S

Wishing on Snowflakes
A Romantic Comedy Novella

LAVENDER MOON

A steamy small town, childhood friends to lovers, military, romance

BOOKS BY NIKO K

Dark and Suspenseful more your jam? Check out this duet written under my other pen name, Niko K.

Karma Society: The Cape Hazard Duet

Karma's Rule, book 1

Karma's Law, book 2

ABOUT NATALIE PARKER

Natalie Parker resides in the Seattle area with her husband and two rugrats, but is originally a Michigan girl. She always enjoyed writing and noticed she had a knack for it while earning her Psychology degree and has always been an avid reader, but never thought of becoming an author until one day there seemed to be a story to tell. In her spare time, she enjoys, reading, reading to her kids, drinking coffee, occasional yardwork, listening to music, and writing.

Want to hang out with me and other readers? Join my Facebook Reader Group.
Natalie's Backstage VIPs

Want to get all the good news first?
Subscribe to my Newsletter

Follow me on Social media

ACKNOWLEDGMENTS

Greys Promo, it was an absolute privilege to get to work with you guys and I thank you so much for all you have done to get the word out. Jenn, Dusty and the rest of the ladies with Smutty Author Resources, you guys are a wonderful gift to the indie author romance community. Thank you for your selfless time and efforts to help get the word out on this story.

My Roadie Crew, thank you all so much for believing in what I do enough to post to your profiles. Your very precious time is a gift that I am so thankful for. Thank you thank you thank you for all you do!!!

Naly Tham, thank you for being a resource when I was researching. I really appreciate you taking the time.

Michelle, thank you again for talking me off the ledge after a tough year and stepped everything up without blinking. You're the best PA this pain in the ass could ask for and one of the most wonderful friends. You work happily and tirelessly and I can't express how thankful I am for you.

Katy, my editor, I don't deserve all you do. You do so much and not only are you okay with it, you insist on it. There's no one more hard working and hard loving than you and I thank you so much for working on yet another one of these stories and being my friend. You're stuck with me as there's seriously no one like you.

My book wife Lizzie, thank you once again for letting me borrow Leo from your brilliant AF Wishbone Tattoos series.

Thank you for the work you did on this book and all the others. I love you so much.

My beautiful Buttsnack Paula, thank you for being one of the bestest friends ever and for whipping me into shape when I need it - so, all the time. Thank you for all your help whether you offer it, I ask politely for it or tearfully beg for it. Love you.

Lori thank you for such a breathtaking cover. I love working with you so much and I hope you have a lot of pride in what you do because I do.

Wander Aguiar, thank you for the perfect photo that represents Luna and Kaleb so perfectly. I'm so glad I finally got to work with you and it won't be the last time.

Readers, Bookstagrammers, bloggers, all of you who read, reviewed, and posted about this book, thank you. Those of you who read it, thank you so much. Those of you who picked it up and decided it was a DNF for you, thank you for giving me a chance.

Printed in Great Britain
by Amazon